DUTY HONOR
DECEIT

DUTY HONOR DECEIT

By
J. Lissner

Leathers Publishing
A division of Squire Publishers, Inc.
4500 College Blvd.
Leawood, KS 66211
Phone: 1 (888) 888-7696

Cover by Angela Steward

ISBN: 1-58597-044-1

Library of Congress Catalog Card No. 00-131144

A division of Squire Publishers, Inc.
4500 College Blvd.
Leawood, KS 66211
Phone: 1 (888) 888-7696

Dedicated to God,
the giver of all gifts.
May I never forget,
the glory is Yours.

ACKNOWLEDGMENTS

I would like to thank my family for their constant encouragement: Adrienne Lissner, Lee Lamming, Tom Lamming, Amy O'Brien, Kevin O'Brien, Chris Lissner, Dawn Lissner, Ken Lissner, Bernadette Lissner, Cindy Hartley, Larry Hartley, Kathy Lissner Grant, Michael Lissner, Rachel Lissner, Billy Richerson and Jake Richerson. Your belief in my ability to complete this process has meant a great deal to me. My special thanks to Adrienne, Lee, Amy, Ken, Cindy, Michael and Rachel, who read and reread my manuscript many times. Your ideas, insights and expertise have been greatly appreciated.

J. Lissner

*"Beware of false teachers who come
disguised as harmless sheep,
but are wolves and will
tear you apart."*

Matthew 7:15

CHAPTER 1

"NAME?" the corporal at the check-in desk requested.

"Zeus Galahad Malone," the scraggly-bearded man growled. He was thin and lanky with pasty-white skin and deep-set eyes. His thin red hair hung unevenly in oily clumps around his bony freckled shoulders.

The corporal stared at the orphan's filthy appearance. A brown stain smeared across Zeus's mustard-colored shirt. Duct tape choked the ragged holes where buttons had been. A scraped knee peered out of his lime green pants.

"M. . .M. . .alone? The. . .the orphan?"

"Yeah."

The corporal whiffed the air and coughed. His eyes watered and his stomach churned. He scrunched his nose. "What's that smell?"

"Machine oils and sewages."

The corporal's eyebrows met. "What?"

"I's works ta gets here's." Zeus shoved his callused hand in the corporal's face. A clear, black residue shimmered under the bright gym lights.

The corporal swallowed. He could not take his eyes off the orphan's left pinkie. The finger was severed below the top joint. The little stump was covered with torn cloth and duct tape. Blood seeped through the cloth. The corporal's voice cracked, "I. . .ID card."

Zeus pulled a small switchblade out of his sleeve and popped it open.

The corporal jumped back, holding his breath.

Zeus cut a strip of duct tape on his shirt. He removed his ID card from inside the tape and handed it to the corporal.

The corporal exhaled and took the card. It slipped in his sweaty fingers and fell to the floor. He leaned down and bumped his head on

1

the arm of the chair. He winced, grabbed the card firmly, sat up and inserted the card into the computer. "State your complete date of birth for voice recognition." He handed Zeus a microphone.

"July tenth, 2200."

"Right eye here for retina verification."

Zeus placed his steel blue eye in front of the scanner and waited for the computer to beep.

"You're in the Alpha unit. Report to Sgt. Susan Leiman over there." He pointed to a tall, muscular blonde at the first table in the corner.

Zeus had hacked into OTS records before his arrival. He was aware of his assignment. He grabbed his ID card, turned sideways, pushed another recruit out of his path and passed between the two tables. He stood at the table marked "Alpha" and fiddled with the switchblade in his pocket.

He felt a bump on his shoulder, pulled out the knife and swung around. His heart pounded. He scanned the room and the hundreds of potential antagonists. No one was taking a defensive stance around him. He swiped the steel against his pants. His sore pinkie twinged as the blade popped into its home.

"Excuse me." A woman passed in front of him.

Zeus felt he was in a vice and the crowd was slowly squeezing him. He could not believe, after all he had been through, Officer's Training School was his only option. The man in front of him saluted and stepped aside.

"Name," Sgt. Leiman demanded from behind her desk.

"Zeus Galahad Malone."

She coughed at the rancid smell burning her nostrils. "How did you get here?"

"Two transports, one budgin garbage ships and portable repairs center," he growled back.

"What?" she asked, unfamiliar with his thick accent.

"Transports, garbage ships, repairs center."

She nodded, hoping she had understood. She covered her mouth and nose. "Change BEFORE you report at thirteen hundred."

"Budgin gots noth'n ta change ta."

Leiman entered her recruit's arrive in her system. "All cuss words, including 'budgin' are not permitted at OTS or by any Corps personnel."

"Huh?"

"Malone, you will clean up both your mouth and your attire before you report."

"Ain'ts budgin gots noth'n ta change ta."

"What?" She ignored the budgin and tried to understand what he was saying.

"Ain'ts budgin gots no's other clothes," the orphan insisted.

"What?" she said, frustrated by his accent.

Zeus tore a bit of thumbnail and spit it on the desk. "Ain'ts gots noth'n else!"

Leiman brushed the dirty black nail off her desk. "Where's your luggage?"

Zeus flung his handmade leechrat bag at her. She stared at the unevenly sewn animal skins. The bag was pieced together with strands of wire and thread, then closed at the top with twine. It, like Zeus, was covered in a thick oily residue and reeked of sewage.

"Where's the rest, Malone?" she sighed, coughing slightly.

"Budgin alls I's gots."

"Budgin is not an acceptable word here. You will stop using it."

"Budgin ain'ts reports yet."

Leiman glared at him. "Malone, it's not smart to get me mad before we start boot camp."

Zeus refused to answer.

She crossed her arms and sat back.

No response.

"I'll wait." She pulled her chair closer to the desk. "When you report, you'll answer and obey or be discharged for insubordination." She thumped the bag. "Empty it."

He grabbed the bag, yanked the knot open and dumped the contents onto the desk.

Leiman stared at what appeared to be an assortment of useless items: duct tape, some pieces of rope, an oddly shaped stone, two additional knives, bits of scrap paper covered with written notes, a small antique portable computer, a slingshot, rocks, some torn pieces of cloth, two carved pieces of wood, a whittling project in progress and four computer-data chips.

She stood and leaned toward him. "Where's the rest of your things?"

3

"Ain'ts budgin gots noth'n else," he spit through the gap in his lower teeth.

Her jaw locked. "Sgt. Baker."

"Yes," the burley man next to her answered.

"This is one of our new recruito. . .Malone. Take him, clean him up, burn his clothes, issue his sweats early and get him ready to report."

Baker stood and straightened his uniform. "You want him to report here when we're done?"

"No. Here's his entrance packet." She tossed it at him. "Go over it with him. Explain, in detail, the parts about respect. I'll handle things here until you return. Malone, I'll see you at thirteen hundred in front of the Alpha barracks. You better review your manual. . .carefully."

"Come with me, Malone." Sgt. Baker turned and marched forward. Zeus followed in angry silence. Baker waited until Zeus was a few paces behind him, then stopped abruptly, swung around and let Zeus bump into him. The sergeant yelled in the recruit's face, "You will always salute a superior before you leave his or her presence. Do you understand, Cadet?"

"Yeah."

"In the future, Cadet," Baker bellowed, "you will respond to each and every statement made to you with 'yes, Sir'; 'no, Sir'; 'yes, Ma'am'; or 'no, Ma'am.' Got it?"

"Yeah."

"I said respond to me with 'yes, Sir' or 'no, Sir.' "

Zeus's upper lip flared. His jagged, brown left incisor poked out like a fang. "Ain'ts reports yet."

"Follow me, Malone. But trust me, you'll pay for that comment."

* * *

Sgt. Baker motioned for Sgt. Leiman to leave her check-in desk.

"Wait here," she said to her recruit and walked over to her partner. "Where's our boy now?"

"Sonic Cleaning Chamber."

"What?"

"I tried to clean him up." Baker shook his balding head. "That stuff won't come off. It's hard to understand that kid. Between his accent and the cuss words, what little information I got took forever. I'm still not certain I understood everything. He claims he did wash before he came."

4

She frowned, remembering the rancid smell. "Do you believe him?"

"I guess. I had him shower four times, and he still reeked. Even cutting off his hair didn't help. That's why I took him to sonic clean-up."

"What's causing that stench?"

"Malone told me he worked for his passage on a garbage ship. There was a break-down, and he had to go into the sewage chamber to fix it."

"He sure smelled like trash. So I'd believe him, except why wouldn't it wash off?"

"Supposedly he went straight from that to a repair cruiser. He worked for his passage, without protective gear, oiling components." Baker rolled his hazel eyes. "According to Malone, the repairs required a pressurized oiling wand. The tech said that would have forced the oil and raw sewage into his skin."

"Great." She crossed her arms. "Did you talk to him about respect?"

"Hopeless." Baker cracked the knuckles on his left hand. "He's willfully defiant. I wouldn't count on cooperation from Malone." He cracked his right knuckles. "That kid was carrying four knives. Two switchblades, one in his pocket, one up his sleeve, a bowie knife tucked under his shirt and a lock blade duct-taped to his inner thigh."

"An innocent orphan. No murdering network member there. Anything else I should know?"

"His body is a mess. I hope he flunks the physical."

She raised her eyebrows. "Is it possible?"

"He has one scar after another. There are cuts, abrasions, welts. Even some weird markings on his chest. I've never seen anything like it. On. . .uh. . .his right upper chest," Baker tapped his brass name-plate, "is what looks like a crude arrow." He touched his The United Corps insignia. "On the left is a number of circles that form a sloppy sort of pyramid design. I'm sure it's some sort of Kalopso thing."

"I've heard the crime network tattoos its people."

"I have, too. But these weren't tattoos. They looked raised, like they were cut into his skin."

"I hate the idea of having a Kalopso plant in our unit. How did we get ourselves into this?"

Baker nudged his partner. "The commander said it was her way of showing how much confidence she has in us."

5

"Oh, yes. Her two best drill sergeants."

"More like biggest idiots. This is going to be a nightmare." Baker twisted his neck to crack it.

"Are you going to do that cracking thing for the whole ten months?"

He twisted his lower back. There were three loud pops. "Only if it bugs you."

Leiman punched Baker's upper arm. "It is going to be a long term. I can't get rid of you, but maybe Malone will flunk the physical."

"I doubt it. The Kalopso is smart. They've sent someone who looks like a poor abused soul, so the bleeding-heart liberals will say he's had a hard life and just needs to be given a chance. I'll bet he'll have a lot of minor health problems, but nothing we could kick him out for."

"They sure sent him with nothing. All he had was a bunch of junk."

"I'm kind of surprised they sent him with so many knives."

She peered around the bustling gym. No one was too close or appeared to be paying attention to them. Just to be careful, she lowered her voice. "Do you think it's a warning to us?"

"Yes. . .no. . .I don't know. I've heard the network doesn't send subtle hints. Members threaten you to your face."

"Great. I'm looking forward to that." Leiman turned. "Come on, we're already behind on check-ins."

Baker stepped beside her. "If we can help it, I don't think we should leave him alone with anyone. I wouldn't have left him with the tech, but Lt. Cmd. Zeigler came in and dismissed me."

"I agree. Let's keep a tight leash on Malone. If possible, one of us should keep an eye on him at all times."

"OK."

"I'm not sure which is worse, check-ins or Malone."

They smiled at each other and simultaneously said, "Check-ins."

*   *   *

Zeus glanced at the clock on the wall, then bolted away from the confines of the sonic chamber. The orphan took some deep breaths of fresh air. It was noon, and he had to report at one o'clock. His stomach growled for the umpteenth time. He blinked at the sun as he scanned a small tree for edible rodents.

The United Corps' base was located on the largest continent on the planet Darris. The area was warm and moist and with ample vegetation. Zeus had never been in such lush surroundings. His orphanage on Velcron was in a dry, arid area. He had attended college in an industrial area. Most of the plants on Darris had a yellow hue that gave the area a golden glow. He could see why this base was referred to as the Golden Star for the Corps. Given the abundance of vegetation, he was certain there must be plenty of game to catch. However, time was limited. Zeus decided he would again have to settle for safety over sustenance.

He eyed the South Gate and walked toward it. The guard at the gate snickered at Zeus's new recruit crew hair cut and stopped him. "Cadets are not permitted off the Officer's Training School side of base."

"Huh?"

"You are only allowed on the OTS side of base."

"Budgin military rules," he muttered under his breath. Zeus trotted off on Honor Street between the Medical Building and Supply Warehouse. One thing he did like about The United Corps, they clearly marked everything. TUC Mess Hall. TUC Officer's Housing. Computer Center. OTS Flight Hangars.

He continued on until Honor Street stopped on the north side at the edge of a forest. Two squirrels darted up and around a distant tree. Zeus's stomach growled. He wished he had a watch, but it was a luxury he could not afford. Unfortunately, today time was not in his budget either. He rubbed his gut and turned west to check out the Obstacle Course. That had potential to be interesting, especially the ropes dangling over the mud pits. The orphan could not resist. He leaped up on the log, grabbed a rope and swung over the brown muck.

A black sergeant called, "You'll have plenty of time for that."

Zeus froze. Where he was from, penalties for minor infractions were often brutal. He wondered the consequence for unauthorized use of military equipment. The orphan chewed off a piece of ring-finger nail and spit. A bulls-eye through the chain links in the bridge.

The sergeant walked away.

Zeus waited another moment, shrugged and continued his surveillance. He jogged along Main Street past a series barracks, each one identified by its unit name: Tau, Tango, Sigma, Sierra. He followed the alphabetical barracks to his unit, Alpha. Recruits were beginning to assemble. He decided he had better stick around.

Zeus looked for a spot to wait. The most secure location was the front of the barrack. He leaned against the building to ensure no one could approach him from the rear. A tall, muscular man walked in front of him and turned away. He hated snobs who looked through him as if he did not exist. The orphan observed every detail of the man. His shoes were perfect black mirrors reflecting all the colors and shapes around them. His fingernails were rounded and pink, not bruised and peeling like the orphan's. A man in brown shoes walked up to Mr. Shiny Shoes.

"Richard, it is a pleasure to be reacquainted," Mr. Shiny Shoes shook hands.

"It's Apollo, correct?"

"Yes, Apollo Christiani. We were introduced once on campus."

"Was I sober?"

"I am delighted to see another Hadley man in the Alpha unit." Apollo smiled. His dark olive skin made his perfect white teeth stand out.

Zeus ran his tongue along his sharp, uneven teeth. The orphan felt this pompous man was flaunting his wealth with his smile.

"Are you prepared for August Agony?"

Apollo straightened his tailored collar. "How does one make preparations? I cannot fathom over a quarter of the unit unable to survive boot camp."

"As they say, make it through Double A, and you're on your way."

"Double A, OTS, TUC, I am already nauseated by abbreviations." Apollo brushed an insect from his curly black hair.

"I agree. Memorizing the entire manual was a waste of time. It must have been written by a noncom." Richard changed the subject. "Have you seen the orphan man they admitted?"

"No, I have not. I pray he is assigned to another unit."

"Pray? You're not one of those preachy Christian guys?"

Apollo dark brown eyes scanned the crowd. "Christian, that is affirmative. Preachy, that is a negative."

"Why? What do you gain from religion?"

"There are many benefits and advantages, such as hope, guidance, strength to face the unforeseen."

"You'll need your strength if you encounter the network's orphan slob."

"Have you encountered him?"

8

"I was standing beside him at check-in. He smelled like trash, and his clothes looked like that's where they came from."

Zeus glanced down at his OTS-issued sweats. He was relieved he did not have to meet the whole unit in his greasy, second-hand rags.

"He must never bathe." Richard curled his broad, flat nose. "He pulled a knife on the corporal at the desk. He speaks like an idiot in between the cuss words. He's got network written all over him."

"What other expectations could you have from someone without any family ties?"

"They're all animals." Richard ogled a buxom brunette standing on the sidewalk. "It's not possible for an orphan to learn to control his primal violent and sexual desires. They should all be castrated so they can't reproduce."

"That is an interesting solution. The orphan's letters of recommendation were limited to one, written by a college coach. The coach is an unknown; however, that is a moot point when one considers how remote and common Alto College is." Apollo followed Richard's gaze and eyed the pretty woman. "You have discriminating tastes."

Richard clicked his tongue. "Beautiful. I can't understand why they admitted him."

"The Corps was coerced by public outrage. His grades were superior. He was a marathoner, a distance runner in track and," Apollo held up a finger, "an undefeated maxor. I observed visuals of his bouts. He is an unbelievable fighter. He has lightning speed."

"Big deal. So he can look impressive against other small-time schools. There were probably only three athletes in the whole college. That's no reason to let him into Officers' Training School. OTS prides itself on taking the best of the best, not the best of the insignificant."

Zeus shoved his hand in his pocket to feel the cool steel of his switchblade. He wished he could introduce these shiny-shoed bastards to his closest friend, "The Little Lady." He liked to gently stroke her smooth surfaces while turning and flipping her until she warmed and became one with his hand.

Apollo's dark eyes squinted in the sun. "Zeus established a new universal collegiate record as a maxor, and his marathon times are fantastic. Marathon times are not related to the school he attended. I can assure you, no one in the Corps desired his attendance. OTS attempted to discover any excuse not to admit him; however, his entrance exam scores were outstanding. The press coverage was merciless. The board was browbeaten into admitting him. The military cannot afford any additional negative press, especially regarding the subject of discrimination. Our pristine image is already tarnished. We cannot jeopardize losing any more public funding."

"I suppose." Richard checked out the legs of a woman walking by. "It's still not right."

"What prompts you to state that? He received acceptance, not on his ability to make an excellent officer; however, simply because it was political suicide to reject him. He cheated on his entrance tests. He is a Kalopso member and a network spy. He appears and smells worse than the scum from my yacht. He can barely converse, with the exception of cuss words. I cannot fathom why the Corps would not consider him as an outstanding prospect."

"No matter what the political environment, how could they?"

Zeus seethed while the two men discussed his unworthiness. Despite his disgust for their snobbish, self-righteous attitude, he was having difficulty focusing on the conversation. His empty stomach was again demanding attention. He could feel the digestive acids churning around searching for something to latch onto. Finding nothing, the gases built up and expanded his stomach to a painfully large size. He wished he could take a needle and with one pop, release the pressure. Instead, he repeatedly burped the useless gases into his pasty, dry mouth.

*　　*　　*

Sgt. Leiman blew a loud whistle. "Form five rows of ten." After a few minutes of counting and luggage moving, five haphazard lines were formed. "Stand at attention." All the cadets, except Zeus, stood tall and straight. "You," she pointed to the first person in the line. "How many people were supposed to be in each line?"

The new recruit stood stiffly. "Ten."

At this response, the sergeant planted herself in front of the recruit and glared at her. "You will address me as Ma'am, each and every time you address me. Do you understand?"

The recruit leaned away from the pushy sergeant. "Yes, Ma'am."

"Louder."

"Yes, Ma'am," she responded in her loudest voice.

"What's your name, recruit?"

"Candy Wang, Ma'am," her voice squeaked.

Sgt. Leiman shoved her face close to Candy's. "Why are you leaning away from me?"

Candy's face turned flush.

"In the future, cadets, you will answer each time you are asked a question. Do you understand?"

"Yes, Ma'am," the group answered.

"Count the people in these lines," the sergeant ordered.

Candy turned to begin counting. Sgt. Leiman yelled in her ear. "You did not answer my request, Cadet Wang. Each time a sergeant or officer speaks to you, you will respond."

Candy gulped. "Yes, Ma'am." She counted, sorry she had chosen to be in the front line.

"Out loud, so I can hear you, Wang."

"One, two. . ."

"You did not answer my request. In the future, if a cadet does not show the proper respect for a superior, he or she will be required to do some form of exercise to refresh the memory. Do you understand?"

"Yes, Ma'am," they responded.

"Wang, resume counting."

"Yes, Ma'am. One, two. . ." Candy reached the end of the second line and realized eleven people were in that line.

Sgt. Leiman strolled over and put her face in the face of the last cadet in line. He was of equal height, with curly blond hair. "What is your name, Cadet?"

"Victor Petroff."

"Cadet Petroff, you did not answer me with 'Ma'am.' Drop and do ten pushups."

Victor dropped and did pushups.

"Cadet Petroff, I gave you an order and you still did not respond correctly. You will do twenty pushups."

"Yes, Ma'am."

"Petroff, you will start over and count out loud."

"Yes, Ma'am. One. . .two. . .three. . ."

Sgt. Leiman spoke over the cadet's counting. "In the future, cadets, when you are given an exercise, you will count out loud. Do you understand?"

"Yes, Ma'am," they answered.

The line-up took fifteen minutes, with Sgt. Leiman ordering pushups until the Alphas had achieved five straight lines of ten. When the fifty cadets were properly lined up, she introduced herself and Sgt. Dennis Baker. The sergeants were of equal rank, but it was apparent that Sgt. Leiman had seniority and Baker deferred to her.

Baker stepped in front of the Alphas shaking his head. He had been holding an InfoPad and flipped it on. "I am going to call roll. If you are not assigned to the Alpha Unit, you need to leave, now." No one moved. "Good. When I call your name, step forward and say, 'Here, Sir.' Do you understand, cadets?"

"Yes, Sir."

Sgt. Baker called names, looking carefully at each cadet. Sgt. Leiman also paid close attention. Both sergeants would attempt to identify each Alpha by their last name before the end of the day.

"Malone, Zeus Galahad."

"Yeah."

"It's thirteen hundred and you've reported." Sgt. Baker marched over to him. "Now your butt is mine, and you will respond with 'yes, Sir,' understand?"

Zeus peered down at him. "Yeah, Sir," he said slowly and indignantly. He refused to use the sharp, crisp voice the sergeant wanted to hear.

"I can't hear you, Cadet."

"Yeah, Sir," Zeus snarled through pursed lips.

"Drop and do fifty pushups for your earlier lack of respect."

"Yeah, Sir." Zeus dropped and counted.

*　　*　　*

The men stood in their muted green underwear waiting for their entrance physicals. A petite black woman entered. Dr. Sarah Bentley was the chief medical officer on base. She had been ordered to personally oversee the orphan's medical review and needs.

"Malone," she called when it was his turn.

Zeus meandered over, handed her his ID card and hopped onto the table.

"Since your last physical, have you had any changes in your. . ." Her voice trailed off. She stared at the huge pink scar that crossed from his left pelvis to his right rib. Dr. Bentley flipped through Zeus's medical

12

history. She found no note in his file about an abdominal injury. She scratched her brow. "What happened to your stomach?"

"Knifes fight."

"Who treated this?" she asked.

"I's did. Ain'ts no hospitals ins the ghetto."

"So you laser sealed it yourself?"

"Ain'ts no laser sealers ons Orphan's Row."

Bentley bit her lower lip. "Then exactly how did you treat it?"

"Fish'n line, needles and alcohols. Can'ts discharge me's for thats," he said in his thick accent.

She listened carefully, concentrating on each word. "Let me get this straight. Instead of using a laser sealer, you got drunk, then sewed yourself up with fishing line?"

"Uses alcohol ta sterilize wound, needle and nylon. Ain'ts for drink'n, Ma'am." He blew his rancid breath in her face.

Dr. Bentley gagged. "Would you repeat that?"

"I's sterilizes with alcohol. Don'ts budgin drinks."

She shook her head. "Addition to file." She scanned the scar. "Note, injury was not laser sealed. Stitched up by the patient."

Dr. Bentley listed numerous visible scars, contusions and abrasions on the orphan's body. When she was finished with the visible marks, she scanned him with the orthopedic scanner and listed previously broken bones. She noted a healed fracture on his left wrist that appeared to be excessively calcified. Bentley assumed, since it was consistent with a hairline break, Malone had not realized it was broken and received no medical attention for the injury. The same was true for the cracked collarbone and broken ribs. After noting the third rib, she stopped.

She looked up from the file perplexed. "Was there some damage to your ID card?"

Zeus watched her every move. He did not like people close to him or touching him. "Huh?" Her question made no sense.

"None of your injuries are in your medical file. Did your ID card get damaged in some way?"

"Nope."

The doctor willed her voice to sound neutral. "Cadet, how did you get all these broken bones? Who's setting these things? And why aren't they noted in your medical file?"

"I's budgin broke 'em in fights and ats works and I's sets 'em."

"I'm sorry, I'm having some trouble understanding you. Would you repeat it?"

"Broke 'em fights. I's sets 'em."

Dr. Bentley's brown eyebrows met over the bridge of her nose. "You've got to be kidding. How could you possibly do that?"

The orphan refused to dignify her comment with a response.

Sgt. Baker's nostrils flared. He marched over and yelled in Zeus's ear, "Malone, you will not disregard officers' requests. You will answer when you are spoken to. Drop, start counting, and don't stop until you hurt so bad you need a doctor."

"Yeah, Sir." The orphan hopped off the table and counted aloud.

Dr. Bentley shook her head at the sergeant and motioned him over to the corner. "You're not helping. I'm having enough trouble with him as it is."

Baker stood his ground. "Look, Doctor, that kid's got to learn respect. Maybe if he's tired, he'll be more polite."

Dr. Bentley was about to tell the sergeant never to question her, when she stopped herself. "I know he's making us a little crazy, and you're trying to protect me, but I need to earn the respect and trust of my patients. OK?"

Sgt. Baker looked at his shoes and shook his head. "Sorry. Do it your way."

Dr. Bentley patted him. "You'll have plenty of time to pick on him later."

Baker thought about the future opportunities, raised his eyebrows and grinned. "Malone, stop and stand to."

The orphan stopped and stood wondering how he had gotten himself into this. A bunch of budgin idiots. As the doctor walked back over, Zeus glared at her. "I's snaps 'em backs ins place. Ones crack. Sames ways they's sets bones for budgin centuries."

Bentley had studied the archaic method and was shocked to realize the orphan must be telling the truth. The scanner confirmed it. There were no traces of caladrom in his bones. Current orthopedic treatments used caladrom and had for the past one hundred years. She cringed as she pictured this man trying to "crack" his collarbone back in place. The orphan had to be crazy. As soon as the Alphas left, she would contact Cmd. Yoggi and insist a complete mental health work-up be done. Until then, she should get a detailed list of his previous injuries. Surely the volume of fights his body suggested would indicate some mental instability or antisocial behavior.

Dr. Bentley continued to make conversation as she documented Malone's body. "You set them all yourself?"

Zeus paused, looked at Sgt. Baker and replied, "Thems bastards ats the clinic sets my's femur. . .Ma'am."

Bentley nodded, trying to ignore his insulting vocabulary. The scanner confirmed caladrom present in his left femur. She consciously softened her voice. "Why not the rest of them?"

The orphan grew more indignant. He yelled, "Yous profession don't treats the poors and indigent. Tooks me's three budgin weeks ta earns cash ta gets a leg set."

Dr. Bentley chewed her lip nervously. She wanted to defend herself and her colleagues, but she did not know of anyone who had ever treated an orphan. Numerous medical school friends had called to comment on her treating one. As the horror of the truth sank in, she dropped the scanner. The noise startled her. She took a moment to regain her composure.

She had not noticed his teeth, until he spoke with his mouth open. She stood to get a better look. Her voice cracked. "No dental care, either?"

"Nope, Ma'am."

She struggled to maintain her professionalism. In her nicest voice, Dr. Bentley requested, "Open your mouth, please."

Zeus eyed Sgt. Baker. He tried to open his mouth while shielding his teeth with his lips and breathing through his nose. The cool air stung as it passed over the exposed roots. Dr. Bentley looked inside in dismay. A quick scan revealed only a few teeth intact. The rest were missing, cracked or chipped. There was a visible infection and numerous sores from jagged teeth.

"Nurse." She sighed. "Call Dr. Jones. Tell her I'm sending Malone up for immediate attention."

Zeus wondered who Dr. Jones was and what "immediate attention" meant. His mind raced. They would not dispose of him this quickly.

CHAPTER 2

AS ZEUS DRESSED, he tried to prepare some possible counterattacks. Sgt. Baker waited, then led him up two flights of stairs. Cadets were not allowed to use the elevators. As the pair walked up the steps, the orphan memorized his surroundings.

A standard stairwell with doors on each floor and solid concrete walls. The only exits would be down on the first floor. The fourth floor appeared to be similar to the second floor, where the examinations were taking place. Room 402 was catty-corner from the stairwell. At least there is easy access to the stairs and a possible exit. The room number was above the door. The door had a standard OTS name plate, "Dr. Barbara Jones, DDS."

Zeus did not know that dentists had DDS after their names and assumed it was another unfamiliar military abbreviation. The orphan had no idea what to expect. He had heard mouth torture was excruciating. He surmised Bentley had seen his infected tooth and realized it was already painful. Perhaps they were going to force him to chew ice or do something else that, on the surface, could not be construed as torture. Something they could get away with, while still forcing him to think twice about staying. He was ready. He was not quitting. Zeus had too much at stake.

A young woman was waiting for the two men when they entered.

Baker came to attention and saluted. "Dr. Jones, I am Sgt. Baker, and this is Cadet Malone." He turned to the orphan. "Malone, you will salute an officer or sergeant each and every time you see one. Understand?"

"Yeah, Sir," the orphan responded with an annoyed tone and a poor salute.

Dr. Jones, still unaccustomed to military routines, forgot to salute back. Doctors and medical personnel were the only people not

16

required to go through basic training or boot camp.

"Thank you, Sergeant," she said. "Where should I send him when I'm done?"

Sgt. Baker glanced around to see who else was in the office. He saw only the doctor and her assistant. Baker had seen visuals of Zeus's maxor bouts and determined Dr. Jones and her assistant would be no match for the orphan. "If you'd like, Doctor," he looked her in the eye, "I'll remain here until you're done."

Jones assumed he was being polite. She was not inherently prejudiced. It had not occurred to her to treat the orphan differently. "That won't be necessary. This could take a long time. I know you're busy today. I'll contact you when he's ready to return."

"Yes, Doctor." He saluted, turned and left. Sgt. Baker always obeyed officer's orders. He also knew how to get around them. He would have Sgt. Leiman come and check on Malone in a few minutes and other sergeants after that, as he deemed necessary.

Zeus was relieved to see Baker leave, because he was not easily intimidated. Zeus put his left hand in his pocket and stroked his switchblade. All he knew was this woman called herself a doctor. What the private did, he could not determine.

"Zeus, follow me," she chirped. Dr. Jones called her patients, except the high-ranking ones, by their first names. It made people more relaxed and comfortable around her.

He followed, memorizing his escape route. The smell of disinfectant irritated his empty stomach.

She motioned him into a recliner.

He burped sour acids as he sat, studying his surroundings. There were dozens of lasers and sharp instruments he could not identify. The red hair on the back of his neck stood on end. In all his years of dealing with the network, he had never seen or used any of these tools. As a survivor, not much fazed him, but right now, Zeus was scared. He knew he could withstand pain; he had had a great deal of experience with that. However, the unknown made him nervous. He would be ready to defend himself. The orphan ran his sweaty fingers across the smooth surface of his concealed weapon.

Dr. Jones asked her customary first-visit question, "When was the last time you saw a dentist?"

"Never." At least I know what type of doctor she is.

"Never? Do any of your teeth hurt?"

"Nope." He wasn't about to tell her which teeth were perfect for torturing.

"All right. Well, sit back and let's have a look," she chirped.

The private's hands shook as he attempted to put a paper bib around the patient's neck.

Zeus noted the private's apprehension and assumed he was being forced to assist in the upcoming torture. Zeus would use that knowledge when the time came. He needed more information on his opponents, then he would plan his defense.

The orphan slapped the bib to the floor. "Huh yous budgin do'n?"

Dr. Jones patted Zeus's arm. He grabbed her hand and threw it back at her.

"It's nothing to be worried about. The bib is just to keep your clothes clean."

Zeus gasped. She was openly admitting there would be bloodshed. Perhaps she was testing him to see how far he would go before retaliating. She was not going to discourage him that easily. He defiantly allowed the private to put on the bib.

"Sit back and relax," Dr. Jones stated.

Zeus obeyed. The chair reclined, not an advantageous fighting position. He stroked the calming steel of the Little Lady. He was amazed they had not checked him for weapons. They had underestimated him. He would use that to his advantage as well.

"Would you like to listen to some music while I'm working?" Dr. Jones asked.

"Huh?"

"I have access to a wide selection." She handed him the headphones.

"Nope." Zeus pushed them away. He intended to listen to everything they said.

"Then we'll get started. Open your mouth, please," she asked sweetly.

The orphan had never heard of a polite abuser. Perhaps that was her trademark. He opened his mouth only slightly, knowing that's not what she wanted.

"Would you open wider for me?"

Dr. Jones examined his mouth briefly. She picked up a reflection scanner and a sharp pointed hook.

Here we go, the orphan thought, fingering the steel in his pocket.

The doctor saw the visibly infected molar. The right side of Zeus's mouth was red and swollen from the infection. She laughed to herself. Military men think they are impervious to pain. "You're certain none of your teeth hurt?"

"None." He knew it would not matter in a few minutes.

She dipped the scanner into a clear solution and put it into his mouth. The drops of moisture should have felt good to Zeus's dry mouth, but the smell of antiseptic nauseated him. She turned the instrument around and tapped his front teeth with blunt end. He could taste the metal mixed with disinfectant. She continued tapping back toward the abscessed molar. Two teeth before the molar, Zeus felt discomfort. She tapped the tooth in front of the molar. He winced. She lightly touched the infected tooth. Excruciating pain shot through his face. It felt like she had driven a spike from his tooth up through his eye socket. He yanked the Little Lady out, opened her claw and jammed it against the doctor's throat.

Dr. Jones remained composed as the young private rolled his chair away from the orphan's knife. Dr. Jones carefully laid her instruments down on the tray. She felt the blade catching on the skin of her neck. Her voice was quiet. "Now, Zeus, please put the knife down. I'm sorry I hurt you."

"Budgin yous. I's ain'ts gonna lay here whiles yous torture'n me's." He pushed the blade into her skin.

She focused on keeping her voice tranquil. "I don't know where you got the idea I wanted to hurt you. I don't. I'm a dentist. My job is to fix your teeth." She could feel from the closeness of the blade that the orphan was not convinced. This scenario was never addressed in dental school. Not certain what to do, she continued to explain. "You have an abscessed tooth. It is badly infected. That's the sensitive one I touched." The blade was still pressed tightly against her skin. Talking seemed her only option. "I need to start you on an antibiotic."

That registered with the orphan. Zeus was aware he needed an antibiotic. He had tried to obtain one; unfortunately he could not afford the black-market price. The tooth had gotten worse. He knew the infection had spread.

Instinct told Dr. Jones she was on the right track. "Are you aller-

19

gic to any medication? Are you taking anything currently?"

He tried to determine if she was telling the truth, but he refused to answer or loosen his grip.

"Zeus, I can't help you if you won't let me." Think, she thought, what would persuade him to trust me. Where would he have gotten the idea that anyone in OTS would mistreat him? Of course, she had never been through boot camp or seen the abuse the staff forced the cadets to endure. She decided to try some logic.

"I guess you haven't felt welcome here; however, you're an intelligent man. Consider this. The entire universe is watching to see how the military treats you. Do you really think we'd get away with blatant abuse? If you don't survive, the press would have a field day, and I might be out of a job. If you do get out, the public will want to know how you were treated." She felt him relax slightly.

Dr. Jones decided medicating him was her best option. "You've got to have an antibiotic. Your infection is spreading. If it goes into your eye socket, you might lose your sight," she lied. "Let me start with the antibiotic, and then we'll talk about the rest. At least, tell me if you're allergic to any medications or currently taking any."

If she wanted to hurt him, why was she asking those questions. He was not certain he believed her, but it did not hurt to answer. "Nope."

Good. I'm making progress. I just hope my assistant does not blow this. "Private, please prepare the antibiotic," she emphasized the word antibiotic. "I'll need three cc's of meliline."

The private was about to correct her, when he caught her eye and understood. "Yes, Doctor. Three cc's of meliline." He turned his chair toward the drug cabinet.

"What yous do'n?" The orphan flashed the knife at him.

Dr. Jones redirected Zeus to herself. "He's just getting you some antibiotics. They're right in the cabinet. Nobody's going to hurt you. There's nowhere for him to go without passing in front of your chair. You're completely in control here."

Zeus puffed out his chest. He was in charge.

"Zeus," Jones continued, "I'm sure you've heard of the antibiotic meliline. Let my assistant get some out. You can verify for yourself that's what we're giving you."

Her bluff was working. Zeus had not heard of meliline; however, he would never admit that. "I's checks it."

20

The private reached into the cabinet and handed the orphan a vial. Keeping the knife centimeters from the doctor's face, Zeus read the little bottle. "Yous put poison ins."

"Well. . ." she searched for something to say. "It does have the customary lavender tinge."

"Budgin cheap dyes."

"You could smell it." She hoped he had no idea what antibiotics smelled like. Offering to let him smell the contents was a risk she would have to take. "Since you're familiar with meliline, you know it has a distinct odor." The drug did have a pungent smell; unfortunately, it smelled like the other sedatives in its group. She was hoping he would not know that. "Would you like me to open it, and you can smell it?"

Zeus waved the knife in front of her and handed her the lavender liquid. "Open its."

As she broke the seal, the odor wafted through the air.

That is a distinct smell, he thought. Besides, what she said earlier made sense. They could not overtly hurt him, and if he did not cooperate, he would be discharged. He could not leave; that would be a voluntary dismissal. His only choice was to concede. There were others counting on him to succeed. Zeus was pleased he had made a statement. He was not going to let anyone push him around. As Dr. Jones had said, he was in charge. "Three cc's, no mores."

She took an injector, filled it to three cc's and gave it to Zeus to verify the amount. "Which arm do you want it in?"

"Right," Zeus responded. He was left-handed. "I's watch'n yous." He flashed the knife so the reflecting light danced in her eyes.

"I'm getting a sterilizer." She swiveled slightly to reach the sterilizer, swiveled around and cleaned a spot on his upper arm. "This won't hurt." She injected the liquid into his arm.

Within seconds, Zeus realized he had been outmaneuvered and deceived. "Yous budgin b. . ." his voice trailed off as the sedative took effect.

As soon as his grip relaxed, Dr. Jones snatched the knife and breathed a sigh of relief. "And we thought it was going to be a boring day," she joked to the private.

"Do you think he's really out?" the private asked.

Dr. Jones lifted his arm and let it drop listlessly to the armrest.

"I'd say he is completely harmless. We should report this and then get to work on his mouth."

The private rolled his chair away. "We still have to work on him?"

"Yes. You've seen his mouth. He's in desperate need of dental care. You go take a break," Dr. Jones instructed.

"You're going to stay alone with him?" He pointed to the orphan.

"He'll be sedated for hours without a counter-stimulant. It's policy never to leave a tranquilized patient unattended, and I gave him almost double the usual amount. Simply fetch me a ComLine, so I can report this." She strapped the monitor on Zeus's arm and took readings. Dr. Jones was relieved everything appeared normal.

They heard a voice from the waiting room. "Dr. Jones? This is Sgt. Leiman."

"I'm in the first room on the right," she called out.

Leiman entered and saluted. "I wanted to check on my recruit."

"I'm afraid you've missed all the excitement." Jones patted her patient's hand.

The private blurted out, "That crazy orphan pulled a knife on us."

"What?" the sergeant exclaimed.

"He's a little less agitated, now that I've sedated him." Jones rechecked his vital signs.

The private quickly told Leiman the entire story.

"We were just getting ready to report it. Who do you report something like this to?" the doctor inquired.

Sgt. Leiman pulled out her ComLine and punched in Cmd. Yoggi's extension. "The top."

*   *   *

Cmd. Cheryl Yoggi walked briskly to the medical building. She was tall for her Asian heritage and took long strides.

Dr. Bentley was surprised to run into Yoggi at the elevator. "I was going to call you later, after I had some more test results on Malone. There are a few problems." Bentley attempted a salute. If she had been following regulations, she would not have spoken until after she had saluted and the commander had given her permission.

Yoggi was aware medical people were a breed of their own. She had long since given up trying to get them to comply with regulations. She appreciated Bentley's attempts at following the rules. Many doctors felt they were above even trying. The two were on friendly terms and each respected the other's abilities.

"Don't tell me you had trouble, too." Yoggi's slanted eyes widen.

"Fourth floor." The elevator whined softly. "Is Barb having problems upstairs?"

"You might say that. Malone pulled a knife on her."

"Are they all right?"

"Yes, everyone's fine. You didn't tell me our new dentist has nerves of steel. I could use more like her on the front lines."

"Barb overpowered Malone?"

"More like outsmarted him." They stepped out of the elevator. While they were walking, Cmd. Yoggi explained what had happened.

"I may have a possible explanation for his behavior," Bentley said as they entered the room where Zeus was sedated.

Dr. Jones was busy draining pus from Zeus's abscessed tooth. "Hi, Sarah. What explanation do you have?"

"Barb, are you OK?" Bentley squeezed her shoulder.

"Yes, I'm fine." Thick yellow pus tinged with red meandered through a clear tube and into a micro-beaker. "What's your explanation for his behavior?"

"He's starving. Whether it's lack of food or a condition, I don't know. But I think it's lack of food. If my tests are accurate, it has been at least three or four days since he's eaten. Some possible side effects: irritability, poor judgment, overreaction. Do any of these sound familiar?"

"You didn't say delusional. He actually thought I was going to torture him."

Bentley tapped the half full micro-beaker. "Is that all from the one abscess?"

"Yes."

"No wonder he's nuts, between that tooth and no food, who wouldn't be?"

Yoggi diverted her eyes from the bloody pus. "Best guesses, doctors, could either starvation or the infected tooth be the reason for his erratic behavior?"

"With an infection this large, and with as many nerve endings as there are in the mouth and so close to the brain stem, it's very likely to have temporarily made him highly agitated, I suppose, even violent." Jones adjusted the tubing and continued draining. "I'm not yet certain if the infection has spread beyond the mouth. I was going to have Sarah check it before deciding which antibiotic to use."

Dr. Bentley flipped on her scanner and moved around to the side of the chair. She waved the wand slowly over and around the sleeping patient's head. "Infection acute in the molar has spread to the gums. . . mouth. . .inner cheek. . .you'll need to drain that area as well. Nothing else."

Dr. Bentley paused, then added, "I'd recommend a shot of benoltal, followed by a round of oral boosters."

"Good, that's what I thought."

"I checked what I can with the scanner. All indications are that he's had periods of starvation his whole life." Bentley slid the wand into its holder. "There are only a few known diseases that could account for his low blood sugars. I have essentially ruled them out. I have a few more sophisticated tests to run; however, I'm ninety-five percent certain right now. It's possible he's anorexic and self-starving, but I doubt it. His problem is he's poor. When I first started to examine him, I thought he was crazy." She pulled up his shirt to show them the scar on his stomach. "He told me he stitched it himself with fishing line."

"You're kidding." Yoggi ran her finger down the long, smooth scar tissue.

"No, and his tests confirm his story."

Yoggi could count each of the orphan's ribs. "We're in for a lot more than we expected. Any suggestions for how we should proceed."

Sgt. Leiman jumped in. "Can't we declare him medically unfit and get rid of the problem?"

"That's not very compassionate," Dr. Jones stated.

"It's also not medically accurate. He's not unfit. He's starving." Dr. Bentley lightly pinched Zeus's emaciated belly. "There's not a gram of fat on him. The treatment, if you will, is simply to feed him, which hardly qualifies as untreatable or difficult to administer. I believe those are the stated reasons I am allowed to use according to OTS bylaws."

"It's also political suicide." Yoggi framed an imaginary box. "I can see the headlines now, 'OTS takes poor, medically deprived orphan and kicks him out for starvation.' No, I realize you want him out, Sergeant; we all do, but we're going to have to do better than that."

"Yes, Commander."

"However, this information could be used later, to support other reasons. I want those of you involved with him to dictate reports on all your encounters with Malone. Sergeant?" She turned to Leiman. "You and Baker send me daily reports of your observations. I want details, both good and bad. If you two observe only negative things, we'll appear prejudiced. Be sure and note all the positive things he does."

"Yes, Commander," she snapped. Just what I wanted, more reports. I already hate this kid.

"We're going to need everything to get him out of here. Dr. Jones, I'm impressed with the way you've handled Malone so far. Keep up the good work."

"Thank you." Jones set the micro-beaker on the counter.

Yoggi stood at the head of Zeus's chair. "How's your schedule for the rest of the week?"

"Basically empty. I understand that's typical. The staff is too busy the first few weeks for dental appointments." She scanned the orphan's mouth. "I obviously need to see Zeus some more."

"Good. Get those teeth fixed ASAP." Yoggi drummed her fingers on Zeus's headrest. "Did you take a before picture scan of his mouth?"

"Yes, before I started draining his abscess."

"Do it daily of your progress. How long will it take you to finish him?"

"There's a lot to be done here. It's not usually recommended to work on a patient for more than a few hours at a time. I also have some problems I'm not certain how to deal with. I'll have to contact a couple of experts. Then I will need to order whatever I don't have in supply. Supplies can take up to a week to come in. If I order a rush job, I might be able to get them in three or four days. To be honest, Commander, I'm new at this. I've never seen or heard of anything like his mouth. I'm just guessing, but I'd say two to three weeks, if I worked on him daily."

"Do the best you can. I want the universe to see the things we did for him before we kicked him out. Anything visible will help. Dr. Bentley," she turned to her, "along those lines, get him gaining weight quickly. Take his weight now, and monitor it regularly. When he leaves here, that man better be in the best health he's ever been in."

"Good. I was going to talk to you about that. Until Malone is at acceptable blood-glucose levels and within the normal fat reserves range, I don't think it's wise to push him beyond his limits." Dr. Bentley peered at Sgt. Leiman out of the corner of her eyes.

"What exactly would his limits be?"

"Only he could tell us that. It's possible he will be dizzy, light-headed, nauseated. There could be vomiting, muscle cramping, even fainting. He doesn't have the reserves to be physically pushed for hours a day." She glanced at Sgt. Leiman.

"You've got to be kidding. Let him decide when he's had enough? He's in boot camp." Leiman stomped her foot. "He's supposed to be miserable."

"It could be medically dangerous for Cadet Malone," Dr. Bentley stated flatly.

"Commander, I've got forty-nine other recruits who are depressed an orphan is in their unit. If Malone is allowed to decide when he's had enough, the Alpha's morale will be shot."

"I agree. He's not the only cadet here. Doctor," Cmd. Yoggi suggested diplomatically, "until his tests are normal, perhaps you could set some guidelines for Malone. State the maximums the sergeants can push him to."

"I'm sorry. My first obligation is to my patient. I'm not making a recommendation. I'm stating a medical necessity, and that's exactly how I'm putting it in my report."

"I realize you want this to be by the book, but we've got to work together to get him out of here. No one wants to be responsible for problems with Malone. You won't be a scapegoat. I'll support you. Don't worry, you have plenty of witnesses." Yoggi swept her arm around the room.

"Commander, I'm sorry." She bit her lower lip. "This isn't CYA medicine. It's basic human rights and compassion. I don't care if I do take the blame or make you and others angry. What you're asking me to do is wrong. You talk about fairness to the others. How fair is it that Malone has starved most of his life?"

Cmd. Yoggi put her hands up. "OK, OK, calm down. I don't want you to do anything you feel is morally wrong. What about setting some limitations for the sergeants?"

"You may think I'm being pigheaded, but I can't set limitations. Every patient is different. He may be able to do ten pushups one day and fifty the next. Or pushups will be fine and sit-ups won't. I can't set guidelines for when Malone will feel nauseated or dizzy. The only one who will know when he feels those things is Malone."

"Let a cadet decide." Sgt. Leiman rolled her eyes.

"Can't you defer him to next year's class?" Bentley asked.

"No, I'd wish I could. My superiors have stated that is not an option. The Corps would receive another year of bad press. Plus TUC would appear to be putting Malone off."

"I sympathize with the sergeant's predicament. I will treat him aggressively. I suggest for the next few weeks. . ."

"Weeks?" Sgt. Leiman threw her hands up. "Boot camp only lasts four weeks."

Bentley shrugged. "I suggest we schedule his visits to Barb and me during the most physically demanding periods of the day. He'll have to miss something; it might as well be things he can't do. Besides, think about it; the more often he eats and the fewer calories he burns, the faster he'll gain weight."

"Nobody gains weight in boot camp," Sgt. Leiman retorted. "We have floating sergeants steal the units' food supplies."

"Sergeant, you listen to me carefully." Bentley shook her finger at the sergeant. "No one is to take away Cadet Malone's meals until I tell you he's healthy. You and Baker work it out, or I'll write you both up. You will see he gets exactly what I prescribe. Nothing less. I'll be telling Malone everything I've told you. He will decide if you're pushing him too hard, and he will eat at least three meals a day. No exceptions. Got it?"

"She's got it," Yoggi interjected. "Doctors, get him healthy as fast as you can. I want you both to report to me at the end of the day."

"Yes, Ma'am," Bentley answered as Jones nodded.

Cmd. Yoggi took her ComLine out of her pocket. "Patch me through to Capt. Haden." She held the ComLine to her ear.

"Capt. Haden," he quickly answered.

"It's Cmd. Yoggi. Cadet Malone pulled a knife on Dr. Jones. I want you to get a security team over to her office right away. I don't want any more problems."

"Yes, Ma'am."

"Excuse me." Dr. Jones set down her instrument. "If you bring an armed guard in here, Zeus will never trust me."

"And it will look bad," Sgt. Leiman added.

"Good point. Capt. Haden, get your team over here. Make sure he's unarmed and the room is cleared of all weapons before he wakes up. You and your team can set up a monitor in here. Then stay out of sight and watch him from the next room. Do the same thing when he's with Dr. Bentley."

"Yes, Ma'am. We're on our way."

The Commander put her ComLine in her pocket. "Come on, Sergeant, let's get out of here."

*   *   *

"Zeus, can you hear me? Zeus, this is Dr. Jones." She gently shook her patient.

Zeus's eyes slowly began to focus on her face. At first all he could see was the outline of her brown hair around a hazy white oval. Her voice sounded shallow and distant as he tried to remember where he was. Slowly her hazel gray eyes came into focus and her voice seemed more real and less dream-like.

"Zeus, this is Dr. Jones. Can you hear me? It's time to wake up."

"Dr. Jones?" He kept repeating the name in his head. Something told him he should know that name. Dr. Jones, Dr. Jones. . .the tooth torturer. He jumped up out of the chair. Still groggy, he became dizzy. His long legs felt like wet noodles. He grabbed the armrest for balance. Dr. Jones caught him and eased him into the chair.

"Calm down. You're fine. Just relax a minute and get your bearings."

Zeus felt the burn of vomit in his throat. He choked back the acid. He could not defend himself in this condition. The words of his Kalopso trainer echoed in his ear. "If yous hurt or can'ts win, stall and waits for a better times." Zeus took some deep breaths to settle his empty stomach.

"Everything's fine. No one is trying to hurt you."

Her melodious voice seemed incongruous with the horrible thoughts he had of her. How could she continue to sound so sweet after what she had done to him? Then Zeus thought, what has she done? He quickly took stock of his body. Everything was there and nothing hurt.

"Budgin bastard. Huh, yous do's ta me's?"

Dr. Jones ignored the insult. "Take a look." She rotated the chair to an upright position and handed him a mirror. "I think you'll be pleased."

28

"Pleased?" Maybe she had given him a mind-altering drug.

Zeus grabbed the mirror and stared at his own reflection in shock. He was startled at his short hair and clean-shaven face. He hardly recognized himself. He had had the beard and scraggly hair since puberty. He was about to panic about why Dr. Jones had needed access to his skull when he remembered the shave and haircut by the barber. Zeus had only glanced at himself while being shaved and had not looked since.

"How do they feel?" Dr. Jones was eager to hear.

"Huh?"

"You're light-headed from the sedative. Give yourself a minute. You'll feel better."

Zeus rubbed his eyes and focused on his reflection.

"Are any of your teeth still hurting?"

"Stills hurt'n?"

"I never intended to harm you. I'm here to fix your teeth. I've drained your abscesses and started you on an antibiotic. There were two other teeth with exposed roots. One I had to pull, and the other I can save. I've smoothed all the rough edges and sealed the cuts inside your mouth. I've cleaned everything up and started two root repairs. I also gave you six temporary crowns. That should protect things until I've had a chance to fix them." She could see he was dumbfounded. "Go ahead and check."

Zeus sheepishly opened his mouth. He was dumbfounded. He put his finger in the corner of his mouth and looked at the infected molar. The redness and swelling were gone. The tooth was covered with a small white cylinder. He took his finger out of his mouth; his hand shook as he lightly brushed his cheek over the molar. No pain. He laid his hand over the cheek. No pain. He pressed his hand hard on his face, moved his fingers and pressed around the area. Still no pain.

"I want to thank you for making me feel like a real dentist today. I just recently graduated and was afraid I'd be stuck doing routine check-ups for years."

"Huh?" He lowered the mirror.

"I enjoyed working on you."

He stared at her.

"Does it hurt?" she inquired.

He shook his head.

"Try biting down a few times and tell me how it feels."

Zeus obeyed tentatively at first, and then bit as hard as he could. The molar did not hurt. None of his teeth hurt. He was stunned. Ever since he was a child, he had always had problems with one tooth or another. "Ain'ts hurt'n. . .none a thems." He quivered. He looked at her gratefully confused.

Dr. Jones thought he was close to tears. "You're welcome." She smiled warmly. "I'm glad I could help."

Zeus returned her smile. Out of habit, he shoved his hand in his pocket. The Little Lady was missing. Then he remembered. His heart raced. "I's blade. . .I's thoughts yous. . .I's thoughts. . ."

"It's all right." She patted him on the shoulder. "No one got hurt. I know you were in a lot of pain and you haven't eaten. Anybody could be confused under those conditions."

"Huh?" Why was she showing him compassion and understanding? What had he done to deserve this? What did she want from him? He felt like he had to force himself to breathe.

"Here, let me show you what I've done and what I'm going to do in the next few weeks." She could hardly contain herself as she showed him a scan of his mouth. "This is what it looked like before." She pointed to the picture. She went through each tooth describing what needed to be done. She explained the problems she intended to consult the experts on and how everything would be at completion. "Isn't it exciting? You're going to have a new mouth with a beautiful, healthy smile."

The corners of his mouth turned up. Nothing had made him more aware that he was poor. Starving was bad enough. When toothaches prevented him from enjoying what little food he had, Zeus felt cheated. He was always jealous of people with good teeth.

"Do you have any questions?"

He shook his head, picked up the mirror and stared at himself. The more he thought about a new mouth, the bigger the grin got on his face.

"You ought to show off those dimples more." Jones watched Zeus methodically check each tooth in his mouth and verify its proposed treatment on the scanner. His face beamed and his eyes sparkled.

He had three teeth to go when he slowly lowered his head, frowned and handed her the mirror.

"What's the matter? Is there something wrong with that one?"

"Crap, I's can'ts affords none a it. Budgin, takes me's forever ta pays for the crap yous done taday."

Dr. Jones ignored his atrocious vocabulary. She was impressed he was offering to pay for his own care. Paying seemed honorable knowing he did not have enough money for food. "Don't worry. Medical and dental are part of the OTS package. Trust me. Check your handbook."

As required, Zeus had memorized the handbook before entering OTS. The orphan protested anyway. "Handbooks don't apply ta me's."

"Of course it applies. You're an OTS cadet. Why wouldn't it?"

This woman was totally crazy. "I's orphan."

"I fail to see what difference that makes."

"Budgin plenty."

"Well, it doesn't matter here." She slapped the arm of her chair.

Zeus twitched. "Not ta yous, budgin most. I's have ta pays for what yous done."

"I think this is another misunderstanding. Trust me. This is covered."

"I's orphan. Ain'ts gots no insurance. Ain'ts noth'n covers."

Dr. Jones was shocked at how ingrained his acceptance of prejudice was. It delighted her to inform him otherwise. "Cmd. Yoggi was here while you were asleep. She wants Dr. Bentley and me to give you the best, most aggressive care we can. You are covered for all the medical treatments you receive at OTS."

"Cmd. Yoggi says I's ain'ts gots ta pay fors this?" He tugged at the corner of his mouth.

"She didn't say it quite like that. She did say your treatments were courtesy of the Corps."

The orphan looked dazed. "Yous budgin sure?"

"Yes, I'm certain." She nodded. "You'll return here tomorrow."

He sat up, stiff backed, in the chair. "Put me's ta sleep tamorrow?"

"I hope not. I don't normally sedate my patients. I was hoping we could trust each other."

"Huh, I's do's?"

"I'm sorry, what did you say?"

"Trust me's?"

"You just have to relax and cooperate. I won't intentionally hurt you. If something hurts, tell me. I'll make sure it doesn't. If there's something I can do to make this easier, talk to me. Visiting the dentist is not meant to be a frightening experience. I don't know where you got the idea I would purposely harm you. I won't. I hope you believe that."

"Yeah."

"Good." She smiled. "If you'll trust me, I'll trust you, and I won't need to sedate you. Deal?"

Zeus nodded.

"When you feel well enough to walk, I'm going to escort you down to Dr. Bentley's office."

"I's fine." He stood. He did not want to appear weak or out of control.

"Take it slow."

CHAPTER 3

ZEUS OBSERVED EVERY DETAIL of the medical examining room. There was an exam table, two chairs, a rolling stool, a counter with cabinets, a sink and a trash can. He opened each cabinet. There were only a few sparse supplies. He checked underneath the table. His head swirled.

He rolled onto the table and lay still until his equilibrium returned. He ran his tongue along the smooth surfaces of his temporary teeth. What was going on here? Were they trying to gain his trust until they had an opportunity to kick him out? Were they genuinely going to be kind and fair? Never. People were not that way. . .no one but Emily. He had trusted only her, and that relationship had cost him more than he was ever willing to pay again. Today's confusion was similar to the frustration he felt the first day he met Emily. His thoughts wandered back to their first meeting.

*   *   *

Red Top scurried after the leechrat. His lanky limbs rattled in the wind. The scrawny boy's only chance for eating was catching the brown rodent. "Got yous." He grabbed the short rubbery tail. It brushed his pinkie and slithered through his fingers.

The animal's coarse, uneven fur stood up. The leechrat's large head turned to bite with its huge mouth and sucking lips. The light blinded the animal's beady red eyes. It sniffed its the enemy. He was still close. The leechrat ran to the safety of an old ventilation pipe.

Red Top rubbed his swollen belly, stared at the dark tunnel, then crouched low and followed his prey into the hole. The light grew dimmer and dimmer until he was engulfed in darkness. Red Top heard scraping and scratching. He crawled slowly, scooting his hands on the rough surface. His left fingertips bent back. He turned right, groping his way around the twists and turns of the pipes.

There was a slight movement beneath his palm. Red Top paused, pressing down hard. He carefully bent his fingers around an insect, scooped it up and popped the morsel in his mouth. He closed his eyes and tried to guess what he was eating. He could hear the crunching and feel the grit between his teeth. Water bug. He licked his hands, then sat quietly, straining his ears to hear the scratching. It was close.

He moved toward the scraping. The sounds grew closer and more frequent. Now he heard the constant sound of nails clawing on metal. The leechrat was trapped. I have got him. Unfortunately, he had not considered how to blindly catch a leechrat. Red Top sat down, blocking the exit. He rubbed his aching knees, wondering how he could get the rodent.

He sniffed the air for his prey, but a sulfuric odor dulled his nostrils. The boy heard the panicked animal scratching. It seemed to mock him. In frustration, he flung himself at the noise.

The leechrat bit down hard in self defense. The boy felt the animal's sharp teeth pierce his naked thigh. It's powerful mouth sucked hard. Red Top screamed with glee and plopped back on his bottom. Luck was with him. The rodent had locked its jaws on his bony leg. Lunch was ready.

He pulled his knife out of the only pocket left in his shorts and popped open the blade. Red Top held the animal's tail, felt for the body, then plunged the blade into the leechrat. The child sat in the darkness and devoured the raw flesh, chewing and grinding the rubbery tidbits, licking every drop of blood from his hands and thigh. He would save the bones for later, when he was desperate. He could chew the bones when nothing else was available. With the ache in his gut gone, Red Top leaned against the pipes and took a nap.

He heard a scream and his eyes jerked open. Red Top rubbed his eyes to help them focus, then remembered the pipes. There was nothing to see. He sat still and concentrated on slow, shallow breathing.

Red Top listened to the voices above him. Someone had not completed their work for the day and was being punished. If he did not return to his work unit soon, he too would be beaten.

He felt slowly around the tunnel. He was surprised to feel three openings leading away from the upward pipe. Which one goes back to the mines? He put one of the leechrat bones in his mouth and chewed. He savored the mangy flavor a moment, took a deep breath and headed down the middle tunnel.

He continued through the pipes, stopping at each pipe that angled upward. Red Top listened to the mine noises above him. A whip cracked loudly. Red Top dropped the bone he was chewing and scampered though the darkness. The screams and moans chased after him, echoing endlessly with the faceless victim's pain. When the noise stopped, so did Red Top. He sat and tried to calm his pounding heart. If he did not return soon, he would be next. He wanted to chew his bone for comfort. It was gone. He had lost the precious item. Red Top scolded his weakness. The bone was too valuable to lose for fear without threat. He vowed never to be weak again.

He sniffed the air. Something was different. He could feel a breeze tickle his thin red hair. Red Top licked his finger and raised it. The knuckle side cooled slightly. He headed that way thinking, I'll follow the breeze to the mine opening.

His hands passed over a large bump and he headed up an incline. The new pipe was cool and smooth to the touch. He made a steady climb in silence. At last his eyes began to focus. He followed the light to a metal grate covering an opening.

He peeked through it into a large room and saw a waxing yellow moon through the window. He panned the room. It was dark outside. The moon was only a sliver. There were no fires or lanterns, yet the room was flooded with light. There was a strange glowing box on the table with funny squiggle lines and a similar smaller pad on the counter. The box talked, and a preteen girl talked back to it. He sat mesmerized, silently casing the room.

The girl with long auburn hair went over to an oddly shaped hole in the counter. She placed a long skinny glass under a shiny metal thing sticking out of the counter. She said, "Water on," and filled the test tube with water. "Water off."

Red Top was overcome with thirst. He kicked in the air return vent, jumped down and waved his open knife in the girl's face. She pulled away, shaking. He grabbed the test tube of water and drank it in one gulp.

He whirled around behind her, put the blade to her throat and nicked her. "Mores." Red Top felt a tear fall between his knife and thumb. He pushed the girl to the hole in the counter. "Mores."

"Water on," she said and it began to flow.

Red Top pushed her aside and jumped on the counter. With his left hand, he waved the knife at the girl. With his right, he grabbed an empty beaker off the counter, filled it with water and gulped the precious fluid. He kept his gaze and switchblade on the girl as he continued to refill and chug the liquid treasure.

Then a sharp pain gripped his gut. He clutched his side and buckled over. His stomach forced the clear brown water up his throat and into the sink.

"Ohhh," Red Top groaned and fell to the floor. The knife bounced and rolled under the counter. Red Top crawled over and quickly retrieved his knife.

The girl watched. Should she call for help? The adults would certainly take him away. No. This was her chance to talk to somebody. Anybody was better than the endless loneliness. Perhaps if she were kind, he would not kill her. And if he did. All the better. She had failed numerous times to commit suicide. He appeared capable of completing the job. Death would be welcomed. She had nothing left to lose.

She knelt beside him. "Are you all right? You probably drank too fast. Let me help you to the bed."

Red Top was too confused to argue. He clutched his weapon in his sweaty palm and allowed her to lead him to a long thing covered with blankets. She laid him down. He had never felt anything so soft. It was not like the ground he was used to lying on.

She stared at his knees. "You're all cut up." She went over, opened a cabinet and took out a box. She placed it on the bed and pushed a button. A red light blinked.

Red Top waved his knife in her face. "Yous a witch."

"No, please," she squeaked. "I'm trying to help you."

He did not retract his weapon.

"Let me show you." She picked up a wand. She tucked her dark red hair behind her ear, put the wand to the cut on her throat and pressed a button. A green ray appeared. She moved the light around the cut. It disappeared. "See, it's all better. And it doesn't hurt."

The boy's eyes widened, perplexed. In the mines, a nick could take weeks to heal. Curious, he demanded, "Me's?"

"Yes, I can help you."

He shoved his bony left knee at her while still flashing the knife in her face.

She waved the magic wand over his wounds. His skin twitched as each cut sealed shut.

She maneuvered the green light over each new sore. "My name is Emily Malone. What's yours?"

"I's a Arrow." He touched the arrow scar on his left shoulder.

"That's what they call you?"

"Red Top," he pointed to himself with his left thumb. The top joint bent backwards and sideways.

"That must hurt. Let me fix it." She put the sealer down and got a medical scanner out of the kit. She held the scanner over his thumb.

The box talked, but he could not understand it.

"Computer analyze thumb," Emily stated. A light blinked as she passed the scanner over his thumb.

Red Top jerked away. He could not understand the words.

"It's scanning. This happened a long time ago! Why hasn't it been fixed?"

"Me's budgin fixes." He tapped himself.

"I'll make it all better, like your knees."

"Fix." He offered her his thumb.

"It will hurt a little. I don't have any pain suppressers."

"Fix." He was fascinated at the prospect. The broken thumb had made it more difficult to complete his work in the mines.

"Put your thumb in here." She demonstrated.

He complied and felt pressure surrounding his appendage. The box beeped and talked again.

"This is the part that will hurt," Emily told him. "Try and stay still. Computer, continue."

The boy held his breath as he felt a pinching and heard cracking. Emily looked at the screen. "The worst is over. Now it will take awhile to flood the site with caladrom. I still don't understand what your name is."

"I's Red Top. Yous Emily."

Her face wrinkled. "Red Top is your name?"

"Red Top. Thems in my's unit calls me's Red Top."

Emily glanced at his bright orange-red hair. She twisted a bit of her long auburn locks between her fingers. Her constant prayers for another family echoed in her mind. She trembled and stood abruptly.

"Huh?" he asked. She appeared upset, but he had no idea why his name would bother her.

37

"Oh, Red Top." She threw her arms around him. "I'm so glad you finally came. I've been waiting so long."

He yanked his thumb out of the box and pushed her away. "Huh?" He had not planned on ending up here. He had gotten lost

"I've prayed and prayed for another family, someone to talk to, that they," she motioned to the door, "wouldn't know about. And you jumped right out of the air vent. I'm so happy you're here."

"Huh?" He did not have to understand all her words to realize she was a crazy witch.

She was so excited she did not notice Red Top was slowly moving away from her. "We must be related, even if it's generations and generations ago."

"Huh?" He stopped at the farthest edge of the bed and stared at her completely perplexed. Perhaps she spoke a different language and the words just sounded the same.

She was aglow as she explained how she knew his arrival was providential. "Only a small percentage of the entire population is red-headed. And we both are. It's a sign that we're related. Plus not many individuals jump out of environmental systems. Only God can take credit for this."

"Huh?" He was so confused, he could think of nothing else to say.

"God must have known you're exactly what I need."

"Huh?"

Emily moved beside him on the bed. "Didn't God send you?"

He jumped up. "Ain'ts knows God," he sputtered, bumping into the counter behind him.

"You don't know Jesus?"

"Nope." He shook his head vehemently.

"Oh, the Lord works in mysterious ways." A smile beamed across her face. "We must both need each other. That's it. We can help each other. That's what families do. Oh, this is so perfect. I can heal you and you can keep me company."

Red Top tuned her out as he looked carefully around the room. He stared at the magic light. He paused at the glowing box on the counter. His heart pounded at the wonder of unlimited water on demand. He bent his newly repaired thumb as he eyed the contraption that fixed it. Lastly, he fixed his gaze on Emily. She was a strange witch with unspeakable power. He would be brave. He would face the fears and confusion and learn her secrets.

"How old are you?"

Her voice startled him and he flinched. "Olds?"

"Yes, I'm ten."

"I's a four circle." He lowered his head, ashamed a petite girl was at a higher number than he was.

"What's a four circle?" She guessed he was approximately her age.

Red Top pointed to the four circles branded on his right shoulder. "I's do light dig'n ins a mines. Huh yous do?"

"I study, mostly by myself." Her voice trailed off. She focused on the blue polka dot bow on her shoe.

Confused, he grabbed her dress collar and pulled it down. Emily froze, barely breathing. "I's ain'ts gonna rock yous." He stared at her chest. There were no brands. Nothing to identify her work unit or job function. He had thought since she was trying to avoid some authority that she was also a slave. "Yous ain't gots no work brands."

"Is that what those are?" She took the med scanner out again. She waved the scanner over his shoulders and listened to the description. "They were burnt in?"

"Yeah. Yous ain't gots none."

She straightened her dress. "No."

"Huh, yous do?"

"I study a lot. You know, physics, chemistry, botany, medicine." She gestured to the first aid kits. "Things like that."

"Huh?"

"Math and science?"

"Huh?"

"Reading, writing and dictating?" She pointed to the computer.

"Huh?"

"Don't you read?"

"Read?"

"You know, ABC's."

"Huh?"

"What do you do all day?"

"Light dig'n. Four circles." He puffed up his chest. He had recently been promoted.

"Digging what?"

"Thems shiny blue rocks."

"What rocks?"

Red Top put his bony hand in his pocket and pulled out the rocks he used in his slingshot. He fingered through them until he found one with a small shimmering teal vein and handed it to her.

She took the rock and examined it closely. It appeared to be a normal everyday stone to her. "Do you mind if I analyze it?"

"Huh?"

"Let the computer scan it?"

"Computer?"

She hopped off the bed. "Can I take it over here?"

"Yeah." He followed her to the glowing box on the counter.

She placed the stone in front of the screen. "Computer, analyze rock contents and report."

"Igneous rock of granite. Composed mostly of quartz, feldspar and colemanite with one vein of boorix. Overall specific gravity."

"Computer, stop. Boorix? You're mining boorix?"

"Blue rocks." He fingered the teal streak.

"Computer, what is boorix used for?"

"Boorix is the main mineral in various alloys used to make light-weight metals for satellites, flyers, floating cities, transport vehicles. . ."

"Computer, stop." She curled her hair behind her ear and peered at him with her blue eyes. "Who do you work for?"

"My's taskmaster is One Eye."

"No, what company?"

"Company?"

"Who pays you?"

"I's works, One Eye feeds me's. I's don'ts, he's budgin beats a ap out a me's. 'Cept when they's no foods, likes now. Ain'ts noth'n : nobody ta eats. Huh feeds yous?"

"The director of the orphanage feeds me." Emily handed the rock to Red Top.

He slipped the stone in his pocket. "Huh, yous got ta do ta eats?"

"Nothing. I don't like eating."

"Ain'ts noth'n better'n eat'n." She was very strange. He had never met anyone who did not like eating.

"I'm not allowed to sit with the other kids. They all tease me in the cafeteria."

"Don'ts matter, if I's eat'n."

40

"I get sick a lot." She hid her face. "It hurts my stomach, throat and mouth."

Red Top frowned. He did not understand; however, he was too fascinated by the talking box to care. He had seen the mysterious letters before, but no one knew how to decipher them. "Huh?" He touched the words on the screen.

"Don't you read?"

"Huh?"

"Are all your computers audio?"

"Computer?" He stroked the air above it reverently. He was careful not to touch her magic tools without permission. Who knows what booby traps might be present on such amazing things.

"Yes." She nodded.

"Audio, huh?"

"Audio means what you hear. Do all your computers just talk to you?"

"Ain't gots no's computers." He held his hand near the box.

"What about InfoPads?" she picked up the object on the counter.

"Huh?"

"Books?"

"Huh?"

"Do you know your ABC's?"

"Huh?" He stomped his foot in frustration. There were too many things to learn in a short time.

"A." She wrote on the pad.

"A," he verified.

"B," she demonstrated.

"B."

"C."

Red Top was in awe. She knew the secrets of the strange lines. He and the other children in the mines had spent hours trying to unlock their secrets. He pulled his knife out and showed her the letters on it.

Emily read, "Made on Earth, 2207."

His jaw fell open. This Emily Malone knew all kinds of strange magic. "Yous a witch?"

"A witch? No, I was reading."

"Read'n?"

"Yes, that's what letters are for. See," she touched the a in made on his knife. "A."

"A," he repeated. Then he saw the similar squiggle in Earth and pointed to it. "A?"

"Yes," she exclaimed. "A."

"A, a!" Even if she was not a witch, Red Top wanted to learn her secrets. Witch or no witch, she had lots of magic and secrets. "More, more," he begged.

Emily pointed to the letters on the knife and identified each one. When she finished, he questioned, "E, e?" because the two symbols did not look the same.

"That's a capital letter, and this one is lower-case."

"Huh?"

"Every letter can be drawn two ways." She demonstrated each letter on the InfoPad as he repeated them back to her.

The challenge was fun. They laughed and played through the night. Red Top insisted all the games had to do with the letters and their sounds. He was determined to unlock their secrets. If he could learn her secrets, he would be powerful in the mines.

"Mores, mores, mores, mores, mores." He giggled with each jump up and down on the soft, springy bed. "More letters, more letters."

"That's all there is."

"Ain'ts no's mores?" He frowned.

"We could read."

"Read letters?"

"You want to hear my favorite story?"

"I's want ta read letters."

"I'll read the letters in my story."

"Yeah, reads story."

"It's about Sir Galahad, the purest knight of the round table." Emily skipped over to the counter and picked up the InfoPad. "In this story, Galahad finds the Holy Grail." She sat on the bed beside him.

"Huh?"

"Haven't you heard of King Arthur and Camelot?"

"Huh?"

"I like Arthurian legend, because they were kind to widows and orphans."

Red Top listened as Emily read the story. He was fascinated with the moving pictures, colors and music. The fact that he did not understand a great deal of the story did not diminish his joy. Emily let him

42

push the buttons to advance the screens, change to the computer reading and replay the scenes. Red Top insisted they replay the story four times before Emily grew tired of it.

"Let's pretend you're Galahad and I'm a damsel in distress. Then you can save me." She jumped up on the counter. "Help, help."

Red Top popped open his switchblade and fought fearlessly with the air. He was ready to rescue her, when the box on the counter beeped.

"She'll be coming soon!" Emily jumped off the counter. "Computer. . .stop alarm."

"Huh?"

"The director. If she finds you here, she'll take you away. You have to hide." They looked around the room for a safe hiding place. The only area Red Top could see was inside the cabinets. He tried to crawl into one.

"No, not in there." She jerked him away and slammed the door. "Please don't ever get in one of those."

Red Top shrugged, assuming there was bad magic in the cabinets.

Emily twisted around frantically trying to find a hiding place. She scooped up the air return vent. "You have to go back up in there."

Red Top attempted to jump up and grab inside the open space. He was too short to reach it. Emily dragged the chair over. Red Top stepped on the chair and jumped. His hands landed inside the open vent and squeaked as he slid unsuccessfully onto the chair. He tried several times as Emily watched the door. Realizing their time was running out, Emily hopped on the chair and pushed Red Top as he jumped. He fell and bumped her to the floor.

"We don't have much time." Her sea-blue eyes filled with tears. "Wait until I'm ready and let me help you." She stood on the chair. "On three."

"Huh?"

"Tell me when you're ready." She closed her eyes and prayed silently. *Please, God, don't let them find my brother and take him away.*

"I's ready," Red Top leaped with all his might. Emily pushed his bottom as she stood on her tiptoes. When he began to slide down, she begged, "Use my head to push yourself up." Red Top put his foot on her head and used it as a step. At last he was inside the vent. "Here, take the vent." She handed it to him and picked up the screws. "How will I get the screws in place?"

The door opened, and both children froze. Red Top breathed quietly as One Eye had taught him. Emily rushed over to the director, hoping she would not notice the chair or vent.

She was a portly Asian woman. "How are you doing today?" the director smiled.

"Fine, thank you."

"Good." She stroked Emily's silky hair. "Here are your vitamins." The director handed Emily the pills.

"Thank you," Emily moved quickly through the door and into the hall. The door shut and locked behind them.

Red Top waited in silence. Emily had not told him what to expect or what to do. He continued to hold the grate in place. His arms grew heavy. He pretended he was the brave knight, Sir Galahad, stopping the evil forces of the black sorcerer from finding him. His imagination sustained him for a time, but his arms grew weak, the grate slipped over and over. In the end, the evil magic of the sorcerer won. The grate fell to the floor with a loud clank and settled between the counter and the sink. Red Top scurried to hide in the darkness of the vents.

He sat waiting, uncertain what to do. He had no idea how to get back to One Eye and the Arrow work unit. Plus, he wanted to take with him the magic faucet that produced unlimited water. If he brought that, One Eye would give him lots of food and might not beat him for missing his work detail. Red Top sat pondering his options. He heard the door open again.

"How does your tummy feel?" the director asked sweetly.

"Fine, thank you." Emily glimpsed up and saw the vent grate missing. Her stomach swished and gurgled.

"Do you want me to stay with you awhile?"

"No, thank you. I think I'll read."

"Call me if you get sick." The woman hugged Emily.

"I will," Emily lied, returning the hug. She watched as the director left and the door shut. Emily stared at the empty vent. Her breakfast jumped into her throat. She gagged as vomit stained her dress. She curled herself into a ball and methodically swayed as she moaned a sorrowful mantra.

Red Top waited to be certain the evil director was not returning. Cautiously he peered out of the open vent and saw Emily huddled on the floor. He jumped down and knelt beside her.

Emily lifted her head. Her hair was glued to her face with vomit. "Galahad, you didn't leave me?"

"Yous OK?" he tried to get her to uncurl enough for him to see.

"It happens a lot. I'll be fine."

"Huh?"

"I threw up from eating again." She cried. "I try not to. Honestly I do. I can't help it."

"Threw up, huh?"

Emily sat up to reveal her vomit-stained dress. She made a puking noise and demonstrated.

"Don't cries. Lots left on yous clothes. Yous can eat it again."

"What?"

"Ain'ts bad. Yous got food." He pointed to the regurgitated chunks.

The smell seared her nostrils. "Yuck, I don't want to eat it."

"Huh? Saves it for later?"

"No. I have to wash it off."

"Yous don't eats it, ever?"

"No. I don't even like to eat it the first time."

"Me's? I's eats?"

"You want to eat my vomit?"

"Yeah." He was excited at the prospect. There were large brown bits of oatmeal still on her dress, and he had no other prospects for the day.

Emily scrunched her face wondering how he was going to eat her vomit. "I. . .I guess."

Red Top leaned over and enthusiastically licked Emily's breakfast from her dress. His belly had been aching for hours. He was determined not to miss any of the precious substance. He held her dress in place and meticulously licked each section. At first, Emily was afraid of his strange behavior. After a while, the long licking stroke felt comforting, like a cat bathing its young. She relaxed in his arms and fell asleep. Red Top continued licking until the flavor was gone from the fabric.

When he finished savoring his meal, Red Top looked at his sleeping friend. He felt safe with her. He laid down with her and went to sleep.

The computer on the counter beeped, waking them both. "Galahad? May I call you that?"

"Me's Galahad." He jumped up and pounded his chest.

Emily smiled, tucking her hair behind her ear. "She'll be back soon. Will you stay while I'm at lunch?"

"Lunch, huh?"

She sighed. Why did she have to have three meals a day. "Time to eat again." She went over to the closet and stepped behind the door.

"Me's lunch?"

"If they find you here, they'll take you away, and I'll never see you again." She changed her dress. "I'm afraid when I'm alone."

"Me's hides," Galahad positioned the chair under the open vent. He was determined not to leave without her secret magic.

Emily helped him inside the vent. "Here." She handed him the InfoPad. "You can look at this while I'm gone, but you have to be quiet. No noise."

"Visual card offs." He turned off the sound.

"Sound driver off," she corrected. "Sound is what you hear with your ears. Visual is what you see with your eyes."

"Sound, hear, ears. Visual, eyes. . ." he trailed off as the door opened.

Red Top waited in the vent looking at the pictures in the story. The time went by quickly.

Emily returned after lunch and waited until the door was shut. "Galahad? Are you still here?" she called into the vent.

"I's here." He leaped down.

Emily twisted her auburn hair in her fingers. "Are you going to leave me?"

"Gots ta eats."

"I know. I tried to sneak something out for you, but I couldn't. She caught me. They keep track of everything I eat. Where do you get food?"

"One Eye. Gots ta works first. He's gonna beats a crap outs a me. Ain'ts works taday. Gots ta works two shifts ta eat."

"Oh. How long is a shift?"

He held up three dirty fingers. "Three loads. I's miss a shift, I's gots ta do it before I's can eats."

"Oh, how many have you missed?"

He scratched his head. He did not know how to keep track without the darkness of night. "Two, I thinks. I's lost. Can't gets back."

"How did you get here?"

"Thems tunnels."

"The venting? I didn't know it went outside the building complex." Emily fiddled with the hem of her pink dress. "Can't you return the way you came?"

"Darks. Ain't sees. Ah, no's visual."

"You don't have a flashlight?"

Galahad frowned. "Flashlight, huh?"

"Something that gives light in a dark room."

"Fire?"

"Is that how you see in the mines?"

"Fire torch."

"No flashlights?"

"Huh? Magic lights?" He pointed to the light fixtures around the room.

"Well, it's like that, only it's portable and uses fluorescent laser illuminaries."

He clenched his fists. He hated not understanding. "Huh?"

"I don't have one to show you. It costs money."

"Money, huh?"

"Like drayka," she explained to her bewildered friend. "You know drayka."

He ground his teeth. "Huh?"

"Accounts you buy things from. I'm only allowed to request things I can use in my research, and I can only research things that win contests and make money."

"Huh, huh, huh?" He stomped his foot.

"It's kind of complicated. I'm a prodigy." She sighed and stared at her bowed shoes. "I have to study all day long, by myself." She sniffed to stop her nose from running. "Every contest I win, the orphanage gets money for me to continue working. I also get grants and stipends for any original or advanced theories that are published. So as long as the supplies requested will lead to grants, stipends or contest entries, they give them to me."

"Huh, huh, huh?" Galahad pounded his fists on the counter.

Emily jerked back.

He lowered his voice. "I's no beat yous."

"You're my knight in shining armor." Emily threw her arms around him. "I'm safe when we're together."

47

He peeled her off his body. "Huh, feed yous at contests?"

"Yes."

"I's goes ta contest, gets foods?"

"It doesn't work like that. You have to be able to read and have progressed through Prodigies for the Future hierarchy. You have to win so many contests and earn so many points within each level. I'm at level six; that's the highest one. It's only at the top two levels that any substantial drayka are involved."

"Huh?"

"It doesn't matter. You have to go, or they'll be even madder."

"I's lost."

"Let's pray about it."

"Huh?"

Emily knelt beside her bed and folded her hands.

Galahad knelt and assumed the magic prayer position.

"Dear God, thank you for bringing me a brother. Please help Galahad find his way back to the mines."

"Huh, me's?"

"You could say, 'Amen.' "

"Amen."

Emily twisted her long hair around and around her finger. With complete faith, she waited patiently for some inspiration. An idea popped into her head. She leaped off her knees and to her supply cabinet. "Maybe the refractor I used to make the laser model could be used as a short-term flashlight." Emily removed a polished disk from the cabinet.

"Huh?" He shook his fists. "Teach." He hated being confused. It made him feel vulnerable.

"It would take a long time to teach you all those things. When can you return?"

"Yous comes ta mines? Brings magic ta me's?"

"I can't leave this room." She fought to control her tears. "If I'm lost, they'll come looking for me. Maybe you could mark your trail and return another day." She unscrewed the laser and attached the first piece of the crude flashlight.

"Mark trail, huh?"

"Put arrows in the pipes." She drew an arrow. "Let them point you in the right direction."

"Darks, I's can'ts sees."

48

"I'm making you a temporary light source. You can use that."

"One Eye takes it."

"Hide it in the pipes, near the exit."

"Huh, exit?"

"Where you go out."

He hopped on the counter, rotated his head in the sink and searched the faucet for water. "I's takes magic water? One Eye not beats a crap outs a me's."

"I don't have anything to carry large amounts of water in. Maybe you could bring him a little and I'll try to get them to order something to carry water in."

He jumped off the counter, wishing he had the magic. "One Eye beats a crap outs a me's. I's not works."

"I'm sorry." Her lower lip quivered. "I shouldn't have kept you here so long. It's all my fault." Tears welled up in her eyes and blurred her vision.

"Not yous fault. No's food and water ins a mines." Red Top shoved his hand in his pocket and stroked his knife. "One Eye's mad, we's too hungry ta work goods. He gets beats. We's get beats."

"One Eye sounds mean," Emily switched on the makeshift flashlight. She walked over and held it out to him. "See, you turn it on like this."

Galahad turned the light on and off, on and off. He was fascinated with Emily's gadgets.

"Don't waste the energy, or it will stop working. I think you have only a few hours of light. Maybe you should only turn it on at intersections."

Galahad turned the flashlight over, memorizing every detail. Without looking up from his new toy, he asked. "Intersections, huh?"

"The places where two or more pipes converge."

"Converge, huh?"

"Where one pipe meets another pipe."

"Oh."

"You could crawl in the dark, except when you have to choose a direction. Then turn on the light, mark where you came from like this." She showed him. "Mark the pipe you went into like this. If you come to the same place again, you can X that one and try another pipe. Sooner or later, it will lead you to the mine. Then, when you want to return, you can follow your arrows to me."

"Yous smart."

"I'm going to miss you." She hugged him.

He tightened, but did not push her away. "I's wants a wat'r."

"Oh, I forgot." She opened the cabinet and got out the largest plastic beaker with a lid.

"I's do's it?"

Emily handed him the beaker

"Wat'r on." The faucet complied, and he proudly handed it to Emily.

"I wish you didn't have to go. Here's your flashlight, marker and water."

"I's be's back if One Eye lets me's."

"I know God will let you return. You're the answer to my prayers. He gave me the idea and helped me make the flashlight quickly. He'll protect you until you come back. God promises if you ask, you'll receive."

She said so many strange things. "God, huh?"

"The person who made you."

"Kalopso mades me's."

"No, the network's not God. They're nothing like God. God is good and kind. He doesn't beat you or hurt you. God knows everything about you, and he still loves you."

"God's gots magic?"

"It's not really magic. God's a person, sort of. When I'm afraid, I ask Jesus to be with me, and it makes me feel better."

"Jesus, huh?"

"He's God's son. He'll be with you in the tunnels. If you're afraid, talk to Jesus."

Galahad punched the palm of his hand. Being confused was so frustrating. "Huh?"

"I'll teach you next time. I don't want you to get in any more trouble because of me."

Red Top climbed onto the chair.

"I'll miss you." She stepped onto the chair beside him and hugged him. "I'll wait for you."

"I's tries ta come backs."

She helped him into the vent. "Good-bye, fair knight," Emily said for the first of many times.

Dr. Bentley had researched any possible conditions relating to the orphan. She had contacted experts on starvation, drug abuse, anorexia, rare food-absorption diseases and psychological disorders with violent tendencies. She had numerous tests to run. She entered the room next to Zeus's.

A sergeant stood and saluted.

"Relax." She waved to him to his seat. "I want to verify the security measures are in place before I start examining Malone."

"Yes, Ma'am. I've cleaned out the room and gotten the sleeping gas set. Remember, if it's safer, we'll gas you both. If not, we'll come in and stun him."

"Yes, I understand." She bit her lip. "That man makes me nervous."

Capt. Haden entered. "What do you expect, Doctor. He's an orphan."

Her head whipped around to face him. "He's also starving."

"So that gives him the right to pull a knife on his dentist?"

"No. I'm well aware you're anti-orphan. You've made that abundantly clear in the staff meetings."

"And proud of it. I hope I get a chance to show him why my nickname is Little Hitler." He ran his fingers through his light blond hair. "I'll show him how we Aryians rid the universe of substandard beings."

"What is your problem?" Bentley said in disgust.

"I've got fifteen hundred new recruits. Men and women who deserve to be here. Instead of helping them, I'm here heading up the orphan protection patrol."

Dr. Bentley rolled her eyes.

"We're really no different. You want him out as much as I do. Admit it. Malone is everything I said he would be: a violent, disruptive, undeserving pain in the rear. We're all going to regret it before he's gone."

"Well, I hate to admit one thing, I do feel more comfortable knowing you're in here."

"No hesitation, Doc. He gets out of line, I'll gladly take him out."

CHAPTER 4

DR. BENTLEY ENTERED and sat in the swivel chair beside Zeus. "Hello, Cadet Malone. I'm sorry to keep you waiting. Are you feeling better after seeing Dr. Jones?"

"Yeah. Ah. . .yeah, Ma'am."

Dr. Bentley was relieved at his compliant tone. "Good. I want to ask you some questions and examine you a little more in-depth. A few of your tests were out of the normal range. Your blood glucose level was nonexistent, indicating you haven't eaten in days. Is that correct?"

He shoved his hand in his pocket. The Little Lady, she was gone!

"When was the last time you ate?"

He frantically checked his other pockets. "Ain't yous budgin problem."

"Actually it is. I'm trying to help you the way Dr. Jones did. She's in charge of your mouth. My job is to get the rest of you healthy."

His eyes narrowed. "Huh, yous do with my's knife?"

She concentrated on not squirming and thought of Capt. Haden next door. "I haven't seen it."

"I's tells the press yous take my's things."

"I'm certain it will be returned. Probably later today. Plus, the sergeants issue you a knife to use while you're camping out for the first month."

He clenched his new teeth. "I's wants mine."

"I will mention that to Sgt. Leiman. However, knives aren't necessary in the doctor's office. You may use it out in the field, but not in here. Now, when was the last time you ate?"

Zeus crossed his arms and glared at her.

Dr. Bentley bit her lower lip. "You have to cooperate, if you intend to stay here."

"Ain'ts sure."

She softened her voice. "I realize this is difficult. Please try to remember."

"Caughts a rat before I's got ta Zinian. Gots there's July twenty-seventh."

"And on Zinian?"

"Budgin metal everywheres. Noth'n ta catch and trash wents straights ta recycle'n."

Dr. Bentley paused, trying to assimilate the knowledge that his diet was derived from rats and garbage. "I'm sorry. You must be hungry." She walked over to the counter and opened the blood monitor kit. "I have one test that must be run on an empty stomach. As soon as that's completed, I'll feed you."

Zeus's head shot up. Feed me? His mind raced while his stomach did cartwheels.

"I'll hook you up to the blood monitor and give you something to drink. I'll monitor your readings for about thirty minutes, then you'll be able to eat."

Zeus heard nothing beyond I'll feed you. His hunger pangs had been unbearable the last few days. It had been years since he had been a week without one good meal.

Dr. Bentley pulled the blood monitor over and strapped it onto his arm.

Zeus jerked slightly, thinking, budgin sedative is making my reaction time slow. How long is this going to last? Then he thought about the prospect of eating and relaxed. He could smell the aroma and feel the food filling his empty gut.

"I need you to lie down." Dr. Bentley gently guided him to a reclined position. "You'll feel a slight vibration. Are you ready?" She was positive she did not want to surprise him.

"Huh?" He could not stop thinking about eating.

"I said, you'll feel a slight vibration, OK?"

"Yeah."

"Good." She activated the monitor and checked the readings. "Everything seems to be in working order. Is it comfortable or do I need to adjust it?"

Zeus was dismayed at the question. How much discomfort could a monitor cause? He shrugged.

"Great." Dr. Bentley adjusted the table to an upright position. She handed him a beaker of clear fluid. "Try to drink it as quickly as possible."

Zeus hesitated. He smelled it cautiously.

"It's glucose, a form of sugar. It won't hurt you."

He was familiar with glucose and how it tasted. He would not be fooled like he was by the dentist. He stuck his finger into the beaker and tasted the solution. Yes, that's glucose. He drank the solution in one gulp.

Dr. Bentley rose to leave. "I'm going to verify everything is recording properly. I'll return in a bit. There is an InfoPad beside you. It has a variety of selections in memory. Feel free to look or listen to anything you wish."

The orphan waited until she left, then picked up the beaker and licked the inside of the glass, pressing his tongue to the bottom of the container. He licked it until the last drops of sustenance were gone. Zeus relaxed on the table and concentrated on his body being nourished. He savored eating. It was odd, having all the sensations of eating except the fullness in his belly. It had been years since he had had a liquid diet. As the pain in his gut subsided, his mind wandered back to Emily giving him the same substance.

*   *   *

Galahad crawled through the venting. In a few visits, Emily had become the most important person in his life. They were family. For the first time, he looked forward to seeing someone. She gave him compassion, friendship, and most importantly, intellectual stimulation. He had never challenged his mind before. One Eye punished him for thinking. With Emily, he was free to use and expand his mind. He was no longer a nameless, faceless, expendable mine worker. Seeing and learning from Emily had become his reason to live. His mind did not have time to fixate on his miserable conditions. Instead, he practiced the alphabet or counted by ones, fives and tens. He drilled himself about everything she taught him.

As he wound his way through the pipes, he rehearsed telling Emily the names of the objects around her room. Sink, faucet, computer, counter. . .what was the thing she slept on. . .he could not remember. He racked his brain and rounded the last curve to her room. He peered through the vent. No one else was there. Galahad gave the signal of knocking on the metal.

Emily jumped up from her desk. "It's safe, but be careful, I'm trying to fix the grate."

Galahad eased the grate open and jumped down.

Emily threw her arms around him. "I've been waiting. I have some presents for you."

Galahad awkwardly returned the hug. "Presents huh?"

"Gifts."

"Huh?"

"Something I want to give you to celebrate us becoming brother and sister." She took his hand and led him over to the cabinet. "I convinced them I was studying nutritional elements and how they're absorbed in the digestive track. They think I'm trying to put vitamins in the aquifer to boost the nutritional value of the plants."

"Huh?" Galahad punched his left fist in his right palm.

"I had them order the equivalent of food for you."

"FOODS! I's eats?"

"Sort of. You drink it." Emily poured some thick clear liquid into a beaker. "They wouldn't give me anything that looked edible. The director monitors my diet carefully."

"Soups?"

"Kind of." She handed him the beaker. "This one is pure glucose. It will taste very sweet."

Galahad drank it in one gulp. He had never had sugar before. His face scrunched up at the overpowering sensation in his mouth.

Emily giggled at his funny face. "Maybe I should cut it with some of the other elements."

"Huh?" He swiped his mouth with the heel of his dirty hand.

"I'll try and make it taste better."

"Don'ts care. Thems yella bugs tastes worse. I's drink foods."

"You can still have it. I'll simply make it taste better." She picked up a group of bottles. "These each contain a chemical necessary to the human body. Like this one is sodium." She sprinkled a little in her hand, licked her finger, dipped it in the salt and licked again. "You try it."

Galahad licked a bit of the white granules. "Tastes likes sweat and limers."

"What are limers?"

"Thems scaly things has three tails."

55

"It's an animal?"

"Yeah."

Emily peered out the window. She had never seen a limer. She wished she could go out and play with the other children. She forced the thought from of her mind. "I'll run some tests to determine the nutrients you need and don't need. I have to be careful what I order. If I ask for too much, the director will get suspicious."

Galahad's eyebrows met. "Just needs foods."

"Yes, but what kind? If you have enough sodium in your diet, then I shouldn't ask for that. Plus, you'll be stronger if I give you the right things."

"I's gets stronger and One Eyes not beats me's. I's beat budgin bastards."

"You want to beat him?" Emily went to the cabinet and got out her medical kit.

"Yeah. I's Galahad." He put his fists on his hips and flexed his muscles. "I's beats budgin bastards."

"No." Emily shoulders drooped. "That's not what Galahad represents. He wasn't better because he was stronger, he was better because he was kind. He never took advantage of those who were weaker."

"I's beats budgin bastards. I's be stronger. I's be best."

She fussed with the blood filter on the bed. "Jesus says to turn the other cheek. It's not kind to hurt others."

Galahad scrunched up his face. "Yous don't wants ta beats budgin bastards?"

"No, I don't want to hurt anybody," she said softly.

"Yous little, yous weak. Knows yous can't win. I's win for yous."

"You don't want to be like the Kalopso."

His eyes popped out. "Yous knows members?"

"My father prosecuted a few. That's why they killed my family." Emily dropped her gaze as tears streaked her milky white cheeks. She shook as she remembered her exposure to the network. "Do you know some Kalopso members?" She took a breath and exhaled in slow, choppy bursts.

"Two squares and bosses they's K. I's sees them. They's gives One Eye food ta feeds us. They's bosses. They's eats first."

She wiped the moisture from her nose. "Then they're not your friends?"

"Ain'ts gots no friends." Galahad sat beside his petite tutor. "Yous my's friend?"

"Yes, brothers and sisters are best friends." She threw her arms around him. Emily feared the Kalopso. She was relieved Galahad was not in the network.

"Yous help me's be's K?"

"What?" She picked her head up off his chest.

"I's be's strong. Gets more foods. I's member, I's gets ta be's two square. I's be's boss. I's give outs food. I's eat first."

"You're not mean like them."

"I's be mean. Be boss. Takes care a yous. Yous not be's alone. Yous be's with me's."

"You would take care of me?"

"Yous sister. I's take care a yous." He squeezed her closed to him. She melted into his protective embrace. It was the first time he had hugged her. "We'll take care of each other."

"I's bring water ta two square, theys let me's join K."

"Is that how it works."

"If I's lucky. Yous teach me's more magic? Yous help me's?"

"I. . .I guess. . .Please don't leave me." She sobbed onto his dirty chest. "I'll help you. I promise."

"Yous smart. Yous helps me's get water ta two square?"

"Yes. I'll have to think of an excuse for them to order me more supplies." The alarm on the counter beeped. "The director will be coming soon. You better hide."

*　　*　　*

Dr. Bentley picked up her dinner and sat down in the recording room next to the terminal. "Computer, analyze drug screening on patient Zeus Malone." She broke the seal on her prepackaged meal. She despised eating at her terminal. She preferred leisurely gourmet dining with the proper ambiance.

The computer beeped. "Two substances found, meliline and locabar. Molecular structure. . ."

She put the cloth napkin in her lap. No matter how hurried or pathetic her meal, she refused to use a flimsy paper napkin. She always carried a fine linen napkin in her purse and kept three in her office locker. "Computer, stop. Access patient's medical file. State possible sources of drugs."

"Meliline administered by Dr. Jones at. . ."

"Computer, stop. Is there any possibility of previous meliline in system?"

"None detected."

She dipped her fork in the creamy white potatoes, at least that's what the package called them. The steam tickled her lips as she blew on her poor excuse for cuisine. "What are the possible sources of locabar?"

Dr. Bentley ate as she listened. "Locabar is commonly used to coat a variety of pills."

"Both controlled and uncontrolled tablets?"

"Affirmative."

"Are there traces of controlled substances in Malone's system?"

"Negative."

She opened her fruit juice. She kept a large supply of her favorite brand in the break room. "State most probable source of locabar."

"Vitamin supplement ingested approximately forty-one hours ago."

"State remote possibilities."

"The substance, Kerowin, also known as the ghost drug. Molecular structure. . ."

"Skip molecular structures. State effects of ghost drug."

"Highly addictive. Produces euphoric-like state and increased energy levels. Progressive kidney deterioration with long-term use."

"Computer, set monitor and scanner to run complete kidney function tests and analysis."

"Tests scheduled."

Dr. Bentley twisted and turned her fork in her fruit compote. One taste of the potatoes convinced her to skip those. "State ways to detect ghost drug."

"Is detectable in blood only while desired effects are present. Is sometimes traceable in the urine for approximately thirty hours after ingestion."

"State all other pertinent facts."

"Ghost drug is sold illegally. It is the drug of choice for individuals who must submit to random drug testing. It is difficult to detect and easily available on the black market."

Dr. Bentley poked something that appeared to be a cherry. "Computer. Assume patient is taking the ghost drug. How would I confirm addiction?"

"Run urinalysis daily and monitor kidneys for decreasing functions."

"Schedule daily urinalysis and kidney screening for Cadet Malone."

"Tests scheduled."

"Are there any other remote possibilities for locabar in system?"

"Negative."

"Computer, analyze glucose absorption tests in progress."

"Glucose is following absorption curve for a starving individual."

Dr. Bentley leaned back in her chair. Malone was a mystery. Why would he have traces of locabar, yet still be starving. "Could a ghost drug addition produce Malone absorption curve?"

"Negative."

"Does the drug affect appetite in any way?"

"Affirmative. Addicts are perpetually hungry. Kerowin addicts are frequently overweight."

Well, that certainly did not fit Malone's physical state. Bentley decided to still run daily urinalysis and the kidney screening; however, she mentally dismissed Kerowin addiction. "State other possible. . ."

The alarm beeped before she could finish her thought. "Thirty-minute glucose absorption test complete," the computer stated.

"Alarm off." She gladly pitched what remained of her so-called meal and tossed her napkin in the laundry bin. The laundry personnel always knew when she had to work through a meal. She was perpetually teased about her napkin fetish. "Computer, prepare passive transport system absorption test for Cadet Malone."

"Test ready."

Dr. Bentley grabbed a banana off the counter and scurried into Zeus's room. "How are you feeling?" she asked Zeus.

"Fines. . .Ma'am," Zeus added, remembering how he was supposed to answer.

"No side effects from the solution?"

"Nope, Ma'am."

"Good. For the next test, I need you to eat this. The banana is easy on the stomach and, like all fruit, is absorbed through a passive transport system."

Zeus's eyes sparkled as she handed him the banana. He had seldom had fresh, ripe fruit before. At times he had treated himself to the rejected, spoiling fruits or vegetables at the grocery stores. Sometimes he had found half-eaten ones in the trash. The banana was beautiful. Zeus eagerly peeled the yellow prize and ate the banana, savoring every bite. When he finished eating the meat of the banana, he gnawed the insides of the peel.

Dr. Bentley could not decide what to do. Should she stop him because what he was doing was pathetic or let him continue, because he was enjoying it so much? Before she made up her mind, the orphan had devoured all except the outer peel and laid it on the table.

"Uh. . .we'll wait another thirty minutes and see how you are digesting and absorbing the banana. If everything appears normal, we'll move on to more difficult things to digest and the active transport system. We'll be doing the same thirty-minute test for rice, vegetables, meats, dairy and fats."

Zeus repeated in his mind: rice, vegetables, meats, dairy and fats. I get to eat them all, in the same day. I hate doctors and hospitals, but if she's willing to feed me, I'll do anything. I wonder what kind of rice it will be and how much. It will have to be a decent amount, since she's testing me. And vegetables, I wonder if they will be fresh like the banana. And meat, will it be raw or cooked? Dairy, I've always wanted to try yogurt. The one time I had milk, I loved it. And fats. Fats? How do you eat fats? Who cares, whatever it is, I want it. The more Zeus thought about the foods, the bigger the smile on his face became.

Dr. Bentley could see he was pleased and decided now was the best time to complete her exam. "Cadet Malone, since you're feeling better, I'd like to finish my exam."

"Yeah," he quickly corrected himself. "Yeah, Ma'am." He did not want to jeopardize future food. He normally would not cooperate with a doctor. This time, when he felt perturbed, he repeated to himself; rice, vegetables, meats, dairy and fats. Rice, vegetables, meats, dairy and fats.

Dr. Bentley ran scans and tests of every major organ. Everything appeared normal and healthy. She had expected to see more signs of starvation, like poor bone and muscle mass. He appeared emaciated and lacked body fat, yet his organs showed only slight signs of nutrient deficiency.

"Tell me a little bit about your diet over the last few years."

"Yeah, Ma'am." He clenched his jaw. He hated doctors and their nosy questions. Rice, vegetables, meats, dairy and fats. "Hunts anything. Plenty a scraps ins the trash arounds campus."

Bentley set her scanner in her lap and gave him her undivided attention. "Did you stay around campus after graduation in June?"

"Nope. Stays where I's works."

"And you ate out of the trash there?"

He concentrated on the fullness in his belly. It was worth a few nosy questions. "Nope. Ain'ts noth'n there's."

"What did you do for food the past few months?"

"Tries ta find rats. Goes ta cans when I's gots time."

"How often was that?"

"Budgin two ta three days."

"You seem in pretty good health for eating only a few times a week."

"Tooks vites when I's don't eats."

"What are vites?"

"Vitamins." He pounded his fist on the examining table.

Bentley flinched and held her breath. She remember the guards next door, exhaled and continued. "Then you ate every day?"

Rice, vegetables, meats, dairy and fats. "Nope. Budgin couple a days."

"I'm a bit perplexed by your test results. None of your organs show major signs of starvation, but you have dangerously low fat deposits. Do you know why?"

"Tooks vites."

Dr. Bentley bit her lip and she pondered his response. "What type of vitamins did you take?"

"All kinds. Vites C and B, calcium withs D, folic acid, spectrum antioxidants and high potency multivite."

"You took those every day?"

"Nope. . .Ma'am." He resented her line of questioning. Zeus was trying to remain civil, or she might not give him the rice, vegetables, meats, dairy and fats. "Tooks what I's had. Tries ta takes multi and C daily."

"If you could afford the vitamins, why not buy food?"

He clenched his fists as he kept repeating to himself what she was going to feed him. "Buys expired vites ons the black market. They's cheap. Bottle of two fifty last me's two ta three months. 'Bout twenty drayka a day ta takes all a thems. Can't gets a budgin balance diet for twenty drayka a day. Best ways ta gets the crap I's needs."

"That's actually brilliant. So you were hungry, but your body had all the things it needed to work efficiently. You were only missing calories."

"Yeah."

The timer on the monitor beeped. Dr. Bentley rose to leave. "I need to go check your readings in the recording room. I'll return with the rice in a few minutes."

Zeus wondered if she intended to question him for the next two hours. Now that the hunger pangs were gone, he was not certain the food was worth the aggravation.

* * *

Cmd. Yoggi flipped on her computer screen. "Hello, Doctor. Have you finished your tests?"

"Yes. They are textbook for a periodically starving individual. No surprises."

Cmd. Yoggi rubbed her eyes. "And the drug tests?"

"All negative. There is still one possibility, but it's a long shot. If Malone is addicted, it hasn't been for very long; otherwise, he'd have reduced kidney functions."

"You're certain?"

"I have consulted with starvation and drug experts all over. Everyone concurs."

"What's his medical condition?"

"Excellent, except for his lack of fatty deposits."

Cmd. Yoggi tilted her chair and crossed her arms. "I'm not a doctor, but I thought starvation caused some major organs to atrophy or whatever."

"It usually does. Malone has kept healthy by taking vitamin supplements for years."

"And you believe that his health condition is plausible with that story?"

"Yes. There were experiments on long-range pilots doing essentially the same thing. Malone's results were consistent with those findings."

"So what's the treatment plan?"

"I need to see him daily. I'm going to continue checking for the ghost drug. I will administer fatty boosters. And I'm sorry, he needs a high-fat diet and to watch his exertion levels."

Cmd. Yoggi rubbed her throbbing temples. "What are his exertion levels?"

"Only Malone knows at any given time how he feels."

"Great."

"I realize this isn't what you want to hear, but consider this. If that kid falls over and dies from overexertion, the press will roast OTS and TUC."

"Yes, they would. How long do you need?"

Dr. Bentley winced. "A few weeks to get him out of the critical range and a couple of months to get him into the normal range."

Yoggi body tensed. "Any other good news?"

"He is the most socially inept and abrasive person I've ever met."

"For example?"

"I told him I was going to fatten him up and he could stop any physical activity he needed to. He was suspicious and unappreciative at best. Malone has a major temper. I could see that being his Achilles heel. I was glad to have the security patrol next door."

"Did he try anything?"

"No. He makes me nervous. I get the feeling he could snap at any moment. Sgt. Leiman and Sgt. Baker had better be careful."

CHAPTER 5

ZEUS STROLLED OVER to the gym. The gym had twelve identical workout areas. The Alphas were in G2. Zeus stayed in the shadows a moment to assess his new surroundings. Sgt. Baker's and Zeus's gaze met. Zeus walked over to his drill sergeant. "I's here, Sir."

Baker noted the orphan's compliant tone and decided to give him the benefit of the doubt. "Cadet Malone, you have missed the meeting in which proper reporting and saluting were demonstrated. From here forward, you will enter, salute and wait until you are given permission to speak. Do you understand?"

"Yeah, Sir."

"The correct response is, 'Yes, Sir,' not, 'Yeah, Sir.' You will answer correctly. Understood?"

Zeus paused and concentrated on his pronunciation. "Yes, Sir."

"We are currently performing fitness evaluations. We need to determine your overall fitness. This includes every muscle, ligament and tendon group in your body, plus cardiovascular and endurance assessments. Dr. Bentley has informed me of your restrictions." Baker gritted his teeth. He could not believe what he was about to ask. "Are you feeling well enough to start your evaluation?"

Zeus focused on his words. "Yes, Sir."

"There's a treader open over there. The machine will take your retina scan and give you on-screen instructions. Warm up and start jogging. If you feel tired," Baker fumbled over the last words, "you can stop."

"Treader, huh, Sir?"

"Cadet Malone, you should have responded by saying, 'Yes, Sir,' or 'No, Sir.' Then if you have a question, request permission to ask it. Drop and do ten pushups, NOW."

Zeus dropped and began counting aloud as he did his pushups.

"Cadet Malone, you will do twenty pushups. You did not respond with, 'Yes, Sir.' "

"Yes, Sir," Zeus snapped. He would not forget basic disciplinary rules again. He was a fast learner. In his world mistakes cost a great deal more pain than pushups. When he had completed his twenty, he stood. "I's asks question, Sir?"

"From now on you will speak properly. 'May I ask a question, Sir?' "

"May I's ask a question, Sir?"

Sgt. Baker rolled his eyes. "Close enough. Granted."

"Treader, huh, Sir?"

"You'll speak properly starting now. I said the one that was open."

"May I's ask question, Sir?"

"Go ahead."

"Two is opens. Treader, huh, Sir?"

"I don't have time for grammar lesson right now. Are you saying you don't know what a treader is?"

"Yes, Sir."

"A treader is a treadmill. It is the empty machine," he pointed to it, "you can jog on."

"Yes, Sir."

"Dismissed."

Zeus raced over and leaped on the treadmill platform. His legs were stiff and tight from days of travel. He could not wait to stretch his legs and move. He hoped the running would help him relax and think.

Zeus jogged slowly for seven minutes. Then the screen instructed him to jog at a comfortable pace until his heart rate was within his target range. Zeus felt fantastic. He was rested, well fed, and his tooth did not hurt as the air rushed past it. He continued to pick up speed until he was in full stride. He was euphoric as he felt his legs stretch, his heart pound and his head clear. The cadet to the right finished and reported to the weight-training area. Zeus was relieved to see him leave; now there was no one behind him or on his right and a wall to his left. Knowing he was safe, the orphan turned his thoughts inward.

* * *

"Did you show Two Square your water?" Emily asked.

"One Eye tooks it." Galahad stomped his foot in frustration. "Tells Two Square he finds water."

65

"One Eye isn't very nice."

Galahad punched the air. "I's gets stronger, beats budgin bastard."

"Did One Eye tell you to go get more water?"

"Yeah."

"I have an idea. I'll give you lots of water. I ordered this bag for you to carry it in." Emily opened the cabinet and pulled out the light-weight brown sack. "They think I'm studying potential water sources for crops. Leave the bag somewhere in the vents. Tell One Eye you can't make any more. Then, in front of Two Square, challenge One Eye to a water-making contest. When the contest starts, go in the sewer, get the bag and show them the water."

"One Eye beats me's for not giv'n hims the water. Be's mad I's shows Two Square."

"I don't know what else to suggest." Emily nervously twisted her hair around her finger. "Does it matter if Two Square thinks the water is from One Eye?"

"I's wanna be K." He pointed to himself. "Two Square gots ta want me's. I's get water, Two Square gives it ta work units, we's mine more rocks, and K gives Two Square more foods and power. I's wanna be two square. Two squares is stronger and gets more foods."

"Oh," Emily curled her silky hair behind her ears. "Helping some-one is enough for me."

"I's help one circles, not beats them, lets them eat when I's a square."

"You'd take good care of them, like you do me."

"I's be's good square. No drug'n and beat'n."

Emily pushed those images out of her mind. Galahad's life fright-ened her. "Do you want to see the aquifer model I'm trying to build?"

"Yous teach?"

"I'll try. I understand how it is supposed to work, but I can't get the pieces to stay together. I'm not mechanically inclined." Emily held his hand and led him to the corner of the room. "See this down here is supposed to represent an aquifer."

Galahad studied the large glass aquarium from every angle. He even laid on the floor and observed it from underneath. The bottom of it was filled with rocks and water. Next was a thick layer of rich, black soil. On top, lush green plants. On the side of the aquarium was a group of pipes, a pump and an engine. "Huh?"

66

"An aquifer is an underground water source, usually in layers of rocks or pebbles. Look through the glass. See the water pools between the rocks at the bottom. Yet, the top is dry. Feel it."

Galahad crumbled some topsoil in between his bony fingers. "Ain'ts wet, huh?"

"When it rains, the water drains down to the bottom," Emily took a large watering can of dyed water and poured it on the model. Slowly small drops of red became visible in the water. "The top layer dries quickly in the sun, while the majority of water pools underground."

"Secret magic wat'r place."

"Kind of. What I'm trying to do is get the water out of the bottom and up to the dirt layer. Like a sprinkler system, only from underneath. It's not hard to get the water to spray up on the top." She turned on the pump.

Galahad watched the dyed water sprinkle the dirt. "Red wat'r!"

"The trick is to water from the bottom. It's less wasteful. Planets that have limited water sources don't want the water to come up to the surface where animals, insects and evaporation take it away from the crops."

"Evaporation, huh?"

"What the sun dries up or takes." Emily turned off the pump. "If this worked, it would make the plants have stronger root systems, which forms a healthier plant, plus it could potentially allow planting in arid areas where building a biosphere isn't practical."

Galahad studied the picture of Emily's computer-generated diagram and her model. She had equipment and tools laid out on the floor in front of the picture.

"That's my hypothesis." She tapped the computer screen. "I built it, but it doesn't work. I can't figure out why. In theory it should work."

"I's likes tools and build'n. Like play'n." He touched the shiny, new instruments and devices.

"Can you make it work?" Emily asked hopefully. The director was getting more and more frustrated with her failures.

"Don'ts know. Yous teach. I's build." Galahad sat down, spread his long legs and scattered the tools and aquifer pieces in front of him.

They worked together through the night. The time flew by. Emily explained and taught as Galahad fiddle and tweaked with her model.

"This is a laser torch. It's used to melt two objects together. . ."

The computer beeped.

"Computer, offs." Galahad stood quickly and moved the chair under the vent.

"I forgot to tell you, I got hinges to keep the vent cover from falling," She grabbed the brown water bag and filled it as she spoke. "I haven't requested the drill or fasteners yet. I was afraid to ask for too much at once. I'll try to get a ladder or step stool, too."

Galahad wished he could stay, but knew he had to go. He jumped inside the vent.

"Here's your water." Emily lifted the bag waist high. She tried to push it over her head. The weight forced her to step backward, and she bumped into the counter.

Galahad hopped down, grabbed the bag, pushed it into the vent and followed after it.

"Good-bye, fair knight."

* * *

"Malone. . .Malone. . .Malone!" Sgt. Baker came beside him screaming. "Malone, what are you doing?"

"Run'n, Sir." Zeus slowed his pace.

"Answer when I call you, Cadet."

"Huh?" He was unaccustomed to being addressed by his last name and had not trained himself to listen for it.

"I ordered you to follow the on-screen instructions."

"Yeah, Sir."

Sgt. Baker scanned the screen. He was surprised to see Malone within the defined parameters. The screen gave his pulse rate at fifty-six beats per minute with a target of sixty-five to seventy-two. Sgt. Baker assumed the treadmill computer was malfunctioning. "Stand down."

Zeus gave a confused look.

The sergeant bellowed in his ear. "Stop running now!"

Zeus leaned his head away from the loud noise. He stopped and stepped off the platform.

Sgt. Baker reached for Zeus's wrist to take his pulse. Zeus jerked his hand away and took a defensive stance.

"At ease, Malone," Sgt. Baker snapped. "In the future, Cadet, you will obey both my spoken and unspoken orders. Drop and do fifteen sit-ups."

"Yeah, Sir."

"The correct response is 'Yes, Sir,' not 'Yeah, Sir.' You will do thirty sit-ups."

"Yes, Sir. One, two. . ."

Zeus rose, his eyes glaring and his nostrils flaring. After years of dealing with prejudice and abusive authority figures, the orphan knew he had to control his desire to punch Sgt. Baker. Why had he put himself back in a position where authority figures had permission to abuse him at will? The sergeants had total control, and if he disputed them, he could be discharged for insubordination. That's just what they wanted. Zeus had no intention of giving them the satisfaction. It would not be his weakness that led to a dismissal.

Baker needed to establish his authority early, especially with someone as aggressive as Malone. Respect for authority was critical for overall boot camp success. Baker would not show fear. He grabbed the orphan's wrist and took a ten-second pulse. Forty-eight? That could not be right. He took a full one-minute pulse. The same.

"Malone, what's your resting pulse?"

"Ain'ts certain, Sir." Zeus had never seen a reason to know his pulse and saw no reason why Baker needed the information.

This kid was going to be a royal pain in the rear, Baker thought. He flipped out his ComLine and punched in Dr. Bentley's extension.

"Dr. Bentley."

"Doctor, this is Sgt. Baker. What's Cadet Malone's resting pulse?"

"Sergeant, it's past midnight. I'm home getting ready for bed."

"I'm trying to follow your orders, Doctor. We're at the gym doing fitness evaluations. I can't do that without accurate information."

"Give me your extension, and I'll call you in a few minutes."

Dr. Bentley returned the call quickly. "Thirty-nine! I hadn't noticed before. I have a resting pulse of thirty-nine."

"Thirty-nine? Are you sure?" Sgt. Baker walked away from Zeus and over to Cadet Wang, who had playfully kicked a friend as he had walked by. Sgt. Baker pointed at Cadet Wang, pointed to the ground and put his hands up to signal her to do ten pushups. She acknowledged him, dropped and counted.

"It was monitored for the entire time he was here. It ranged from thirty-four to forty-five and hovered consistently at about forty. Wow!"

"Doctor, could this be caused by either the starvation or the infection?"

"No, it shouldn't be. Is Malone where he can hear me?"

"No, just a moment." Sgt. Baker paced over to Zeus and pushed the speaker option on his ComLine. "He can hear you now. Go ahead."

"Malone, this Dr. Bentley. We're a little surprised at your heart rate. Do you run or hike or do some other cardiovascular work out regularly?"

"Yeah, uh. . .yes, Ma'am." Zeus wiped the sweat from his forehead with his wrist. "I's runs 'bout six ta seven kilometers ta works. And manual labor, eight ta twelve hours. And I's do marathons in season."

"Sgt. Baker, are you there?"

"Yes, Doctor."

"What you heard would account for low pulse rate. I'd say his heart is in great condition. What target range did the computer assign him?"

"Sixty-five to seventy-two."

"I'd like him to keep it below sixty-five for now. Let me see how he does with that. Have a copy of his fitness evaluation sent to me. I'll let you know if I want any other changes."

"Yes, Doctor. Baker out." Just what I need, more instructions to remember about Malone. "Malone, get up there, time a five-minute warm up and then continue your evaluation. I'll change your target range."

"Yes, Sir." He hopped on the platform and resumed jogging. He felt like he could go on forever.

Sgt. Leiman had been watching the orphan. Now that she was finished with the other cadets, she wanted to check on his progress. She went over and read the screen. Malone had been running for thirty-three minutes. His heart rate was sixty-three and had not increased in twelve minutes. Sixty-three was his exertion plateau. Leiman was impressed. It was the lowest she had seen all day. Plus, he had an exceptional stride and good speed.

"Good job, Malone!" she exclaimed. "Keep going, you're doing great."

Zeus was dismayed at the compliment and encouragement. He broke his stride, and the momentum forced him to lose his balance, stumble and almost fall off the end of the treadmill. He faltered a few steps, then regained his balance.

Sgt. Leiman chuckled. "Sorry, I didn't mean to break your concentration. Keep up the good work. I want the others to see your form."

Sgt. Leiman brought the other Alphas over and pointed to Malone, "You see that, cadets? That's how you're supposed to look. Full, long, even strides, arms pumping and, after over thirty minutes, a pulse rate of sixty-three. That's the kind of performance I expect before you get out of here. Do you understand?"

"Yes, Ma'am."

Zeus stared at her. He was her example.

"Cadet Malone, you will be leading the run tomorrow. Keep up the good work. Sgt. Baker will finish your evaluation. The rest of you, stand up and fall in."

Zeus thought, what type of place is this? He had to do everything he was told without question, just like in the mines, the K-Club or his jobs on Orphans' Row. Only instead of beating him or starving him, the people in charge had him perform a few simple exercises. They fed him, clothed him, fixed his teeth, complimented him, encouraged him, used him as an example and wanted him to lead the run in the morning. Zeus was beginning to think the dentist had given him a mind-altering drug.

CHAPTER 6

THE ALPHAS WERE SPREAD OUT around the camp. Tents and camping gear dotted the forest floor. Zeus had never lived in such lush surroundings. The smell of the damp leaves; the variety of vegetation and wild animals; the canopy of trees; the trickling stream, all inspired him. It was like Emily had described the Garden of Eden. Zeus had caught more game this morning than he used to catch in weeks.

He saluted Sgt. Leiman.

"At ease."

"Request permission ta asks questions," he said.

"Granted."

"Huh, animals we's eats? I's clean? Yous want thems in big pot? Greens, huh?"

Here we go again, Leiman thought. "Malone, one question at a time, and go slow." She hated dealing with Malone and his communication problems.

"Huh, animals we's eats?"

"Something about the animals we eat?"

"Yes, Ma'am. Huh animals?" He tapped the pile of bloody carcasses beside his dirty boot.

Leiman exhaled a long, bewildered sigh. "Try again, Malone."

"Budgin we's eats, HUH?" He was sick of no one understanding what he had to say.

"Drop and do fifty."

"Yes, Ma'am." He did not mind the punishment, especially when the cool, yellow moss tickled between his fingers. He minded the conversations. Talking was frustrating. He wanted to conquer it. To stop slipping up.

"Malone," she lectured when he was done, "you will not be permitted to disgrace yourself or this unit with your vocabulary. You will carry yourself with the honor and dignity befitting a member of this unit and the Corps, got it?"

"Yes, Ma'am." He grinned. No one asked him to be honorable or dignified. The sergeants told the unit to stand tall and proud, but never spoke to him individually. He assumed the comments did not apply to him.

"About the animals, what's the problem?"

"Eats animals, huh?"

"Malone, I don't have time for this today. We have to report to the parade grounds in thirty minutes." She put her fingers in her mouth and whistled loudly. Zeus leaned away from the ear-piercing noise. "Which one of you is the orphan translator?"

Apollo jogged up and saluted.

"Are you the one who's figured out part of Malone's speech?"

"Yes, Ma'am, a limited amount."

"What's he saying? Malone, repeat it."

"Animals we's eats, huh?"

"Something pertaining to the animals we are to consume," Apollo offered.

"I got that! What about them?"

"Ma'am, this is not my expertise. I have made a few limited observations."

"Such as. . ."

"Huh always relates to a question. Zeus pluralizes many of his words. Ain't is for all negatives."

"You're further than the rest of us. You figure out what he saying and report to me." She turned to the cadet behind her.

"Yes, Ma'am." Apollo faced the orphan. He found the exchanges with Zeus to be like a challenging puzzle. "Is the question posed in reference to the animals?"

"Yeah." He stomped his foot.

Apollo rubbed his dark olive skin from his chin to his ear. He frequently scratched his ever-present stubble when he was thinking. "Huh is not a word we comprehend. Who, what, where, when, why, how. Remember we discussed reconstructing your sentences using clarifying words."

"Ain'ts none."

"Very well. Articulate your thoughts with an alternate word besides huh."

Zeus put his hand in his pocket and fiddled with his switchblade. The Little Lady always understood him. "Which." He raised his head. "Which."

"That denotes a question as well. Which is an additional word for your clarifying list." Apollo repeated Zeus's original question in his head. Animals we eat, which. "You're inquiring which animals we're eating?"

"Yeah."

"I assumed you caught them all for us to consume."

"Budgin," Zeus growled. They had come full circle with no more clarity than when they started.

"Malone," Leiman said without turning around. "Twenty-five. Drop."

"Yes, Ma'am. One. . .two. . .twenty-five."

Apollo waited. Zeus was much more interesting than his predictable peers. Zeus stood. He was one of the few men close to Apollo's height. "Why would we not consume everything you caught?"

"Gets. . .gets. . ." Zeus fumbled, trying to describe the problem without incurring more pushups. "Goes ta crap hole lots."

Apollo rubbed his jaw bone. "If the incorrect animals are consumed, we will have diarrhea?"

"Yeah."

"Which animals will produce diarrhea?"

Zeus hated this. Why did not they understand him? "Sgt. Leiman, which ones?"

Apollo face lite up in recognition. "You were asking Sgt. Leiman for instructions on which ones will result in gastrointestinal distress?"

"Yeah." Finally.

Leiman turned around. "Good work, Christiani. You too, Malone. I wondered if you'd be concerned about which animals were edible. None of these are." She kicked a gray-bellied rodent. "All varieties of squirrel are fine. The snakes you have here are fine. There is one with yellow rings around its tail. That one will make you sick. Forget the birds. Sometimes it's hard to tell them apart. Now go on to your next question."

"I's skins?"

"State the phrase with a question word," Apollo instructed.

"Who? I's skins?"

"No," Sgt. Leiman answered. "I want you to teach the others how to skin them."

"Yes, Ma'am."

"Next question?" She rolled her eyes. Simple conversations with Malone took hours.

Zeus went through the question words Apollo had given him. Again none of them seemed to apply. "Bigs pots?"

"Pick one of the words Christiani gave you to choose from."

"None rights. Adds water ta big pots."

Apollo read between the lines. He enjoyed deciphering Zeus's unique approach to things. Apollo nodded. "May I, Ma'am?"

"Go ahead." She glanced at her watch, annoyed at the delay.

"If I am not mistaken, Zeus is inquiring about preparing stew in a big pot."

"Yeah."

"As opposed to what?" she asked.

"Cooks and eats."

"What?" She squeezed her head in her hands. Malone was so incredibly tedious to deal with.

"Consuming them directly off the grill?" Apollo offered.

"Yeah."

"That's easier," Sgt. Leiman stated.

"Ain'ts gots 'nough."

"How many edible ones did you catch?"

Zeus divided the carcasses, then counted the good ones. "Sixteen."

"Stew," Sgt. Leiman answered. "Are we done?"

"No, Ma'am." Zeus dropped his eyelids. This was humiliating. These conversations made him feel like an idiot.

"Go ahead."

He repeated the question words to himself, carefully composing the question. "Greens and craps in stew, which?"

"Herbs, spices and vegetables for the stew," Apollo offered. "Which foliage is safe?"

"Good job, Malone, you're remembering to ask the important questions. I hope your unit mates appreciate your diligence. You could be the first group to get out of boot camp without experiencing the runs.

We have to go. We'll review plant life when we return. As for you, Christiani, you just got promoted to company translator."

"Promoted?" Apollo quipped.

"This is what teamwork is all about. From now on, you two will march side by side. You try to learn orphan." She pointed to Apollo. "And you learn some English," she said to Zeus. "From now on, Malone, 'huh' is an unacceptable word. You'll get twenty-five squat thrusts every time you use it. Learn the question words from Christiani and use them. Got it?"

"Yes, Ma'am."

"You're dismissed."

* * *

"Emily?" Galahad jumped through the hinged vent and held out his arms. She leaped into his open arms. "I's been wait'n ta come and tell yous the good news. Two Square's let'n me's train ta be's K!"

"Oh." Emily pull her hair behind her ear and twisted and twirled it as she remembered the atrocities the network committed on her family. "Then you were able to dig a well?"

"I's start. Ain'ts founds no water. Keeps dig'n. I's do's what yous tell me's and digs where the computer says. Two Square says I's got magic. Asks ta see me's fight. Says I's mean bastard." He pulled out his knife and fought imaginary foes. "I's fight goods, like Galahad."

"Why did you have to fight?"

"Gots ta be's strong ta be's K. I's strong. I's gets ta be's K if I's work hard."

Emily gazed up at him with her big blue eyes. "Then you're not a network member yet?"

"I's train'n. Gots ta learn ta fights like K, mean and smart. That's what Two Square says when he's teach'n me's. I's gets strong enough, I's gets ta proves ta K I's good."

"What happens if you're not a good fighter or you don't prove yourself?"

"Can'ts join."

"Are you a good fighter?"

"I's good. I's learn round kick." He rotated his leg and hit the wall. The glass inside the cabinets clattered. Emily cowered. His demonstration reminded her of other Kalopso members. She slid down the wall, pulled her knees to her chest and swayed from side to side.

"I's not hurt yous, Emily. I's be's K, yous ain't be's hurt by budgin bastards. I's take care of yous."

She wanted him to stop her painful memories. She knew the Kalopso had power. If her brother had power, he could protect her. The sheltered, safe life appealed to her. At the same time, she felt guilty for being selfish. Her heart pounded as a sheen of sweat covered her body. Emily cried as she banged her head against the wall.

Galahad knelt beside her. "Yous OK, Emily?"

"I don't know what's right." She threw her head against the wall.

"Huh?" He pulled her away from the wall, sat down and held her between his legs. "Yous hurt yous head."

"The Kalopso is bad. They killed my parents." She sobbed into his chest. "But you're not bad. I don't know what's right."

"K ain't bad, they's strong. Strong is goods."

"You don't think the network is bad?" she muffled into his shirtless chest.

"Nope. Feeds us. Can'ts be's bad."

"I guess. Maybe."

"Yous not help me's be's K?"

"If I don't help you, I'd be a bad friend, and that's wrong. If I do help you, then I might be supporting the Kalopso, and I think that's wrong, too. I don't know what to do." She jerked away and pounded her head on the floor.

Galahad pulled her up and held her tightly. "Huh, yous hurt youself?"

"I'm bad."

"Yous ain't bad."

"Yes, I am. That's why I saw my parents and baby brother killed and didn't do anything. It's all my fault," she screamed.

"Yous kills 'em?"

"NO! I was trapped in the cabinet. My dad saw these men coming with guns and hid me in the cabinet. He told me not to say anything, no matter what, and I didn't. I wanted to get out and help them, I really did. The cabinet was safety-latched one shelf above me. I couldn't reach it or get out. I wanted to get out. I wanted to see if they were dead. I kicked and scratched, but I couldn't get out. It smelled terrible." She could smell the memory of decaying flesh in her nostrils. Her gut churned and she burped. Her stomach tightened, then punched its contents through her mouth and onto Galahad. Emily curled herself into a ball and swayed in his arms. She coughed and choked long after her stomach was empty.

"Yous ain't bad, Emily. Budgin bastards, thems bad." Galahad did not know what to do to stop her dry heaves or comfort her. Emily confused him. She was so strange and unpredictable. "I's K, I's get thems for what they's done ta yous. I's make thems suffer. Ain't gonna lets no one hurt yous."

Emily put her head in his lap as her hiccups from crying continued. He listened to her inhaling and sniffling. Galahad patted her between her shoulders until she collapsed into a fretful sleep. He looked hungrily at the vomit in her hair and on the floor. Galahad wished he had asked if she wanted the vomit or if he could eat the regurgitated morsels. His empty stomach growled while he waited.

An hour later, the alarm beeped. "Alarm off." Emily rubbed her eyes. "Galahad?"

"I's here. Takes care a yous." He tentatively relaxed his hold.

"I thought you'd leave once you knew the truth."

"Huh?"

"About what happened." She wrapped her hair behind her ear, pulled her sticky hand away and stared at the brown paste.

"Yous ain't bad."

"Then why didn't I stop them from killing my family?"

"Stuck ins the cabinet. Budgin bastards killed yous family. Yous gets out, they's kill yous."

"Then you still want to be my friend?" She tried to stand, and he pulled her back. "I have to change. The director will be coming soon." She had reprogrammed the alarm to give them a thirty-minute warning.

Galahad released his grip. "Yeah. Yous smart and good. Yous feed me's. Help me's with med kit. Teach me's."

"It's just like my therapist said." Emily changed her outfit behind the cabinet door. "He told me I could tell a true friend what had happened, and the person would still like me." She jumped out, half-dressed, and threw her arms around him. "Galahad, you're my first true friend! We're like family."

"Family?"

"We could adopt each other as brother and sister."

"Family." He liked the sound of that. He had never had anyone he trusted before.

"Yes. I take care of you and you take care of me. I'll help you with anything you need."

"Yous give me's food ta be's stronger? Help me's be's K?"

"Yes. I have food for you to drink on the counter." Emily grabbed a hat, put it on and stuffed her hair inside it. "You better hide, now. You can drink it while I'm gone."

"I's eat yous puke?" he climbed into the vent.

She scrunched her face. "If you want to."

"I's wait for yous."

"I'll return soon, fair knight."

*   *   *

Sgt. Leiman and Sgt. Baker entered Cmd. Yoggi's office and saluted in unison. She returned their salutes and motioned for them to wait. Yoggi was expecting strategic insights into Cadet Malone's dismissal. They had none. They had nothing to say that she wanted to hear.

"Sergeants, I'll be right with you. Get something to drink while I finish this report."

"Yes, Ma'am." They saluted and walked to the common area where drinks were available.

Leiman grabbed a disposable cup and filled it with water. "At least this is going to be an informal meeting, and we'll be able to speak freely."

Baker pulled the tab off a juice drink. "Yeah, I'm saying as little as possible."

"Chicken."

"I prefer to tell my company commander things she wants to hear." Baker crumpled his trash, aimed and threw the trash into the wastebasket. "You're the lead sergeant."

"Great. Now you want to take a backseat." She walked beside him to Yoggi's office dreading the meeting.

"Backseat, nothing. I don't even want to be present."

Cmd. Yoggi popped her head out her door. "Come in, Sergeants. I've been eager to see you."

There was a small sitting area on the left side of the office. Yoggi took a seat in one of the chairs and motioned for the sergeants to do the same. Her office was simply decorated, clean and clutter-free.

Yoggi straightened her skirt. "Tell me, how goes it with the first orphan ever admitted into OTS?"

Sgt. Baker remained silent, and he hoped to stay quiet the entire meeting. Unless Yoggi indicated he was to speak, he had no intention of doing so.

"Not bad, Commander," Sgt. Leiman said, wishing she could avoid the inevitable. "He's not what we expected."

Yoggi crossed her legs and carefully observed her sergeants. Baker kept a watchful eye on Leiman. He seemed uneasy and acted more like an observer than a participant in the conversation. Yoggi was concerned that Leiman had instructed Baker to allow her, the senior sergeant, to do all the talking. "What is unexpected about Malone?"

"He's in good physical condition, does what he's told and doesn't complain."

"How bad has it been complying with Dr. Bentley's orders?"

"No problem. He's never brought it up. Malone's not asked to rest or slow down once. If you ask me, we're not pushing him hard enough."

Yes, Leiman was doing all the talking. "I'd like you both," Yoggi paused on that word, "to speak freely." She looked directly at Baker. "You're certain he understood the doctor's instructions and that you were required to obey them?"

Baker twisted in his seat. He wished she had not encourage him to speak so early. He would never be able to avoid substantial contributions to this conversation. "I spoke to him myself about the doctor's limitations and made certain he understood if he was tired or feeling bad he could stop."

"I see," Yoggi said as much about Baker's comment as the sergeants' responses. Leiman had relaxed and Baker was fidgeting. Baker was attempting to avoid her questions. Yoggi rested her gaze on Baker and waited for him to continue.

When Leiman did not offer anything else, he added, "Besides, Malone's jumped in a number of times to relieve other Alphas."

"Have you noticed he only helps the women?" Sgt. Leiman asked.

"I hadn't noticed. But now that you mention it, I guess I haven't seen him relieve a man."

"Interesting." Yoggi pondered a minute. It was not what she had anticipated hearing. "We know he's willing to be a team player, he's tough, and he's not a slacker. What else can you tell me about him?"

Baker cracked his knuckles nervously. He wished he had not done that. He reminded himself not to crack his knuckles in front of superiors, especially because she was looking straight at him. What could he say to Yoggi that was safe? He intended to leave the bad news for Leiman to state. "He's a great hunter."

"A hunter?" Yoggi's eyebrows met. "What are you two doing out there?"

"Nothing out of the ordinary," Sgt. Leiman snapped, annoyed. She quickly realized Baker was leaving her with the negative things to say. "Malone interprets things differently than we do."

Yoggi could tell this train of thought was not particularly important. The best way to get a good picture of the situation was to stop interrogating her people and listen. She relaxed in her chair. "Go on."

"We were having a discussion session over breakfast. The usual get-to-know-the-other-members-of-your-group chat. I've been doing this for eleven years, and I've never experienced such strange sit-downs."

"I may want to hear about those later. Go ahead with the hunting."

"One of our cadets, Christiani, complained about the small rations we're providing. Sgt. Baker asked for suggestions, and Malone speaks up. Which is highly unusual."

"Why?"

"Malone never speaks unless we order him to." Leiman placed her cup on the small table. "It took awhile to understand him, but Malone suggested we catch some of the wild animals around the camp and eat them. A number of the others objected, questioning how. Malone ignored their comments and asked, if he saw an opportunity, did we want him to catch some. We both gave him permission, assuming he'd never have time to hunt. Within minutes, there was a half-dead squirrel laying in front of me."

Sgt. Baker continued with the play-by-play. "We're sitting around talking, and Malone whips out his slingshot, loads it with a rock and shoots. Bam!" He clapped his hands. "A squirrel falls down meters from Leiman's foot. You should have seen the look on her face when it fell out of the sky. Then Malone casually goes over, cracks the thing's neck and returns to his seat, as if it's normal. Which apparently it is for him. It was unbelievable. Our entire group was stunned and shocked."

Sgt. Leiman threw her hands up. "I asked him what he was doing. Malone reminded me we had instructed him to catch anything he saw available, so he had. I would have been furious, except I don't think he was being disrespectful. It didn't seem to matter to him whether he caught anything or not. After all, Malone's getting full rations. If anything, he was confused by our surprise. It seemed natural and predictable to him. Don't you think so?" She turned to prompt Baker.

"Yeah, I agree. I don't think he anticipated our reactions. Hunting like that was definitely something he'd done hundreds of times. Nobody uses a slingshot that good without lots of practice, and at a moving target. I was under the impression he was amazed the rest of us weren't doing the same thing."

"I'm surprised he didn't slit its throat," Yoggi muttered.

"Malone's been teaching the unit to hunt. He says slitting an animal's throat wastes valuable blood. Plus open wounds allow parasites to get in. You only slit the throat of animals you can't crack the neck on."

"Oh, how foolish of me." Cmd. Yoggi rolled her brown eyes. "What did you do with the dead squirrel?"

"That's when Christiani speaks up again," Sgt. Leiman said. "He's hungry and wants to know if the animal's edible, which it is. He says, 'I don't know about the rest of you, but I'm impressed. If Zeus is willing to kill them and we can eat them, why not let him? For that matter, teach me how to kill them, too. If we're supposed to spend another three or four weeks out here, we've got to supplement our diet, and it seems pretty effortless Zeus's way.' "

Cmd. Yoggi wanted a picture of the whole Alpha unit. "Christiani sounds like he has potential. What do you think of him?"

"Probably one of our best recruits." Leiman turned to her partner. "So far he is our best chance at a second lieutenant ring." Only the two best cadets from each class received the rank of second lieutenant and an OTS ring. It was one of the only military honors the general public was impressed with.

"I agree. Christiani has good leadership skills, is an excellent communicator, and I think he's physically and mentally strong enough to do more than survive. He's also big," Sgt. Baker added to explain his cadet's obsession with food. "I'm sure the rations we're giving him are less than he snacks on daily."

Normally size is irrelevant. Cmd. Yoggi was surprised Baker mentioned it. "How tall is he?"

"It's not just that he's tall," Leiman answered. "He's stocky and big everywhere."

"Everywhere?" Cmd. Yoggi raised an eyebrow.

Leiman grinned from ear to ear. "I try to know everything I can about my cadets."

Baker chuckled. "He even has big thick hair."

"Hair, that man has fur," Leiman said. "His nickname is Black Bear."

"Enough about the Black Bear. What did the Alphas decide to do about Malone's hunting?"

"With Christiani's leadership, they decided Malone should continue hunting. In thirty minutes, he'd caught six more animals. All in the same nonchalant way. Today we actually have leftovers."

"Leftovers? Aren't you keeping that boy busy?"

"We are," Sgt. Leiman stated emphatically, "but no matter what we're doing, he's hunting."

"It's amazing. We'll be jogging along in full packs, he'll see something and whip out his slingshot." Baker pulled out a pretend slingshot, loaded and shot it. "You hear thunk. He goes over, cracks its neck." Baker twisted an imaginary neck. "Or stabs it, then throws it over his shoulder with the rest of 'em." He pretended to tie a rope around an animal's neck and toss it over his shoulder.

"Then," Leiman added, "Malone returns to formation without missing a beat. I've never seen anything like it."

"He kills things while he's jogging?" Cmd. Yoggi questioned in disbelief.

"He stops and steps out of line to shoot the slingshot."

"That's nothing compared to what he caught earlier today. We sent him out with Christiani and Petroff to collect firewood. They ran into one of those wild boars. The kind that gored the cadet last year. He killed it with a knife and his bare hands."

"Actually it took two knives." Sgt. Baker held up two fingers. "Malone explained it to us. You can't break a wild pig's neck. It's too thick." Baker acted out each description as he spoke. "You hit it a few times in the head with the slingshot and throw your first knife into its side. When it turns to try and remove the first knife, you jump on its back and slit its throat with your second, bigger knife. Then, when it's dead, you retrieve your first knife."

"It's turning on a spit right now."

"And we were worried about feeding this kid!" Cmd. Yoggi's short, perfectly rounded fingernails clacked as she drummed them on her mug. "The way he hunts, how could he possibly be starving?"

"Malone was asked that in our last sit-down. There isn't as much game in the ghettoes, and apparently lots of competition."

"Do you believe that?"

"I don't know what to believe with that kid." Leiman picked up her drink, thinking how confused Malone made her feel.

"What else does he say?" Cmd. Yoggi asked.

"Very little." Sgt. Leiman shrugged. "Half his vocabulary consists of huh and cuss words. It takes forever to have a conversation with him. He's constantly hitting the deck for unacceptable words."

"Does he talk about anything personal?"

"Not much. He never speaks unless spoken to. No chit-chat. Answers with looks, grunts or, one-word answers. He's definitely a loner."

"A few of the other Alphas have said he's so quiet, it makes them nervous," Baker add.

"That's what Dr. Bentley said," Yoggi interjected. "Malone talks so little it bothers her."

"If you don't mind my asking, what's Dr. Jones say about him?" Leiman inquired.

"Jones says he's a little quiet, but she's had no problems with him." Yoggi sipped her coffee. "You two will get a kick out of this. Malone puts his switchblade on the counter before he sits in the chair. Apparently it's a sign of trust, or respect, or something."

"After her first experience with him, I'm sure Dr. Jones appreciates that," Leiman smiled.

"You think we should tell her Malone always carries more than one knife?" Baker wondered.

Yoggi peered at Baker. "Are you certain?" She did not like the idea of an armed orphan on base.

"Ask Sgt. Taylor. He met a few trying to sneak in and steal our supplies. You know the drill, Ma'am. We tell the recruits they better take care of their supplies, because we're not giving them any more. Then at night, one of the floating sergeants comes in, steals things, and we get to make them pay for being careless with the taxpayers' money."

Leiman smiled; that's what made her job fun. "Only it didn't work. As usual, these kids are so tired, no one thinks about guard duty. Our provisions were sitting out in plain sight, free for the taking, or so Taylor thought. Malone was watching from the tree. He jumped out of the tree and grabbed Taylor from behind."

Yoggi's face scrunched up in confusion. "What was Malone doing up in the tree?"

"Sleeping," Leiman explained. "He says it's the safest place. He can see the supplies, tents, our entire perimeter, and anyone coming and going. Malone says it also gives him the element of surprise. Which, of course, it did."

"Anyway, so Taylor flipped him and the two of them start fighting. Taylor tried to scare Malone by pulling a knife. Only Malone pulled his own knife, threw it at Taylor's hand and disarmed the sergeant. Then Malone dropped Taylor to the ground and put his switchblade to the sergeant's throat." Baker held an imaginary knife to his throat.

"That's how Cadet Malone brought Taylor to me, hand bleeding, with a knife pressed against his jawbone." Leiman said. "I ordered Malone to stand down, and he did."

Yoggi furrowed her brow. "I don't like the idea of Malone attacking OTS personnel. It sounds as if Sgt. Taylor could have been seriously hurt."

Leiman took a drink and reminded herself to be professional. It had upset her when Malone brought her boyfriend to her bleeding. Right now she was a sergeant and Malone was her cadet. "In Malone's defense, Ma'am, Taylor was not in uniform, but night blacks. Malone had never seen him before. Besides, we told them they needed to protect the supplies. We can't penalize this kid for listening and following instructions because we didn't expect him to."

"No, of course not," Cmd. Yoggi waved her hand. "It just bothers me to have anyone, especially an orphan, so capable of attacking others."

Leiman remained silent and waited for Baker to chime in.

"We are going to be teaching them all that," Sgt. Baker noted.

"You're right." Yoggi swished the coffee in her mug. "We can't penalize Malone for knowing how to defend himself before you've taught him."

"I'd also like to point out, Malone could have hit Taylor in the eye or anyplace else." Baker crossed his ankle over his knee. "I've been watching him throw that knife. He could hit anyone anyplace he wants to. He chose to disarm the intruder with a small cut on the hand and turn him over to his superior. It's exactly what we're going to teach him."

"You are correct. I still don't like it."

"I'm not saying we like it either," Baker emphasized. "There's no question he's going to pass the survival training."

"Sergeant," Yoggi snarled, "may I remind you, I don't expect Cadet Malone to be here nine months from now, for the final survival test. You two are supposed to be finding his weaknesses and leading him to a discharge."

"Ah, Cmd. Yoggi." Leiman took a deep breath. She had been dreading this moment for days. "I don't think Sgt. Baker and I are dealing with his weaknesses. We're kind of hoping he flunks out or can't fly. He's not going to have any problems making it through what we have to teach him."

"That's not what I want to hear, Sergeants," Yoggi slapped the armrest.

Both sergeants sat up straight in their chairs. "Yes, Ma'am."

Yoggi noted their stiff posture. She did not want to alienate her frontline people and softened her tone. "I realize you two are doing the best you can. You're doing exactly what I ordered. You have to keep treating and evaluating him fairly. If we don't, OTS will be devoured by the press."

Cmd. Yoggi tapped her foot. She raised her pointer finger. "Let's zone in on the things he can't do. If you think about it, he's lived survival his whole life. Given what we know about him, boot camp seems to be another version of his everyday life. What about his marksmanship, his flying, the obstacle course?"

Baker was relieved he was not the lead sergeant. Leiman was squirming as she answered. "Malone's a fair shot. He's got great times on the course, and we haven't had our rotation in flying yet."

"I'm a little surprised at the shooting. From what you've described, he should be proficient at weapons. It's another survival skill. I would have expected him to be a good shot."

"My guess is he's never used weapons like ours," Baker offered.

"No matter how good a marksman you are, it takes awhile to get the feel of a new weapon."

"Good point, Sergeant."

"But he does know weapons," Leiman added. "He took the six-caliber Phase Stun Gun apart and reassembled it fast."

"That leaves us two things he might not be proficient at, flying and school. TUC has spent a great deal of time checking out Orphans' Row where Malone lived. Supposedly, most orphans are functionally illiterate. Malone can obviously read. How's his comprehension of the OTS manual?"

"Good, as far as I can tell. It's not like he appears to be reading on a grade-school level," Sgt. Leiman answered.

"I was grilling them earlier today on the flight manual. Malone seemed to know it as well as anyone else." Baker shook his head. "He's not illiterate."

"I still don't see where studying fits in with the hard physical labor, knife slinging, hunting and surviving. How could he possibly be starving and afford a computer? Plus, if he lived on the streets, where'd he keep it?"

Sgt. Leiman rested her chin on her fist. She had spent hours trying to figure Malone out. She offered the only conclusion she had come up with. "It's like he had a mentor or someone who helped him."

Yoggi raised an eyebrow. That was the first idea that made sense. "Perhaps from the Kalopso network? Has he mentioned anyone?"

"No, Ma'am."

Yoggi scratched behind her ear and contemplated this new twist. One piece of the puzzle did not fit. "If he is member or had a mentor, why wouldn't whoever it is feed him?"

"I don't know," Leiman answered. She had not thought about that. It annoyed her when she could not figure things out. Malone was driving her nuts.

"We seem to have lots of questions." Yoggi needed to push without hassling her people. Paranoid personnel do not work as effectively. She focused on being casual and nonchalant. "I need answers. Does he seem to be relating better to either one of you two?"

Sgt. Baker grinned, looking at Sgt. Leiman. He knew it was not him.

Leiman gazed at the floor. "I hate to admit it. I think it's me."

"Why you?" Yoggi picked up her mug and took a drink.

"I don't know. He seems less defensive and more comfortable with me."

"You and all the women."

Yoggi's head shot up. "What do you mean?"

Sgt. Leiman instantly understood. "I don't get that feeling, Commander. Malone's never made any inappropriate suggestions or gestures. Nothing sexual of any kind. I have fairly good instincts in that area. I don't get that an uneasy feeling, at least not with Malone."

"What do you mean, at least not with him?" Sgt. Baker snarled.

Leiman swatted an imaginary fly. "Oh, there's always a few who have to make comments, wink or whatever."

"Who?" Sgt. Baker squeezed his armrests. "I'll make sure they're too tired from now on."

"Thanks, anyway. I'm certain I can handle it on my own."

Cmd. Yoggi had experienced what Leiman described. Yoggi agreed, getting anyone else involved implied weakness on Leiman's part. "Sgt. Leiman, do you feel comfortable chatting with Malone and getting him to open up?"

"Yes, Commander. I'll try, but he's not much of a talker. He doesn't talk to anyone. I'm figuring when school starts, it won't matter."

"Then you get along with him?"

"I don't think anybody gets along with Malone," she stated. "He's completely antisocial, with no communication skills. You should hear him at our sit-downs. It's a miracle if he says two sentences, and that's only when we force him. His big weaknesses are social and communication skills."

"I'm curious. What does he say in your sit-downs?"

"Let's see." Baker watched a unit marching outside the window. "The other day we asked them about their college majors. Malone answered with two words, 'physics, computers.' That's all he said, no embellishments whatsoever. He didn't even bother to use 'and.' "

"You should have heard today's sit-down." Leiman smirked.

Cmd. Yoggi smiled. She was pleased the sergeants were comfortable again and wanted to encourage it. "Go ahead."

"The topic was to talk about your family's heritage and background. Malone gets up, says 'ain't gots none,' and sits down. So I'm encouraging the others to ask some questions or give him a little sympathy.

That's when Christiani chimes in. Christiani made up an entire historical background for Malone."

"It was hysterical." Baker grinned and rubbed his balding head. "Malone is descended from great and noble hunters. In ancient times, they were known as the Order of the Boar and had a knife as their family crest. Christiani takes Malone's idiosyncrasies and ad libs for about five minutes, giving each trait to one of Malone's supposed ancestors. The Alphas were buckled over laughing."

"How did Malone handle it?" Cmd. Yoggi asked.

"Fine. He chuckled a little. The whole spiel was typical Christiani. It was funny; it perfectly roasted Malone, and yet there was nothing disrespectful or insulting about it. As an example, Malone doesn't talk much. Christiani makes one of his relatives a monk living in silence as a dedication to God."

"Is this Black Bear kid, Matthew and Victoria Christiani's son?" Yoggi asked.

Both sergeants nodded.

"He sounds like a natural-born diplomat."

"He is," Baker answered. "He has charisma, a good speaking voice and a friendly, outgoing personality. People immediately gravitate to him. I don't know how he does it. No matter what he says, he comes out looking good."

"I still can't figure out how he pulled off the Bible bit without alienating anyone." Leiman pictured the surreal incident in her head.

"What did he do?"

"Another classic Alpha sit-down," Sgt. Leiman answered. "They were to tell the group someone who was important to them. Everyone else is talking about their girlfriends, boyfriends, parents and family members. The usual. Christiani stands up and says God is important to him. He proceeds to ask if anyone is interested in doing a weekly devotional with him."

Yoggi's jaw dropped. Christians represented less than ten percent of the population. Having faith and worshipping a higher being was out of style. People of faith were considered behind the times and unable to accept humans as THE force in the universe. "He says he's a Christian and wants to hold a Bible study in OTS, and nobody commented?"

"Smith, who's supposedly a friend of Christiani's, made a crude crack about it." Leiman rolled her eyes. "Smith asked if Christiani was going to try and convert them all. Christiani wasn't defensive or embarrassed. He explained his faith was a private thing. That he had no intentions of evangelizing to anyone. If there were others who wanted to worship, they could come to him later privately."

"Amazing!" Cmd. Yoggi exclaimed. "I don't think of ever heard of anything like that."

"No, the amazing part is after Christiani spoke, what?" Baker looked to Leiman. "Four or five people stood and said they'd like to join him in whatever it is they do."

"Four or five sounds right."

Yoggi glanced at the floor, shaking her head. She could not get a good feel for the Alpha unit. The more they spoke, the more confused she became.

"I know it's hard to imagine, but if you heard this kid, you'd understand," Baker said. "I don't believe in all that stuff, yet the way he talked, I almost wanted to join."

"He's right, Commander," Leiman said. "No matter what Christiani says, you want to agree with him. I have a feeling if he told them it would be great to jump off a cliff, a bunch would follow him into suicide."

"Sounds like an interesting group."

Baker cracked a knuckle, then stopped himself. "We both think it's the weirdest unit we've ever had."

"Malone's running around killing everything. Christiani's leading everyone in prayer. I'm afraid to ask, does anyone else stand out?"

"Smith." Sgt. Leiman curled her nose as if she were smelling something rotten.

"What's his problem?"

"He's a first-class jerk. Smith's got a big mouth, and he's constantly using it. He loves to put people down and insult them. His primary target is Malone."

"That sounds like a volatile situation."

"We're trying to keep it under control, but it's not easy. He's so prejudiced he puts Little Hitler to. . ." Baker cleared his throat. Sergeants were only to refer to officers by their rank and name. "I'm sorry, Commander, that was uncalled for. I. . ."

Cmd. Yoggi waved him silent. "Don't worry about it. I'm well aware of Capt. Haden's nickname and his blatant hatred of orphans. If Cadet Smith is worse than Haden, you two better keep them separated. Malone's liable to kill him."

"We're trying," Leiman stated. "Smith's so stupid, he looks for opportunities to get another zing in on Malone."

"And Malone?"

"He ignores it. I don't think Malone's looking to provoke anybody. Do you, Baker?"

"I agree. There are a number of others who have publicly stated anti-orphan attitudes. Malone does his best to avoid them. He's got a thick skin. He ignores them. I've never heard or seen him retaliate."

"And if these individuals pushed Malone or started a fight?" Yoggi raised her eyebrows.

"Malone will beat the crap out of them, or worse."

"That's what I'm afraid of." Yoggi's career was already on the line. A murder, or unexplained accident in the Alpha unit, was sure to end it. "Do you two think Malone's a killer?"

"I don't know," Sgt. Baker said. "Everything he's done, with Dr. Jones, Sgt. Taylor, and a few other things I've seen, implies to me he's going to defend himself well. But his knee-jerk reaction doesn't appear to be to go for the jugular."

"No, I can see that, too," Yoggi said. This orphan kid was difficult to read.

"I don't see him starting anything, either. Malone's too cool and in control to do something stupid. On the other hand, if someone like Smith forced him into an altercation where he had to defend himself, do I think he's capable of killing? Yes. If he had to, I don't think he'd hesitate. He's a survivor, and I don't see him going down without a huge fight."

"If you put it that way. Yes, I think he could kill, if he had to. But then," Leiman added almost to herself, "so would I, and I don't think of myself as a killer."

"Good point. Anybody is capable of killing in self-defense. I guess the question becomes, is Smith, or anyone else around here, willing to push him to that point?"

"Smith could possibly be dumb enough," Baker sighed in contempt.

"I don't know." Leiman cocked her head in thought. "My experience with people like Smith is they're all talk. I've found they're chicken when it comes to real guts. I don't think Smith has the balls to face Malone. I'm positive he doesn't have the guts for a one-on-one confrontation."

"Either way, we don't need those kinds of problems. I want you two," Yoggi pointed to each of them, "to talk to Smith and anyone else who is verbally abusing Malone. Encourage them to knock it off. Give them the team-player lecture. Explain to them it doesn't help get him discharged, and could hurt the OTS image of being fair and impartial. Reassure them we are trying to take care of the problem and would appreciate their help and cooperation."

"Yes, Commander," the sergeants replied.

Yoggi looked at her watch. She had lost track of the time and had another meeting to attend. "Is there anything else either of you wish to add?"

"No, Ma'am."

"All right," Cmd. Yoggi stood. "You're dismissed."

Both sergeants stood and saluted.

"And good luck, it sounds like you need it."

CHAPTER 7

THE SELF-DEFENSE AREA SMELLED of sweat. The air was heavy and moist. The sparring mat was in the center of the room. Bleachers were on one side of the large mat. Six smaller mats and twelve punching bags lined either side. Sgt. Taylor entered the room and whiffed the musty scent.

Sgt. Ryan was waiting on the dingy green mat. Ryan had been an intergalactic maxor champion. He was considered one of the greatest maxor fighters of all times. "How's it going between you and Leiman?" the burly Sgt. Ryan asked his assistant.

"Great." Taylor grinned. "I never thought I'd be in love. I'm a little nervous about today."

"Why?" Ryan pulled his headgear on over his light brown hair.

"It's bad enough being an OTS rookie without everyone knowing we're dating. I don't want to be accused of evaluating the Alphas unfairly. Cmd. Yoggi said she doesn't mind us dating, but she and Capt. Haden have made it clear, it can't interfere with our work." Taylor tightened his protective helmet, popped in his mouthpiece and met Ryan on the middle of the sparring mat.

The two men faced off. Maxor fighting was Taylor's passion. A maxor combined all known fighting styles: boxing, wrestling and martial arts. Taylor lived for the physical and mental challenge of a good bout.

Taylor bobbed around. "I've been wondering, what brought the intergalactic maxor champion to OTS?" The words were muffled through Taylor's mouthpiece.

Ryan was accustomed to people speaking with a mouthpiece. "I'd done it all in the ring. Got all the money I need." Ryan jabbed and hit Taylor in the chin. "Fight'n is the only skill I got, and there ain't much call for that in the business world."

"Do you like it here?"

"You bet. I love tak'n rich, spoiled brats and put'n them in their place. The cockier the better." Taylor tried a kick, and Ryan dropped him on his back. Ryan towered over his buddy. "I like the irony. An uneducated guy like me, teach'n those college snots a little respect. I can't wait to get my hands on Malone." Ryan punched the mat beside Taylor's head.

"I'm glad he's not carrying a knife this time. I can't wait to see him fight in the ring." The rookie popped up and stood ready.

"Yeah, well, you can work with him. I'm not associating with an orphan."

"I'm sure I can handle it for the few weeks he's here." Taylor jabbed his superior and knocked him to the ground.

Ryan jumped up. "I should never have taught you that, Bulldog."

"I'm a fast learner."

"Is that why they call you Bulldog, 'cause you're easily trainable?"

"My brother said I reminded him of our pet bulldog. The name just stuck."

Ryan looked at Taylor's black face. His lower jaw extended out beyond his upper lip. Ryan burst out laughing. "You do have that same pushed-in face bulldogs do."

Taylor landed a rib kick. "Watch out for my bite."

Ryan chuckled as the Alphas filed in. The Alphas sat on heavy plastic bleachers in front of the dirty gray mat. Ryan spit out his mouthpiece. "This is your introduction to self-defense. I am Sgt. Ryan, your head instructor. And the Bulldog over there," he smiled at his assistant, "is Sgt. Taylor. We'll be dividing you into groups according to your abilities. Novices with Sgt. Taylor, and the rest with me. Now, which one of you is the orphan?"

Zeus stood. "Here, Sergeant."

"You, orphan boy. Get up here. Let's see what you can do."

"Yes, Sir." Zeus moved to the center of the mat.

"I hear you've never lost a fight, orphan scum. You're about to lose your first one. This is a demonstration of self-defense, so make it good for your. . .buddies," he said mockingly.

"Requests permission ta asks question?" Zeus sized up his opponent. Ryan was heavy set with well-defined, bulging muscles. He had the weight advantage. Zeus's advantages would be youth and speed.

Ryan put his face in the cadet's and bellowed, "You address me as Sir, you worthless piece of scum. Drop and give me fifty."

"Yes, Sir." Zeus counted out fifty pushups and returned to attention. "Ask your question."

The orphan did not appreciate Ryan's obvious insults and anti-orphan attitude. Zeus slowly and indignantly asked, "Rules, huh. . .Sirrr?"

The sergeant was enraged by the lack of respect and intended to teach Malone some. He shoved his face near Zeus's. "Survival."

"Yes, Sir." Zeus was more confident with survival as the only rule. Maxor rules limited his ability. "I's ready. . .Sirrr."

Ryan had planned his first move to be a direct kick to the chest followed by a palm slam between the eyes. This combination left an opponent coughing on the floor with tears running out of the eyes. Perfect for putting orphan trash in its place.

The two men faced off. Oddly, Zeus did not stand in a starting position. He stood nonchalantly and strolled around, instead of bobbing like the teacher.

To catch the orphan off guard, Ryan struck quickly, but Zeus was ready, and it was Ryan who ended up flat on his back. Sgt. Ryan sprang up determined not to let the orphan see he had felt the blow.

Zeus was not fooled. The man was over forty, practically ancient as far as Zeus was concerned. He was too old to be a challenge, and too stupid to get mad at. The cadet returned to his seat.

"Why, you SOB, one good move doesn't make you a fighter. Get back over here."

The orphan walked slowly to the center of the mat and stood in a casual stance. Zeus had learned to stand ready in this position. His opponents assumed he was not prepared and would try to get in a hit thinking Zeus would not counter-attack. His stance was Zeus's version of a surprise attack.

"Come on, you orphan bastard, start."

Zeus realized the best offense could be an enraged defense, so he taunted the sergeant to further flare his temper. "Yous start, Sirrr. I's let yous gets in one hit."

Ryan was seething. He ground his teeth. "You just tell me when you've had enough." Ryan took a quick two-step with a reverse turn to hit Zeus in the kidneys.

Zeus parried and jabbed with a right and two kicks to the gut. Ryan returned fire, but Zeus blocked him. Again, the orphan got in two solid blows to the face. The "teacher" was now bleeding. Determined not to lose the respect of the Alphas, Ryan decided to try the neck-lock-leg slam. The move was illegal in the ring, because it could break an opponent's neck. Ryan figured Malone would not have encountered it or know how to defend against it.

Zeus parried perfectly, recovered and counter-attacked in the blink of an eye. In three minutes, the sergeant's blood was splattered across the mat. One eye was swollen shut, he had a fat lip, and his nose bled profusely as he lay dazed on the mat. Zeus towered victoriously over Ryan with his knee firmly pressed on the sergeant's chest, his fist a hairpin away from Ryan's bleeding nose.

Zeus paused, jumped up, mockingly stood at attention and shouted, "I's had enough, Sir," and returned to his seat.

The air was thick with fear. Sgt. Ryan had been the Maxor champion for eight straight years. He was considered one of the greatest fighters of all time.

Taylor had watched hundreds of fights and had never seen anyone like Malone. He could not identify the orphan's style or some of his moves. Taylor went over and helped Ryan to his feet. He handed Ryan a towel. "I'll call Dr. Bentley."

"Give me a minute, I'll be all right," Ryan pressed the towel to his nose. His pride would not allow him to seek medical attention while the Alphas were present.

"Are you sure?"

"Yeah, go ahead and start separating them. I'll help you in a few minutes."

Sgt. Taylor could not resist a challenge. "Let me try and fight him."

"You can't beat him."

"I know."

Ryan blew some bloody snot in the towel. "Wasn't that knife fight enough?"

"He caught me by surprise. I still want to feel what he's like in the ring."

Ryan understood the mentality and shrugged. "Watch it. He's fast!"

Bulldog walked over to the silent, stunned Alphas. "Come on back over here, Malone." He smiled. "I may regret this, but I've got to spar with you myself."

Zeus was instantly aware of the difference in the two sergeants' attitudes. Zeus willingly moved to the center of the mat. Taylor was younger, but in theory had inferior abilities to the senior sergeant. However, Zeus never underestimated an opponent. Being overconfident could cost him his life on the streets.

Bulldog's fight was similar to Ryan's. Zeus quickly disposed of the opposition. In minutes, Taylor fell down on one knee. Zeus stepped away to allow him to stand before attacking again.

"That's all right, kid." Taylor wiped the blood from his lip with the base if his thumb. "I'm convinced you could beat the crap out of me. I've never seen that last move before. Did you pivot before you hit me?"

"I's half pivots and strikes, Sir."

"Show me that again." Taylor applied pressure to the corner of his lip.

Zeus positioned himself to hit him again.

Taylor objected. "Whoa, Malone, not me, the bag. I still want to be able to kiss my girlfriend after today."

Everyone except Zeus laughed. He was not accustomed to conversational quips. Zeus demonstrated his kick on the bag numerous times.

"That is a powerful kick. In fact," Taylor wiped his bleeding lip again, "I may need a short blast of the laserseal. Sit down. You'll be assisting me when I teach the novices."

Zeus's face lit up. "Yes, Sir!" Zeus was amazed Taylor suggested he help instruct. It was beyond comprehension for him to be in a position of leadership or authority. Zeus did not believe Sgt. Ryan would allow him to assist in teaching. He had experienced too much prejudice not to be aware of how it worked. By the next session, Ryan would come up with some excuse why Zeus could not be an instructor.

Zeus was glad he had been singled out to spar with the sergeants. He was impressed by Taylor's abilities, fairness and professionalism. He had learned Ryan was blatantly prejudiced and Taylor was open-minded. He had also shown the other Alphas he was a force to be reckoned with. The exhibition would help deter direct anti-orphan aggression. To accomplish his mission at OTS, Zeus needed to avoid trouble. He would continue to focus on his goal and ignore the rest.

*   *   *

The Alphas lined up in front of their barracks. When the first trumpet call of the Corps' anthem sounded, each soldier snapped to attention. A roll of the drums was followed by one bass drum beat. At the sound of the single beat everybody stomped their right foot and sang. The second drum roll finished and the bass beat again. The group stomped its left foot and snapped a salute. At the end of the song, the drum roll and bass beat were repeated. They stomped their right feet as the salute was completed and the group yelled, "We are proud to serve."

Sgt. Leiman stepped out of formation and in front of her partner. "What's wrong with Christiani?"

"I don't know, I've been wondering that myself. He's way too quiet." Baker spied Apollo's tall figure standing rigidly next to Zeus. Malone always looked pale next to Apollo's deep olive complexion.

"I know, I haven't been correcting him for speaking out."

"Me either. That's not like him. I'd hate to lose him." Sgt. Baker squinted in the bright morning sun.

"I agree. Is he looking to you?"

Sgt. Baker put his hand up to shade the sun. "A little. I'd like to talk to him."

"Great, he's yours. I'll take the rest of them on to the course." Sgt. Leiman turned and bellowed to the group, "Alpha Company, follow me."

"Christiani, get over here," Baker ordered.

Apollo jogged over and saluted. "Yes, Sir?"

"Let's take a little walk," Baker led them.

"Yes, Sir." Apollo fell in abreast.

"You've been quiet, what's up?"

Apollo lowered his head. "I've been contemplating, Sir."

"About what?"

"Who I am. Who I want to be." Apollo sighed in frustration. He knew they hated him mentioning his faith. But he was desperate, and talking helped him. "Who God expects me to become."

"We give you time for that?"

"No, Sir." The corner of Apollo's mouth curled up slightly. "A miniscule amount."

"What's got you thinking?" Baker motioned him over to a tree and sat down.

"I have been listening to people speak in reference to Zeus and some of the others." Apollo sat and leaned his head against the rough bark. "Sir, do you perceive me to be similar to Richard?"

"Be specific?"

"Prejudiced. Conceited. Self-important. A snob."

"You're not like Smith."

"I am not convinced of that, Sir. I have been pondering statements I have made in reference to Zeus and orphans in general. I am not proud of my conduct. It is not limited to Zeus's life. We, I make pronouncements about others' inferiority. Victor maturing in a room he shared with his sisters. Candy working in a fast food restaurant."

"You mean Smith only wants to associate with rich people?"

"How amusing. Your perspective is contrary to my own. I do not consider the Smiths wealthy. Upper middle class perhaps; however, certainly not in my class. I suppose attending Hadley makes a difference." Apollo paused as he heard himself. He put his head in his hands and rubbed his aching forehead.

Sgt. Baker remained silent. He liked cadets to figure out their own problems. He stroked the dew-coated grass until Apollo lifted his head.

"I apologize, Sir. That comment is precisely what I am attempting to address. Judging people based on income, class and university affiliations. Those are not good barometers of an individual's character. I have avoided contact with poor or lower class individuals. I attended the finest preparatory schools where upper middle class was the lower end. There were scholarship cases at Hadley; however, not affiliated with my fraternity. I did not associate with them." Apollo tossed a stick. "I speculate that at some level I have envisioned the lower classes as composed of lazy individuals who do not apply themselves. I am aware that is not the case. If anything, they have worked more diligently and had less opportunities."

Sgt. Baker listened and chuckled to himself. As numerous people had stated, Christiani was long-winded; letting him speak uninterrupted could take all day.

"My church at home was in an affluent area. We contributed to charity projects; however, I never had contact with the underprivileged. The church on campus was similar. I do not consider my responses toward the less fortunate as a reflection of my religious attitudes." Apollo stared at the grass in front of him until the individual blades became a sea of melted yellow.

Baker waited to be certain Apollo had paused long enough for him to speak. "I think you're learning some important lessons. I don't want to discourage that. It's a lot of what OTS is about. The question is, what are you going to do?"

Apollo took a deep breath, still looking at the murky grass. "I believe God is instructing me to befriend Zeus and others I have excluded."

"Why is that a problem. You get along with everyone, except Malone. He doesn't like anybody."

"That is not my concern, Sir. I realize the majority of the Alphas will not alienate me for associating with Richard's clique. Unfortunately, the reverse is not true. There are individuals who will be judgmental, even appalled, if I befriend Zeus and the others."

"This is an odd unit because of Malone. People have divided into smaller groups more than usual. I think once Malone is gone, you'll unify."

Apollo turned to face his superior. "I am unconvinced, Sir. I have been in popular groups. I am familiar with their interworkings. Once cliques are formed, they are challenging to infiltrate or divide. I cannot envision Richard and the others associating with Victor or Candy or anyone else they consider common. My groups would critique everything about everybody. . .their clothes, their hair, their voice, their family income. Everything. Richard's clique is no different. If anything, they are more vicious."

"Then you'll have to choose."

"Yes, Sir. That is why I am distressed." Apollo picked a single blade of grass and tied it in tiny knots. "I had opportunities to befriend some of the scholarship people at Hadley. Some invited me to functions or festivities. I fabricated excuses to avoid attending."

"Why are you certain Smith's clique is the group to be in? And even if it is, there's only four or five of them, which means there are about forty other cadets that are jealous, resentful or angry. The way I see it, you can have forty true friends or five superficial ones."

"I never considered it from that perspective." Apollo tossed his knotted blade and picked a fresh one.

"Tell me, in these groups you were in, what happened if someone lost his or her money or was scarred in an accident?"

"If I were to surmise, they would be ostracized from the group. In high school, a friend's father was arrested for embezzling public funds. After that, I did not associate with him much."

Sgt. Baker pulled out his InfoPad and pretended to read the schedule. It was best to let cadets come to their own conclusions.

"I was a poor reflection of friendship." Apollo leaned his head against the tree.

"What's your definition of a friend?"

"An authentic friend would be loyal, not superficial. I would probably add nonjudgmental, someone I could be genuine with."

"You've never been yourself around your buddies?" Baker scrolled down his schedule without reading it.

"No, Sir. I am typically the perfect clique member."

"It doesn't sound like you have much freedom in these groups."

"The goal is to be homogeneous."

"Isn't that stifling?"

"Yes, Sir." Apollo slumped down against trunk. "What did I perceive as the advantage?"

"Security."

"That is extremely shallow."

"The time has come for you to grow up and look at things differently." Baker turned off his InfoPad and slid it in his pocket.

"Yes, Sir. I have read former cadets matured more during OTS than throughout the rest of their lives combined. I am beginning to understand why."

"There's a lot more to being a good officer than physical fitness and flying. Return to camp and think about it. We'll be there at thirteen hundred." Sgt. Baker stood.

Apollo rose and saluted. "Yes, Sir, and thank you, Sir."

"If you need to talk, next time come to me." Sgt. Baker returned the salute.

"Yes, Sir." Apollo smiled as he thanked God for Sgt. Baker.

*   *   *

Galahad and Emily sat on the floor playing mazes. He liked the twists and turns the computer took him through. He loved to see how fast he could speed up the program and still win. Galahad was almost to the end of another puzzle when the door opened. The director and two men with tailored suits walked in. No one ever came to Emily's lab before lunch. The two children jumped up. Galahad scrambled to hide, but it was too late. He had already been seen.

"Who are you?" the director demanded.

"I's Galahad."

"Emily, come over here." The director motioned Emily to the floor beside her.

"Yous not touch her." Galahad took his fighting stance. His Kalopso mentor had been teaching him well. He quickly sized up his opponents. The men were not much taller than he was and appeared weak and overweight. To him, the woman posed no threat. He had never met a strong, healthy woman and assumed all women were weak.

"He's an orphan." The blue-suited man surmised from Galahad's accent and attire.

"Get him," the gray-suited man lunged at him. Galahad round-kicked Mr. Gray Suit in the face and followed with a punch to the left kidney. The man fell to the ground without any retaliation.

"I's K fighter. I's beats the crap out of yous."

"You're a member of the Kalopso?" the blue-suited man asked.

"I's strong. Gots K friends."

"Then I'm one of them. I'm a full member."

"Budgin bastard."

"I can see you've been trained by us."

"Huh?" Galahad never dropped his guard.

"Only the best fighters are K, and those were good hits."

"I's beat the budge out of yous."

"Not likely," the man pulled a 3-caliber PSG out of his pocket.

"No, don't hurt him," Emily jumped in front of her brother.

Galahad pulled his knife, popped open the blade and flashed it at the blue-suited man.

The man laughed at the boy's audacity.

Galahad, furious he was being mocked, pushed Emily clear, threw his knife and hit the man in the shoulder. As the knife hit, Galahad kicked the weapon out of the man's hand, and the gun fired at the ceiling. Galahad followed with two blows to the man's face.

The director watched in terror. Galahad's eyes filled with rage as he turned toward her. She ran out the door screaming, "Help! Help! Guards."

"You better hide." Emily pulled the chair under the vent.

"Yous come, too. . ."

The door opened and three guards burst through. One leveled his gun and stunned Galahad. He fell against the wall and slid to the floor.

"We's better take hims ta the boss." A guard grabbed Galahad by the arms and dragged him to the door. The director helped the two injured men up and followed the guards out the door. She locked Emily in her room and scurried to the boss's office.

The boss looked up from behind his large, hand-carved desk. "What's this?" he asked as the guard presented the stunned prisoner.

The blue-suited man held his bleeding shoulder. "That brat claims he's K and fights like we've trained him."

He relayed their short altercations as the boss chuckled. "You had a gun, and that kid beat you with a knife?"

"I've never seen anyone so fast."

"Check his brands," the boss ordered. "Tell me what unit he's in."

The guard turned Galahad over. "He's a five circle for the arrows."

"Get his two square up here," the boss demanded. The guard nodded and left. "Where was he?"

"In Emily's room," the director answered nervously.

"How'd he get in there?" the boss demanded.

"I. . .I don't know," she stammered.

"You're supposed to know," the boss slapped his desk. "We need her. The big boss says he wants positive orphanage press. He wants to see her winning those contests and encouraging donations and public funding. She's not supposed to associate with that trash." He spit at Galahad on the floor.

"I'm sorry. I'll keep her controlled."

"She's lost the last two contests. In the last one, we got no money at all, not one drayka," he snarled. He rose and leaned over his desk. "Are you failing me?"

"No!" She shuddered. "I'll work with her. She'll do better. I promise."

The door opened, and the arrow's two square walked in behind the guard. "That yours?" The boss pointed to Galahad on the floor.

"Yeah. I's told yous 'bout him. Digs the well and fights mean."

Galahad lay motionless as he listened to the voices above him.

"How long ago did he dig the well?" the boss asked.

"Few moons."

"You said he disappears to do his magic?"

"Yeah."

"He's been seeing Emily for months," the boss yelled at the director. "You're failing. That's why she's losing."

"No! How? She's locked in and they're locked out."

"You're not controlling her. She pukes and screams constantly. Her therapist says she's made up an imaginary brother. Only he's not so imaginary."

"I'll find out and see it doesn't happen again."

The boss pointed to the director. "If I have to answer to the big boss for your mistakes, you'll pay with a level four."

The director swallowed hard. Level fours were the most sadistic, long, drawn-out tortures the network could come up with. "It won't happen again," she promised. "I'll stay with her myself."

"I want to know how that trash got in. Put him in the box." The boss motioned to the restraints in his office. "Then wake him up."

Galahad heard the conversation and felt his body being picked up. He pretended to still be stunned. He was not going in the beating box. He could take anything but the box. Fear and anger welled up inside. He peeked out of his closed eyes as his two square had taught him. The guard threw Galahad over his shoulder. Galahad remained limp and waited until he was put down. When his feet touched the floor, he grabbed the guard's gun, head-butted the man and kicked his legs out from under him. Galahad turned to face the others in the room.

"Him big K boss. Yous not fight," Two Square yelled at his pupil.

"Huh?"

"Huh yous gets here?" Two Square asked.

"Magic."

The Kalopso boss aimed his PSG at the boy. "Put down the gun." Galahad held his ground.

"I wouldn't either, kid." This orphan could be useful. The boss rose slowly and methodically, keeping his eyes on the weapon. "You want to be K?"

"I's strong. I's be's K."

"I'll make a deal with you. You win in the ring, I'll let you train under me. Then if you're good enough, I'll let you join."

"Red Top, it's what yous wants. Do it," Two Square advised him.

"Deal," Galahad handed his weapon to a guard.

"You're going to fight him." The boss pointed to Two Square. He wanted to test both Galahad's fighting ability and his loyalty to the network. The Kalopso code stated no friendship was greater than one's loyalty to the network. He wanted to see if this boy could fight well against his mentor.

"I's beats him," Galahad stated. He would prove himself not just to any K boss, but the big boss. He would win for Emily.

"Take them to the ring," the boss ordered the guards.

*   *   *

Sgt. Leiman and Baker stood behind the firing line. Leiman handed her partner Malone's last target evaluation.

Baker clicked his tongue. "He's definitely improving."

"An impressive learning curve for a guy with no weapons experience."

"How did he do on his other two drills?"

"Malone just returned from Dr. Bentley's. He's only taken one rotation."

Baker watched Cadet Petroff's form as Victor aimed and fired. "How far behind is Christiani?"

"Christiani? I thought he was still with you."

"What?" Baker was immediately alarmed.

"I paged him. When he didn't respond, I figured you told him to put his ComLine on messages only. I told him to check in as soon as he was done with his current assignment."

"I ordered him to go to camp and said we'd be there in about an hour." Baker checked his watch. "That was two hours ago. And I never told him to turn off his pager." Baker jerked his ComLine out of his belt. "Cadet Christiani, connect." He listened to it ring five times. "No response."

"He probably fell asleep. Turn up his volume."

Baker pushed the button for maximum receiver's volume and waited. "No answer."

"I guess it's a good thing Christiani is catching up on his sleep, because he's in for a long night."

Baker was visibly upset as he slapped his ComLine shut and clipped it in place on his belt.

"What's the big deal?" Leiman asked. "So he misses target practice. His shooting isn't that bad."

"That's not what I'm worried about."

Leiman stood in front of him. "What?"

"Christiani told me he hadn't been nice to Malone. What time did Malone leave Bentley's?"

Her gut sank. "I never checked." Concerned, she took out her ComLine. "Dr. Bentley, connect."

"Dr. Bentley."

"This is Sgt. Leiman. Doctor, what time did you dismiss Malone today?"

"Awhile ago. I don't remember the exact time."

"It's important. Take a guess. How long ago?"

"Between half an hour and an hour ago."

"Could you be more specific?"

"I realize this comes as a surprise to you, but Malone isn't my only patient. In fact, I'm way behind because of him."

"Never mind, Doctor. Leiman out." She shut her ComLine slowly and met Baker's eyes.

"If Malone were smart, and I think he is, he wouldn't have any direct confrontations."

"If I were him, I'd arrange some unfortunate accidents for my adversaries. Something that wouldn't look suspicious or point fingers at him."

Baker yanked his ComLine out and pressed redial. "I'm going to try again to page Christiani." Baker felt a tightness in his chest. He should never have sent Christiani to camp alone. "No response. I'm going to leave it on for a few minutes."

"What difference does it make? If Malone took care of things, it won't matter." She leaned over and pushed Baker's off switch.

"You're right. He'd complete the job."

"You want to go to camp and check on things?"

"Yeah. I think I will." Baker turned and ran.

"We'll be about fifteen minutes behind you. It's time to wrap up here."

Baker did not respond. He broke into a full jog and headed toward the woods.

CHAPTER 8

SGT. BAKER LISTENED for any unusual noises as he entered the Alpha's Camp. All he could hear were the songs of the insects and birds singing and chattering about him. "Christiani," he called out as he entered the first of the twenty-three cadet tents. It was empty. He wished he could remember which tent was Christiani's. He sealed the tenth tent and marched to the next one. Nothing.

He ducked down and entered the nineteenth tent. Apollo was on his knees slumped over a crate. "Christiani? Christiani?" Baker shook him.

"What?" Apollo rose. His legs wobbled. He stumbled and knocked over the crate. "Yes, Sir?"

Baker grabbed him, picked up the crate and sat Apollo on it. "What happened?"

"Happened, Sir?" Apollo rubbed his knees.

"What have you been doing?"

"Praying, Sir."

"For two and a half hours?"

"That substantial an amount of time cannot have expired." Apollo checked his watch. "My perception was only a few minutes had passed."

"We had a schedule change. Sgt. Leiman called you to the range. Why didn't you answer your page?"

"I. . .I never heard it." Apollo checked the ComLine on his belt. The light was on. He unclipped it and verified the sound, not the vibration function was activated. "I. . .I am also confused, Sir. Perhaps it is not functioning properly." He held it to his ear.

Sgt. Baker pulled out the unit on his belt, "Christiani, come in." Apollo jerked the receiver from his ringing ear. "It seems to be working now." Baker said annoyed.

"Sir, I am at a loss to explain the discrepancies. I never heard my ComLine."

"Sgt. Baker? Sgt. Baker?" They heard Sgt. Leiman calling.

"Over here." He stepped out of the tent and motioned her over. "Everything OK?"

"Fine," he snarled.

Leiman nodded. "We got a few more changes."

"Christiani?" Sgt. Baker popped his head in the tent. "Go get some chow. I'll deal with you later."

"Yes, Sir." Apollo saluted the sergeants and trotted off to the food line.

"Did he fall asleep?"

"Says he was praying the whole time, it only felt like a few minutes, and he never heard the pages."

"Oh." Sgt. Leiman looked at her coworker out of the corner of her eye.

"Yeah. Can you pray for that long?" Baker watched as Apollo got his food.

"How would I know? Hey, thanks for volunteering to take this one." She nudged him, gloating.

"I gotta learn to keep my mouth shut."

"What did you give him?"

"Nothing yet. . .I may go easy on him."

"Oh?"

"He just walked past Smith's group and sat down with Petroff and Cane."

Sgt. Leiman turned and looked. "That last two and half hours may have been well spent."

"I didn't figure he'd do anything this quickly."

"At least he's not a hypocrite."

"You're right. And he's not a liar." Sgt. Baker crossed his arms. "If he fell asleep, he doesn't realize he did."

"I agree, Christiani would take the punishment before he'd blatantly lie."

"And he did seem surprised when I said I'd called him. What do you think we should do?"

"We?" She put her hands on her hips. "You took him. He's yours."

"Yeah, yeah. A couple of hours ago, you said you'd wished he'd opened up to you. I'll give him to you."

"Nope, you know how it works. The first sergeant a cadet opens up to becomes his confidant. Unless he switches, he's yours."

"You're enjoying this, aren't you?"

"You bet. It's great not having to deal with a rookie. I haven't been without a trainee in three or four years. If it were anybody else, I would have to deal with it."

"Am I supposed to take that as a compliment?"

"Yes." Leiman faced him. "Even though this has been a weird unit, it's been easy working with you. I don't have to check on you or stop to explain things. You know what you're doing, and I can trust your judgment."

"Thanks, I agree. I've had trainees the last few years. What a pain in the rear. Still I wasn't psyched about this assignment."

"Afraid I'd lord it over you?" She raised her eyebrows and smirked.

"Yes. I didn't want you looking over my shoulder; questioning everything I did. And you haven't. I told my wife yesterday how well this is going. I can see why you beat me in the awards."

"Just barely, but I did beat you. I keep thinking, once Malone is gone, with the two of us working together, we should sweep the awards."

"Exactly what I was thinking." Baker intertwined his fingers and cracked his knuckles loudly. "I think Christiani has a good chance at one of the two lieutenant commissions."

"Me, too. A lot of good leadership skills there."

"And integrity. He just went over and is helping Wang with clean-up."

"If Christiani put his mind to it, with his communication skills and charismatic personality, he could have the Alphas unified in a day."

"Maybe I will keep him."

"It's not like you have a choice."

*　　*　　*

Sgt. Leiman knocked on Taylor's door. He greeted her with a glass of champagne and a bunch of flowers. She accepted the bouquet in one hand and the goblet in the other, then wrapped her arms around him and pressed her lips to his.

Taylor closed his eyes and pecked his way to his favorite nibbling spot, her earlobes. "Gees, I've missed you Sues."

"I thought I'd go crazy waiting to see you." She walked forward, guiding him backwards to the couch. He felt the seat cushion at the base of his knees and sat down. Leiman fell on top of him and tipped his glass. The pink champagne bubbles popped as they skated down his arm.

Taylor jerked his arm. "That's cold." He leaned forward to put the empty glass on the table as he kissed her.

"I love you, Brian," she cooed.

"It's more than that for me, Sues." Taylor was nervous about bringing up the subject of commitment. Current social customs stated that once a couple said amour to each other, they were dating exclusively. He hugged her tightly and gazed into her hazel-gray eyes. "Amour."

"Oh, Brian." She laid her head on his chest. "I've been thinking about that, too. I didn't want to push you into anything permanent. I feel the same way. I don't want to see anyone else." She ran her fingers up his neck.

He twitched. "I get chills every time you do that."

"Amour, honey."

"Amour." He exhaled and his shoulders relaxed.

She lifted her head. "A little nervous there, Bulldog?"

"I've never said that to a woman before."

"Is that what the flowers and champagne are for?" She set them on the table.

"That and I've missed you." He cupped her face in his hands and pressed his lips to hers. They wrapped their arms around each other and kissed passionately.

"I can't believe we're only a week into boot camp. It's never seemed this long before."

"You feel so good in my arms."

"Umm, amour." She pecked at his neck.

"Amour." He stroked her hair.

She felt peaceful nestled with him. No work, no worries, only the two of them. She listened to his heart and felt his quiet breathing. Taylor's stomach grumbled.

"Are you hungry?"

"As a matter of fact, I am."

"What did you fix us?"

"Some of my famous Tageen stew," he boasted.

"Is it ready?"

"It can wait a few minutes." He placed his hand under her chin, gently lifted her head and kissed her. Taylor's stomach gurgled.

She patted his belly. "Well, some of us apparently can't wait."

Taylor lifted her off his lap and onto the couch, then strolled into the kitchen.

She called after him, "Is there anything I can do to help?"

"Sure. Why don't you set things up?"

Leiman meandered in and locked her arms around him. "Let's eat on the couch. That way I won't miss a moment in your arms."

"Works for me." He watched her walk out of the kitchen.

She brought in a full glass of champagne and set it on the counter beside him.

"Can you heat the rolls?" He sprinkled some gravy thickener in the pot.

"It's possible." Leiman open the rolls, placed them on a plate and put them in the LaserOven. "So tell me how your first days working with OTS cadets went."

"Relatively uneventful, except for my run-ins with your boy Malone. Every time I see that kid, I end up at Dr. Bentley's."

"I forgot about that." She turned his head to face hers. "Your lips look fine. How do they feel?"

"Fine. The doctor only sealed a few centimeters."

She kissed him until the LaserOven dinged. "They appear to be in top-notch working order, but I'll need to run a few more tests."

"You just tell me when and where, I'll be there."

Taylor ladled the stew onto the plates, and Leiman added the rolls. He picked up the plates. "Grab the fruit out of the Coolie, will you?"

She got the cut fruit, followed him to the couch and wiggled in close to him.

"Sues, you should see him fight. Unbelievable! That kid is amazing." Bulldog spoke quickly. "I don't consider Ryan or myself amateurs, but still, we never hit him. He dropped us both in minutes. Neither one of us touched him. The annoying part is, it isn't even hard for him. Malone never takes a stance. He moves in ways and combinations I've never seen before. It was incredible to watch. Talk about strong. There is no way I can stand up, if he kicks me good. Malone is just amazing."

"I think you said that." She dipped her roll in the gravy.

"I've never seen anyone like him. I can't even identify his style. Ryan can't, either. I wish I had more time to talk to him, have him show me a few things. I watched him work the bag. Gees, talk about power! I gotta learn some of those moves." Taylor looked at his girlfriend. She was grinning from ear to ear. "What? What are you smiling at?"

"You."

"What?"

"Bulldog, you crack me up. You're completely energized, talking about how Malone fights. I can't imagine being that thrilled about someone giving me a fat lip."

"I'm sorry. We can change the subject."

"It's OK. You're kinda cute like this." She touched her fork to his nose. "Will you get a chance to work out with him?"

"Yes and no. Ryan is pretty prejudiced. He doesn't want Malone assisting him with the advanced Alphas. Says he won't work with an orphan." Taylor took a bite of stew.

"You think he's jealous?"

Sgt. Taylor nodded, put his finger up, then swallowed. "He was furious after Malone dropped him. I was impressed with how Malone handled it. He could easily have beaten the crap out of Ryan."

"Did Ryan deserve it?" She blew the steam from the potato on her fork.

"Oh, yeah. He was insulting Malone the whole time. Both times, with Ryan and with me, that kid stopped as soon as we went down. No malicious or vindictive hits. Nothing extra. Anyway, Ryan is jealous of how good he is, but he'd told me before your unit arrived, Malone was going to be in my group. I don't get it, Sues. I can't understand hating someone before you've met them."

"Me neither. We've got a couple of those in our group. Completely anti-orphan. Doesn't matter what Malone does, they've already decided. They're rude and insulting. It would be one thing if he deserved it, but Malone's not doing anything to provoke anybody."

"What's Malone doing?" Taylor popped an entire roll into his mouth.

"Basically the same thing he did with Ryan; nothing. He ignores it. Never comments. He just goes about his business. Anyway, back to the first question, are you going to work out with Malone?"

"Like I was saying, yes and no. Yes, I'll be working with him. I told him he could assist me with the Alpha novices; and no, I won't get a chance to have him show me anything." Taylor tossed his fork on his plate.

"Why not?"

"In the advanced group, there's always some free sparring, but with beginners, everything is basically standard. I kind of feel bad. Malone knows he belongs with the advanced group. The fact is, he could teach Ryan and me."

"It's not your fault." She stroked his thigh. "Ryan's in charge and he made the decision."

"I know. What would you think about me sparring with him a few times? Maybe having him show me some things?"

"Sure, why not? If he wants to and he can find the time, why should I care?" She fed him a piece of meat from her fork.

Taylor swallowed the morsel and winked. "I don't want you feeling uncomfortable. Everyone knows about us."

"As long as you don't order him and he doesn't miss anything, I don't see how that's a conflict of interest."

"What about Yoggi?" Taylor asked, uncertain of OTS protocol. Every commander had their own little quirks.

"I'd ask her. See if she minds, especially because it's Malone."

Taylor picked up a small juicy bit of ripe red fruit and placed it in her waiting mouth. "She's busy. Is that OK?"

"You probably shouldn't see her. I usually talk to Simb, her secretary. I tell him what I want or need and let him give her the message. If Yoggi wants to discuss it with me, she'll call me in. If not, she appreciates my respecting her time limitations and lets Simb give me the answer. I don't think it's a good idea to take up the company commander's time, unless that commander wants me to."

"What about going through Little Hitler?"

"If it were any other cadet, I'd say you need to go through Haden, but not Malone. Yoggi wants to be personally informed of what's going on with him. We're reporting on Malone directly to her, not through Haden. She knows Haden's prejudiced. We report to him separately."

"Thanks, Sues." He pecked her on the cheek. "I'd never have thought to leave a message with Simb."

"You tell Simb about those fights the way you told me, and he'll convey your enthusiasm to Yoggi."

"Thanks. You're brilliant. How'd I get to be so lucky?"

"It must have been your good first impression," she teased, with a wink.

"Ha, ha." He tickled her abdomen. "So maybe I was a little drunk and said a few stupid things."

"A little drunk? A few stupid things?"

"OK, OK, I said I was sorry. You were a knock-out that night, both literally and figuratively." He put his fist to his chin.

Leiman smiled smugly. "You earned it."

"Yeah, am I ever going to live that down?"

"Probably not."

Taylor took a gulp of champagne and set the glass down. "So, how's it working out with Baker?"

"Good. I can see why Yoggi picked him to be with Malone. He's a great drill sergeant."

"How about the seniority thing? I know you were worried about that."

"No problem. Baker acknowledges I'm the lead sergeant. He's not trying to get into a power struggle, and I'm not trying to control him or treat him like a rookie." She poked Taylor lightly.

"You're cruel," the rookie answered.

"I told Baker I appreciated his taking a back seat after being a lead sergeant for years. We talked things over. We're working more as a team. I respect him and know different techniques are effective. I told him to do things as he saw best. He doesn't need to come and check with me; I'll tell him if I have a problem. He seemed pretty relieved by that."

"I'll bet."

"Baker is easy to work with, and we seem to think alike on the important issues. With trainees, I go from problem to problem. With Baker, there are no problems. He controls things before they get out of hand, which is important with Malone in the unit."

"How is it going with Malone?"

"Good, I guess. He's not what I expected." She leaned into him and maneuvered his arm around her.

"What did you expect?"

114

"I figured he'd be a jerk. Stirring things up. Trying to cause trouble. He's not. Does what he's told. Learns fast. Keeps to himself."

"What about the starvation thing? How often is he sitting out?"

"None. Hasn't dogged it once."

"You're kidding. That's amazing. If I'd been given the option, I would have sat out some of the drills in boot camp, and ours only lasted two weeks."

"I know, he's tough." She lifted her head and leaned until their gaze met. "Do you know what work brands are?"

"No." He shook his head. "Should I?"

"I just wondered. It came up in one of the Alpha's sit-downs. Baker lets them chatter more than I do. Malone has two sets of whatever they are, one on each side of his chest. On the left is a group of circles and the other side is arrow. The doctor noted they were made from burns. Someone asked him what they were and he said, 'work brands.' Whatever that means. The group was too confused to ask him what a work brand is. He said it like everyone should know."

"You think they're Kalopso markings?" He put his hand on her shoulder and pulled her close.

"That's my guess. We have a lot of communication problems with Malone. Even when he answers, I have no idea what he's saying. We tell him what to do, and he thinks he's doing it, but he's misunderstood, or he stands there, completely confused by our orders. It's like he doesn't speak English."

"Does he scare you?"

Leiman jerked away, her eyes glaring.

Taylor held up his hands. "I know you can take care of yourself, Sues. I just mean. . .Gees, I saw the kid fight, and I've seen him with a knife. . .I can honestly say, he makes me a little nervous. . .and. . .and I do worry about you." Taylor lifted his arm and held it up until she leaned on his chest. He folded his arm around her.

"I know you do."

"And remember, that's a good thing."

She nodded as she rubbed his chest. "Whatever wrongs Malone has done, I can't believe there weren't extenuating circumstances. You should see his med file. He must have had a terrible life."

"Is he making you feel sorry for him?"

"No, that's probably why I do. Malone never complains. He's not asking for special treatment, and he's never said a word to me or anybody else about his past."

"Then you want him to stay?"

"On the one hand, I think he deserves a chance, like everyone else." She paused.

"And on the other hand. . ."

"I don't like having a Kalopso plant in my unit."

"You're certain of that?"

"No. My life would be a lot easier without him. He may not be dogging, and he does whatever he's told, but he's not a team player. He doesn't work well in groups, and he scares half the unit. Most of them don't want to be near him. How am I supposed to unify a group like that?"

Taylor kissed her head and stroked her hair.

"You can hear the sighs of relief when Malone reports to the doctors. Once he leaves, things go more smoothly."

"My guess is he doesn't trust anybody. The kid's probably never had a break in his life."

"I'd be surprised if he had. I'm just not sure we're the ones to give it to him."

"So you'll be glad when he goes?"

"Mostly." She sighed as she kicked off her shoes. She laid her head in his lap and propped her feet on the arm of the couch.

Taylor twiddled with her hair. "What are you going to do?"

"I'll keep going the way I am. I'm conscious about treating and evaluating him fairly. Baker is, too. Other than that, what else can I do?"

"Nothing, I guess."

"What did you think of him?"

"I was impressed he didn't get in extra hits when we fought. The question is, why'd he stop?" Leiman outlined his chin with her finger. Taylor grinned. "If he's doing that to trick or manipulate me, I'm going to feel differently than if he did it because he wanted to."

"Sure, what's his motivation? I think the same thing about why he came here."

"I don't think I'd go some place where everyone there wanted me gone, unless I was being paid to."

"I agree. Why OTS, when it has a terrible reputation for class cast-

116

ing and prejudice?"

"I'd say he was doing it to stir up trouble, except you say he's not. I can't figure him out." He lifted her and nuzzled in beside her horizontally.

"I'm tired of talking about Malone. We only have tonight, and then I won't see you for a whole week."

"Well, then, we'd better store up enough loving to last that long."

CHAPTER 9

SGT. TAYLOR TROTTED OVER to Cmd. Yoggi's office. He was thrilled to see Simb at his desk.

"Hi, Taylor. I heard through the grapevine you've had a few rookie encounters with the orphan."

"Simb, I'm amazed how much you know about what's happening on this base."

"What can I say?" Simb puffed on his fist and rubbed his chest. "It's a gift. What brings you here?"

"I was hoping you'd talk to Cmd. Yoggi for me about Malone."

Cmd. Yoggi rounded the corner from the kitchenette. "Something on your mind, Sergeant, ahum?" she fumbled on the name. The man was familiar, but she could not remember who he was.

Bulldog turned and gulped. He was not prepared for this contingent. "Sgt. Brian Taylor, Ma'am." He stood tall and saluted. "I don't want to take up any of your valuable time, Commander."

"That's all right. I've been thinking about Malone all day. Maybe a little more input would be helpful. Why don't we chat while I eat lunch." She held up a sandwich.

"Yes, Ma'am. Thank you." Taylor said, uncertain if it was a mistake coming to her office.

"Do you want to grab something out of the break room?" She flicked her head in that direction.

"No, Ma'am. This will only take a minute."

Yoggi stared at Taylor's pushed-in face. Then she remembered. Leiman was dating the bulldog. "You're Sgt. Leiman's friend, aren't you?" She motioned him to the comfortable chair by the coffee table.

"Yes, Ma'am." Taylor grinned. Susan would get a kick out of him being referred to as her friend.

"And from the smile on your face I'd guess that friendship is progressing." Yoggi picked her drink up off the desk, carried it over and sat down across from him.

Taylor smirked as he tried to look professional. "Yes, Ma'am. Thank you for asking."

She set her cup on the table. "I'm happy for both of you. Sgt. Leiman's one of the best people I know."

"Yes, Ma'am. I think so, too."

"Well now, you've obviously met the infamous orphan. Tell me about your encounters with him."

"The first time, I was trying to steal the Alpha's supplies, and Malone jumped me from behind."

"Yes, I heard about that from Baker and Leiman. It sounds like Malone handled himself pretty well. What did you think?"

"I was impressed. Malone throws a knife like a pro."

"How badly were you hurt?"

"A minor cut on the hand." Taylor twisted his hand in the air. "I don't think he was trying to hurt me, just disarm me."

"Is Capt. Haden aware that you and Sgt. Leiman are in a relationship?"

Taylor titled his head. He was confused by the question. "Yes, Ma'am."

"Was anyone sick that night?"

Taylor's eyebrows met over his pug nose. "No, Commander."

"I'm trying to figure out why you were assigned to infiltrate the Alphas." Cmd. Yoggi took a small bite of her sandwich.

"I was assigned to an area. I didn't know who I was stealing from at the time. Capt. Haden has said he doesn't want me to substitute for the Alphas. Once I've stolen their supplies, I'll be assigned to another group."

"Oh, that's right. I'd forgotten at the beginning the floaters are given areas. And the rule is, any supplies missed, you're required to go back and take?"

"That's the rule. I'll be ready for Malone the next time, Commander. I hadn't expected anyone to come at me out of the trees." Taylor scratched the nap of his thick black neck. "I was told the first few nights cadets are too tired to protect anything. And it was true, for everybody except Malone."

"You said that was your first encounter. What else have you done with him?" She took another bite, then laid the sandwich on the table.

"I assist Sgt. Ryan in hand-to-hand. I met Malone a few days ago when the Alphas reported for their self-defense intro. Malone briefly sparred with Ryan and me. The fights were brief, because Malone beat us that fast. He's amazing." Taylor leaned forward, his eyes gleaming. "I've never seen anyone fight like he does. He has no style Sgt. Ryan or I could identify, and he combines moves in ways we've never seen before. He is unbelievable." Taylor smacked his leg.

"I can tell you were impressed. He beat Ryan and you." She took a sip. "Was Ryan feeling OK?"

"He was, until Malone broke his nose." Taylor leaned back in the chair, chuckling.

"Did you try and stop Malone? Is that how you got involved?"

"No, Ma'am. I requested permission to spar with Malone." Taylor gave an animated recap of the fights. "Commander," he concluded, "it was like Malone was swatting flies." He waved his hand in the air. "And unfortunately, I was one of the flies." He clapped his hands together. "Ryan and I aren't exactly amateurs, but it was effortless for him."

"No, I've seen Ryan, and I've heard you're almost as good. I guess Ryan will have a lot of help in the A group."

"No, Ma'am." Taylor dropped his head. He wished the subject hadn't come up. "Sgt. Ryan decided I should work with Cadet Malone."

"I thought Ryan always taught the advanced group. Why isn't he with the Alphas?"

"He is Commander." Taylor twisted around in his chair.

"Malone is supposed to be in your group? Is that what you wanted to speak to me about?"

"No, Commander." He nervously smoothed his pants. "I told Malone he could assist me. I. . ."

"Ryan has a problem with Malone?"

"He felt I might do a better job with Malone."

"You mean he's prejudiced and won't work with Malone."

"Commander, I've had no problems working with Sgt. Ryan. . ."

"And you don't want any." She understood. Tattling on another sergeant would make it difficult for Taylor to work in OTS. He might as well hang himself, and she did not want to put him in that position. "I'm not going to speak to Ryan or anyone else about this conversation. I respect your loyalty to Sgt. Ryan."

"Thank you, Ma'am." He exhaled loudly.

"However, I have to know what's going on with Malone. If Ryan has a problem with Malone, then it is better for you to work with him. I need to keep open-minded people dealing with and evaluating Malone. I informed the staff, if anyone had a problem with Cadet Malone, to have Capt. Haden reassign them. Sgt. Ryan would have been following those orders."

Taylor's shoulders relaxed. "Yes, Ma'am."

"I'd prefer my people to be honest about whether they are prejudiced or not. I chose Leiman and Baker as the Alpha's drill sergeants because they aren't anti-orphan. I assumed Ryan assigned Malone to you for the same reason."

"I have no problems with Malone being an orphan, Commander."

"Good, I'm glad to hear it." She picked up her sandwich. "What other encounters have you had with him?"

"None, Ma'am."

She put her lunch down and looked at him. "I'm perplexed. What did you want to ask me about?"

"I was hoping to spar with Malone a few times. If he doesn't mind. I don't want to order him, and I know there isn't a lot of time available. Maybe have him show me a few moves."

"Obviously you're not prejudiced, if you're willing to have him teach you." Cmd. Yoggi was impressed with Taylor's evaluation of Malone's talents. "Does Malone know you admire his skills?"

"I think so, Commander. I commented to him, but Malone didn't say much."

"Did Sgt. Leiman tell you what I want from whoever has contact with him?"

"No, Ma'am."

"I was telling Leiman and Baker I wanted Malone to open up a little. The sergeants were going to try to befriend him, maybe get some more insight into how he thinks. . .and how he got here. They were going to try, but weren't confident he'd open up."

"Leiman said he was kind of quiet and kept to himself."

"Maybe if he spoke to someone one on one more as an equal, or as a teacher, he wouldn't feel so threatened." She tapped her leg. "Since you're not his drill sergeant, you could joke around more, do some male bonding, ask for advice about fighting, stuff like that. Perhaps

121

tell him not to think of you as a sergeant. Get rid of the rank barrier, and hopefully we can get some answers out of him. Would you feel comfortable doing that?"

"Yes, Ma'am." Taylor answered enthusiastically. "Fighting's like that, anyway. You can't spar and be worried about rank. I've already told him to teach the Alpha novices as he sees best, and I'd use that as part of his leadership evaluation. All I need is to see if he's willing to spar with me personally."

"Good work, Sergeant. I'm pleased with how you're handling this. I agree let's not order him to do anything. Did you get the feeling he'd be willing to show you some things?" She placed the last bite of bread in her mouth.

"I think so. The only problem I see is time. None of the cadets have much free time in boot camp."

"Ultimately, I'd like to see you with him for one-hour blocks. Enough for warm-ups, with chit-chat, sparring, discussions about sparring and cool-downs with chit-chat. Now to arrange that." She paused, picked up her drink and took a few sips. "Have you fought in the All-Military annual bouts?"

"Yes, Ma'am." Taylor sat up straight in his chair. "I've come in second, the last three years."

"Excellent, how about first this year?"

"That's what I want Malone for. I think a few lessons with him could put me over the top."

"And in theory, we should assume Malone would be fighting in the All-Militaries this year. How about inviting him to start practicing for it with you?"

"Great! When can I start?"

"Very well. I'm certain with your genuine enthusiasm, your interest will not seem contrived. As Malone's sergeant of hand-to-hand, invite him to sign up for the All-Military competition and, as we would do for any cadet, arrange for a practice schedule with his sergeants. I'd like to see two or three times a week, starting as soon as possible. You are to report to me after you've worked out with him a few times. Cpl. Simb will schedule that for you. Any questions or anything you'd like to add?"

"No, Ma'am."

"You're dismissed."

Taylor stood and saluted. "Thank you, Commander."

She flipped him a salute as he turned and left.

Cmd. Yoggi looked at her watch. The discussion had run longer than she had planned; however, it had been extremely productive. For one thing, she was impressed with Sgt. Taylor. She would not forget his name again. He had a good attitude, followed protocol, tried to make his superiors look good, evaluated fairly, participated in military functions and seemed confident and capable. Cmd. Yoggi also thought Taylor had the best chance of getting answers out of Malone. She had not considered having the orphan prepare for the All-Militaries before, because she did not anticipate him being around that long.

*   *   *

"Hey, Taylor." Sgt. Leiman grinned. "What are you doing at the firing range?"

"I took your advice and went to talk to Simb. Only Yoggi overheard. She called me into her office."

"How did that go?" Leiman latched the safety on her rifle.

"Fantastic." He clapped his hands and rubbed his palms. "She wants Malone to sign up for the All-Military maxor fights and spar with me two or three times a week. I should be able to learn some things in that time."

"What's in it for Cmd. Yoggi?"

"I'm supposed to talk to him without the rank barrier. See if he'll open up a little."

"You certainly couldn't be any less successful than I've been." Leiman held up her rifle and waved it at Zeus. Zeus pointed to himself. Leiman nodded and pulled the rifle to her.

Zeus trotted up and saluted.

"At ease, Malone," Leiman ordered. "Sgt. Taylor has a proposition for you."

"Yes, Sir?"

"I've been thinking about the cracked lip you gave me. That was a great hit. Are you interested in training for the All-Military maxor fights?"

Zeus's face went blank. He thought the staff would not waste time preparing someone they intended to discharge before the competition. He also assumed they would not let him represent OTS if he was around. He was too perplexed by the request to answer.

"If you need a little time to think about it," Taylor stated, "you can let me know."

"No, Sir," Zeus answered. He did not need time to think.

"OK." Taylor assumed he was answering the original question. "If you change your mind, let me know."

Zeus realized he had not responded correctly. "No, Sir," he tried to convey the misunderstanding. "I's mean yes, Sir." Only it sounded like yes, he would tell Taylor if he changed his mind. That wasn't what he wanted to say. He clenched his fists. "Budgin, I's wanna fights."

"Drop it, fifty," Leiman ordered.

Zeus complied, frustrated he could not remember to avoid cussing.

Taylor shook his head at Leiman. "Is this an example of the communication problems you were talking about?"

She rolled her eyes. "Malone, it's a good thing they don't give points for language skills during those fights. You'd lose in the first round."

Zeus stood. He eyes fixed downward. "Yes, Ma'am." He hated always being mixed up when he talked.

"What weight do you fight in?" Taylor asked.

"Super Heavy Weight."

Both sergeants looked at the emaciated orphan. "What?"

"Fights ups," Zeus explained.

"And you've never lost?" Taylor eyebrows raised.

"Ain'ts gots ta do's with weight."

"This isn't like the college kids you're used to fighting," Sgt. Taylor reminded him.

"Uses ta surviv'n ons the Row. "

"I see your point. Ryan is a Super Heavy Weight, and you didn't have any problems dropping him. Can you fight by the maxor rules?"

"I's can."

"All right, Malone, I'll see you get signed up for the fights, and then we'll start practicing. You see," Taylor clicked his tongue and gave a half-wink, "I have a little pull with your lead sergeant. I'll work it out so we can spar a few times a week."

"Taylor, get out'a here." She swatted him on the rear. "We've got work to do. Malone, return to your rotation." She turned to Taylor. "I'll look at our schedule and send you some available times to choose from. Try to keep your lips away of his fists."

He nudged her. "Anything for you, Sues."

124

*   *   *

Galahad's heart pounded as he follow his mentor and the Kalopso boss's guards. He was glad Emily had fed him earlier. He felt invincible. They marched into a large, auditorium-style room with a ring in the center and seating above. In the ring, two men fought with knives. The spectators sat on lounge chairs and placed bets on the fights. Galahad focused on Two Square's weaknesses. Galahad was determined not lose. If he won, he would be trained by the Kalopso and on the road to providing for Emily's safety and happiness.

The victorious knife fighter left the ring, and the loser was dragged off to be thrown in the body pool. As Galahad stepped into the ring, he asked the magic God/man Jesus to help him. Emily had assured him praying brought on His magic.

Galahad and Two Square faced off. The only rule was survival. The crowd favored the larger, older man. Two Square did not want to look weak in front of his boss. He hated hurting his favorite pupil, but this was war. Galahad round-kicked at his mentor's face. Two Square bobbed and responded with two jabs to Galahad's face. Galahad landed a left under-cut and a knee to the groin. Two Square pulled his knife. Galahad's knife had been taken from him earlier. Two Square took aim and threw the blade. Galahad winced and grabbed his shoulder. Blood spurted between his fingers and the knife. Two Square clipped Galahad's legs out from under him. Galahad fell on his back as blood splattered on his face.

The crowd booed and yelled, "Put him in the box." Galahad stood up and pulled the knife from his shoulder. As he prepared to fight again, he glanced around the room and saw various kids in boxes. The box terrified him. He could not stand the thought of being restrained and helpless at the same time. He was not going in one of those. He no longer felt the pain of his shoulder. He charged Two Square with every ounce of his will. He jabbed and kicked mercilessly until his mentor lay helpless on the floor.

"Put the loser in a box and bring the kid to me," the boss's voice said over the intercom. Panting and bleeding, the victor was brought before his master. "You fight well. Why do you want to be in the Kalopso?"

"K strongs. Strong is good. I's strong."

"What's the most important thing to the K?"

"Loyalty. I's be loyal. Not fail yous. I's be's strong for yous."

"What if you have to fight a friend?"

"Two Square friend. K's better. No's friends better than K."

"Kid, you've got potential. Show me how you got in here."

"Stupid if I's don't belongs ta show yous magic."

"And if you're in?"

"I's be's loyal ta yous. Yous boss, show yous."

A whole-hearted belly laughed shook the boss. "I like you, kid. You're hurt. You're completely surrounded, and you've still got the rocks to negotiate. You're strong, and I'll let you join. If you're loyal to me, I'll reward you."

"I's be's loyal."

"Good. Now show me how you got in."

"Goes under club, through air and heat'n vents ta Emily's room."

"Show me," the boss said. They followed the director to Emily's room.

Emily lay on her bed crying. The smell of vomit filled the room. She looked up as the door opened. When she saw Galahad, she ran over to hug him.

Galahad stepped away and turned to the boss. "I's helps Emily?"

"Can you make her stop crying?"

"I's stop her." He held his sister. "Emily, we's did it. I's strong. Boss let me's join K!"

"How did Emily help you?" the director demanded.

"She's a K?" Galahad asked of the director.

"She's a member. Answer," the boss ordered.

"Give me's food. Cure me's with magic. Help me's be's strong."

Emily clung to her brother. "Galahad, no, don't tell them."

"He's K boss. Gots ta be's loyal. Ain'ts no punishment bad enough if I's ain't loyal."

"That's right, boy. What's your Two Square call you?"

"Red Top."

"I like you, Red Top." The boss would not acknowledge an orphan with a name like Galahad. It would humanize him and put him on the same level as the superior Kalopso members. "You're a good K member. Show me how you got in."

Galahad showed them the hinged vent. "Crawls through ta mines."

"What does she feed you?"

Galahad took him over to the beakers. "I's drinks foods."

"What is it, Emily?" the director demanded.

Emily refused to answer.

"You're failing to control her again," the boss snarled through clenched teeth.

"I's not fail, boss," Galahad stated boldly. "Emily, he's K boss. Yous answer for me's."

She looked at her brother and only friend. It was wrong not to help him. "Sodium, potassium, protein, glucose and a few other vitamins."

"What do you do for her?" the boss asked Red Top.

"Takes care of Emily. She's weak. Not screams when I's sleep with her. Helps her build for contests." He showed them the aquifer model.

"Is that the model that got her accepted to the semifinals for the centennial agricultural symposium?" the boss asked.

"Yes," the director conceded.

"The once-in-a-century, million-drayka prize, the regional boss expects her to win?"

"Yes. She can do it." The director hoped for mercy.

"Emily, can you make this thing work?" the boss asked.

"Not without Galahad's help. The semifinals are only six months away. I'm doing extensive research on geological engineering, but I'm not good at the mechanical things."

"Red Top, you built this?"

"Emily tells me's how, and I's build."

"If he helps you, can you make this work?" The boss lightly kicked the model.

"Yes," Emily frantically prayed her friend would not be taken away.

"Is it good enough to win?" he asked the director.

Emily answered instead. "My aquifer will redefine agriculture throughout the galaxy. The other contestants aren't proposing anything this dramatic. That's why they let me compete."

"What do you need him for?"

"I can only create the aquifer theoretically. Galahad does the building and is making the model for my presentations." Emily wanted to ensure Galahad's daily presence and added. "Plus, I can't think when I don't sleep. Galahad helps me sleep."

"Red Top, you're going to work for me," the boss said. "You're going to take care of Emily and see she wins that contest. If she loses, you're in the box. If she wins, I'll take care of you both. I'll see you're trained to be the best K fighter that ever lived."

"Emily wins," Galahad assured him.

"I know you won't fail me." He glared at the director. It was the last time they saw her. Her failures were not acceptable. "Red Top, show my guards the vents entrance outside."

"I's show thems."

"Seal both entrances," the boss said to the guards. "Then bring Red Top here." The guards nodded and led Galahad to the door.

"Good-bye, fair knight." Emily sniffed.

CHAPTER 10

SGT. TAYLOR HAD BEEN PLANNING this supply run for days. He hated his new reputation as the guy Malone jumped. If any sergeant was outdone by a cadet, it was cause for teasing; however, being a rookie made it much worse for Taylor.

Tonight, he was ready. He had kicked himself over and over for underestimating Malone. This time he was going in armed with a three caliber PSG. He would check the trees and disarm Malone — of both his knives. He intended to capture the orphan, gag and tie him up for the night. That would give Malone time to think about his mistakes. Bulldog had prepared five gags and ropes, and they were ready and easy to reach in his gun belt.

He quietly sneaked up and scanned the encampment with his Surveyor/Recorder. The SR detected and identified life signs, metal, most weapons, vegetation and other pertinent information. It told him the equipment he wanted was a hundred and twenty meters southeast of him and was guarded by two cadets on the ground. Taylor tugged his infrared night goggles off his head and over his eyes. Each guard was holding a PSG. The SR picked up one human in the tree above the bulk of the supplies. Malone. Taylor scanned the tree. The SR noted only small amounts of metal, an amount consistent with knives.

Tonight is my night, he thought. A noisy storm was blowing in. The leaves rattled and thunder clapped off in the distance. With any luck, Malone would be asleep and not hear the guards fall when he shot them.

Taylor slowly moved closer to the guards and put himself in position to fire. PSGs were only effective at stunning their victims if the laser band had a direct hit on the intended target. If the shot hit interference from other objects, the ray could be defused or deflected.

The sergeant took half an hour to get in the perfect position to shoot both guards and be in range to get Malone out of the tree and on the ground quickly. Taylor did not want to stun Malone, it was not as sporting; however, he was prepared to and presumed he would have to.

Taylor fired two silent shots in secession. A bright burst of lightning followed by a bang of thunder muffled the sound of the guards falling. Taylor approached the tree.

The orphan was perched on a thick branch. He stuffed his hand in his pocket and united with the Little Lady. He held his right hand over her claw as he pushed the button. The blade opened, and he eased it out until it locked in place. He watched as a murky gray blob moved beneath the tree. He did not have the advantage of infrared goggles.

Taylor, on the other hand, could easily make out his opponent's facial features and the knife in his left hand. "Drop the knife, Malone."

Zeus dropped the knife in his hand.

"And the other one."

Taylor pointed the PSG at the orphan. The other knife dropped to the ground. Taylor aimed the weapon with his right hand and picked up both knives with his left hand. He tucked the knives in his gun belt. "All right, slowly come down out of the tree."

Zeus descended to the lower branches keeping plenty of leaves in front of him. He was not giving Taylor a clean shot. When he got to the lowest branch, as a strategic ploy, he positioned himself as close as he could above the sergeant.

"Not this time, Malone." Taylor stepped away.

Perfect, Zeus thought.

Taylor aimed his PSG directly at Malone. "Drop out of that tree."

Zeus dropped. The instant his feet hit the ground, he attacked with a round kick, sending the stun gun flying through the air. The orphan used the surprise to his advantage and followed with a left jab to Taylor's face. Before Taylor could recover and counter-attack, Zeus grabbed his knife out of the sergeant's belt and put the knife to Taylor's throat.

Taylor was more stunned than the two motionless cadets on the ground. Everything had gone as planned, yet in the blink of an eye, he had been disarmed and checkmated. He dreaded the sergeants' meeting in the morning. He thought, I'll never schedule another raid on the Alphas the night before a meeting.

"Malone," Sgt. Taylor conceded as his hands were being tied with his own ropes, "You're good. Crap, you're good."

"Yous a slow learner, Sir. I's gets a better kick from a distance." Zeus jerked the rope tight and pushed Taylor toward Sgt. Leiman's tent.

*   *   *

Sgt. Leiman heard a familiar voice outside her tent. "Sgt. Leiman, requests permission ta speaks, Ma'am." At first in her sleepy state, she could not place the voice. Again the voice requested permission to speak.

"Malone, granted," she answered excited. She had anticipated this for days. She was hoping her cadet had taken Taylor prisoner again. The first incident had given her a great deal of pleasure teasing her boyfriend. This time, the two of them had a bet. The loser would take the winner out to LLardo's, the most expensive restaurant on the planet.

"I's caught him try'n ta steals supplies, Ma'am," Zeus yelled in his best cadet voice. He knew his sergeant would be thrilled with his gift. She had told the whole unit about her bet, and that she did not like to lose, especially to Sgt. Taylor.

Sgt. Leiman stepped out of her tent. "Good job, Malone." She faced Bulldog in triumph. "Why, Sgt. Taylor, what brings you to the Alpha encampment?"

"Just trying to earn enough money to afford dinner at LLardo's," Taylor quipped.

"How'd he get you this time?"

"I thought I had him covered, and the next thing I knew he disarmed me." He cocked his head toward his warden, adding in an annoyed tone, "Malone, don't you ever sleep?"

"Not when my's Sergeant's honor's at stakes." He tightened his grip on the prisoner.

"Thank you, Malone," she said, genuinely flattered. "You caught him, Malone. What should we do with him?"

Taylor was starting to get nervous. Leiman loved practical jokes; this could not be good.

Zeus had no idea what to suggest. He had barely spoken for years. He had never been involved in a practical joke. He did not want to disappoint Sgt. Leiman. He blurted out the only thing that came to mind, "Ties him ups?"

"Yes, we could tie him up. . .and leave him some place interesting. . .like the crap hole."

Sgt. Taylor started to squirm, he did not like the mischievous tone in his girlfriend's voice. Zeus tightened his grip and pushed the blade against Taylor's throat

"Hey, Malone, do you know how to hog tie?" she asked smiling.

"Don't knows hog tie'n, but I's ties him so he's ain't leave'n, Ma'am."

"Come on, Sues. I admit it, you've won," Taylor begged. It was drizzling and he did not enjoy the prospect of spending the night in the rain in the crap hole.

"Start tying, Malone," Leiman ordered. "I plan to get more than a dinner out of tonight."

"Yes, Ma'am." Zeus smiled. He was elated as he immobilized the helpless Sgt. Taylor.

"Sues, please, I've got a meeting in the morning, and it's supposed to storm tonight."

"Then you shouldn't have gotten yourself captured or picked better weather."

Zeus could not believe he was getting to play and be part of the fun. Not watch, he was getting to participate. The more he thought about it, the more involved he wanted to be.

"Sgt. Leiman?"

"Go head, Malone."

"Gots gags here."

"We wouldn't want to waste the taxpayers' supplies, would we, Malone?"

"No, Ma'am."

"Sues, this isn't funny any. . ." the rest of Sgt. Taylor's words were incoherent as the gag was positioned in his mouth.

Sgt. Leiman took Zeus aside, "I'm sorry, Malone, he probably deserves it, but I can't leave him tied up all night. He'd kill me in the morning. Besides, with what you've done and the abuse he'll get from the staff, he'll suffer enough. If it's OK with you, I'll leave him there for awhile and then go release him." She watched to see if Zeus appeared disappointed.

He was not. Zeus understood and agreed with her. He was elated she had checked with him first. It implied a rapport of mutual respect.

Before he answered verbally, "Yes, Ma'am," Sgt. Leiman had read his facial expression and knew her plan was acceptable.

"Thanks, Malone. You did a great job tonight. I appreciate this, more than you realize. You go get some shut-eye and I'll take care of Taylor."

"Yes, Sergeant," Zeus answered as he saluted.

Leiman returned the salute. "Thanks again. You're dismissed."

Zeus felt more exhilarated than he could remember feeling. He had never wanted to attend OTS; however, it had been his last available option. Now he was enjoying the entire experience. It was not just that he was eating four times a day, or had whole mouth full of perfect teeth. Zeus liked everything about the military: the saluting, the chain of command, his sergeants, the order, the predictability, the athletic challenge, the flying and navigating, the honor system, the camping out, and everything else. He had never cared where he lived before. Here he wanted to stay.

Taylor was drenched to the bone. He resigned himself to a long, cold night and vowed he would get even. The rain formed small rivers down his back and into his pants. It tickled and he wanted to scratch. The gag was becoming uncomfortable as it pulled at the corners of his mouth. He was miserable. All he could do was wait and plan his revenge.

Taylor felt someone approaching from behind him and wondered what his captors had in mind now. He was livid as he envisioned sleeping in the crap hole.

He felt Leiman's trademark finger swirling around the base of his neck and the warmth of her mouth as she nibbled on his ear. Within moments, he forgot he was cold and angry. She seductively removed his gag and positioned herself to kiss him full on the lips. He instinctively responded in kind.

"Mmm," Taylor murmured, "you are the most exciting woman I've know. Amour."

"Amour."

"How 'bout untying these ropes?"

"I'll have to think about that," she purred, caressing his arms as she moved to untie him. "I want you completely at my mercy."

"No problem," he whispered, "I surrender."

*　　*　　*

Dr. Bentley slowed down at the guard gate. She saw the Alphas and Malone in full packs, jogging. She yanked her controls to the right and slammed her flyer into park. She leaped out, waving her arms. "Sgt. Baker!"

"Alphas, halt," Baker ordered. The company stopped. Baker trotted to the doctor and saluted. "Yes, Ma'am."

She jerked her hands to her hips, fixed her jaw and snarled, "What is Malone doing still jogging and in double time no less? I passed him and the Alphas jogging on my way to lunch over an hour ago."

"Cadet Malone has not requested to stop, Ma'am. If he asks to slow down, I'll allow it, as ordered. Remember, I was not supposed to determine when he was overtaxed."

"Obviously you have not made him aware of his options."

"Yes, Doctor, I have." Baker cocked his head. "Malone, get over here."

Zeus dropped out of formation, ran over and saluted. "Yes, Sir."

"I'll ask the questions," she said, shoving Baker to the left. This way he could not prompt the orphan into any answers. She turned to Zeus. "Malone, what were you doing?"

Zeus hated open-ended questions. With yes or no questions, he had a fifty percent chance of answering correctly. He thought he was in formation correctly, yet he could tell from her tone and Baker's face, no matter what he said, he was in trouble. "Hike'n, Ma'am," he replied, convinced it was not the right answer.

"Thank you, Malone. I could see that. What have I told you about your fatty deposits?"

Zeus had no idea how the two questions were related and again decided he could not answer correctly. "They's low, Ma'am."

"Yes, they're low." She crossed her arms. "And what does that mean?"

Zeus was confused and glanced at Sgt. Baker for guidance. Baker gave none. "Ain'ts eat lots 'til here, Ma'am."

"Malone," Dr. Bentley snarled between her teeth, "what did I tell you about overexertion?"

"Don't."

"Right. Don't. So why are you doing a one-hour hike?"

Baffled, Zeus continued to answer the obvious. "Sgt. Baker orders a hike, Ma'am."

"I don't care what Sgt. Baker ordered. When you get tired, you're supposed to stop."

"Yes, Ma'am."

Sgt. Baker chuckled. "Look, Doctor, he's not even breathing heavily."

"It's not his lung capacity I'm worried about. What's the point of me keeping him away from intensive workouts, if you just push him once he gets here?"

Zeus clenched his jaw. The Doctor was purposely preventing him from training. He hated medical things, and he enjoyed the OTS activities. He forgot about protocol and snarled, "Huh, yous budgin stop'n me's from train'n?"

Under most instances, Sgt. Baker would have severely reprimanded his cadet for speaking in such a manner to an officer. Today he ignored the language and encouraged the orphan's outburst. "Permission to speak freely, Malone."

Zeus ground his new teeth as he blew hot, dragon-puffs. "Huh I's sit'n on my's butt in yous budgin office?"

Dr. Bentley rubbed her temple. "Look what you've done to this poor boy." She shook her finger at Baker. "When I heard you and Leiman were the best OTS sergeants, I had no idea how effective you were. In only two weeks, you have completely brainwashed this man. He actually appreciates you two pushing him to exhaustion. After your indoctrination, Malone couldn't have a non-regulation thought if he wanted to."

Zeus stood tall and proud. "Thank yous, Ma'am."

Baker laughed as Dr. Bentley snarled, "It wasn't a compliment, Malone. You're not supposed to be thankful when people work you to death."

"Ain'ts work'n ta death. Less work than I's use ta."

She turned to the under-fed orphan. "I'm trying to build up your fat deposits. That means you have to expend less energy than you take in."

"Ma'am, I's eat'n more a day than I's eats in a month and I's work'n less."

Dr. Bentley dropped her head. She closed her eyes and bit her lip. "All right. Go over to the infirmary. I'll check you after you've been exercising. If everything looks acceptable and your deposits are rising, you can take your pills at night, and I'll check you once a week."

"Yes, Ma'am." Zeus snapped a salute and smiled.

Sgt. Baker saluted his dismissal, and Zeus raced away elated. Baker turned to the doctor. "Satisfied?"

Dr. Bentley lifted her arms and plopped them on her thick black hair. "How do you brainwash them so fast?"

"Most of them are miserable. Not Malone, he's thriving on it."

"Yes, that's apparent." She dropped her arms. "At least he zinged you, too."

"What do you mean?"

"He doesn't seem too challenged." She shook her head. "I'm willing to bet you won't break him in boot camp."

"I'll take that bet." Baker put his hand out.

Bentley clasped his hand and shook it. "No extra pushing, even if he does check out. Only as much as the others."

"Nothing additional. I understand." Baker held her hand firmly. "And just for the record, I did sit him down and make it clear he could stop." He released her hand.

"I'm sorry. I believe you. It's Malone I don't believe. Every other cadet would be thrilled to sit in my office. Medically, I'm not happy about this, but I can't restrain him. I told you before, he's the only one who can tell if he feels over-taxed and he says he doesn't."

"You sound disappointed."

"No, not really. He makes me nervous."

"That seems to be everyone's comment. Nice talking to you, Doc." Baker put two fingers to his eyebrow and twisted them in an irreverent salute. "I've got to return to my brainwashing."

"I'll send him your way when I'm through." She slid into her flyer.

By the time Dr. Bentley parked and returned to her office, Zeus was waiting for her. She checked his organs and blood. His fatty deposits were up significantly. He showed no signs of exhaustion or stress. The orphan was healthy and getting healthier. She grudgingly gave him the fat storage boosters with instructions to take them at bedtime. The pills were most effective when the body was at rest. Zeus was exhilarated as he left the infirmary.

*　　*　　*

Sgt. Taylor arrived at HQ ten minutes early. He had an opportunity to impress his commander and wanted to take advantage of it, especially since he had failed to steal any of the Alpha's supplies. He paced as he rehearsed his answers. At precisely 13:00 he checked in for his appointment.

"Sergeant, I've been eager to talk to you." Cmd. Yoggi returned his salute and pointed to the chair in front of her desk.

"Yes, Ma'am." He sat formally. They were not sitting informally as they did the last time.

Yoggi was being forced to take the entire orphan situation more seriously. Each day the vice pressuring her to discharge Malone was tightening. "I overheard you and Malone talking. You seem to be taking the right approach with him. It sounded like he was comfortable with you. I must admit I wanted to eavesdrop longer; unfortunately I had a meeting. I'd like to start with your basic impressions."

"Malone is an incredible fighter. If you took the ten best fighters I've ever seen and put them together," he cupped his hands, "they wouldn't be as good as Malone one on one."

"That good?"

"Yes, Ma'am. I can't beat him. I asked him his secret." Taylor raised two fingers. "Malone said two things." He tucked in his middle finger. "Be smart first. I'd say that's his fighting motto."

"What does he mean?"

"Think about what you're doing. Assess and evaluate your opponent, be unpredictable, stuff like that. He told me any maxor who uses a method, like judo or karate, is stupid. He thinks the same of trademark combinations like Ryan's backhand with a leg tuck."

Yoggi crossed her legs and laid her hands in her lap. "As another fighter, what's your opinion of that?"

"It's true. I can't figure out how to fight him or where his weaknesses are. We've sparred four times, and he's never used the same combo more than a few times. The minute I figure one thing out, he changes his method, delivery and combinations."

"I can see why that would be smart. It makes it impossible for you to defend or attack. What's the second secret he gave?"

"His stakes are higher. If I do poorly, I only lose. He's used to fighting for his life against gangs, knives, swords, guns, he even mentioned fire. Mistakes for Malone are fatal."

Cmd. Yoggi drummed her fingers on the desk. "I'm a little concerned about you sparring with him. Dr. Bentley says you're becoming a regular customer."

Taylor cleared his throat, embarrassed. "Yes, Ma'am. Malone's never really sparred before. What kept his skills sharp are his life."

"I still don't like an orphan taking out his aggressions on one of my sergeants."

"Malone's not trying to beat the crap out of me. He's constantly tapping me to let me know he could have nailed me. I zig when I should zag," Taylor bobbed his head, "and walk right into his fist, or knee or whatever. Malone will even tell me beforehand what he's going to do and how to defend it. Then he's so fast, he's two moves ahead of me." Taylor dropped his head. "Afterwards I have to go see Dr. Bentley."

Yoggi wished she could watch Malone fight. The times had never worked out. Every report she heard indicated he was an amazing maxor. "What about sparring with his college team?"

"Malone didn't spar with the Alto team or run with the marathoners. They wouldn't let him. He was on the teams because he didn't lose. Division money is given out based on the win/lose record."

"What was in it for Malone?"

"One meal a day." Taylor shook his head. "Commander, this kid's got lots of reasons to have a big chip on his shoulder."

"Give me some examples."

"When the teams traveled, Malone flew with the luggage and slept on the streets. When he won, he got an extra meal. He wasn't allowed to watch the others compete. He had to remain out of sight until his event and leave as soon as it was over."

Yoggi put her elbows on the desk, clasped her hands and rested her chin on her knuckles. "Then why would he choose OTS, a place with a reputation for class prejudice?"

"He didn't, exactly, Ma'am. There was this journalism major at his school. She was assigned to do a story on class prejudice within our society. Malone never considered OTS. This woman had him apply, knowing we'd turn him down. She used that as an example of prejudice for her article. It was a fluke the story got picked up on InterPress. In his version, even taking our entrance exam wasn't a part of the original plan."

"I'm supposed to believe that this entire thing is a fluke?"

Taylor grimaced. "According to Malone, when InterPress picked up the story, the professor then assigned the journalism student to do a follow-up story. Malone took the entrance exams as a favor to her. They never figured he would do well on the exams. It didn't occur to them he'd ever get accepted. InterPress kept pushing the issue. Malone continued because he thought it might help himself and other orphans. He never planned on coming, and even when he decide to attend, he wasn't eager to come."

Yoggi drummed her fingers. She had assumed Malone and whoever he was in league with would fabricate a better story. Strategically, it seemed wise to follow the false assumptions. Her experience was, often liars reveal bits of the truth. "Then why did he?"

"This woman convinced him it would be a great way to promote orphan causes and help change a prejudiced system. His original goal was to try and stay a week. They figured the longer he stayed, the more effective the political statement."

"And now?" She rested her elbow on the arms of her chair.

"In his own words, he never wants to leave. This is the best place he's ever lived."

"Great." Yoggi squeezed her temples. Somehow, this sounded like a bit of the truth.

"Malone can't figure out why boot camp is called August Agony. He thinks we pamper the cadets."

"That's a new and unique perspective. Why?"

"Three meals a day, tents, toilet paper. . .he thinks that's the ultimate luxury. Doctors caring for him, new teeth." Taylor stared out the window as he tried to remember other things Malone has mentioned. "He talks about the flight simulators, the computers and the weapons like they were toys. He's got everything he wants right here."

"What does he say about the staff?"

"He's aware everyone wants him out and we're ordered to treat him fairly. That's what impresses him. Our system is designed to evaluate people based on performance, not personal opinions. I'd bet money he won't be discouraged into quitting. Malone's not a quitter, and he's used to no one liking him."

Yoggi sighed. Malone not being persuaded into a discharge also rang true. "The other orphans didn't get along with him either?"

"I'm not certain. I was ribbing him about the way he speaks. He said he had to speak that way. If he didn't, it was like putting a big bull's eye on him saying, beat the. . ." Taylor cleared his throat.

"I'm certain I can imagine what Malone said."

"I'm not certain if the other orphans liked him. I wish I could be more accurate for you, Commander."

"I understand. You're supposed to be sparring, not interrogating him. Don't push him too much, or he'll clam up completely. I heard you ask who taught him how to read. Did he answer?"

Sgt. Taylor eyes bugged out as he remembered his exact, colorful words. "Ma'am, I. . ."

"You may have stated it a little differently. I'm pleased you're able to communicate on his level. You're the only one getting anything out of him."

"Yes, Ma'am." Taylor's shoulders relaxed. "That touched a nerve. I don't know why or who, only he was upset and immediately changed the subject."

"Has Malone ever mentioned anything about the network or gangs?"

"He says he hates the Kalopso; that's the other big nerve I've hit. He went off. We were working on the bag. He was cussing and beating the crap out of it. I thought he was going to break it."

"Anything specific?"

"No, Ma'am, just every bad word in the book." Taylor picked a piece of lint off his shirt.

"That's odd, I thought most orphans were members of the network."

"Not according to Malone. He said most orphans hate the Kalopso, or K as they call it. Although he did say, the ones who belong are fiercely loyal. Then I hit another big nerve. We were sparring and joking with each other. I asked him about the network's reputation for giving people fates worse than death, and snap." Taylor snapped his fingers. "He flew into a rage. He cracked two of my ribs before I got him back to reality."

"He attacked you?"

"I don't think Malone realized how hard he hit me. He seemed surprised I was hurt. He'd definitely administered or experienced the fate-worse-than-death thing. Then he got," Taylor fumbled for the words, "quiet or distant, I can't describe it. It's the only time he's given me an eerie feeling. Like he was remembering something. He said the fate thing works. It's a lot easier to see someone die and get over it, than to watch someone you care about suffer day after day, begging to die."

Yoggi sat up eagerly in her chair. Perhaps Taylor was onto something. "Then what?"

"It was weird. I sat down, because when he'd cracked my ribs, he also bruised my lung. I was having trouble breathing. We just sat there. He didn't say it exactly, he kind of implied he wished they'd killed him instead. I'm not certain, it was just my impression."

She leaned over the desk. "He wished they'd killed him instead of what?"

"I'm sorry, Ma'am, I have no idea. I can tell you this: he's not afraid to die. From what he says, it's because he has nothing to live for."

"Interesting." Her mind clicked with the possibilities. "If we were to assume he's been coerced here by the network, do you think he'd consider defecting to our side? Maybe become a double agent?"

"I don't know." Taylor had never thought about that. "The anger he showed when we talked about the Kalopso seemed real. I've never seen Malone out of control, except that one time. I'm not sure if that's good or bad. What would be in it for Malone?"

She slumped in her chair. "Good point. He's not likely to help us for free. If he honestly does like it here, and I hate to say it, but I think he does."

"So do I."

"I still can't offer to let him stay. I'll have to think about what I could offer."

"I don't think Malone cares about money."

"Good. We don't have any." She laughed. "What does he care about?"

"Being respected. One thing he mentioned that impressed him was Baker demanding he stand tall and proud. He's never been asked to hold his head up and exude pride."

She drummed her fingers. "I guess it makes sense that he'd have an inferiority complex."

"I don't see how we can use that to our advantage."

"See if you can steer the conversation back to the Kalopso and fate thing."

"Tell Dr. Bentley to get ready."

"Do you feel comfortable bringing it up?"

Taylor lifted one shoulder. "Sure, I can handle it."

"If things get rough, change the subject."

"Yes, Ma'am."

Cmd. Yoggi swiveled her chair and peered out the window. It helped her think. "Does he mention any friends?"

"Only his knife, the Little Lady."

She snapped her head around. "He named his knife?"

Taylor shrugged. "He says she's never let him down. Kind of implied everyone else had."

"That may explain his lack of social skills."

"I don't have any trouble getting along with Malone. He's kind of antisocial, but then a lot of fighters are."

"Has he talked to you about where his money was going? I can't figure it out. If he was working full time and getting meals from the teams, why was he starving?"

"He wasn't hungry during those months. It sounded like the one meal a day was all he ate. He starved the rest of the time to be able to afford tuition, books and lab fees."

Yoggi pressed a few buttons and accessed Malone's financial sheet. "Alto tuition isn't that high. We've verified everything Malone spent on tuition, books and fees. Even at minimum wage, he should have had enough money for food."

"Malone told me he couldn't get a minimum-wage job. He worked under the table in manual labor for the sewage company. It's common on Orphan's Row, something he blamed on the network. As an orphan, he got paid one drayka per hour for manual labor, maybe one and a half in the sewers."

"That's a whole lot less than minimum wage." Yoggi picked up her InfoPad and wrote down the monetary figures. She would run a variety of calculations with those figures later.

"The orphans are given jobs the other workers refuse to do, usually ones that are dangerous. Injuries are high, and if an orphan gets hurt, they don't get any medical or disability benefits. They get paid in cash at the end of the day. If they don't make it to the end of the day, they don't get paid."

Yoggi put down her pad. "Do you think that's true?"

"Yes, Ma'am. I've heard of hiring orphans under the table. Plus, from what he says, his needs are pretty basic. Malone hopes to live where he can eat once a day and do some form of work that requires

142

him to think. Living on the streets doesn't bother him."

"What about the lack of medical care?"

"That definitely isn't a problem. He knows Dr. Bentley is helping him, but he doesn't like going and would stop if we didn't make him."

"Anything else?"

Taylor thought a moment. "He has a shoe fetish. Malone likes the idea of having shoes that fit and three different pairs. He talks like it's extravagant."

"That makes sense. I saw the shoes he arrived in." She crossed her hands in her lap.

"He also acts funny around the women."

"I'm not following you."

"I notice it mostly when he's teaching self-defense. Almost everything he teaches the women have to do with protecting themselves against attacks," he looked away from her, "like rape. When we're there, he has a completely different agenda than the rest of us. He's teaching street safety and what he calls life-protection skills."

"Are the women complaining?"

"No, most of them think the stuff Malone is showing them is more practical than what I'm teaching. One of them commented she was more likely to get mugged on the street than end up in hand-to-hand combat."

"Yes, but we're supposed to be training them to protect our galaxy, and hand-to-hand can be part of that."

"Don't get me wrong, Commander. Malone is teaching them their skills. In fact, his group has progressed better than the other units. He's teaching them the skills we require and more. Works them hard. The women have complained about that."

"Then how is it different?"

"The scenarios he presents are more what we'd associate with inner-city violence. I guess he's teaching what he knows."

Cmd. Yoggi checked her watch. She had a little more time before her next appointment. "Do you have anything you'd like to add, any personal opinions?"

"I don't have any problems with Malone. I think he's had a crappy life, and it's made him not trust people, but I think he's an OK guy."

"Do you think he'd make a good officer?"

"Ah," Taylor scratched his neck, "I don't see him as an officer. I could see him fitting in better with some of the enlisted recruits I've had. There were always a few, like me, who originally joined instead of going to jail. I'd say he's kind of like that."

"I'd forgotten that's why you originally enlisted. It makes sense you would understand Malone better than the rest of us."

"The Corps turned my life around. A lot of people like me and Malone get into the Corps and thrive on the structure and consistency."

"I should think he would want freedom and flexibility."

"We've discussed this. We give him feedback. That's important to Malone. He likes it when we tell him exactly what to do, when to do it and how to do it."

"I see. No surprises."

Taylor nodded.

"Anything else?"

"No, Ma'am."

"Thank you, Sgt. Taylor. I'm impressed with your work and your attitude." Cmd. Yoggi stood and walked around to the front of the desk.

Taylor stood. "Thank you, Ma'am."

"You've gotten more information from Malone than everyone else combined. Keep up the good work." She extended her hand. "If he says anything important, call Cpl. Simb. He'll work you in."

Taylor shook her hand. "Yes, Ma'am."

CHAPTER 11

"LADIES AND GENTLEMEN." Sgt. Leiman walked among her troops seated on the ground. "There have been two attempts made on our supplies, and only Malone has been able to stop them. What are the rest of you idiots doing? This is supposed to be a unit. Where is your teamwork?" She paused. "Because you're going to need it. I guarantee you, Sgt. Taylor will not rest until he has those supplies. It seems he's a little upset about being tied up in the rain."

The group cheered and whistled. All the other units were essentially supply-less. The other cadets were counting on the Alphas to continue the sergeant's humiliation. The Alphas were enjoying the notoriety they had achieved amongst the other units.

"It's going to take teamwork to stop Taylor from getting our supplies." Baker cracked his knuckles with an exaggerated motion. "We need suggestions?"

Apollo stood to address the group.

"Christiani, go ahead," Leiman ordered.

"I was contemplating the situation during our invigorating morning run. I propose we allow him to obtain our supplies." Apollo paused for dramatic effect. "Or at least enable Taylor to perceive he has achieved his mission. We amply guard the boxes and crates; however, we place something besides the guns, ammo and provisions inside the containers. Allow him burglarize the decoys and determine his failure afterwards."

"I say we use the boxes as our crap hole, and let him haul that away," Richard offered.

Candy rolled her eyes. "You don't think he'd smell that? Besides he's probably using an SR. The surveyor will tell Taylor long before gets to camp what's inside our crates."

Victor mumbled out loud, "It's too bad we can't get some of that

145

exploding pepper spray, like they use in banks. Once the thief gets so many meters from the bank, the containers explode, and the perpetrator is covered with an itchy, red dye. It takes days for the stuff to wear off."

"Great idea," Richard snapped. "Where do you figure we're going to get the pepper spray, idiot?"

"It was just a thought, Richard."

Zeus was enjoying the game with Taylor. He liked the idea of decoy operation and exploding spray. Numerous people whispered among themselves. When Zeus stood, everyone went silent. "We's make pepper spray crap."

"Do you know how to?" Apollo asked.

"Ain'ts done it before, but the theory's simple."

Apollo's mouth curled upward. "What would we have to do?"

"Makes a trigger device and fills it with poisonous plants."

"I'm convinced we can obtain some cruel vegetation to place in the device. However, do we possess the necessary supplies to construct a trigger mechanism and the proper type of explosives?"

"Watch can be's used as timers, and our weapons gots explosives. Ain'ts hard."

Apollo wanted to encourage Zeus, yet he did not want his compliment to appear contrived. Between Zeus's pride and the chip on his shoulder, few comments were received in the spirit they were intended. Not to mention the number of times the spirit intended was not positive to start with. Apollo had observed how the orphan reacted to various forms of communication and decided he would experiment with praise mixed with personal mockery and see how that method of delivery faired.

"Zeus." Apollo clapped his hands and rubbed them together. "You are a man of exceptional talents. Without your diligence, there would be limited supplies to protect. While the majority of the Alphas were getting our noses wiped, you were learning useful survival skills."

Apollo paid close attention to the orphan's response. Zeus seemed mildly pleased. This conversation combination was worth repeating.

"This isn't like the cheap bombs you make on the Row, orphan boy," Richard snarled. "We have sophisticated equipment here. You're just stupid enough to blow up the whole camp."

Daggers of hate shot from Zeus's eyes.

Others agreed with Richard. One nameless coward voiced, "I don't trust him, either." People looked around to see who said it, but no one claimed the remark.

Apollo spoke up. "I am convinced Zeus can make this successful."

Sgt. Baker wanted to move on before anything else antagonistic was said to the orphan. "Malone, how long would it take you to make a test bag, timer, trigger, the whole thing?"

"Few hours, Sir."

"Good." Sgt. Baker stepped to the middle of the group. "Who's going to help Malone?"

Apollo had never worked with explosives and was nervous trusting the orphan with a dangerous substance, but the basic idea had been his. If he did not volunteer, it would imply he did not respect Zeus's talents. Plus, Zeus never offered ideas he did not have the skills to complete. Apollo rose and in a strong voice stated, "I'm willing to assist Zeus on assembling a demonstration."

Zeus was pleased with the offer, but preferred to work alone. "Don'ts needs helps, Sir."

"Too bad. This is supposed to be a team, and teams work together. Remember, that's how Sgt. Leiman started this conversation. You'll work in a group or not at all."

"Yes, Sir."

"Who else besides Christiani's going to work with Malone?" Baker strolled in silence around the group.

After a few long, tense minutes, Candy said, "I'll help out."

"Good, Wang. Who else?"

"I will," Victor said. He stood more as a protest to Richard than an endorsement of Zeus. He was from the lower class, had lived in a small apartment and had shared a room with his two sisters. Richard had mercilessly teased him. Victor did not take verbal assaults as well as the orphan. He did not know Zeus and had no burning desire to; however, he liked Apollo and trusted his judgment. If Apollo thought it was safe, then Victor was willing to follow along.

"All right, Petroff. You, Wang, Christiani and Malone get to work on the demo. The rest of you, full packs. We're going for a hike."

"Yes, Sir," they yelled.

Candy and Victor both gravitated to Apollo. Without realizing it, they assumed Apollo, not Zeus, would lead the group. The three waited for the orphan to join them.

Instead, Zeus went over to speak to Sgt. Leiman. "Requests permission ta speaks, Ma'am."

"Go ahead."

"Huh, OK with yous, Ma'am?"

"Huh. Twenty-five," she ordered. After he counted out his squat thrusts, she asked, "What do you mean, OK?"

Zeus did not know how to express what he was trying to say. "What yous says 'bout pepper crap?"

She shook her head. He was incredibly tedious to deal with. "Try again," she grumbled.

"Makes the test fail if yous want."

"Oh." Now she understood. "I say Sgt. Taylor is more than capable of taking care of himself. Besides, it was a lot of fun the last time."

Zeus returned her smile. "Yes, Ma'am."

"I appreciate your checking. It was very thoughtful." She gave him a friendly pat on the shoulder.

Zeus flinched, barely remembering to say, "Yes, Ma'am."

"I'm sorry. You don't like being touched, do you?"

"No, Ma'am." He dropped his gaze. Sometimes it bothered him to be so different from the others.

"I respect that and will try to remember not to touch you."

"Yes, Ma'am," he answered out of habit. Then realizing what she had said, he looked at her and added, "Thank yous, Ma'am."

"Go make it work, Malone." Sgt. Leiman saluted as a way of dismissal.

"Yes, Ma'am." He returned the salute and walked to the three people waiting for him.

Apollo stood under a tall tree. Bits of sunlight shown through on Apollo's dark skin and made it appear he had white spots. "Zeus, how should we proceed?"

"By get'n outa my's way."

Apollo cleared his throat. "Does the word teamwork sound familiar?"

"What yous know 'bout trigger switches and explosives?"

"Absolutely nothing," Apollo answered in a pleasant tone. He wanted to be certain not to antagonize the orphan. "Although I have been informed I am a rapid learner."

"If yous ain't. . .kaboom."

"You just guaranteed my complete and undivided attention."

Zeus glared at him.

Apollo sensed the other two waiting for him. "May I suggest, you explain in detail exactly how to construct the exploding device and the supplies necessary to achieve the demonstration. Then we shall inform you what steps in the process are within our capabilities."

"Told yous what I's do'n. Needs rope with wire hidden. Bag or flat container with some leaves. A watch and ammo."

"Very well. I shall obtain the rope and wire." Apollo faced Victor.

"I can get a bag and put some harmless plants in it," Victor offered.

Zeus put his thumb nail between his new, straight, white teeth, tore off a piece of nail and spit it on the ground. "Needs two."

"Two." Victor walked away.

Candy raised and lowered her shoulders. "I guess that leaves me with getting a PSG and some live ammo."

Apollo remained quiet to give the orphan a chance to take charge.

There was a long silence. Zeus wondered why they did not get to work. He fiddled with the knife in his pocket. "I's gets my's own wire," he finally offered.

Apollo gave up. "We shall assemble at that tree with our supplies." He pointed to a yellow-leafed shade tree.

Zeus left to get the wire.

Apollo led Candy toward the supply tents. "One attribute I admire about Zeus, he does not fritter time on unnecessary communication."

Candy returned alone with the PSG.

Zeus was sitting against the trunk of the tree. "Disassemble the rifle and gives me's the trigger mechanism," Zeus said, without looking up from the wire he was stripping with his knife.

Candy sat beside him and took apart the rifle. She was unaware she had seated herself too close to him.

The rule on Orphan's Row rule was always allow enough space to see an attack coming and defend yourself. Certainly not less than arm's distance. Zeus yanked the plastic insulation off the wire. Her closeness made him nervous.

Candy twisted the locking piece off the PSG. She had been waiting for an opportunity to ask Zeus about the other morning. She had always assumed he did not like her or the others. After his help, she was not sure. Maybe he was quiet and needed to talk individually.

"Zeus, can I ask you something?"

He looked at her thinking, not only is she sitting too close, now she's talking.

"Why did you help me on the obstacle course?"

"Huh?"

She placed a blackened pin on the ground. "Everyone knew if I didn't get over that wall, I was out, and you helped me."

"Ain'ts touch yous."

"No, that's what made it perfect. You stopped, ruining your own time, and motivated me in a way no one else could. I must have had a mental block, because I'm not having any trouble getting over the wall now. I wanted to tell you how much I appreciated your help. I'd have been out if you hadn't helped me. Thank you."

Zeus remained silent.

"If I've insulted you in some way, I'm sorry."

Zeus scratched his head. Similar to many of the conversations he overheard, he had no idea how they got from one subject to another. One minute she's saying thank you, the next she's apologizing for who knows what.

"Do you hate me or something?" Candy asked as perplexed as the orphan.

"Huh?" Three unrelated questions in a matter of sentences.

Candy was not settling for no answer. Everyone in the unit was doing that. She was not tolerating no response any more. She would continue to ask until she found out. "Why did you help me?"

Zeus shrugged. She had returned to the first question. How they'd gotten there he had no idea.

"I honestly want to know. Why should you care if I'm discharged or not?"

Apollo walked over and squatted to show Zeus the rope. "Is this what you wanted?"

The orphan took the rope and walked away, pretending to test it. He was relieved to escape Candy and her crazy questioning.

"What, may I ask, were you two discussing?" Apollo tipped his head to Zeus.

"I was trying to find out why he stopped to help me on the obstacle course the other day."

"Zeus assisted you in completing the course?"

"Yes. I'd be discharged without him." She dropped the butt of the rifle on the grass.

"What did he do?"

"I was on the wall, trying to get over it and couldn't. It was my last chance. I'm hanging on the rope crying, when Zeus comes up behind me. He pulled out his switchblade, flashed it at me and, in that really scary voice of his, says, 'I dare you to come down.' I popped up and over that wall so fast you wouldn't believe it."

Apollo's big barrel chest shook as he laughed. "An interesting motivational technique."

"It's strange. I tried to thank him. He barely acknowledged me." Candy put the rifle down. "Do you think he's weird?"

"I attribute Zeus's uniqueness to being from a completely different culture. What is effective interpersonally for us does not produce the same results with him."

"Why do you suppose he stopped to help me?"

Apollo sat beside her. "I could not surmise. I would suggest inquiring with him?"

"I did; he never answered."

"We are pioneers. We are encountering an entirely different culture. Since we are the first ones to interact with an orphan, there are no reference materials. It is a challenge because our only recourse is trial and error." He tapped her on the shoulder. "It is exciting. Don't you concur?"

"Apollo, you're the weird one. I don't need any more excitement or challenges in my life. OTS is providing more than enough. In fact, I wouldn't mind a dull, boring day, right about now."

To avoid contact with Candy and Apollo, Zeus stripped his wire across the camp. He figured they were talking about him, and he did not care. When Victor reappeared with the bag filled with leaves, Zeus was forced to return to the group.

Apollo decided a compliment-type joke might ease the tension. "Well, Admiral Malone, what are your orders, Sir?"

Zeus glared at Apollo smiling innocently. The orphan never quite knew what to do with humor and sarcasm. He was convinced Apollo was not insulting him the way Richard did; however, Zeus's limited social interactions had not prepared him to communicate beyond what was necessary.

151

Apollo rephrased, "What do you require next?"

"Needs a timer."

"You stated previously a watch could be altered." Apollo unfastened his watch. "Can this be modified into a timer?" He held the gold timepiece in front of Zeus.

"What's it do's?"

"It has a number of specialty features. Which functions interest you?"

"Alls."

"It is lightweight; scratch, water and crack resistant; night-readable. . ."

Candy nudged him. "Apollo, you sound like a sales pitch."

Apollo dangled the watch in front of Candy and Victor. He assumed a commentator's voice and demeanor as touched each feature he was describing. "This is a state of the art timepiece. It has a new and improved satellite-linked compass; universal date and time functions; pulse and blood-pressure monitor; oral address and ComLine recall; oral note dictation; and a loud alarm. Yours for this low introductory price of five thousand drayka."

Candy and Victor clapped at the performance. Zeus stared, his mouth open.

Apollo sensed Zeus's admiration and tossed the watch to the orphan. "Thirty-day free trial offers are available."

Zeus caught the watch and looked at it in amazement. "How's it works?"

"Pull up a tree, demos are free," Apollo quipped, pleased he had come up a clever rhyme.

Zeus looked perplexed. "Huh?"

"What," Apollo corrected. Zeus was hopeless. He had not appreciated any of Apollo's verbal banter. Apollo decided they had best return to the business at hand. "The sergeants will give you twenty-five squats for stating huh. I implied we were to sit by the tree."

Zeus sat meters across from the three other cadets.

"I cannot demonstrate long distance." Apollo moved around and situated himself beside the orphan.

In order to see, Zeus had to control his natural urge to push Apollo away. Apollo had incorrectly assumed the orphan needed the information to assemble the timer. In truth, only Zeus's curiosity and fascination were being satisfied.

Apollo showed him the stopwatch with its split times, the compass, the universal time and date feature, alarm, pulse and blood pressure monitor, oral address and ComLine recall, and oral dictation abilities. Zeus listened enthralled.

Apollo wished he could remember the other features once he was aware of Zeus's fascination. Technology was another way to reach the orphan. Apollo would remember that.

"Here, you try it." Apollo handed Zeus the gold timepiece.

Zeus carefully and precisely went through each feature Apollo had demonstrated. The others were impressed by the orphan's memory.

"Will this suffice as a timer?" Apollo asked.

"Want me's ta use this?" Zeus stroked the expensive jewelry.

Apollo reclined on his elbows. "How badly will it be damaged?"

Zeus could not believe the stupidity of the question. "I's make'n a timer for a bomb."

"Oh, as in kaboom, and nothing remains?"

"Yeah. Yous can haves the gold and crystal face. All I's needs is the insides."

Apollo glanced at the other three cadets' wrists. Zeus did not have a watch. Candy and Victor had relatively inexpensive watches. Apollo was positive Victor could not afford another one. Candy may or may not be able to. To Apollo, money was no object. When this watch got ruined, his mother would send him a new one.

"It is only money," Apollo cracked. "Please proceed."

The three laughed, while the orphan remained silent. Zeus did not see the humor in the joke. He rummaged through the toolbox to find something to disassemble the watch.

Apollo attempted to make eye contact with the orphan. Zeus was busy and did not notice. "Zeus?" Apollo waited for him to grunt. "If you are going to be occupied for awhile, perhaps we should also be productive. Is there another task we are qualified to complete?"

"Six long ropes withs wires hid inside."

Victor rose. "How long do you want the ropes?"

More dumb questions. Do they not understand what we're doing? "Long 'nough ta goes 'rounds a supply crate."

"Each one?" Apollo questioned. "What do we need that much rope for?"

"Each crates gots ta be's rigged."

"May I inquire why?" Apollo was willing to be agreeable, but he was not willing to do extra work just to appease Zeus.

"Yous gonna leaves a sign ta Taylor, 'takes me's I's rigged ta blows.' Gots ta do's them alls ta make sure Taylor gets hit."

"Oh, I guess that make sense." Victor walked off with Apollo and Candy to work on the ropes.

*   *   *

The unit sat on the ground. Sgt. Baker ordered Zeus to get up and explain what he was going to demonstrate.

"Each box gots ta be's rigged ta blow and sprays in two ways. First, if Taylor cuts a ropes ta verifies supplies, it blows up ins his face. Second, he picks the thing ups. Motion causes the wires ta makes contact withs the timer. So many minutes later, kaboom. Box here's sets for cut'n." Zeus pointed to the crate near his feet. "That ones," he pointed to his left, "sets for motion. Yous want me's ta cuts it?"

"What's in the bags right now?"

"Sir." Victor stood.

"Go ahead."

"Nothing dangerous, just crushed-up leaves from the tree over there." He pointed to an angular, soft-leafed tree.

"Smith," Sgt. Leiman ordered, "you're so confident this won't work. Get over there and cut that rope. Malone, you sit down."

Zeus stepped out of the ring as Richard approached the crates. Zeus threw his knife. It landed with a thump centimeters from Richard's feet and startled him. Richard glared at the orphan and pulled the knife out of the ground.

"Cut it," Leiman ordered.

Richard leaned over, slid the knife between the box and rope and cut the rope with one strong, clean jerk. The group heard a soft popping sound and then a loud burst. Leaves flew everywhere; in Richard's face, above his head, on his clothes, around his arms and in his eyes and mouth. The leaves went more than two meters in the air and hit numerous people seated close to the box. Richard coughed as plant fragments lodged in his throat and tears ran down his cheeks.

The entire group was amazed and awed. The demonstration was far more effective than any of them had anticipated. Sgt. Leiman leaned over and murmured to Sgt. Baker, "Bulldog is going to kill us."

Apollo applauded. Everyone except Richard joined in.

154

When Zeus saw his sergeants clapping for him, his chest swelled with pride.

Once the group quieted down and Richard stopped gasping, Baker exclaimed, "Unbelievable! After that display, I can't wait to see the other one blow. What do we have to do to that one?"

"Picks it ups. In two minutes, it's blows."

Sgt. Baker walked over, cautiously picked up the crate and moved it to the center of the group. The silence was deadening as each person anticipated the exploding fountain of leaves. The leaves burst into the air, only with no one's body to stop them, they went meters up and then gently floated down to the ground. A few pieces got caught by the breeze and stayed in the air, floating like balloons over a party.

Baker opened the floor up for discussion and suggestions. The Alphas wanted to be certain Taylor had to cut at least the first rope to ensure his face would receive a direct hit. A plan was devised where the supplies would be tied to trees, forcing him to cut the ropes. The Alphas decided that the only way to ensure Taylor would go for the right boxes was to have the real supplies in the rigged crates. The group also decided to stagger the motion timers in case Taylor successfully ran off with some of the crates. With each one bursting at different times, the sergeant's escape would be severely hampered. Plus, the Alphas would have plenty of opportunity to retrieve the stolen items and hopefully recapture Taylor.

"What about Zeus?" Victor asked. "If he doesn't try to stop Sgt. Taylor, Taylor might smell a trap and abort his mission."

"I's let hims beat me's," Zeus offered.

"He'll shoot you."

"PSG stuns don't hurts."

"I was queasy for days after he stunned me," a cadet stated. "Are you sure you want to do that?"

"Yeah."

Leiman cocked her head. "OK. Let's get this set ASAP, in case Taylor strikes tonight."

The Alphas prepared the traps and each night eagerly awaited Sgt. Taylor's arrival. Four nights later, the trap was sprung.

CHAPTER 12

SGT. TAYLOR QUIETLY SNEAKED past the perimeter guards, unaware they did not intend to stop him. The plan proceeded exactly as intended. Zeus jumped Taylor; the two fought briefly. Zeus allowed Taylor to gain the upper hand just long enough to reach for his rifle and fire on the orphan. Even though Zeus was stunned, as a way of revenge, Taylor tied the orphan up and left him in the crap hole.

Taylor's heart pounded with anticipation as he hid in the underbrush. With Malone out of the way, he was certain he could acquire at least a few of the supplies. If he was lucky, he could make a number of trips and take them all. Taylor stunned the last two guards and yanked the top two crates. Crap, he thought, they tied them to the tree to give Malone more time to get me.

He pulled his knife and cut the rope. He heard a soft pop and a loud burst as poison plant fragments shot into his face. Fortunately, he was wearing his night goggles, and nothing got into his eyes. He inhaled some plant toxin and coughed. His face stung from the crushed obsiden stems. He kept his wits, grabbed the top two crates by their ropes and ran into the underbrush.

As he ran, he concluded the poisonous obsiden was worth getting two crates of supplies and putting Malone in the crap hole. He was pleased with his spoils until the rope around the crate in his left hand exploded and covered him with more plant debris.

"I hear him over here," an Alpha guard called.

Taylor left the fallen crate and continued running. The timer on the right clicked. "Crap." Taylor could feel the poison burning his tongue. He spit the fragments out of his mouth as he ran through the woods.

"We've got to be close. Here's one of the crates," a guard called.

Taylor hid in the underbrush until the coast was clear. His face itched and his tongue felt like stiff, dried leather. Hours later, he reported to the medical building in defeat. He thought the night could not get any worse, but it did. The first person he saw as he entered the infirmary was Cmd. Yoggi.

"Well, Sergeant, it looks like you've had another long night, but I think you're doing a fine job. Malone's been living survival all his life. I admire your tenacity and dedication. Just keep the Alphas on their toes for a little longer, and it will all be over."

"Yesh, 'am," he attempted to say with his wooden tongue. Normally he would have appreciated the compliment; tonight it fell on deaf ears. He felt like a failure.

Dr. Bentley heard the voices and came out. "What happened to you?" She looked at Taylor. His face was swollen and green. Even with his dark complexion, his goggles and hat were perfectly outlined in his skin. The skin under his shirt was swelling where minute particles had penetrated the fabric.

"Ob th di an." He tried to say it one syllable at a time.

"Poison obsiden?"

"Yesh."

"Follow me, and let me have a look."

Taylor saluted Cmd Yoggi with downcast eyes.

Yoggi patted him on the shoulder. "Look on the bright side, Sergeant. At least you got Malone and dumped him in the hole." She turned and addressed Bentley. "Where is the troublemaker, and how's he doing?"

"Room three. Fine. Still groggy." Bentley walked Sgt. Taylor to room one.

Cmd. Yoggi entered room three. Leiman was seated at the foot of Zeus's bed. She stood and saluted her superior.

"At ease."

"If you don't mind my asking, Commander, has Sgt. Taylor checked in?"

"Yes, Dr. Bentley's treating him now. He's fine, but you all got him good, very good from the looks of it. My guess is it will take a lot longer for his ego to heal than his face."

Leiman glanced at Zeus's long lanky body lying on the examining table. "Malone is a man of many talents."

"Any of them applicable to the Corps?"

"Not many."

Yoggi sat in the chair across from the bed and pointed to Leiman's seat. "Sergeant, assure Taylor I think he's doing a fine job. Malone is a unique cadet, and no one is able to predict him. I don't believe these little incidences are a reflection of Sgt.Taylor's abilities."

"Thank you, Ma'am. I'm certain Taylor appreciates your confidence in him."

Yoggi nodded to Zeus. "Has he come around yet?"

"No, he's been restless and mumbling for over half an hour. Doc said that's common before patients come to. I thought he'd be awake by now. Taylor must have used a six-caliber PSG."

Cmd. Yoggi watched the orphan lying on his back swaying his body and mumbling every few minutes. "Can you figure out what he's saying?"

"I'm not certain. He's definitely not having pleasant dreams. I've only been able to make out a few words. He said something about finding food. I think I heard 'don't cry,' and he keeps repeating what sounds like the name Emily, over and over."

"I'll be certain to tell Maj. Sato that. Maybe he can get some information out of Malone."

Zeus murmured again. Yoggi leaned forward, straining to hear.

Once the orphan was silent, Cmd. Yoggi relaxed in her chair. "Is that what he's repeating?"

"Yes, Ma'am."

"It sounded like Emily to me, too. I wish we could get some answers from him."

"His being here just doesn't make sense. He had to have a mentor, a group or someone assisting him."

"Maybe she's the person who helped him or sent him here." Yoggi drummed her fingers. "I'll have Simb run a check on the name Emily. Maybe he can come up with a Kalopso member who would benefit from an orphan plant in OTS."

"The Corps has other enemies, too."

"It's impossible to narrow down. Have you gotten anything out of him in the last few days?"

"Nothing, Commander. Malone is tight-lipped about everything."

Cmd. Yoggi was waiting for Taylor to be cleaned up before sending Sgt. Leiman to see him. Yoggi estimated the doctor had Taylor presentable. "Enough about Malone. Would you like to check on Taylor next door?"

Sgt. Leiman smiled. It was thoughtful of Yoggi to keep their relationship in mind. "If you don't mind, Commander."

"Go ahead. If you see Dr. Bentley, ask her to come in here when she's done."

"Yes, Ma'am, I'll send her in. And thank you."

Cmd. Yoggi returned her salute and sat in the chair at the foot of Malone's bed. Normally as a commander, she did not check on cadets in the infirmary; however, her superiors and the entire universe was watching. What was done to Malone might make or break her career.

Zeus kicked the stark white sheet into a tangled ball at his feet. Yoggi walked around to the side of the bed. She had only seen his work brands and stomach scar his first day. Yoggi leaned forward and studied the markings. She lifted her hand to touch his chest as the door opened. Yoggi flinched and looked behind her.

"Sorry. I didn't mean to scare you," Dr. Bentley said.

"I was trying to get a closer look at the burn marks." Yoggi returned to her seat at the foot of the bed.

"That kid's body tells quite a story." Dr. Bentley sat on the swivel chair and rolled over to her patient.

"Doctor, could this stunning cause any problems with his fat reserves?"

"No, nothing significant. . ."

Zeus heard the muffled voices. They were not the voices he expected to hear. It had not occurred to him he would be taken to the doctor for a simple stunning. He expected to wake up at camp. What was the doctor up to? He opened his eyes the width of a thread and peered out to keep surprise to his advantage. Zeus grabbed Dr. Bentley's wrist, twisted it and slammed it into the bed.

Bentley leaned into her pinned arm. "Malone, stop it. I was just trying to examine you."

"Yous budgin bastards."

Yoggi jumped up and tugged at Zeus's hand. "Malone, release the doctor. That's an order."

Zeus jerked Bentley's arm up and threw it in her face. Dr. Bentley took control of her hand just before slapping herself.

"Huh the budge I's do'n here?" Zeus sat up and dangled his legs off the exam table.

Dr. Bentley rolled out of his way as Cmd. Yoggi left the room. Yoggi did not want the situation to deteriorate further and went next door for Sgt. Leiman. She deduced Malone would respond best to his sergeant.

Sgt. Leiman entered and saw Zeus standing on the bed against the wall, holding a scalpel pointed at the doctor. "Malone, stand down," she bellowed. She marched over, grabbed the scalpel and ordered, "Sit down, now!"

Like an ashamed child, Zeus slid down the wall to a seated position and responded with the ingrained, "Yes, Ma'am."

"I think I need a little drill sergeant training," Bentley quipped to the commander.

Leiman sat on the edge of the bed. "Malone, what are you doing?"

Zeus hated when she asked him questions requiring more than a yes or no answer. "Huh, I's do'n here?"

Sgt. Leiman heard the bewilderment in his voice and softened her approach. "Taylor stunned you. Don't you remember?"

"Yes, Ma'am. Huh, I's heres?"

"I wanted to be certain that you were all right. I asked Dr. Bentley to check you out." She knew her personal interest in his well-being was significant to him.

His shoulders relaxed and he straightened his legs out in front of her.

"Your plan worked beautifully. Taylor's next door being treated. His face is green and swollen. He must have taken a direct hit, because his goggles and hat are perfectly outlined on his skin. You did a good job tonight."

"Thank yous, Ma'am."

"I want to be certain you are in tip-top shape for our next altercation. I'm going to stay here and make certain you cooperate with Dr. Bentley. No knives, scalpels or other weapons and no disrespectful behavior. You do what you're told. Understand?"

"Yes, Ma'am."

*   *   *

Zeus jumped down the infirmary steps two by two. The morning sun was bright as he walked briskly passed the track. He heard Sgt. Leiman's voice.

"Get away from me. Keep your poison obsiden to yourself."

Zeus was glad Dr. Bentley had returned his knife. He pulled it out of his pocket, leaped onto the track and waved the open blade in front of Taylor's swollen green-black face.

"Yous ain't touch'n hers."

"Yeah, you tell him," Leiman joked.

Taylor batted the knife out of his face. "I didn't know you had a bodyguard, Sues."

"Neither did I, but he certainly comes in handy."

"Hey, Malone. I'm just curious. What are you going to do if I touch my own girlfriend."

"I's makes lots more hurt than yous face." Zeus threw a playful left jab and stopped it centimeters from Taylor's gut.

"There are some things worth hurting for. And what Sues here gives me, that's one of them." Taylor winked.

"Don'ts kiss her, yous idiot."

"That's all you have to say?" Leiman crossed her arms in protest.

"Crap, Sergeant, don't expects me's ta argue withs that logic. Rock'n is worth hurt'n for."

"Yeah," Taylor elbowed his girlfriend, "I knew another man would understand."

"I should never have let you two spar. You relate too well to each other," she said.

"I's still gets him again," Zeus said to let Leiman know where his loyalties were.

"Yeah, well don't forget I beat you last night." Taylor pointed to his own puffed-up chest. "By the way, how'd you like the crap pit?"

"Yous don't beats me's. Hard be'n bad 'nough ta let yous gets one good shot off."

"You dogged me?"

Zeus nodded and Leiman laughed.

"And you knew?"

"Of course. It was a well-thought-out part of the plan. I assumed you knew by now."

"No. Malone, I hate you." Taylor took a swing at his sparing partner.

Zeus parried. "We's fight lots. How yous figure yous can bet me's? Ain'ts never before."

"I thought you were tired after staying up for days to catch me. Don't you ever sleep?"

"Ain'ts stay'n awake ta catch yous. Sleeps with my's eyes half open. Beat'n yous like fight'n a woman. Ain't worried 'bout lose'n."

Leiman's nostrils flared. "Excuse me, Malone, what do you mean by that?"

Taylor grinned from ear to ear. He realized she could not stand helpless women or being treated like one.

"What, Ma'am?" Zeus was aware she was agitated, but had no idea why.

"What exactly do you mean by fighting a woman?"

"Women's weaker," Zeus defended. "That's why men gots ta do's the fight'n."

"Yeah." Taylor egged Malone on.

Leiman dropped her hands on her hips and huffed. "Are you saying women are basically helpless, and we need men to take care of us?"

"Yes, Ma'am." He was glad she understood.

Leiman clenched her teeth. "You don't think I can take care of myself?"

"Not likes that. No, Ma'am."

Leiman pushed her face close to his. "Why not?"

"Cause yous a woman, Sergeant."

"Yeah, cause yous a woman," Taylor parroted, laughing. He could hardly contain himself. He remembered her ranting on this subject in the past. Unbeknownst to Malone, he had tripped into discussing Sgt. Leiman's number one pet peeve.

"Why does being a woman make me inferior to you?"

"No, Ma'am. Ain'ts say'n yous inferior. Yous weaker. That's why yous gots ta be's protected."

Taylor slapped his leg. Zeus was digging himself a deeper and deeper hole, and Sgt. Leiman was growing more incensed. "Malone, hearing this was worth getting nailed last night. Sues here is going to have you doing pushups 'til you fall over and die."

Zeus had no idea what was going on. He had somehow missed part of the conversation, again. He wanted to ask why she was upset; however, talking was what had gotten him in trouble in the first place. The orphan decided to return to silence. It was the only safe thing to do.

"Get out of here," Sgt. Leiman ordered, "before I do make you do pushups until you fall over."

"Yes, Ma'am," Zeus returned to protocol. He saluted and jogged off, thankful Taylor seemed to understand.

Leiman smacked Taylor on the arm. "I ought to kill you for encouraging him. I think he really believes it."

"I think he does, too. That's what made it so funny."

"I don't know why I love you. You're so obnoxious."

Taylor put his arms around her waist and tried to kiss her with his swollen face.

She pushed him away. "That stuff is contagious. You'll just have to suffer. I'm returning to camp to plan our next attack." She enjoyed winning, yet a part of her hated to see him bested again. "Good luck."

"Amour, Sues." He blew her a kiss. "I can't wait for you to move on base. I get lonely at night."

"Lonely and in trouble." She pointed to his swollen face. "We'll just have to make up for lost time." She winked, turned and walked toward the woods.

*   *   *

The Kalopso boss and an older man entered the auditorium. The older, pot-bellied man took a seat at one of the tables. His flabby thighs hung over the edge of the chair. "How soon before Emily competes for the million drayka?"

The boss took the seat across from his friend. "The semifinals are in a few months. They're picking three finalists. Each one gets a hundred thousand to continue their research. I'm confident she'll get that."

"Then what?"

"A year from now, she makes a final presentation, and the winner is announced at the big centennial celebration." The boss held up his right hand and snapped his fingers twice at the waitress.

"Do you think you can keep her together that long?"

"I have a new secret weapon. One of the orphans from the mines."

"An orphan?"

A scantily clad waitress in high heels stood silently at the table. Orphans were not permitted to speak to members, only respond; no interaction beyond their work. The boss would have ordered immediately except his hefty friend was enjoying the view. He continued his conversation while the other man ogled.

"Remember Emily's imaginary friend? It was this Red Top kid all along. He was crawling through the venting to Emily's room."

"The venting? Why would it connect to Emily's?"

"Actually, the sewers and venting are sort of interconnected in the courtyard. That is how we filter the boorix gas without having to pay for it. We send the gases through the sewers to the public works plant."

The fat man laughed and laughed. "My cousin that I stay with when I'm here. She was hired to identify where the boorix gas is leaking into your sewage system. It costs the taxpayers billions to filter all that gas. She has spent two years and can't find any pipes around boorix."

"And she never will. The pipes we connected will never show up on her maps. The connectors are deep underground, and we've rigged things so our pipes register as underground quartz deposits. She could be looking in the correct places and still not figure it out."

The fat man wrapped his arms around the shapely waitress and pulled her onto his lap. "I figured my cousin was an idiot. Boorix isn't that hard to detect."

"She is. She inadvertently crossed the Kalopso."

The fat man fondled the orphan. The young waitress stiffened, but did not protest. "How does that help Emily?"

"When Red Top sleeps with her, she doesn't have nightmares. She's not puking like she was. And it's perfect. I'm able to manipulate both of them. If she fails, he gets a fate worse than death; if he fails, she does. They're both highly motivated to succeed. Emily is more focused than I've ever seen her."

The man glanced away from the waitress and spoke to the boss. "And you're sure Emily is safe with him?"

"He's protective of her, fiercely protective."

The fat man pressed a sloppy, wet kiss on the reluctant waitress. "Young love is definitely exploitable."

"I've made certain this stays platonic."

"Why?"

"They're both hitting puberty. Emily is given medical exams by the Prodigy board before every competition. I want her to be nice and pure for them. It's much better press for us."

"So you made the boy a eunuch?"

"No, he's too good a fighter. For now, I'm giving him a drug that suppresses his sex drive. It allows him to grow and develop normally. I'll keep him once Emily's gone."

The fat man whiffed an entre going by. "Double scotch. Large prime rib, medium. Everything on the side." He released the waitress. She quickly hopped off his lap.

"Bring an appetizer medley first. Bourbon, now. Some wine with dinner and I'll have the special." The boss swatted the woman on the butt as way of dismissal.

She nodded and left.

"How's it going in the mine?"

"Not good. There was another major cave-in two weeks ago. I thought I'd lost Red Top."

The older man watched the gladiator-style fight while he spoke. "How'd Miss Whinny handle that?"

"Terrible. She had a contest to go to. It was a given she was going to win. I sent her. The stupid brat bawled through her whole dissertation. I lost twenty thousand. She's lucky I didn't kill her then."

"And Red Top?"

"He managed to dig himself out. Dragged a few other workers out with him. I hate losing him in the mines. He's a good worker."

"What's he doing now?"

"Cleaning rooms and controlling Emily. I can't afford to have her blow the centennial contest."

"And after the contest?" the fat man raised his eyebrows.

"Emily, or more specifically I, get a million drayka. She's supposed to go work at a company and oversee the development of her aquifer. She knows too much, and I won't be able to control her there. She's going to have an unfortunate accident on company property. We look good and I get money."

"Brilliant."

The waitress set the drinks on the table. The boss waved her away.

"How's it going in Congress?"

"Not bad," the older man gulped his scotch.

"Do we have enough votes to ensure the emergency funding for the Orphan Relief Agency?"

"ORA is lobbying hard. I've been pushing as much as I can, but there's no guarantee. We may be a few votes short. Then I'll have to reintroduce the measure later."

165

"Crap." The boss watched the ring. Another bloodied loser was being carried out of the ring. "I was counting on the extra funding coming in soon."

"Why? What difference does it make?"

"That cave-in put my production way down. I have a big drug deal I've been negotiating. I need cash to complete it."

"Then you'll need to create a little public panic before the vote next week. Something that will sway the seven or eight who are on the fence, maybe even a couple of others."

"Yes, a good smear would make even the liberals question a reformed orphan's ability to stay upstanding and law-abiding."

"Exactly, like what I did to Carl Kane," the old man boasted.

"I still remember the look on his face when the evidence was being presented against him. Just by watching the InterPress reports, I knew it had to be you." The boss held up his drink and toasted his friend.

"He could never figure out how all those incriminating things got into his possession."

"You set him up perfectly. Your tearful testimony was heartbreaking. After years of personally rehabilitating him and welcoming him into your home. It was," sniff, sniff, "very touching." The boss laughed.

"That was worth a couple of million to ORA. My wife still cries about his 'suicide.' "

"How did you manage that?"

"I got a pardon for one of the inmates."

The waitress served a large plate of steaming appetizers. The boss snapped his fingers, and she quickly disappeared.

"How many times have you set up an orphan?" The boss scooted the platter to the older man.

The fat man chose a succulent piece of meat covered with cheese. He scooped up the morsel. Orange cheese dripped and oozed onto the platter. "Obviously not enough. People still question some of my proposed legislation."

"Any good stories I don't know about?"

"Have you heard about the orphan who went on that rape and mutilation rampage on Zinian?"

"How could I not? It was all over InterPress. Those pictures that were accidentally released. . .was that your idea, too?"

"Naturally." He licked his chubby fingers. "I never introduce a request for more funding without first making certain the public will be receptive. Taxes are a very touchy subject for most people."

"But that rampage started a year before your current bill was presented."

"Yes, but the police didn't apprehend the 'guilty' orphan until two days after I introduced my bill."

The boss jabbed his fork into a fried vegetable. "How do you know so far in advance you're going to need a fall guy?" He dunked his tidbit into the pepper dip.

"I always have a few in the works. You never know when you'll need to create a scandal, so I'm always prepared."

"Some of those bodies had been buried for months."

"I have orphans I've been slowly setting up for years." The old man held up his empty glass to their waitress. She nodded as he continued, "I've got the perfect financial one in place. I can't wait to use it. I've got incriminating things pointing to an orphan woman for the last ten years. When the time comes, she won't have a chance."

"You are the master of the smear." The boss spooned some dip on his appetizer and spread it around.

"Yes, but I learned from the best. I miss old Charlie. His methods were so vindictive and ruthless."

"He was an expert at smearing, but you've done more to cultivate orphan distrust than the rest of us combined."

"How could you say that?" The old man deviously smirked. "Just listen to any of my speeches. I firmly believe there is a way to reform orphans. That's why we must separate them and carefully study the issue. We must never give up or scrimp on the funding of such a noble cause. Why, I myself have spent years studying and researching possible methods of reform."

"I'll tell you the perfect method. It's what we've got right here." The boss slapped the table. "They serve without question, and if they question, we make certain they never do it again."

"We both know the only things orphans are good for are sex and labor. They're subhuman. That's why I insist on keeping them segregated."

The waitress appeared with a new drink. She cleared the fat man's empty glass and scurried away.

"Can you help me?" the boss asked. "I need a graphic orphan scandal in the next few days."

"It will cost you."

"What do you want?"

"Your planet has started a charitable organization to help orphans in the ghettoes here. I want you to volunteer to be on the board and oversee things for me." The pot-bellied man popped a whole fried mushroom drenched with dip in his mouth. The creamy white dip dribbled out of the corner of his mouth.

"That charitable organization is legitimate. It's not one of ours."

The old man swallowed. "I know, that's why I want you on the inside. Trust me, it's the perfect way to find set-up victims and keep an eye on the real orphan lovers." He wiped his mouth with a napkin. "In fact, I want to target them as much as the orphans. If we can discredit the radicals who think we need less orphan legislation, then more people are willing to support my segregation bills."

"I don't like it, but I'll do it. Let me know who I have to contact."

"Deal. I'll get things in motion."

*　*　*

Sgt. Baker stood in front of the Alphas. "With only a few days left in boot camp, you can bet Taylor will be unrelenting in his attempts to steal from us. He's only gotten a few of our supplies. I'd like to humiliate him one last time before we move on base. Any suggestions?"

Candy rose. "Sir, my family owns a locksmith service. I could pick the locks on his office or quarters. While he's stealing from us, we could be stealing from him."

"Or once we're in, we could trash his place," Richard offered.

"And provide visuals for the daily bulletin," Apollo said. "We would want our mischievous antics appreciated."

"How are we going to get Taylor's schedule so we have time to trash his place?" Victor asked.

Zeus stood. The match against Taylor was personal. The orphan was not about to lose. He was amazed at how bad the Alphas were at strategy. "Don't needs Taylor's schedule. I's follows him. When he's ats camp; our other team goes ins."

"Hey, stupid," Richard said, "what about our supplies? He's been bringing in reinforcements. We'll need plenty of people to protect our stuff."

168

"Let's hims has the crap." Zeus waved hand in the direction of the crates. "We's don't needs noth'n for a few days. Alls the other units been live'n withouts that crap. I's follow Taylor, when he's goes ta camp, we's all leaves and goes ta his office or quarters; don'ts matter. Taylor ain'ts gonna believe thems supplies ain't guarded or ain't rigged. He gets mad try'n ta figures out what we's done."

Candy sprung to her feet. "Zeus, that's brilliant! I'll bet he's so paranoid he'll be afraid to take the boxes. What could be more cruel than making him fight his own demons?"

The Alphas quickly accepted the plan and discussed implementation. Candy and three others would break into Taylor's quarters and office. They would pretend to have been ordered to clean the floors with toothbrushes. The three would keep watch, while Candy attempted to pick the locks.

Zeus could easily get into the sergeant's place; however, he did not offer his services. An orphan with good breaking and entering skills would look suspicious. He did not want to give them any reason to think he had broken the law.

The supplies were to be scattered around the camp so Taylor would wonder why the supplies were separated. The last order of business was following Taylor. Eight people wanted to be on the team.

Zeus rose. "Too many peoples. We's gets noticed. I's tag him and I's won't gets caught. Only needs help at the gates, case Taylor leaves and returns ins a different gate."

"What makes you so certain you can keep track of Taylor? Exactly how are you not going to be seen? You're the only orphan here." Richard shook his finger at Zeus. "You stand out. Everyone knows who you are and that we're after Taylor. Anybody is better than you."

Zeus glared and refused to comment.

Apollo started to stand and defend the orphan, but Victor beat him to it. "Where have you been, Richard? There's nothing Zeus has said he could do, that he didn't deliver on. Everything from hunting to the triggers. If Zeus says he can follow Taylor without getting caught, I believe him."

Most of the unit seconded Victor's comment, and Zeus was assigned to follow Taylor. As soon as the discussion was over, Zeus grabbed a ComLine and left.

CHAPTER 13

ZEUS FOLLOWED HIS ENEMY throughout the day. That evening, Sgt. Taylor, Sgt. Ryan and Sgt. Wright, a floating sergeant, set out on another clandestine mission. Zeus reported to Sgt. Leiman. She was leading the trashing group. She had decided to oversee their deviant behavior personally. Everyone else left camp and waited at the rendezvous point.

The three sergeants separated and circled the Alpha's perimeter. They could not figure out why there were no life signs or guards. They continued cautiously toward the unprotected camp. Taylor warned them not to underestimate the orphan. He was certain Zeus was somewhere around those supplies. More than an hour passed before the three men slowly headed into the Alpha camp in their yellow camouflage suits.

They scanned the boxes and crates around the camp while communicating. "I don't like the place being deserted." The hairs on Taylor's neck stood up. "That means whatever they planned required them to leave camp."

"My SR isn't reading anything unusual," Ryan grumbled.

"Maybe we should check the trees and make sure nothing's going to fall on us." Sgt. Wright leaned back and panned the treetops.

"Come on, Bulldog," Ryan adjusted his headlamp and focused it on a crate. "Let's take the supplies and see what happens."

"Crap." Taylor kicked a rock. He was determined to find the orphan's trap. His reputation was on the line. He could not bear another loss to the Alphas. "Wait a minute. What about the ground? They could have buried something."

"I'll check over here," Wright recalibrated his SR to detect things underground.

Taylor and Ryan followed suit. Between the three of them, they dug up an earring, some coins, bits of wire, an old boot, numerous empty scrap cartridges and a bent fork.

"It's got to be an orphan thing that isn't detectable. Keep looking."

* * *

Sgt. Leiman grew concerned. It had been over two and a half hours since they'd broken into Taylor's quarters. The group had turned every piece of furniture upside down; removed all the door knobs and light bulbs inside; removed the toilet seat; taken the doors and cabinets off their hinges; built a small castle with all the boxes, jars and cans of food in the living room; removed everything hanging on the walls; took all the laundry and placed it over the bulbless light fixtures; placed every book, disk and knick-knack around on the floor, and toilet-papered the entire place. When the group was finished, they could barely see or walk across the living room to get to the kitchen, bedroom or bathroom. Once the destruction was complete, they placed a large banner proclaiming, "GOTCHA! BETTER LUCK NEXT YEAR. THE ALPHAS!" and then took pictures for the base bulletin board.

Sgt. Leiman wondered how long Taylor and the others would keep looking for nothing. She and her group met the rest of the Alphas at the checkpoint. The longer the sergeants were fooled, the funnier the joke became. They finally decided to surround their camp and capture the enemy.

As the Alphas moved into SR range, the three realized they'd been had. Sgt. Leiman buzzed Taylor on his ComLine.

"Taylor," he snarled through clenched teeth.

"Gotcha again," she gloated. "You're surrounded. Surrender."

"We're carrying stun bombs. Come in and get us. We'll take you all out and we'll take the supplies."

"Assuming you can get them out of there," she baited.

Taylor put his ComLine on hold and looked at his co-conspirators. "Crap. What do you think?"

"I say we stun them all," Sgt. Wright said.

"But we came for the supplies," Taylor reminded him.

"I say we make a deal," Sgt. Ryan said. "The two of us against Malone. Winner takes all."

Taylor raised his eyebrows. "I'm game."

"It's your call, Bulldog." Wright shrugged. "I'm only here to help out."

Taylor flipped on his ComLine. "It looks like we're at a standoff. Are you ready to negotiate?"

Leiman grinned from ear to ear. She loved the way his devious mind worked. "What do you have in mind?"

"Ryan and me against Malone. If we win, we get all the supplies. If Malone wins, your supplies are safe until the end of boot camp."

"Wait a second," she pushed the hold button. She linked into Baker's and Zeus's lines and explained the proposition.

Sgt. Baker responded, "Two to one. They'll kill Malone."

"No they's won't."

"Malone, how often have you been double-teamed?" Baker asked.

"Often."

"Against fighters like Ryan and Taylor?"

"I's can takes 'em, Sir."

"It sure would be fun to watch," Leiman stated.

"What have we got to lose?" Baker said.

Sgt. Leiman paused. "Malone, are you sure you want to do this?"

"Yes, Ma'am," he said enthusiastically.

"OK," she said, "I'll make the arrangements."

A truce was called. Zeus and the Alphas returned to their camp. The three sergeants removed their safety suits. Ryan and Taylor discussed Zeus's weaknesses and their strategy. The two men decided whenever Malone got hit, the other person was to follow up in seconds. They would attempt to each get in a solid hit, one right after the other, as opposed to each one following up his own blows. The orphan would consistently have to protect two sides and watch both men.

Zeus also contemplated his approach. He was familiar with both sergeants' styles. Taylor would be harder to beat, because the orphan had been coaching him, and he was younger. On the other hand, neither man was used to fighting in a team. Zeus would use their lack of teamwork to his advantage. The two men might get in each other's way and trip over one another.

The Alphas formed a circle with all their headlamps lighting the clearing. The three fighters stepped into the middle of the makeshift ring. Sgt. Wright acted as referee and approached the three men. "What are the rules?"

Ryan glared at Malone and growled, "Survival."

Taylor and Zeus nodded. Taylor added the only rule he and Malone sparred with, "No crotch shots."

Everyone agreed. If a man was down and could not stand in ten seconds, he was out. Except for down counts, Sgt. Wright would stay out of the way. If Taylor or Ryan went down for a count, the other man and Zeus would continue fighting. If Zeus was down, the other fighters would wait for the count. Other than that, no rounds and no stopping until a winner was declared.

Zeus planned to take Ryan out first; then he would be able to concentrate fully on Taylor. The orphan normally did not make the first move, and Taylor was aware of that. As soon as Sgt. Wright declared, "Start," Zeus bolted forward and hit Ryan solidly in the jaw with his fist, then backed up and attempted to round-kick Taylor. Taylor blocked and hit Zeus in the mouth. The orphan tasted blood.

"Goods hit." Zeus smiled. "Yous learns a few things."

"Yeah." Taylor bobbed around. "I'll be teaching you by the end of tonight."

"Budgin yous, Taylor. Yous ain't gots noth'n ta teach me's." Zeus felt Ryan approaching from behind. He ducked and hit Ryan in the gut. Ryan unfazed, followed with a jab to the face. It hit the orphan, but did not land solidly.

As Zeus had predicted, Ryan and Taylor were each taking him on, but not fighting as a team. Ryan backed up as Taylor lunged forward, and the two men collided. The spectators taunted the sergeants.

The fighters regrouped, and the battle continued. The more intense the contest became, the more Zeus enjoyed it. He missed the adrenaline surges he had had when defending himself on Orphans' Row.

Each man gave and received blows. Zeus had a fat lip that was bleeding slightly. Taylor's nose continued to bleed long after Zeus kicked him in the face. Ryan had a bruised jaw and a black eye.

Ten minutes into the battle, Ryan appeared to be tiring. He was not used to fighting without rounds or breaks. Zeus concentrated his efforts on the older man. Six blows later, Ryan was down and out. Ryan's left eye was bruised, bloody and swollen shut. He could barely see out of the right eye, and what was visible was blurred. Sgt. Wright guided Ryan over to a tree by Leiman and Baker.

The Alpha sergeants regretted giving Malone permission to fight when they realized Ryan had a concussion and needed immediate medical attention.

"One of us needs to call Bentley." Baker looked at his partner.

"She is not going to approve of this altercation." Leiman winced as Taylor took a hit in the kidney.

"You're the lead sergeant. You call her."

"Chicken."

Baker pulled a coin out of his pocket. "I'll flip you for it."

"Deal."

Baker put the coin on his thumb and flicked it.

"Heads," Leiman called.

Baker caught the coin in his hand and slapped it on his wrist. He lifted his fingers. "Tails, yes."

Sgt. Leiman frowned as she pulled out her ComLine and entered the code.

"Dr. Bentley."

"Doctor, this is Sgt. Leiman. I need you to come to the Alpha encampment with your bag and a transport vehicle."

"What's the problem?" Bentley asked.

"I think Sgt. Ryan may have a slight concussion and a few black eyes."

"What happened?" Dr. Bentley could hear the noise in the background and added, "What's going on out there?"

"Just a little realistic hand-to-hand combat, Ma'am." Leiman hoped the doctor would believe this was part of boot camp.

Cmd. Yoggi grabbed the ComLine from Dr. Bentley. "Yoggi here. I want to know what's going on, NOW!"

Baker and Leiman glanced at each other. He was glad he had won the coin toss.

"Yes, Ma'am," Leiman gulped. "Sergeants Taylor, Ryan and Wright attempted to steal our supplies. When they failed, Ryan and Taylor challenged Malone to a fight. The winner takes all the supplies."

"Stop that fight!"

"Yes, Commander." Leiman caught Baker's gaze.

Sgt. Baker nodded and walked to the center of the fight and held out his arms. "Cmd. Yoggi's on the ComLine and ordered you two to stop."

"Commander," Leiman said, "they've stopped."

174

"Sergeant, did you and Baker condone this?" Yoggi asked.

"Yes, Ma'am." Sgt. Leiman looked at Baker, Taylor and Zeus as they walked up.

"We'll discuss this when I get there. The doctor and I are on our way. ETA less than five minutes. Yoggi out."

Zeus was not aware of normal OTS rules and did not realize the sergeants were in trouble. The sergeants had endorsed the fight, so the orphan assumed it was acceptable.

Leiman rubbed her temples, put the Alphas in formation and hoped for the best. The ER vehicle flew up. Bentley positioned her flyer so the light shined on Ryan leaning against the tree with bandages over his left eye. The four other sergeants walked up and saluted their commander. Cmd. Yoggi returned their salute and yelled, "Malone, get over here." She wanted to be certain the orphan was not forced to fight before deciding what action to take.

Zeus ran over and saluted. The orphan's thumb would not lie flat against his hand. Instead, it pointed oddly up, making a right angle with the top of his hand. He dropped his right hand and with the left hand felt the break. He located the fracture and snapped his thumb in place.

The loud "crack" sent shivers down Dr. Bentley's spine.

Zeus stood tall at attention and delivered a perfect salute.

The OTS staff members stared at him dumbfounded. After thinking about it, Dr. Bentley grew incensed. "Malone, what are you doing?"

"Sorry, Ma'am. Hads ta fix my's thumb before I's could give yous a proper salute."

"I mean what were you doing fixing your thumb with me right here?"

He was forever stating the obvious when he knew it was not the correct answer. "Was broke, Ma'am." Zeus was confused by her anger. He had taken care of things. To the orphan, the problem no longer existed. He would use the camp first aid kit later to flood the bone with caladrom.

Dr. Bentley snorted like a bull ready to charge. "Why were YOU fixing it?"

Zeus was completely perplexed. " 'Cause it was broke, Ma'am."

Sgt. Leiman had dealt with the unique language barrier before. "Request permission to speak, Commander."

"Go ahead."

"Doctor, Ma'am," Leiman turned to Yoggi, "I don't believe Cadet Malone means any disrespect by his comments. He just doesn't understand the question."

Dr. Bentley crossed her arms and glared. "What part, exactly, doesn't he get, Sergeant?"

Cmd. Yoggi could tell there was no disrespect in Malone's voice, and he appeared bewildered. Before Leiman could respond, Cmd. Yoggi ordered, "Doctor, go treat Ryan. You can yell at Malone later."

"All right, Commander." Dr. Bentley stomped over to Sgt. Ryan under the tree.

"Unbelievable." Yoggi shook her head at Malone. "Have you figured it out yet?"

Zeus hated being lost in conversations, especially when they were directed at or about him. It made him feel powerless and vulnerable, two things he did not like to feel. "No, Ma'am?" He glanced to Leiman for an explanation.

"May I, Commander?" Yoggi nodded and Leiman explained, "Malone, you're not supposed to be setting your own broken bones. That's Dr. Bentley's job."

"Ain't gots ta do noth'n now. Why's she mad?"

Sgt. Leiman explained it again in more detail.

Yoggi listened in amazement. She turned to Baker. "Does this sort of problem come up often?"

"Yes, Ma'am," Baker answered. "There's definitely cultural and language barriers."

Leiman repeated herself, trying to get some understanding out of her cadet. Another blank stare.

"Malone," Cmd. Yoggi interrupted, "I don't care whether this makes sense to you or not. From now on, if you break something, you let Dr. Bentley fix it. That's an order, got it?"

"Yes, Commander." Zeus dropped his head.

"Now," Yoggi handed Taylor a tissue and rubbed her nose. "I want an explanation for what was going on here."

Taylor dabbed his nostril with the tissue. "It's my fault, Commander. After they baited us for hours, we challenged Malone to a fight for the Alpha's supplies."

"And they ordered you to fight?" Yoggi asked Malone.

176

"No, Ma'am. Sgt. Leiman and Sgt. Baker says no, cause they's afraid I's gets beat. I's tell 'em I's can win, and I's can."

Taylor was still in the fighting mentality. "No way, Malone. Your thumb's broken."

"I's fixes it." Zeus flipped his thumb in Taylor's face.

Bulldog stuck out his bloody jaw. "Cmd. Yoggi, request permission to finish what I started."

"Malone?" she asked, "do you want to finish it, too?"

"Yes, Ma'am."

Dr. Bentley stood and stomped her foot. "We came here to stop them. Remember?"

"Oh, come on, Doctor." Yoggi motioned to her. "What's the harm?"

"What's the harm?" Bentley threw her arms in the air. "This man here," she directed her hand to Ryan, "has a concussion, a broken nose, one eye swollen shut, a bruised stomach, and he needs lasersealing in three places. Both of those men are already hurt. How can you even consider this?"

"I'm not hurt." Taylor wiped the red ooze dribbling down his lip. "A little bloody nose doesn't count."

"I's fixes my's thumb. Ain'ts noth'n wrong with me's."

"You men belong in the infirmary, not starting another fight," Dr. Bentley insisted.

Yoggi patted Bentley's shoulder. "They're trained to fight. We'll stop it if anybody really gets hurt."

Bentley pulled away. "What's a concussion and broken nose, fake injuries?"

Yoggi did not need the doctor's approval; however, she would have preferred it. Yoggi had been wanting to watch both men fight for weeks. She turned to her men. "Let's see what you two can do."

"Yes, Ma'am," they both exclaimed, jogging over to the center of the clearing.

Zeus was positive he could win since he had had a chance to rest. If they had continued after Ryan dropped out, it would have been harder. Now it was a guarantee.

Sgt. Wright acted as referee and restarted the contest. Dr. Bentley stood seething by Cmd. Yoggi.

"I'm sorry you're upset, Doctor. Think of this as just another bout in the gym."

"Malone is not just another cadet. And these men are not wearing any protective gear."

"Honestly, the worst that can happen is they spend a few days in the infirmary." Yoggi watched as Taylor round-kicked Zeus in the chest. "I probably wouldn't let it go on, but I'm curious to see how Malone fights and how good Taylor is. I haven't seen either of them fight yet."

"It doesn't matter what I say, does it?" She squeezed her brown eyes shut as Taylor took a blow to the ribs.

When the pair sparred, Zeus usually gave Taylor time in between hits. Today, they were in a bout, and he had the Alphas, his sergeants and Cmd. Yoggi watching. Zeus intended to drop his opponent quickly and decisively. Zeus landed two more hits to the ribs and one to the kidneys.

Taylor knew he was in trouble and tried to defend himself until he had caught his breath.

Moments later, the orphan clipped Taylor's legs out from under him, and Taylor went down for the full count. The second round lasted less than three minutes.

Zeus wiped some blood from his lip as he went over to Taylor and put his hand out. Taylor grabbed it, and Zeus helped him up.

Taylor groaned, grabbing his upper left side, "I hate you, Malone."

"Ribs hurt'n, Sergeant. Yous get'n better. I's think yous cracks one of mine." He rubbed the ribs above his diaphragm.

"Well, that makes me feel better."

Dr. Bentley strolled up to them. "Wonderful. You two both won yourselves a trip to the infirmary. Go get in the ER vehicle."

"Yes, Ma'am." The two men followed Dr. Bentley to the transport.

"That was worth seeing," Cmd. Yoggi commented to Baker and Leiman. "Malone is good. I thought it would take longer against Taylor."

"That is longer for one of Malone's fights," Sgt. Leiman stated, proud of Taylor. "Normally Malone finishes his fights without a scratch."

"Taylor should be good in the All-Militaries."

"Yes, Commander."

"Too bad Malone won't be there. Talk about your ringers." Yoggi turned and strolled to the ER vehicle.

The three patients were in the rear discussing the bout. Cmd. Yoggi and Dr. Bentley could hear the excitement in their voices as they re-played numerous moves and hits.

"You see, Doctor," Yoggi joked, "that's just how little boys play. They certainly don't sound hurt or angry."

The doctor eased the flyer into the air. "I will never understand men or their desire to fight."

"You didn't enjoy watching them, even a little?" Yoggi pinched the air.

"No, Commander, I've never liked violence. I prefer healing instead of inflicting pain," she commented in a condescending tone.

"I'm sorry you were offended. Do you mind dropping me at my house?"

"No, of course not. You go right to bed. I'll stay up and treat the aftermath." She placed the back of her hand over her brow for effect.

"Well, I'm glad you understand how rank works. Upper brass only create problems; it's the lower ranks that are supposed to deal with them."

*   *   *

After Dr. Bentley treated him, Taylor dragged himself to his quarters. It was late, and he was tired. The doctor had given him a pain-killer. He staggered to his door. He was drowsy and defeated. He could not wait to crawl into bed. He put his key in the lock, opened his door and said, "Lights on." Nothing.

He thought maybe the verbal command was out and tried to turn on the lights manually as he walked into the dark room. Two steps in, he tripped on something. "Crap." He tried to remember what he had dropped on the floor. When he stumbled on the second item, his gut sank. He was a neat person and had not left a mess.

He walked cautiously to the main door and opened it completely. The hall light illuminated his living room enough for him to deduce where the Alphas had been while he and the other sergeants checked for booby traps. He cursed Leiman, Malone and the Alphas as he stepped over and around the items on the floor. In the dark, he bumped into a towel hanging from a light fixture.

"Budgin bastards." He reached up and ripped the towel down. All he wanted to do was go to sleep. He stumbled to the bedroom. The blinds were open. The glow of the streetlights outlined the destruction. He stared in angry disbelief at the upside-down bed frame and the mattresses leaning against the wall.

"I'll kill them. How could Susan have let them in? She will pay. If it's the last thing I do, Susan is going to pay."

Tired, sore and groggy, Taylor decided there was nothing he could do tonight. He pushed the debris aside on the floor, rolled up the towel for a pillow, laid down and went to sleep, muttering angry words of revenge.

CHAPTER 14

THE CADETS MARCHED to the Alpha barracks that would be their home for the next nine months. Each unit had an identical building clearly labeled with the unit name above the door. The buildings had three floors. The basement had a large meeting room, supply room, storage area and sergeants' offices.

The top two floors were cadets' quarters, bathrooms and study rooms. Each room was designed for two cadets. The rooms were small and contained two beds, two desks with chairs and computers, two lockers and one small closet. OTS regulations required cadets' rooms to be kept a specific way. The only places for personal items were the closet and desk drawer. An officer could check these areas, and they had to be clean and neat. Lockers were for OTS supplies and uniforms. Each item had an assigned place. Beds had to be perfectly made. Desks could not have any clutter. Computer tapes, notes, pens, etc., were in the desk drawer.

Apollo carried his pack and gear up the stairs to room 205. Zeus followed a few minutes later.

"I hope you are not offended, I chose a bunk without inquiring about your preference. Sgt. Baker ordered me to bunk on the outside wall." Apollo cleared his throat. "Apparently, my snoring is a problem. With his arrangement, nobody is disturbed on the opposing side of the wall."

Zeus cared immensely. The door was in the middle of the hall wall, and his bunk had a better view of the door opening and people coming in. He shrugged to indicate the choice was fine and tossed his gear on his bed.

The orphan sat at his desk and turned on the computer. Zeus was in heaven. He had only had a small antique portable computer to work on. This one was a top-of-the-line computer. It had all the latest features. The computer had a detachable dictation/microphone, keyboard, scanner and screen that could be carried to class. A portable laser quill and writing pad were also attached. The system was capable of both audio and visual communications and recordings. It had both internal and universal electronic mail capabilities. It could be used to contact and speak with family and friends outside the base, but that capability was unavailable to cadets. Cadets were not allowed to have two-way communications with people outside of OTS.

Zeus was so absorbed in the computer he did not notice Apollo leave the room. Apollo went to the storage room to pick up his custom-designed suitcases. Sgt. Baker verified the bags were his and checked them off the list.

"How's it going with Malone?"

"Fine, Sergeant, I suppose."

Baker put down his InfoPad and gave Apollo his full attention. "What do you mean, you suppose?"

"Zeus has not spoken since he entered our room; not a single word, Sir. He threw his gear on his bunk. Since then he has been occupied with the computer."

"That's strange. What's he doing on the computer?"

"It appears he is verifying the system. From what I observed, he is accessing every function and testing it; however, I am uncertain."

"Maybe he thinks it will help him in computer class."

Apollo did not buy that explanation. "How would that assist him in class?"

"How would I know? Malone thinks differently than most of us. Who knows what he's thinking."

"Yes, Sir. I suppose."

Baker clapped Apollo on the shoulder. "Remember, Christiani, you have any problems, you come to me or Leiman."

"Yes, Sir, I understand. I do not believe he would harm me. Zeus is just extremely introverted."

"I agree. I'm hoping you can get him to open up a little. You better get finished unpacking." Baker picked up his InfoPad. "Officers love to hold inspections the first few days."

"Yes, Sir." Apollo tucked the smallest bag under his arm, grabbed the other two bags and returned to his room. Zeus was still absorbed in the computer. Apollo hated to interrupt him, but did not want demerits for their room being out of order. He was already tired and sore enough without any extra physical exertion.

"Excuse me, Zeus." He waited for the orphan to cock his head. "Sgt. Baker stated officers enjoy holding inspections on the first day. He would appreciate our belongings stowed promptly."

Zeus nodded and manually terminated the program he was reviewing.

Apollo could not believe it. Zeus did not even use verbal commands with the computer.

The orphan never considered using the verbal commands. He was accustomed to noise giving away his location. He realized he did not have to be silent here, but out of habit he used the manual buttons.

Zeus unpacked his gear and put it away according to regulations. He followed the instructions to the letter, paying attention to every detail.

Apollo did the same, but was not as detailed. He was too preoccupied with attempting to converse with his new roommate. Since checking out the computer was the first thing Zeus had done, and he was a computer major, Apollo figured that was the best place to start. He made certain he asked an open-ended question. "Now that you have acquainted yourself with our system, inform me about our computers?"

"They's great!"

Two words, oh well, that's a start. At least he seemed excited. Apollo sensed he was on the right subject. "What determines this system's greatness?"

"We's link ta a main frame. Ain'ts separate computers, just terminals."

"I do not comprehend the significance of that statement."

Zeus enthusiastically launched into a detailed explanation of the entire OTS system.

Apollo could hear the excitement in his roommate's voice. He had never heard Zeus talk in such a manner or so much about anything. Not wanting to interrupt, and having no idea what Zeus was talking about, Apollo remained silent except for an occasional "uhuh" or "I see," enough to imply he was listening and interested. In truth, Apollo was bored stiff. Apollo could not believe it. The first time Zeus actually was conversing, and it was incredibly dull and technical. Apollo had not only gotten stuck with an antisocial orphan, but an intellectually technical, antisocial one.

Zeus was basically talking out loud to himself. He had long forgotten his roommate was there until Apollo interrupted him.

"Zeus, may I inquire where your personal belongings are? We need to determine how we are going to arrange the closet."

"Ain't gots noth'n worth crap."

"Oh. . .um. . .well. . .perhaps you should retrieve your luggage. Then we can accommodate whatever you brought."

Zeus did not see the point, but shrugged and left. He went downstairs to the storeroom and retrieved his leechrat bag. He returned and emptied the meager contents on the bed. He put the computer discs, his written notes and the calculator in the center desk drawer. He left everything else in the dirty bag, rolled the bag into a small bundle, tied it with some rope and placed it in the large desk drawer. He tossed the bottom sheet on his bed and tucked in the corners. It had been years since he had helped make Emily's bed. He checked the manual to see exactly how the Corps expected it done.

Apollo watched in perplexed silence. Why had Zeus not brought up his luggage? Apollo was aware his roommate did not have any luxury items, but he expected to see shaving supplies, a few clothes and some other necessities. Plus, why did the orphan keep garbage? When his roommate did not go back to retrieve the remainder of his belongings, Apollo grew frustrated. He had put his regulation things away and made his bed. He could not arrange the closet without Zeus's stuff.

"Did the sergeants misplace your luggage?" Apollo asked diplomatically.

Zeus, as usual, could not follow the conversation. Was Apollo blind? He had just finished putting his stuff away. The orphan gave him a confused look.

"Where are your other clothes and personal belongings?"

"They's pitched my's clothes. Ain't gots noth'n else."

Apollo was perplexed; a few knives, some computer discs, a calculator and trash were all Zeus had brought to camp. Apollo sat on his bed and tried to determine what to do. Perhaps Zeus had sent his belongings. Maybe he thought he would be kicked out so quickly it would not be worth bringing his personal stuff. Apollo could not decide how much space he should leave for Zeus's things in the future. The only choice was to put his things away and deal with Zeus's belongings when and if they arrived.

Zeus saw officers approaching from the window. He did not want to receive disciplinary exercises. Normally he would not care; however, today he wanted to get back on the computer and planned to work on it through the night.

"Puts that crap away." He tossed Apollo's engraved manicure kit at him. "We's got brass come'n."

Apollo quickly stuffed the belongings on his bed into the closet as neatly as possible. Zeus tried to finish making his bed.

"Perhaps since we are in the corner on the top floor we will be one of the last rooms inspected," Apollo said.

"Wrong, Cadet," a voice stated.

Zeus and Apollo both snapped to attention and saluted. Neither man recognized the captain, and they could not read her name tag. Apollo wanted to know who he was dealing with, so he would know how to respond. He was a chameleon and changed his answers and gestures to please each officer. Some officers preferred strict adherence to the regulations; others, blind respect; others, guts. Each officer was unique to Apollo and required a different tone and attitude. Until he knew what each wanted, he was uncertain how to charm them.

Zeus never knew how to play anyone. It had never occurred to him. He followed the rules exactly; that usually brought the most predictable responses.

Capt. O'Donnell returned the salute. "That bed should be made." She pointed to Zeus's half-made cot. "And those items," she pointed to Apollo's personal belongings, "are non-regulation." She hesitated. "Two demerits each."

"Yes, Ma'am," they responded.

Apollo picked up her indecision and lack of military protocol. They must be dealing with one of the non-career teachers. "Ah, Captain?"

"Capt. Katherine O'Donnell." She extending her hand to Apollo.

"It is a pleasure to meet you, Ma'am." Apollo smiled warmly as he returned the handshake. If this had been any other officer, he would have been working off points for weeks. He recognized her name as the computer science professor and realized teachers like her were uncomfortable with military protocol.

Capt. O'Donnell turned to Zeus and extended her hand.

Zeus had been baffled by Apollo's question and even more confused by Capt. O'Donnell's response. Military procedures gave the orphan a script to follow, and that was easier for him. Once they had broken away from protocol, he was uncertain what to do. Zeus was relieved Apollo was behind the captain and prompting him. Zeus shook her hand.

Apollo mouthed, "Say your name," and tugged at his name plate.

At first, Zeus was not sure what his roommate meant. "Oh, Cadet Malone, Ma'am."

"So you're Malone."

"Yes, Ma'am."

Apollo listened to his instincts about people. He felt she would go easier on them if she was comfortable. There was a long pause, as neither Zeus nor Capt. O'Donnell knew what to do next. Apollo realized Zeus would never say anything, and the Captain had obviously forgotten she was supposed to be in charge. Capt. O'Donnell was getting an uneasy feeling, when Apollo offered a joke and the tension faded.

"She means, she presumed you would be uglier," Apollo quipped.

Capt. O'Donnell relaxed. "Something like that."

Zeus was still at attention. The Captain had not given him permission to stand down. Apollo was relaxed and motioned Zeus to do the same. Zeus misunderstood the signals and instead requested permission to ask a question.

"Sure."

Zeus was fairly certain that was a yes. "Yous write articles on computer renaissances waves rebound'n off satellites?"

"Yes." Her eyes sparkled. "You've read my work?"

"Yes, Ma'am."

"Where did you read it?"

"Self-publish section ons the net under satellite waves."

"Oh, do you have an interest in that field?"

"Yes, Ma'am. Does yous theory work ons a system where mainframe supports link-ups through a satellite?"

"It should, why?"

"I's can't gets it ta works."

Capt. O'Donnell beamed as she discussed her favorite topic and Zeus's earlier access into the OTS system.

Apollo listened in amazement. Zeus had had numerous opportunities to compliment the captain. He had not used one of them. How could the orphan waste such a golden opportunity?

Zeus had his own agenda. If her theory worked, along with the one he had adapted from Emily's work, he could hack into anything in the OTS system. All he needed was a few details. Zeus was not certain when he would have time to research the information. If she gave him the frequencies, satellite bouncers and boundaries, he would be able to hack into restricted information faster.

Capt. O'Donnell was not worried about security. As far as she knew, there was no technology available that could be used in conjunction with her work to make it a security risk. O'Donnell was impressed by the intelligence of the orphan's questions. As his questions progressed, Zeus purposely became skeptical.

"Sit down at your terminal and let me show you some things."

Zeus sat in his chair and manually brought up the computer codes. Capt. O'Donnell leaned over his shoulder. Zeus controlled his desire to push her away. She pointed to various sequences on the screen and explained each one. Her hair tickled his ears, and he could smell her breath. Once he realized the extent of her knowledge, he was more than willing to overlook her lack of respect for his personal space. For an hour she taught as Zeus listened and learned with a voracious appetite.

Zeus plugged in the final sequence codes as she instructed. "Incredible. It works!" It was everything he needed and more. Applying her theories would give him immediate access to restricted files. And she had shown him how to obtain the information for other computers. Zeus could potentially apply her theory, along with his own, and in time get into any system in the universe.

"Yes, of course it works," Capt. O'Donnell stated with pride. "This will cut down on feedback loops, satellite breakdowns and terminal slowdowns. All I need is a grant and some time to incorporate the theory into a self-diagnostic device."

"Self-diagnostic?" Zeus forgot she was not planning to used her theory as a hacking tool.

"What?" She crossed her arms disappointed. "Don't you think it can work?"

"Don't knows. Where yous plan'n ta hooks inta?"

"I was planning to program it into the satellite feed chip."

Zeus tilted his head to peer up at her. He considered her theory along her original intent. "Why's not diagnostic chips?"

"I've thought about that. Neither has been tested. I think putting it with the direct satellite feed would be just as effective, while not creating any cross-systeming problems. I'm hoping that will work. If not, then I'll try to hook it into the diagnostic chips."

"Can't tests here. Not withs the stupid frequency for the OTS system."

"Actually, the C874 frequency does make sense. The mainframe is on Tallien, and C874 is a strong band there."

Zeus's jaw dropped as he began to understand the power of the system he had access to. "Frame ins the computer lab's a secondary link ta Tallien's system?"

"It's similar to a secondary link setup, but it's actually a sub-mainframe with satellite boosters."

Zeus chewed his nails and tried to absorb what she was saying. How could OTS's frame be a submain? Only megaframes had that capability. "Tallien's a megaframe?"

"One of the biggest in the universe. Here, let me show you how you can tell." She leaned down and tapped on the keyboard. Zeus was transfixed. She had a great deal of knowledge he was eager to learn.

Apollo listened for more than an hour as he put his things away and made Zeus's bed. He did not want another officer to come in and give their room demerits. All room points were given to both people to promote teamwork and interdependence. After being certain the room was in perfect order, Apollo left to talk to the other Alphas.

CHAPTER 15

THE OFFICERS ASSEMBLED in the conference room across from Cmd. Yoggi's office. Boot camp had been over for eight days. Each teacher had held one lecture for all the cadets and two labs for the Alphas. Cmd. Yoggi had rearranged the schedule to allow each professor time to evaluate Malone before this meeting.

The atmosphere in the conference room was tense. The staff realized the pressures to discharge Malone had increased substantially since the orphan had passed boot camp. None of the usual chit-chat proceeded the meeting. Most of the officers did not have good news for their superior and loathed being the bearer of bad news.

Cmd. Yoggi entered. Everyone rose and saluted. She marched to the head of the table. Cpl. Simb followed behind and sat at her right to take notes.

"Be seated. I don't need to state the purpose of this meeting. We know why we're here. I have received everyone's reports and will go over them in detail after the meeting. I wanted to hear your unofficial thoughts first, before reading the official versions. No one except Simb is to take notes, and there will be no recording of this meeting. Nothing is to be discussed outside of this room. Is that clear?"

"Yes, Ma'am."

"Speak freely about Malone." Yoggi panned the room. "I need honest, gut reactions and feelings. Don't hold back; this is your chance to say what's on your mind. I want each of you to recap your experiences with Malone, then add any personal comments, feelings or opinions. Any questions?" She paused and looked to her left. "Capt. O'Donnell, you begin."

"Yes, Commander. As I told you when he moved into the barrack, Malone is proficient in computers. I spent over an hour with him the first day, and I've met with him numerous other times. He's full of questions, learns quickly and can easily pass my class."

Yoggi frowned. "You're certain?"

"Yes. If he were anybody else, I'd beg for him to be my cadet assistant. One thing's for certain, he's studied and worked on computers a long time. He's questioned me about my work and the articles I've written. He clearly understood the material. He's at a graduate level or above in computers."

"Graduate level or above?" Yoggi dropped into her chair. "That's not possible!"

"Malone's more obsessed with computers than I am. He's been playing with this stuff for years."

"How can that be?" Dr. Bentley asked. "I've examined him. He's starved most of his life. Are you saying, Malone bought computer stuff instead of food? And where was he keeping it?"

"I have no idea." O'Donnell raised and lowered her shoulders. "I'm just telling you, he hasn't picked this hobby up in the last few years. He reminds me of computer whiz kids. They're socially inept and spend their time relating to computers instead of people."

"Well, I think we can all agree he's socially inept." Yoggi grimaced. "Anything else?"

"You asked for my personal opinion. He's crude, and sometimes his speech is difficult to follow. He also has a disgusting habit of biting his fingernails and spitting them out. I can't say I like him, but he's never going to flunk computer class. In fact, he's a highly motivated student. He wants extra work more on his level. He calls or comes to my office constantly asking questions." O'Donnell rolled her eyes. "If I'm not available, he leaves detailed messages. One night he contacted me six times."

Yoggi leaned back and crossed her legs. This orphan confused and surprised her more and more each day. "What types of questions is he asking?"

"He's fascinated with renaissance waves, image echoing, satellite feedback and things like that. First, he wanted recommendations for reading, then he called asking questions about those readings. Now he wants to know how they relate to my work, how it relates to mega mainframes, to regular frames. Everything. Half the stuff, I have to look up. If Malone weren't so vulgar, I'd enjoy working with him. He's extremely intelligent."

"OK." Yoggi exhaled loudly. "Anything else you want to add?"

"He has a strong science background. Malone seems to be cross-referencing a great deal of the information with the other sciences."

"Any possibility you've overrated his science background? If, as you said, he's obsessed with computers, maybe he didn't study the other subjects."

"It's possible, but I don't think so. At the level he's at, it's fairly technical and requires the background."

"Commander, if I may speak?" Maj. Kong stroked his thin, graying mustache.

"Go ahead, Kong."

"Cadet Malone does have a solid science background. I have given my cadets homework from mid-semester of last term. Malone got a sixty-nine percent on his space sciences work. Since over half the cadets didn't pass, that's not bad. I predict he will pass my class with a solid C or better. On a personal note." Kong crossed his arms in disgust. "I don't like him. He's a great deal of trouble and distracting us from teaching the other cadets. I have better things to do than waste hours on one cadet who has no chance of graduating."

Numerous other officers nodded, voicing similar opinions.

Cmd. Yoggi threw up her arms in frustration. "I agree with your sentiments, people; however, no one's giving me any indication that he's in danger of flunking out or discharging. Let's complete the individual discussions, and we'll brainstorm about possibilities later."

"Well," Maj. Patterson proclaimed, "Malone's, without a doubt, going to flunk my speech and PR class. As far as I can tell, he doesn't even speak English. He's crude and has no understanding of how the press or public relations works. His first speech was horrendous. He stuttered and stammered. It was difficult to follow, and his grammar is pathetic."

"And his grade?" Yoggi asked.

"I gave him a zero. Malone would have been better off not getting up. I've instructed him to redo it, but I don't think it will matter. Lastly, I'm with Kong. I say, get him out of here." Patterson flicked his thumb over his shoulder. "We need to deal with the real students."

"Thank you, Major. That's three he'll pass and one he'll flunk. Ritz, you're up."

"I'm sorry, Commander." Capt. Ritz dropped her eyes. "I think if

I gave him my final right now, he'd pass. He definitely studied physics in college. My class is not something you can fake your way through. I usually flunk more students than anyone else. After talking to O'Donnell, I was concerned he was hacking into our files or workbooks, so I conducted my time with him orally. He can't cheat that way. Malone has had lots of physics, and he's going to pass. He's a little weak in the lab."

"Weak enough to flunk?" Yoggi raised her eyebrows hopefully.

"No, he'll do fine, but it appears he's had very little practical time in the lab. My unofficial comment is, I don't like him either. As everyone else has said, he's crude and has an abrasive personality. On the other hand, I was impressed by his intelligence and knowledge. I'd be curious to know his IQ."

"Forget his IQ." Yoggi pounded the arms of her chair. "How did he get so well educated?"

"I don't know. Physics is not considered a subject that can be self taught. Anyone, without an instructor, could become an expert on things like history or political science. That's not true for physics, and certainly not astrophysics at Malone's level."

Yoggi peered out the window as she tried to sort out her thoughts. "Who did he learn it from?"

"I took the liberty of calling a few of the physics professors at Alto College. Most of them, like us, didn't want him there. They did say he religiously went to class and always turned in his work. He asked few questions, and it sounded like the teachers basically ignored him. All except one guy, who saw him in his office a few times and helped him with some things."

"What about his first year?"

"His first physics teacher was surprised he was able to keep up with the work. She said if she hadn't known better, she would have assumed he'd taken at least two years of physics in high school. He appeared to have a working knowledge before he arrived at Alto."

Yoggi's face twisted. Malone's life was a puzzle she could not put together. "Sgt. Taylor told me he either lived in the sewers or on the streets before Alto."

Ritz slumped in her chair. "I don't know of anybody who teaches physics in the sewers."

"I think he was hiding out down there," the balding Lt. Cmd.

Zeigler interjected. "I've always thought that kid was guilty of something. Why else would anybody live in the sewers? He was hiding out from the authorities. I'll bet he was trying to avoid the security scans. The sewers would be one of the few places where he wouldn't run into hidden scanners. It's the perfect place to hole up."

"That's a believable theory." Cmd. Yoggi drummed her fingers on the table. "Except that there are no warrants for his arrest or any cases where he is or ever was a suspect. That avenue has been painstakingly gone over. So who was he hiding from?"

"The Kalopso," Zeigler offered.

"If I were being hunted by the network," Dr. Bentley touched her nametag, "I sure wouldn't go from living in the sewers to getting my name in InterPress for acceptance into college. Plus, applying to OTS would be suicide. Everyone recognizes him now."

"Maybe he made a deal with the Kalopso. He'd go to school. He'd major in computers, so he could hack into illegal places and physics, so he could make bombs. The sergeants said he had no difficulties constructing the explosive device that nailed Taylor." Zeigler rubbed his ear as he pondered his next thought. "Whether OTS was a part of the original plan or thought up later, who knows. All I've got to say is, that kid is definitely hiding something. That's why he doesn't want to talk to anybody. He's afraid he'll slip up."

"Sgt. Taylor said Malone applied to OTS as a favor to a journalism student. He never expected to be accepted, and he never wanted to come. Unfortunately, he likes it now and says he never wants to leave." Yoggi leaned forward. "I have to know which version is the truth."

The consensus was Zeigler's Kalopso theory was more logical. However, without proof, they still could not discharge him. Yoggi decided to continue evaluating his abilities.

"Dr. Jones, how are you doing with Malone?"

"My personal opinion is different from the rest of you. At first, I didn't like him either. He made me nervous and uncomfortable. But now that I've had a chance to get to know him, I enjoy his unique approach to life. I can honestly say I've never had a stale conversation with Zeus."

The officers chuckled nervously.

"Dr. Bentley, I'm going to skip you, since we've talked extensively. Maj. Sato." Yoggi looked to the bearded man. "I'd like you to go next."

"I've had three therapy sessions with him, if you could call them that." Sato stroked his beard methodically as he spoke. "My role here is supposed to be support and guidance to cadets. Malone knows the rules and procedures I'm required to follow, and he insists that I do. He has also requested that everything we do be recorded to keep me from overstepping my boundaries. The time I spend with him is an exercise in futility. He hasn't said one thing worth noting. Most of the time Malone answers with, 'Ain't comfortable discussing that now.' "

"Insist he answers," Yoggi snarled.

"I wish I could. He's smart. That's practically a quote from the guidelines as to when, as a therapist, I'm not supposed to press on an issue. Whatever he's hiding, he's hiding it well. For the most part, I'm wasting my time."

"Any personal thoughts?"

Maj. Sato twisted the end of his beard into a little curl. "I feel the best way to get rid of him is to have everyone document his antisocial behaviors. Have his unit members filing reports to that effect, noting he can't work in a group or as a team member. We can note his lack of effective communications, leadership skills, things like that. A few incidences wouldn't be a concern, but dozens, even hundreds, could be. I can certainly find plenty of literature supporting such behaviors as warning signs of future instability. The sooner we start documenting, the better."

"Capt. Haden, care to comment?" Yoggi flicked her wrist at him. "Are the cadets in his unit complaining?"

Haden fidgeted, conscious he needed to sound objective. Yoggi had ordered him to put his prejudice aside. "There are still a few complaining, but not many. Most of the Alphas have accepted his idiosyncrasies. As for his leadership, it's a unique style. Unfortunately, it's effective. The few missions he's led have been extremely successful. He comes up with reasonable plans of attack, explains those plans and makes certain everyone follows through. Look at his altercations with Sgt. Taylor. The kid doesn't lose. I thought once we forced him to work with the unit, he'd fail. Unfortunately, the last few incidences were as effective as the first ones. When he had to work with the group, he adjusted enough to do the job."

"Being effective does not negate antisocial behavior," Maj. Sato noted. "Has anyone befriended him?"

"No one's really befriended him. Christiani is his designated translator and was assigned as his roommate. He respects Malone. I'd say that's a fair comment for many of the Alphas. Not everyone hates him. A number have noted his helping them. Oddly, he never wants credit for assisting members of his unit. He won't even acknowledge his involvement to the people he's helped."

"Perhaps they're mistaken, and Malone didn't help them," Zeigler offered.

"I wish I could say that was true, but they say they witnessed his involvement. People have even commented while it's happening."

"What do you mean, Captain? Give us some examples," Zeigler questioned. As second in command, it was important for him to be on top of things.

"Sato informed Cadet Connor her father had been in a terrible accident and might not survive. Connor was upset she might never speak to her dad again. Without being asked, Malone set up a two-way ComLine and let Connor speak to her father for about an hour. From what Connor said, it made a huge difference to her and to her dad. Her mother sent word the next day, that the call was the turning point for her dad. He was going to be all right. Malone kept watch while Connor was on the ComLine, left when it was over, then ignored Connor the next day, even when she tried to thank him. There's no question Malone setup that ComLine, and from what Capt. O'Donnell says, he's one of the few who could."

Yoggi's face scrunched up in confusion. "Why deny it with Connor?"

"That's obvious, Commander," Zeigler offered. "Malone doesn't want anyone to know he can hack into a two-way ComLine."

"What difference does it make? Dozens of cadets have done it in the past," Capt. Ritz said.

"Besides," O'Donnell replied, "that's an easy hack job. I'd be disappointed, at his level of expertise, if he couldn't do that. Even if he's never done it before, Malone could figure it out. The method OTS uses to deactivate the cadets' outside ComLines is pretty basic. Lots of cadets have done it. It's not hard to do. The tricky part is not getting caught."

Yoggi slumped in her chair. "Haden, what other things has he done?"

"Well, he's forcing people not to quit, kind of at knifepoint."

Yoggi sat up straight. "Excuse me, what do you mean at knifepoint?"

"An Alpha told me yesterday he's about to flunk out. It seems Petroff got less than ten percent on Ritz's first quiz. You do know how to flunk 'em out fast." Capt. Haden nudged his friend. "Petroff had decided to discharge without attempting to retake the test. Apparently, Malone and his knife convinced him otherwise. Petroff told me he intended to cooperate with Malone the first night, because he was afraid to leave, then discharge in the morning. Only it turns out, the orphan's not a bad tutor. Malone's tutored Petroff until three or four in the morning every night since. Petroff thinks he has a chance to pass now. But again, Malone refuses to take credit for his involvement."

"I guess I'm impressed that he cares about the others in his unit. However," Cmd. Yoggi cleared her throat, "I wish his knife weren't so concerned."

The officers laughed nervously.

"Why wouldn't he want anyone to know he's being a team player?" Dr. Bentley bit her lip. "I would think he'd want everyone to see that."

Dr. Jones threw her hands up. "Did it ever occur to you that maybe Zeus really is a nice guy? His culture is different. Maybe where he's from, it's rude to boast or take credit for helping others. Perhaps, if we want to know more about him, we ought to start communicating in a way and on a level Zeus understands. We're expecting him to adjust to our ways, and from what everyone says, at least he's trying. What have we done to try and make it easier for him?"

"That's a good point. Capt. Haden, has anyone tried to, hum." Cmd. Yoggi couldn't decide how to state her thoughts. "Is anyone attempting to talk orphan with him?"

"The closest things would be Taylor, when they spar, and Christiani, his roommate. Christiani says they get alone fine, but Malone is too quiet and never says anything personal. I'm surprised he told Taylor he lived in the sewers. That's more personal than he usually gets."

"Is there anything else you want to add?"

Haden punched his right fist in his left palm. "Personally, I want him out and I don't care how we do it. I have twenty-nine other units, and I spend ninety percent of my time dealing with Malone. It's not fair to the others, and he's never going to be worth it."

"Message received." Cmd. Yoggi was aware of Haden's personal views. "Thank you for your honesty," she added for diplomacy. "That leaves us with the flight instructors and half the total OTS scores. Please tell me you have good news."

Four sets of eyes stared at the floor. Cmd. Yoggi's gut sank.

Col. Peaks spoke first. He taught Military Strategies and piloting. "He's an above-average student. I've given a short quiz, and he got a. . ." Peaks glanced at his notes, "a seventy-nine percent. Not bad, considering. Certainly not borderline flunking. As far as flying goes, he understands the work and does fine on the written portions. Capt. Mohammadi is his flight instructor. I'll let him detail Malone's flying."

"If he wanted to be a pilot, there would be a chance he wouldn't meet minimum flying standards. Malone's obviously never flown before. His first run in the simulators," Capt. Mohammadi read off his notes, "he bumped the wall eight times, and when he hit interspace, he let go of the controls and spun out. He said, other than on public transports, he's never been off world. During the interspace sensation, you know, those initial seconds of disorientation when the ship jumps to light speed, he completely lost it. I'm so used to it, I don't even think about it." Capt. Mohammadi smiled as he remembered the orphan's reaction. "He had no idea it was coming. He was confused and surprised. Also, mad I hadn't warned him about it."

"Were the other cadets also upset?"

"I've never had anybody else mention it. In the beginning, a lot can't handle the intensity of a Jackel's disorientation, but they know it's coming. However disastrous, even comical, his first fight was, Malone was definitely more prepared the second time. Second time out," Mohammadi glanced at his InfoPad, "he only hit the wall five times. When he hit interspace, he was able to hold on to the controls, but still spun out. Third time, scraped the wall twice, banged the crap out of it once, and he was able to regain control, once he did spin out in space. He's steadily improving. He is clocking in at the simulators at night practicing. He's the only cadet I've ever had who was still on simulators after boot camp. He's about ready for his first solo. I want to be certain he doesn't blow himself up taking a ship out of dock and into space."

"Best guess, do you think he'll flunk?"

"He works hard, has improved fast and, considering where he started, will probably meet the minimum requirements for a navigator/

gunner long before the final tests. The fact is, once we assign them as pilots or NG's, he'll be Zeigler's and Weiss's problem. With his math and science background, he's definitely going to be a navigator/gunner."

"All right, thank you, Captain. That and PR are our only weak links. Zeigler, Weiss, you're the last ones. What have you got?"

"I'm sorry, as far as my class goes, he was teaching it. I couldn't believe it." Zeigler held up a data disk. "I've watched this visual of my class over and over again. He didn't need to cheat to get in. He could ace my final right now. I brought the disk of him in my lab. With your permission, Ma'am?" Yoggi nodded her approval and he inserted the disk and played it.

On the screen a cadet completed a fuel-energy problem in front of the Alphas. After the problem was finished, the group could hear Zeigler's deep voice asking the group, "Is that correct, or does anyone see problems with this answer?" Lt. Cmd. Zeigler paused, then demanded, "You over there shaking your head, what's your name?"

The cadet stood. With the angle of the camera, only the base of the his shaved head could be seen. "Cadet Malone, Sir."

"OK, Malone, you seem to disagree with this answer, what's going to happen?"

"Kaboom, Sir."

"That's right. Christiani, you just blew up your ship. Malone, what's right and what's wrong up there?"

"Ain'ts noth'n right, Sir."

"Get up there, fix it and explain what Christiani did wrong."

"Yes, Sir." Zeus walked to the laser board. He deleted Apollo's work and picked up the laser quill. "Apollo uses the velocity part of the equation as fuel. That's kaboom. Fuel is consistent equations, only seventeen of thems. This here's high grades kinadron." Zeus circled a portion of the equation. "An this, initial velocity." He underlined another portion of the equation. "Jackel's mass and relative density is always 'bout same. Don't change much from problem ta problem." Zeus put a squiggle line under more numbers. "This here has ta be's the space anomaly the ships pass'n through, 'cause it's the only other part of the problem that gots ta do withs mass and density." He put a square around the final portion. "Then yous do the math." Zeus worked out the equation and declared the answer. "Fuel efficiency's been reduced point oh six three percent, Sir."

Lt. Cmd. Zeigler turned the viewer off. The officers sat in silence with their jaws on the floor. Yoggi's fuel efficiency math was rusty. It had been years since she had done fuel consumption problems. When she recovered from the shock of seeing Malone's apparent intelligence, she asked, "Was the answer correct?"

Those who knew nodded as Zeigler stated, "Perfect. No mistakes."

"What about the explanations: high-grade kinadron, Jackel's relative density, all those other things he was saying?" Yoggi paused, trying to accept the orphan's obvious intelligence. Up to now, she had convinced herself the others were exaggerating or misinterpreting Malone's abilities. What she witnessed could not be faked, cheated or misinterpreted. The orphan was not uneducated or stupid.

"Everything he said was a hundred percent accurate. He could pass my final now." Zeigler smacked his armrests. "What are we going to do about him? He obviously can pass. His navigation and shooting are acceptable and improving. If it weren't Malone and his flying were better, he'd be a top seed NG."

"Weiss." Yoggi rubbed her throbbing temples. "I take it you're his in-flight NG instructor?"

"Yes, Commander." Capt. Weiss took a deep breath. "He's in line to be a good navigator, as I'm certain you can surmise from Zeigler's visual. He's apparently never shot before or applied navigation to flying. Navigation seems to come naturally to him, and with his strong math background, it isn't going to be a problem. The shooting is taking him a little longer to get the hang of. As Mohammadi noted, he's not used to the interspace feel and still gets disoriented. He's improved a great deal and has minimal problems now. He's slightly above average in shooting and is improving fast."

"Anything else?" Yoggi stared at her shoe as she listened. Her head was spinning. She felt like she had just hit interspace, was disorientated and could not regain control of her vessel.

"I give everyone a reflex test and peripheral vision test. Malone has phenomenal reflexes and peripheral vision, which is common in good fighters. They tend to develop those skills in the martial arts, and they're easily transferable. He'll be a better than average NG as soon as he has more space time and can learn to compensate for the interspace feelings."

The commander raised her head and shook it to clear her thoughts.

"Any chance he'll never overcome it?"

"I don't think so. I've had cadets discharge when they couldn't overcome a Jackel's interspace feeling, but they don't usually improve the way Malone has. A typical interspace discharge would be someone who blacks out, pukes, or both during the interspace shifts. Malone's never done any of that. The kids who do, they can't stop it. My experience is they get worse as we go faster, not better, as Malone has. They also don't clock in time at night; it's all they can do to recover for the next day. Unfortunately, Malone's not getting sick."

"Weiss is right," Zeigler growled in disgust. "I've never seen one adjusting the way Malone is that couldn't learn to control it. The question becomes, Commander, what are we going to do about him?"

"That's a very good question. I'm open to suggestions. Everyone can speak freely."

"I'd like to ask a question of Dr. Bentley." Maj. Patterson waited for the commander to nod her approval. "How accurate are your medical findings? What's the error ratio for your tests? There is no way that kid's been starving. Look at his educational background."

"I'd agree." Bentley shrugged. "Except I've done tissue samples of all his organs, not just the major ones, and tested them myself. Then I retook the samples and sent them off to two separate labs, each with different testing techniques. All three came back virtually the same. He's starved on and off his entire life. Every single organ shows signs of that. I also have had a total of eight different experts read the results; they all came to the same conclusion."

Sato stroked his bead. "Maybe he falsified the results."

"I checked. You can't. If I tested him at age ten or eighty, the results would be the same. The way tissues and organs form is directly related to the nutrition the body receives. As far as him setting his own bones, sewing himself up, et cetera, those tests are equally conclusive."

Patterson frowned. "I still don't see how that's possible."

"I have no explanation for how he can be educated and still have his medical history. Unfortunately, I state facts, irrefutable facts."

"Has anyone gotten any personal information out of this kid? I want answers, people. Who taught this kid how to read, work on computers and do advanced physics? Why is he here?" Cmd. Yoggi's temper and tone rose with each question. "Who's he working for or with? Why help the others and then burn the bridges? Answers, anyone?"

200

Nervous silence was her only response.

"Taylor, Leiman and Baker, what are they saying?" Yoggi growled.

"The same things you're hearing from us, Commander," Capt. Haden responded.

Yoggi banged the table with her fists. "I want answers!" No one dared to speak. She grabbed her ComLine and punched in Sgt. Leiman's code.

"Sgt. Leiman," she stated, slightly out of breath.

"Leiman, where are you?" Yoggi demanded.

Leiman was glad she recognized the commander's voice. From her perturbed tone, it would not be a good idea to ask Yoggi to identify herself. "On a hike, Ma'am."

"Where?"

"About two kilometers past the north entrance, Ma'am." Leiman was racking her brain trying to figure out what she had done wrong.

"Have someone else lead the hike. I want you in my conference room, NOW!"

"Yes, Commander. I'm on my way."

"Where's Baker and Taylor?"

Leiman realized the topic must be Malone because the commander had asked for Taylor. "Baker was going to do some work in his office, and Taylor, I guess, is teaching hand-to-hand at the gym. If you'd like, I'll track them down for you."

"No, you get to the North Outer. I'll have Simb pick you up there."

"Yes, Commander, I'm on my way."

"Yoggi out." She turned to Simb. "Grab a flyer and go pick up Leiman. The rest of you take a ten-minute break."

CHAPTER 16

SGT. BAKER WAS THE FIRST of the three sergeants to report in to the officers' meeting. He was glad he had worn his good uniform this morning. The other one had a small tear in the pocket seam he had never taken the time to repair. He would repair it that night, before he got caught in a room full of officers without a perfect uniform.

Taylor interrupted his workout with the Sigma unit and jogged over in his sweats. He entered and saluted the room. He had never been called in front of so many officers in his life. He was certain he was in trouble for failing to pilfer the Alpha's supplies. He stood straight and saluted.

Cmd. Yoggi pointed to an empty chair. "Take a seat. Leiman's on her way. We've been here all morning discussing Malone. How are you two getting along?"

Taylor exhaled, relieved he was not being disciplined. "Great, I think, Ma'am. What exactly do you want to know?"

"Has he told you who taught him how to read or how he became so well educated? Anything about his background?"

"I've tried. We mostly talk about fighting." He looked around as he heard the door open. Leiman and Simb entered and saluted. Taylor was careful not to make eye contact with her. If their eyes met, they might smile, and this was not the time for that.

Sgt. Leiman was uncomfortable entering a roomful of brass sweating, in dirty boots, shorts and a T-shirt. She took the chair Yoggi motioned to and sat down.

"Continue, Taylor," Cmd. Yoggi ordered.

"Yes, Ma'am. We mostly talk about fighting in one way or another. The way he talks to me, he doesn't sound educated. I thought he was supposed to flunk out."

"I don't think that's going to happen. That's why I called you three here. I want some answers. Zeigler, show them your visual. I'd like your comments on this, sergeants."

The three sergeants watched in awed shock.

When it was over, Leiman asked, "Is any of that accurate?"

"One hundred percent correct." Zeigler snapped.

"Wow!" Taylor exclaimed. "Do all the cadets talk like that?"

"NO! Malone is doing very well academically. What about you, Baker, any comments?"

"No, Ma'am." Baker shook his head. "I'm amazed. I figured he was failing his classes. Especially navigation, he's having so much trouble flying. I just assumed he wouldn't know that stuff. Where'd he learn that?"

Cmd. Yoggi pounded her fist on the table, spilling numerous drinks. "No more questions. I want answers. You people are here to bring me answers."

"Yes, Ma'am," they responded.

"What do you know about his background? How did a poor, starving laborer get advanced knowledge in computers, physics and the sciences?"

The sergeants remained silent.

Cmd. Yoggi waited to give them a chance to think and then interrogated Leiman as the lead sergeant. "You were supposed to get to know him, make Malone trust you and open up. How's that going?"

"I have spoken to him a number of times." Leiman gulped. "Malone seems more relaxed and less tense when we speak. He recently told me he's having problems flying and asked for my help. It may not sound like much, but it's a big step for him. I think there is small amount of trust, but I don't think he really trusts anyone. He does seem to care about me and respect me. Is almost. . .protective," she fumbled for the word.

"What are you talking about, Sergeant?" Lt. Cmd. Zeigler demanded. "Does this orphan kid have a crush on you?"

"Oh, no, Sir. Not like that. He told Taylor," she explained, being careful not to use Brian's first name, "that the reason he was protecting our supplies so vigorously was because my honor was at stake."

"Specifically your honor, not the Alpha's?" Zeigler questioned. "Sure sounds like he's attracted to you."

"No, I don't think so. Malone's, well, not encouraged our relationship, but kinda, I don't know, what would you say?" Leiman looked to Taylor. "He, sort of, wanted to be certain everything was OK between us."

"I know this is difficult for you two," Yoggi said to her nervous sergeants. "Tell us anything personal you know about him and anything about his life before OTS."

"He's done manual labor most of his life." Taylor touched a finger with each thought. "He worked his way through school. Got the name Zeus after a street fighter on Velcron. Doesn't have a girlfriend, in fact, Malone's never mentioned anyone specifically by name. Says he's been fighting to survive since he could walk. Has weird ideas about women. Is. . ."

"Wait," Cmd. Yoggi interrupted. "What do you mean, he has weird ideas about women? Since this kid's arrived, everyone notes strange behaviors toward women. First, it was only relieving the women in the unit. Leiman talks about him being protective. Taylor, you joked before about Malone being Leiman's bodyguard. What exactly is he saying to you about women?"

"Well," Taylor swallowed hard, not wanting to provoke the female officers. "Malone thinks all women need to be protected."

"Malone looked me in the eye and told me I couldn't take care of myself," Leiman declared in an exasperated tone. "When I asked him why, he said it was because I was a woman."

"What?" Cmd. Yoggi exclaimed.

Dr. Bentley laughed, "I could understand him saying it about me, but why does he think you're helpless?"

"Malone thinks all women are helpless," Leiman replied.

Taylor avoided eye contact with everyone, hoping not to comment further.

Unfortunately, Yoggi noticed. "Taylor, has Malone explained some of his views to you?"

"Yes, Ma'am. After we talked with Leiman, I asked him about it."

"You didn't tell me that," Sgt. Leiman interjected, perturbed.

"You were mad enough with his first comments. I didn't see any reason to get you more upset."

"What did he say, Sergeant?"

"Well, Commander," Taylor squirmed. "Remember, I am just telling you what Malone thinks. These are not my views. He thinks, he says, women are weaker, and. . .and. . ."

"Is this somewhat graphic?" Cmd. Yoggi asked.

"Yes, Ma'am." He hoped Yoggi would dismiss the topic.

"We're all adults here, Sergeant. Now what did Malone say?"

"HE said," Taylor wiped the sweat from his forehead, "women have to be protected because. . .because women have periods, can get pregnant, have breasts, and can be raped, Ma'am."

"What!" Every woman in the room screamed.

Leiman stood and leaned toward her boyfriend. "You didn't tell me any of that."

"Sues, if I believed that stuff and wanted a helpless women, I wouldn't have picked you. I'm just telling you what Malone said."

"Did Malone say what the aforementioned list had to do with being helpless?" Cmd. Yoggi demanded.

"He tried to explain it to me, but I had no idea what he was saying. It was one of those conversations with Malone where we weren't speaking the same language. His examples I agreed with, but I could never see how those things had anything to do with his conclusion."

"What things?" Leiman plopped in her seat, fuming.

"Yes," Cmd. Yoggi demanded, "what examples?"

"He asked if I was stronger than a woman, and I answered yes. He asked," Taylor hesitated, looking at Cmd. Yoggi.

"Out with it, Taylor." She no longer cared how uncomfortable he was.

"He asked if Leiman was being raped, would I stop the guys. And I said yes, I'd help a woman, even if she were a stranger. Then he said, 'See, that's my point.' "

"What does that have to do with anything?"

"I don't know." Taylor shrugged defensively. "I tried a couple of times to understand him. We finally gave up and went back to sparring."

"Oh, there's a typical male solution," Sgt. Leiman snarled. "I don't understand this important point you're trying to make, so let's just go fight instead of talking about it."

"It makes sense to me," Taylor snapped back.

"All right, that's enough," Cmd. Yoggi yelled. "Sato, what do you make of all this?"

"Malone seems to think that because he's stronger, he should rule. Might is right. Survival of the fittest. That basic mentality."

"I don't agree," Dr. Jones interjected. "Zeus didn't say, 'Because I'm stronger, women have to do what I want,' or 'I survive by taking advantage of the weak.' He said women had to be protected from people like that."

Yoggi's head throbbed. "OK, let's get off this subject. Who taught him how to do physics and computers? Taylor, what do you know about that?"

"I didn't even know he could talk like that. He's never said anything to me about studying, reading, things like that."

"What about you, Baker?"

"I don't know anything. Malone and I tend to get into it with each other. That kid has a temper."

Yoggi tried to contain the throbbing in her head by pressed her fingers on her forehead. "Give some examples of what you get into it over?"

"Now that I think about it, what usually makes him mad is when I push the women, in his mind, too much. He'll try to step in, and I'll order him back in line. Then he just stands there fuming."

"I've heard his face gets as red as his hair when he's mad."

"Malone doesn't hide it well, that's for sure."

"Ever discussed this with him?"

"I've been working on his defiant attitude. He's gotten a little better. I went up to him about a week ago, after returning him to formation a number of times, and said something like, 'You don't like me, do you?' He snarled, 'No, Sir,' and then surprised me by adding, 'but I respect you.' I figure that's as far as I'm going to get, and that's fine with me. I'm not trying to win any popularity contests out there. If he's willing to listen and follow orders, that's all I care about."

"Then he never talks to you out of formations or necessary conversations?"

"No, he never talks to me."

"Leiman," she questioned. "Do you have problems with him overprotecting the women in your unit?"

"No, Commander."

"That really bugs me," Sgt. Baker offered. "Leiman goes out there and pushes and bellows at those women and Malone doesn't flinch. Me, I say, 'Women, line up,' and he glares at me as if to say, 'Don't you dare yell at them.' I can't win, and Leiman can't do anything wrong.

That kid drives me crazy."

"Is he angry when you're pushing him or ordering him around?" Yoggi asked.

"No, he doesn't seem to care."

"He does take this female protection thing seriously. It's kind of strange and sweet," Dr. Jones commented.

"You may think it's sweet, Dr. Jones," Baker retorted, "but some of the women in our unit are tired of being patronized."

"And some of them are milking it," Leiman added. "I overheard a group of women talking. They were saying if you're tired or you don't want to do something, just pretend to cry, and Malone will do it for you."

"Well, he's consistent, even if it is strange. Sato, work on figuring some of this out," Cmd. Yoggi ordered. "I want you to start seeing Malone daily, at least for the next week or so. No matter how uncooperative he is, you keep grilling him."

"Yes, Ma'am."

"Taylor?" She turned to him. "Increase your training for the All-Militaries. I want you to spar with him daily. See what you can learn about his background, especially his education."

"Yes, Commander."

"Leiman, keep trying. See if there are any women in your unit he might open up to and have them chat with him."

"I'll do my best."

"Dr. Jones." Yoggi pointed to her. "You seem to get along with him. Strike up some conversations and try to find out who helped him with his physics and computer training. Anything about learning, a mentor, or things like that. The rest of you," Yoggi swept her hand around the table, "in the next week, I want you to give the Alphas your finals from last term. Grade Malone's. If he passes, you're done. If he gets below a forty percent, I want everyone's graded. Report Malone's class standing and the odds he'll pass by the end of the term. You flight people, same basic concept. By this time next week, I want to know for certain if that kid is capable of graduating. Every one, start talking to him. Find out everything you can about his past. Any questions?"

"My final is their graduation speech," Patterson said. "Do you want him to do that, or should I grade the one he's correcting?"

"Who cares? Of course, he's going to flunk speech and PR. Un-

207

fortunately, you're less than two percent of the total scores. Malone can get a zero from you and still pass. You don't need to do anything."

Patterson nodded.

"Any other questions?" Yoggi paused. "I want you all here next Tuesday, oh eight hundred. You're dismissed."

*   *   *   *

Galahad dragged himself down the K-Club hall. The boss had assigned him to clean one floor of the K-Club and manage the food on that floor. He had passed out the evening rations hours ago. Unlike the other one squares in the club, Galahad checked on his girls at least once a day.

He hated his job in club and longed to spend more time with Emily. The aquifer model had been working perfectly for months. He was now taking apart and rebuilding an old computer.

He took a deep breath and entered the women's dingy sleeping room. Four steps in, his tattered shoe stepped in a wet pool of red. Galahad clenched his fists. He insisted his rooms be kept meticulously clean. Emily had taught him it was a way of cutting down on germs and diseases. His girls were the healthiest in the club.

He glared around at his girls. "Huh?" He pointed to the blood stains.

Whippy, a twenty-year-old woman, limped forward. "I's gots a crazy." She turned her thigh. In the ripped, jagged edges of her costume was a large bruise. In the center of the blackish-purple cluster was a gapping hole. Red rivers with bits of flesh meandered down her leg.

"Budgin bastard." Galahad stomped his foot and punched his fist in his palm. The more he lived with Emily and heard about kindness, the more he hated the life he and the others were forced to live. He took a deep breath and did as Emily has taught him. He held out his arms. Whippy could come to him or not. With him, the girls had a choice.

Whippy ran to the teenager, threw herself in his arms and sobbed. Galahad could do nothing but hold her shaking body. He waited, counting the minutes until he could re-immerse himself in Emily's world. Whippy relaxed, sniffed and wiped her nose on his dirty shirt.

He patted her. "Lays downs, I's helps yous."

Whippy leaned sideways, wincing as she bent her swollen leg and reclined on the barren floor. The other women pressed in around them, waiting to see what Red Top would do.

Galahad pulled his ratty backpack off and stuffed his hand in the outside pocket. He pulled out his medical supplies: a small needle, fishing nylon, a rag and some gin. He handed the torn cloth to one of the younger girls standing nearby. "Gets it's wets."

The girl trotted off through the missing door to the one basin in the bathroom.

He slid his backpack on over his shoulders. Not all the women could be trusted. Galahad called to the senior woman in the room. "Old Lady yous help."

A tall, oriental, thirty-year-old woman stepped in front of him. "Huh?"

"Sits on the floors against the wall. Spread yous legs. Whippy, yous put yous head in her lap." When the women were set, he took the wet cloth and gentle cleaned the wound. Galahad was angry the boss would not allow him to use Emily's medical supplies or kits on the women, but he said nothing. It would be disloyal to speak negatively about the boss or the Kalopso.

"Huh?" He pointed to Whippy's thigh.

"Don't knows. I's gots a bad trip an don't remembers noth'n."

Galahad nodded as he threaded the needle with the clear nylon. He laid the rag on the floor. He held the needle and thread over the cloth and poured the booze on the sutures.

"Holds her," he said to the mature oriental woman. "Got ta cleans it." He positioned the rag under the cut and poured the alcohol into the wound.

"Ahhhhhhhhh." Whippy twisted her leg.

"Holds her leg," he said to three larger girls standing around. The assistants knelt down and positioned themselves around Whippy.

"I's got ta sew its." Galahad took a deep breath, held it and punctured her skin. Whippy screamed as the needle pierced her and the thread dragged over her tender flesh.

As he sewed, Galahad tried not to think of the boss's callous attitude toward the orphans. He had begged the boss to let him laserseal his women. He'd tried and tried to convince the boss the girls worked better if they were sealed. The boss did not care. It was the one thing he felt Red Top did wrong — pamper the girls. The boss would not allow them to be pampered further. They were orphans and should be treated as orphans.

When he was finished sewing, Galahad placed the wet rag on Whippy's swollen thigh. He realized the cool rag would not help. It comforted the girls to think he was doing something.

Galahad removed his backpack and stuffed his supplies in the outer pocket. He thought of his empty stomach, then pulled his own meager rations out of the pack and handed them to Whippy. "Yous eat. Helps the pain."

Her eyes filled with tears as she took the priceless gift. She could offer him nothing in return. He wanted to run away to his computer and forget about the club. Instead he patted her back while she ate. If he left before she was done, the bigger girls would take her prize. When she was done, he gladly got up.

"Tries ta sleeps. I's check on yous later." Galahad unlocked the door, left and locked the door behind him. At least he still had Emily. No one could take that away from him.

*   *   *

Apollo slid into the pilot's seat and clipped his belt. His solo simulations scores were excellent. He was considered a top-notch pilot. The next set of scores were from randomly picked pairs. Apollo wanted good simulator scores so he could pick a top NG as a flight partner. Without a good NG, Apollo did not stand a chance at one of the two lieutenant commissions.

Zeus hopped in the seat beside Apollo.

Apollo's heart sank. Great, he thought, I get stuck with Mr. Silence, and he's a lousy gunner. It is bad enough I have to room with the orphan. Apollo sighed, then decided to make the best of things and smiled at his current partner.

Zeus chewed his ring fingernail as he finished his navigational preflight check.

Apollo cleared his throat and attempted to make eye contact.

The orphan turned around and verified the weapons on board.

Apollo "accidentally" flipped on the interior lights.

Zeus plugged in the flight coordinates.

So much for catching Zeus's attention. Exasperated, Apollo launched the mock ship and practiced his inverted roll. He could not wait to get off the simulators and into a real flyer. The adrenaline rush was not the same when there was no risk involved.

"Six enemy aircraft approach'n." Zeus rotated his seat up into the mock gun turret and armed his weapons.

"Any space anomalies or gravitational fields around?"

"Grav field in quadrant D six, Delta six. Theys gonna get there before we's do's. An asteroid fields 'bout fifteen minutes at full speeds in S twenty-three, Sam twenty-three."

"Will we arrive at the asteroid belt before those fighters intercept us?"

"Maybe."

"Maybe is unclear to me. Could you elaborate?" Apollo snarled. How was he supposed to get a good score with an inexperienced person.

"I's might be able ta boosts engines ta goes faster."

Apollo took a deep breath and reminded himself this was just one drill. Everyone had a few low scores. "What would you like me to do?"

"Punch it ta the belt. Tells me's if theys get within five minutes a fire'n range."

Apollo fed the coordinates in and flew at full speed. When Apollo was nervous or excited, he had a tendency to babble. He rattled on and on about the unrealistic odds of OTS drills. "What a ridiculous drill. The enemy aircraft will engage us moments before we. . ."

"Shuts the budge up."

Apollo faked a cough. "I apologize." When he could not stand the suspense anymore, he asked, "What are you attempting to accomplish?"

"Shuts up, I's think'n."

Apollo questioned whether he should have listened to Zeus. The other ships now had a chance to surround them. The asteroid belt was their only hope. Apollo tried to reassure himself that Zeus never offered solutions he could not achieve. If he could not talk to Zeus, he would talk to God.

Apollo prayed until he heard Zeus say, "Increase speed. We's enter the belt at C sixteen, Charlie sixteen."

Apollo complied, amazed the ship was increasing speed. "Charlie sixteen, complying."

They safely entered the belt minutes before the enemy ships were within firing range. "Now at least we have an opportunity for some modicum of success." Apollo maneuvered the ship behind some large floating rocks. "The odds are currently six to one. If we immobilize one or two ships, we should earn an acceptable score. Plus we will receive credit for entering the asteroid belt safely. The increased speed is excellent. You never cease to amaze me."

Zeus had been working on responding to people when they made comments to him. A suggestion Dr. Jones had made. Responding was simple enough. He was amazed at how effective little comments could be. "Aah, glad yous like it."

"Liked it. I loved it! You are the navigator. Where do you want me to go?"

"Yous want coordinates, or yous sight fly'n?"

"I can manage either way. I am less proficient at sight and would prefer to practice that." Between Zeus's talking and successfully entering the belt, Apollo was feeling jovial. "Pick a rock, any rock and I will hide us behind it."

"On screen."

"If, correction, when we engage, do you shoot more accurately from one angle or another? I will attempt to position you as best I can."

"Top, left."

"Top, left. I will attempt to accommodate."

The men destroyed two of the enemy's ships and incapacitated another one. Each time Zeus chose a rock for them to hide behind, it perfectly lined them up to attack one lone ship without alerting the others. After the third time, Apollo was convinced it was not a coincidence.

"I am impressed. . .again. How are you accurately predicting the other ships' locations?"

Zeus was nervous about providing too many details. "Manual says we's can alter ships computers and engines as necessary." He hoped that would satisfy his roommate.

"I surmised you altered our ship's computer and engine. How could that reveal the enemy ships' locations, when the asteroid belt is interfering with our sensors?"

Zeus thought, I'll have to tell him sometime. He carefully considered what to say. He did not want it to sound like he was cheating. "We's on a simulators."

"And the significance of that would be?"

"Same programs run'n this ship is run'n all thems, too."

"Oh." Apollo paused, still confused. "Restated, you hacked your way in?"

"Yeah."

"I must spend more time studying computers," Apollo quipped. "You are quite the prodigy."

Zeus forgot to comment. He was stunned at being called a prodigy. In the orphanage, they were always calling Emily a prodigy. After all she had taught him, he thought maybe she would be pleased he was called that, too.

"Are you currently capable of determining the location of the other three ships?"

"Yeah."

Apollo grinned from ear to ear. "This altercation is turning out to be quite enjoyable. Reveal them to me."

Zeus transferred the information to Apollo's main screen. "Rotate down here." Apollo insisted. Zeus complied, and his seat rotated from the gun turret down to copilot's position.

"Shall we go on the offensive, partner?" Apollo offered Zeus his hand.

Zeus shook it with pride. Having a partner made him feel more a part of OTS's traditions. "I's say we's take this bastard out next." Zeus tapped a blip on the screen.

"I am hesitant because this vessel," Apollo pointed to another ship, "is so close. Can you determine if they are able to communicate with one another?"

Zeus pressed a few buttons. Apollo could not figure out what he was doing or how he was reading the trash on his screen. Zeus trained himself to read everything in computer language. Reading the computer codes was the best way to verify if information was accurate. Many OTS programs read one way, while keeping the true information hidden. By not looking at the reader's screen, but on the program level, Zeus could see hidden text.

After a few minutes, Zeus said, "They's communication is unpredictable. On and off."

Apollo stared at the control panel in front of him. "Therefore, we cannot be certain, up front, if one vessel can alert the other."

"We's can."

Apollo whipped around to look at Zeus. "How?"

"It's a budgin program. Them ships gots ta follow set parameters. Ain't likes real people. Computers is predictable."

"How do we, or more accurately, you, predict what those ships are going to do?" Apollo flicked the screen.

How could Apollo not understand. "We's simulate a fake simulation."

"I simply must spend more time studying computers." Apollo shook his head as he watched his partner running fake simulations. He recognized Zeus was reading computer language, but that was all he could figure out.

"We's fire on the first ship, the second one comes after us."

"Can we destroy the first ship before the second attacks us? I would prefer fighting one on one."

"Ain'ts sure. Depends on how good yous fly, and I's shoots. We's ain't gonna have lots of time."

"Let us speculate about attacking this ship first?" Apollo touched the blip off by itself. "We would receive credit for destroying another ship before we had to engage the other two."

"Takes longer ta circles back, but makes sense."

"A reasonable plan." Apollo maneuvered their ship toward the lone enemy.

In the end, they destroyed five of the six enemy ships before being taken out. They would receive an excellent score for this drill.

Apollo was ecstatic. He leaped out of the flyer and bounded over to walk beside Zeus. "Great job, partner. The perfect, untraceable scam. That was such a superb deception, I am uncertain what you did, and I was present. The brass will never figure it out. You are a fabulous con artist."

The orphan's face flashed red with anger and blended in with his short buzzed hair. Why did he bother to help these bastards? He did not need a high simulation score. He was passing and would get a lousy pilot no matter what he did. Zeus stormed out of the building and fumed as he stood in formation.

* * *

Apollo and Zeus sat on their bunks cleaning their boots. Zeus was contemplating how to hack into OTS's mega mainframe on Tallien. As usual, the room was silent. Apollo dreaded the cold, non-responsive silence of his roommate.

Apollo chipped a piece of dried mud off his boot. This is ridiculous. I cannot live like this. If it were anybody else, I would ask what the problem was. Then it occurred to him, what have I got to lose? Zeus will not hurt me, and he cannot possibly improve on his silent treatment. Asking for an explanation offered no downside. Even anger would be better than total silence. Apollo took a deep breath. "Zeus, may I inquire about something?"

The orphan glared at the interruption. He was trying to concentrate.

Another enthusiastic response. Oh well, here goes nothing. "What may I inquire is the problem?"

No response. Just a blank stare from a confused man.

Apollo felt like a scolded child sentenced to silence. He was determined to clear the air. He decided Zeus must still be angry about his flippant joke the previous night. Zeus had misinterpreted the comment as Apollo accusing him of cheating. Apollo had apologized profusely, but apparently to no avail. He would try again. "I can comprehend your displeasure over my scam and con artist comment."

Zeus dug a pebble out of the bottom of his shoe. He thought they had cleared that up.

"In a way, it was more of a compliment than an insult."

Zeus grimaced. How could Apollo's joke have been a compliment?

Apollo put down his boot. "I was impressed by your expertise in the simulator. It did not occur to me you would misinterpret my comment because I do not perceive you as a cheater. I understand why you would be defensive, and in retrospect, it was a foolish remark. It has become obvious you are honest. You are more than proficient enough in the technical classes to graduate. I was under the impression you were hacking as a favor to me, so I could choose a more qualified NG. And I appreciated what you did. A great deal. I thought it was a sign of the friendship we are developing. That is why I was not cautious when I spoke. I was joking. In my culture, joking is a type of verbal play that friends engage in."

The orphan smiled. The remark did seem like a compliment the way Apollo explained it. Zeus shrugged at Apollo's ability to manipulate words. Apollo was a word hacker. He did to words what Zeus did with computers. Apollo could change people's perceptions and make them hear whatever he wanted them to hear, a verbal hack job. Apollo programmed people to perceive situations according to his own agenda. Zeus would have to be careful, or he might be convinced of things he did not want to be.

Apollo was ready to tear his hair out. Another entire conversation with Zeus, and the orphan had not spoken one word. Exasperated, Apollo threw down his cleaning brush. "I am perplexed. What is the problem?"

"Huh?"

"Why will you not speak to me?"

" 'Bout what?"

"Any topic would be acceptable."

"Huh?" Zeus brushed his boot. He had been communicating.

"Obviously, I have been conversing on the wrong subjects. There are a great deal of cultural differences between us; however, I do not see any barriers that would prevent our friendship. What did you and your previous roommates discuss?"

"No rooms. No roommates."

"When you were in the orphanage, what subjects did you and the children in the next beds speak about?"

"No beds."

"I am confused by your no beds comment." Apollo picked up his boot and brush. "Where did you sleep?"

"Ons the ground, in the mines, ons the street."

"What type of orphanage did you reside in?"

"Don't makes no difference, they's all the same."

Apollo was not normally at a loss for words, but he was now. Apollo considered his responses and decided humor was his best ally. He laughed and shook his head. "When you contemplate our situation, it is rather humorous."

"Huh?"

Apollo tried to acknowledged Zeus's sparse upbringing without embarrassing or pitying the orphan. "The two of us assigned as roommates. We represent an unlikely pair. I am arguably the wealthiest individual in OTS, and you are without a doubt the poorest."

It worked. Zeus was not offended or ashamed, only surprised. "Yous the richest person here?"

"I speculate I am correct."

"Don't acts it."

"Thank you, I will accept that as a compliment. I assure you, there is a large difference between people who pretend to have wealth and those who have achieved it." Apollo wisely changed the subject. "What topics did you and your teammates converse on? You must have spoken to them in practice or at meals."

"I's told not ta goes ta practices. Thems bastards don't let me's in the mess hall. They's let me compete cause I's don't lose."

"I apologize. I am at a loss for words."

Zeus smiled and waited. Apollo was never at a loss for words. Zeus wanted to see if Apollo actually was.

Apollo rubbed the stubble on his chin. "It is no wonder you do not trust us. I realize Richard and his clique have been disrespectful; however, not all the Alphas are cruel, vindictive, prejudiced imbeciles. Zeus?" Apollo looked his roommate in the eye. "I pray you believe me. I do not consider myself superior to you. I am definitely not smarter, faster, or more proficient in computers. Money does not make me, or anybody else, superior, simply more blessed. It is no wonder you do not choose to converse with me. Please trust me, I honestly do not perceive you as inferior."

So much for Apollo having a loss for words.

"Do you believe me?" Apollo asked.

"Yeah." Zeus believed Apollo, because Apollo did not treat him as inferior. The people at OTS continued to baffle to him.

"Then we're friends?"

"Yeah, I's guess." Zeus shrugged.

"For myself, that implies we converse together, assist one another, share our thoughts, complain when we're frustrated, and so forth. Does friendship have a similar connotation for you?"

Zeus nodded as he put down his shiny boot and picked up the muddy one.

"I am baffled about you. Between us, there are so few similar points of reference. Are my topics of discussion perplexing to you, and therefore, responding is confusing, or are you extremely introverted?"

"Mosts the time, I's got no idea what yous talk'n 'bout. Talks a lots and needs a dictionary ta understands yous."

"I apologize. You are not the first individual to state I was verbose and I speak the intellectual English of an Aquaian. Plus to exponentially make matter worse, my mother was extremely particular about how I converse. I was required to use complete sentences, articulate clearly and an entire host of other rules."

"Huh?"

Apollo concentrated on speaking in what his mother termed simple English. "Lots of individuals state I talk too much and I use big, confusing words."

"Yeah." For once, what Apollo said make sense.

"I apologize. If I spoke more clearly and you, therefore, had some idea what I was saying, then would our communication problems be solved or are you extremely introverted?"

"Ain'ts never thoughts 'bout it's. I's talks more in the last few weeks than I's talks in years."

"Great." Apollo dropped his clean boot. "You are the quietest person I have ever encountered, and this is your idea of being outgoing and wordy."

"Ain'ts say'n that. Didn't have no choice if I's could talks. Hads ta be's quiet."

"Then God's purpose for placing me here is apparent."

"Huh?" Zeus tossed his brush on the bed. He was sick and tired of being confused. "I's can't follow noth'n yous say. How yous get ta that?"

"I was contemplating, thinking, we have a great deal to learn from one other." Apollo was conscious not to imply he was superior, but they would work as a team. They had made some progress and he did not want to offend Zeus's ego. "I can assist you in the social stuff, and you can tutor me in the sciences. Deal?" Apollo held out his hand.

"Yeah." Zeus shook Apollo's extended hand.

"If, or more accurately when, I am too verbose," Apollo corrected himself, "talk too much, just inform me."

Zeus nodded.

"If you do not understand, inform me, I will rephrase my sentence."

Zeus nodded again.

"You're not being charged by the word."

"Huh. What's that's mean?"

"It was another poor excuse for a joke. To me, you are acting as if it costs you to speak."

"Oh." Zeus shook his head. It would be nice to have someone translate what all the others were saying.

"I'll wager, it will be significantly easier for you to learn general communication than for me to comprehend astrophysics."

"Goods." It was comforting to know he was not as lost as Apollo was in astrophysics. That would be depressing.

"Advanced communication requires at least a two-word answer."

Zeus was please he followed the joke this time. "Very goods." Zeus counted the words off on his fingers.

Apollo chuckled. "Is there perhaps a sense of humor hidden below that stoic exterior? I'll wager you have been consistently amused as you have observed all us spoiled brats suffering."

Zeus flashed his sparking white teeth as his dimples appeared. "Heck, yeah." He held up one finger for each word.

Apollo was beginning to think this relationship had potential. "All quizzes require three-word answers and, for graduation, it is four."

CHAPTER 17

CMD. YOGGI WENT to the kitchen sink for a glass of water. It was after midnight. She still had plenty of work to do. During the day, much of her time was spent explaining to superiors why the orphan was still in OTS and what she was doing to get rid of him. She thought she would scream if she heard the name Malone one more time. She stepped to the sink. "Water on." Yoggi heard a familiar gurgling and stepped away as water shot out of the faucet.

"This is just what I need." She slammed the cup on the counter. "The basement flooded again." Yoggi stomped over to the basement door and opened it. "Lights on." She peered down at the water sparkling just below the first step. Yoggi slammed the door and went to kitchen computer to look up which unit was on duty. It was the Alphas. She dialed Leiman's code and waited.

Sgt. Leiman's hands fumbled around on the nightstand. She picked up her ComLine and pressed the audio button. "Sgt. Leiman."

"It's Cmd. Yoggi. Sorry to wake you. My basement's flooded again."

"I'll get the Alphas and be right over, Ma'am."

"Thanks. I'll see you in a few minutes. Yoggi out."

"Crap." Leiman banged the ComLine on the nightstand.

* * *

Cmd. Yoggi wandered down to the bottom of the basement steps. Sgt. Leiman waded through the water and saluted.

"Sorry to ruin your evening." Yoggi stared at the glistening liquid centimeters above the lowest step.

"I'm certain it doesn't make yours, either, Ma'am."

"How is it going?" she asked as Zeus walked up and saluted.

"Requests permission ta speaks, Ma'am."

Yoggi rubbed her temples. "Go ahead, Malone."

220

He was annoyed she interrupted his flight simulations. He needed all the extra practice he could get. "Why yous not fix this, Ma'am?"

Sgt. Leiman was ready to kill him. She would again have to go over things not to say to an officer.

"Thank you, Cadet," Yoggi responded sarcastically. "Of course, we've tried to fix it. The plumbers say it the city's problem, and the city says they don't have a problem."

"Whats the city looks at?"

Leiman knew Zeus never questioned or commented on things he did not have personal knowledge of. "Commander, may I?"

She leaned casually on the banister. "Go ahead."

"Malone, do you know how to fix this permanently?"

"I's think I's can, Ma'am."

Yoggi's eyes lit up. Perhaps his years in the sewers had taught him one thing she could benefit from. "What do you need to fix this?" She motioned to the ankle-high water.

"Tools and show me's the intake and outtake, Ma'am."

"Our tools are upstairs in a drawer. Follow me, I'll show you." Yoggi headed up the stairs. Her plumbing problems had progressively gotten worse. She was willing to give even Malone a great deal of leeway if he could fix the flooding permanently. "What do you mean by intake and outtake?"

Zeus followed behind Sgt. Leiman. "Where's water enters and exits the house, Ma'am."

"I have no idea where the water enters or exits the house. I guess I thought they came and left through the same spot. When the plumbers came, they turned something off in the basement. I thought they called it the main valve."

Zeus stopped on the top step. "Yous ain't turns the main valve offs?"

"I haven't done anything," Yoggi defended.

"That's why we's ain't make'n no progress. The water's still on. Where's a budgin valve?"

"Malone, that will be three demerits." Leiman whipped out her pocket InfoPad and noted the punishment.

"Yes, Ma'am."

"What does a valve have to do with you making progress?" Cmd. Yoggi asked.

"Stops any more water froms come'n in, Ma'am."

"Oh." Yoggi squeezed past Leiman and Zeus and descended the stairs. Yoggi stopped on the last stair, rolled up her pants and kicked off her shoes. The water was cool and the floor slick as she waded her way to the far corner. "They did something over here." She waved to the far wall.

Zeus marched over to the main valve and turned it off. "Ma'am, may I's make a suggestion?"

"What?"

"Yous see water ins a basement, turn this ta off." He showed her the manual shut off. "Instead a two meters a water, yous mights only has a few centimeters."

"Are you sure?"

"Yes, Ma'am. I's certain."

"Why wouldn't someone tell me that? Leiman, have you ever heard of this?"

"Yes, Ma'am. I've turned off my water before."

Yoggi put her hands on her hips. "Why didn't you tell me that or turn it off?"

"I'm sorry, Commander. I always assumed you or Mr. Yoggi would have taken care of that."

"Well, I won't forget. Come on, the tools are upstairs." She led them to the kitchen and opened the tool drawer. There were a few screwdrivers, a hammer, some small needle nose piers, a drill, screws, nails, nuts and bolts.

Zeus stared at the useless items in front of him. "Where's the rest of thems?"

"What do you want?"

"Automatic ratchet set? Wrenches? Scrapers? I's use manual sets. What's 'bout. . ."

Cmd. Yoggi shook her head to each item. "This is all I have." She shut the drawer.

"Don't Mr. Yoggi gots noth'n?"

"Mr. Yoggi is an editor. He can barely hammer a nail into the wall. This is all we have."

"Ma'am, if I may offer," Leiman grinned. Bulldog had teased her mercilessly when she had complained about bailing out Zeigler's basement. "I think Sgt. Taylor has most of those items. If you'd like, I'd be happy to call him and have him bring them over."

"Call him up," Yoggi ordered.

Sgt. Leiman pulled out her ComLine and punched in Taylor's extension.

"Taylor," he mumbled.

"Hi, I'm at Cmd. Yoggi's. Malone thinks he can fix her plumbing problem and needs some of your tools." Sgt. Leiman pushed the speaker option on her ComLine. "Tell him what you need."

"Needs a ratchet set, one withs at least a three centimeter, some. . ."

"If you two think I'm letting you get me again, you're wrong. I'm going back to bed."

"Taylor, this is Cmd. Yoggi. You get your tools and your butt over here, NOW! I want this mess fixed."

"Yes, Ma'am," he gulped, jumping out of bed. "I'm on my way, Commander. What tools do you want?"

"Just bring them all." Yoggi snapped the ComLine off. She wanted the mess fixed and to go to bed. If it had been any other cadet, she would have gone to sleep and had the sergeants report in the morning. Malone she needed to observe and evaluate personally. "Malone," she turned to him, "what were the other things you said you needed?"

"Intake and outtake, Ma'am."

"I don't know, what do they look like?"

"Gots a flashlight, Ma'am? I's find thems outside."

"Yes," Yoggi led them to the garage and grabbed her dirt-stained flashlight off the shelf. "Here." She handed it to him, turned on the outside lights and opened the garage door.

"I's be back."

"We'll tag along," Yoggi stated authoritatively. "I want to know where these things are in the future."

The garage opened to the side of the house, and Zeus started searching there. He walked slowly, moving the light around the side of the house, through the yard to the street and then back again. He continued around the front of the house. As the group rounded the corner, a flyer pulled into the driveway.

"That's Taylor." Leiman smirked. "I'll go tell him we're over here." She went over to her boyfriend.

Taylor turned away from her and grabbed his toolbox out of the flyer. "You're enjoying this, aren't you?"

"Every minute." She took the tool harness he handed her. "Come on, they're around this way. Yoggi's tired and mad."

"Thanks, I heard that in her voice." Taylor shut the flyer door.

"See how much fun this is?" Leiman winked and walked in front of him.

Taylor approached Cmd. Yoggi, put down his toolbox and saluted. "Ma'am."

"Sorry to wake you. I can't imagine why you wouldn't have believed Leiman and Malone," Yoggi smirked.

He glanced at Leiman. "Just paranoid, I guess."

"Thanks for coming. Why don't you see if you can help Malone?"

"Yes, Ma'am." Taylor trotted over to Zeus.

"Malone, what are you doing out here?"

"Look'n for the intakes and outtake."

Taylor laughed. "You idiot, around here it's always by the street, usually in the front of the house. Come on. I'm not waiting all night for you to find it."

The women followed the men to the front sidewalk and stopped at two metal plates in the grass.

"I's think it's intake." Zeus handed the light to Taylor. "I's checks it first."

"Why do you think it's intake?" Taylor asked.

"Ain'ts no female crap, TP or crap ins her basement."

Yoggi put her foot on the metal plate. "What do you mean by female crap?"

Leiman quickly answered before her cadet could say anything else insulting. "I think he means feminine hygiene, Ma'am."

"Oh, that actually makes sense." Yoggi removed her foot. "If there's none of that, toilet paper, or other things in the water, and there never is, then the problem must be from the water coming in. I can't decide if I should be pleased or terrified that something Malone said actually made sense to me." The women made eye contact and chuckled. "Proceed."

"Yes, Ma'am." Zeus bent over one of the dingy plates. "Taylor, yous bring a power wrench?"

"Yeah." Taylor put the toolbox down, opened it and handed the wrench to Zeus.

Cmd. Yoggi wanted to understand what was being done in the hopes that after tonight, even if Malone could not fix it, she would be able to explain the problem to the city or a plumber. Yoggi looked at the two identical metal plates in her yard. "How do you know that one is the intake?"

Zeus pointed to the inscription. "Says 'Intake,' Ma'am."

Cmd. Yoggi glanced down as Taylor shined the light on the raised lettering. "You're right, it does. Live and learn."

Zeus removed the bolts, pried the large metal cap off and flipped it onto the grass. A pungent, rotten-egg odor wafted through the air causing Yoggi's eyes to water.

"What is that smell?" She covered her nose and mouth with her hand.

"Sulfur, Ma'am," Zeus answered. "Requests permission ta asks a question."

"Go ahead."

"Taylor, yous gots a headlight?"

"No."

"Needs a light. Yous gots a rocks ta come down with me's?"

"Lead it, Malone," Taylor snapped, then looked to Cmd. Yoggi for approval.

"Go ahead," she nodded.

Zeus grabbed a number of tools and secured them in his belt. "Grabs the ratchets." Zeus crawled down into the hole. "Ma'am?"

"Yes?"

"We's gonna need towels, Commander."

"I'll go get some." Yoggi turned and headed for the house.

Taylor followed Malone down. "I can't see a thing," he objected.

"Feels for the rungs, yous wuss."

Yoggi returned with four towels, and the women watched at the open hole. They could hear the men's boots clank on the rungs.

Sgt. Leiman looked down at the darkness. "Taylor could never refuse a challenge, especially one from Malone."

"Are you sure you're going to be able to control that man?" Yoggi nudged her.

"I'm certain I can't, Ma'am." Leiman chuckled.

"Ow, budgin," they heard Taylor yell. "Something's biting me."

"Leechrat. Crap, Bentley gives yous a shot."

"How do I get it off?"

"Don'ts drop the light, yous wuss. Yous have ta wait."

The women glanced at each other.

"Yous idiot, gets off me's."

"I can't see. Sorry, is that better?"

"Yeah. I's hit bottom, yous gots ta be's close. It's tight, I's guide yous."

"Watch your hands, Malone."

"Budgin yous, Taylor."

"Get the leechrat off."

"I have a feeling they don't realize we can hear them," Yoggi interjected.

"I'll tell them." Leiman leaned over the open hole, hoping to silence Taylor before he destroyed his career.

"No." Yoggi pulled her away. "I want to see how Malone handles things. Don't worry about Taylor. I know how men talk. I have a husband and two brothers. Besides, I ordered Taylor to talk on Malone's level. This is the most enlightening experience I've had with Malone."

"Budgin, it's corroded. I's gots ta clean the bolts. They's a mess. This is gonna takes awhile."

Cmd. Yoggi groaned. It was late, and she wanted to go to bed. She was about to tell Leiman to report to her in the morning when Taylor spoke again.

"How do you know about this kind of stuff? I consider myself pretty handy, and I don't know anything about it. In fact, I don't know anyone who does."

"I's lives and works ins the sewers on Velcron. Moves a light right, little more, OK."

"What were you doing living in the sewers?"

"First I's try'n ta gets out. Then we's live'n there cause it's safer than the streets. Rats who bite yous are lots smaller and more predictable down here."

"There's an orphan community in the sewers?"

"Nope, we's on my own."

"We? Who were you down there with?"

"A friend."

"Of the female persuasion?"

"Ain't likes that."

"What did you two do down in a sewer?"

"Survive."

"Why'ja quit living there?"

"Gots tired of not see'n the sun, smell'n fresh air."

"It's no wonder a night in the crap hole didn't phase you. It felt like home."

"Ain't gots no home."

"Where did your friend go?"

"Thinks she's deads."

"Sorry. . .ouch, something just ate off half my arm."

"It bleed'n?"

"Yeah, I think a little."

"Give me's the light. Looks like yous met a sewer eel. Tries ta stop the bleed'n. Attracts leechrats."

"Did you bring a first aid pack down?"

"Heck, no. Time for yous ta meet my friends, anyway. Holds the light, I's try ta hurry."

Cmd. Yoggi decided not to go to bed. She was learning too much about her orphan cadet. After the men were silent for a number of minutes, she faced Leiman. "I think we're going to be here awhile. I'll go get a couple chairs."

Cmd. Yoggi returned with two lawn chairs, drinks and popcorn. "What are they talking about now?"

"Some maxor fight." Leiman opened one chair and offered it to her commander.

"Oh, then I didn't miss anything." Yoggi put her drink in the holder on her chair. "I called Dr. Bentley to come over. I have a feeling she'll be needed."

Leiman sat, and Yoggi handed her a soda. "Every time Taylor gets near Malone, he ends up at Bentley's. Broken ribs, laser sealing, black eyes. That kid is a menace."

"Not to mention pepper spray, leechrat bites and eels," Cmd. Yoggi added. "Does it bother you they understand each other so well?"

"It makes me a little nervous. I won't miss Malone, that's for sure."

Fifteen minutes later, Dr. Bentley strolled up and saw Yoggi and Leiman lounging in the chairs, eating and drinking. "You two certainly appear to be working hard."

Leiman stood and offered her chair to the doctor.

"Hi, Doc, have a seat," Cmd. Yoggi chirped. She had gotten her second wind. "There's another chair in the garage," she told the sergeant. "Why don't you grab the Doc a drink?"

"Yes, Ma'am." Leiman headed to the garage.

Dr. Bentley sat. "What are you two doing out here?"

"Listening to Malone and Taylor." Yoggi tossed a kernel of popcorn near the open hole. "And when that's not entertaining, getting to know Leiman better."

"Malone," they heard from the dark hole, "why didn't you just ask Yoggi where the intake and outtake were?"

"I's did. She don't even knows ta turns off the water main."

Taylor laughed. "No wonder she always has more water than everyone else; she's been leaving it on. Crap, that's funny."

"She don't seems that stupid."

"Think about it. Is it smart or dumb not to know? She's got the money and rank. Why should she bother? Whenever she has a problem, she calls up a couple of us grunts and we get stuck down in this pit. If I had the rank, I'd send some other poor slob down in this crap hole, too."

"Ain'ts never thoughts 'bout it like that."

Bentley accepted the drink from Sgt. Leiman. "You really never turned off your water?"

"Does everybody know about this but me? You knew about it, too?"

The doctor nodded. Yoggi tossed a piece of popcorn at her. The kernel bounced off Bentley's knee and hopped on Leiman's seat just as she sat down.

"Of course, when my basement started to flood, I found the water main and turned it off. I can't do much, but that's easy."

"Ow, crap. I got bitten again," Taylor complained. "Why'd you tell Yoggi I had the tools?"

"I's don't. Leiman did."

"Man, that woman has a mischievous streak. She hates this duty. I've teased her about having to drag her butt outa bed and bail out basements. Now she's got Yoggi dragging me out of bed and sending me into the sewers. And with you, no less."

Leiman lowered her head, hoping the men would be finished soon.

"Yous whipped," they heard Zeus say.

"And proud of it," Taylor answered.

"Well, that's sweet," Bentley interjected.

228

"Laugh all you want," Taylor insisted. "It'll be your turn some day."

"Not me's, Taylor."

"That's what I used to say. I was so certain that I'd never settle down, I recorded a bachelor creed and gave it to my brother as a guarantee. He's going to roast me when he finds out how serious I am with Sues. The deal was, if I ever got serious, he got to show the disk to my girl. Susan will kill me. I'm not sure how to prepare her for some of the things I've said in it. I was a first-class jerk to women."

"How yous know yous brother still gots the disk?"

"Got it? He says he watches it whenever he needs a good laugh. He's been waiting for years to show that disk."

"What's ons it?"

"A few of my past dating rules."

"What they's?"

"Rule one is if a woman doesn't respond to your advances quickly, find another woman. Wooing is too much work, costs money, and there are plenty of willing ones out there. And that's about the nicest one."

Dr. Bentley swatted Leiman's arm. "I guess you and Taylor will be having a long conversation when you get through here."

"Yous idiot, why yous record it?" Zeus questioned.

"I was convinced I'd never fall in love. I've totally broken every one of my rules with Sues. The first night I met her, she belted me."

"Crap."

"A right cross to the jaw. It was a great a hit, too. My jaw hurt for weeks."

Leiman fidgeted in her seat, wondering how much worse things could get.

"I knew about the right cross," Yoggi interjected. "In fact, I thought about giving you a commendation for it."

"Taylor wasn't the only one I belted that night," Leiman bragged. "There were a few others involved."

"Yous idiot, that's what impressed yous? If I's look'n for a woman, it a be ta rock, not fights."

"I was impressed with Sues before she belted me. It took me forever to get her to date me after that. I had to bribe another sergeant to let me sit by her on a transport last summer."

Leiman squeezed the arms on her lawn chair. "I didn't know about that or the disk."

"Yes, Taylor's in for a long talk tonight," Dr. Bentley said.

"What yous do ta gets her mads? I's done withs this one. Moves the light down."

"Is that where you want it?"

"Yeah."

"It's tradition that new sergeants are taken out and gotten drunk. We were out drinking and playing pool. By the end of the night, I was completely plastered. In my drunken state, a couple of the guys convinced me Sues was an easy mark."

"Uh oh."

"Yeah, I propositioned her, and bam, she nailed me in the jaw. . .Quit laughing, you stick. . .Aw, crap, I deserved it."

"What's a great lady like her wants with yous?"

"I'm not like that anymore. There's not a woman alive I'd risk losing Sues over. She's too incredible. Believe it or not, that stuff doesn't even appeal to me anymore."

"Yous whipped bads."

"See, he does love you," Yoggi commented. "I know it's been a long night, Sergeant, but I've learned a great deal about Malone. I appreciate your patience."

"And I appreciate the entertainment," Bentley joked. "I can't wait until someone asks me, 'what did you do last night?' I can honestly answer, 'I got called in the middle of the night to go sit on lawn chairs in Cmd. Yoggi's yard, drink pop and eat popcorn while listening to Taylor and Malone down in a sewer discussing women. Thanks for calling me over, I wouldn't have missed this for anything."

"I'm glad you're enjoying yourself." Cmd. Yoggi drummed her fingers. "I just wish they'd finish."

"That's the lasts one." Zeus stated.

"Wow, Sgt. Leiman," Bentley exclaimed, "You certainly have taught that boy to follow orders."

"He's been a challenge," Leiman replied.

"Which one?" Yoggi asked.

"Both!" Leiman chuckled.

"Does Malone talk to you like this?" Yoggi pointed to the hole.

"No, never, and certainly not for this long," Leiman answered. "He usually says only what he has to and then shuts up. Taylor says they joke some, but I don't think he talks to Taylor this much, either. My guess is it's mostly because they're stuck down there in the dark without much else to do."

"Well, isn't that the only way to get men to talk?" Dr. Bentley interjected.

The women laughed. "You mean discussing the ball game doesn't count as an intimate conversation?" Yoggi asked.

"Up, up, yous idiot," they heard Malone yelling.

Moments later, Taylor's mud-streaked head appeared. He leaped out of the hole. Three leechrats had their teeth locked onto his flesh. Sgt. Leiman jumped up and attempted to pull the largest leechrat off his back.

"Ouch, that hurts." Taylor jerked away.

Leiman put both hands around the body of the rodent and pulled hard. "Hold still; I can't get a good grip."

Meanwhile, Zeus popped out of the hole and rolled in the grass. Four leechrats scampered in every direction. He saw Leiman trying to remove the leechrat from Taylor's back and Taylor battling one on the front of his thigh. Neither person was having any success. The more they squeezed and pulled at the frightened animals, the tighter the leechrats clamped their teeth.

Zeus grabbed one of the towels, twisted it in the air and yelled, "Stand back, Leiman!" As soon as she was clear, Zeus snapped the towel, hitting the leechrat on the spine. The leechrat instantly let go and turned to bite the towel. The women looked bewildered.

"Snap reflex." Zeus cracked the towel at the rodent hanging onto Taylor's shoulder. It too turned to bite, fell and scampered off.

"Turn around." Zeus twisted the towel again.

Taylor pivoted. "Just watch where you're hitting."

Zeus cracked the towel. "Ain'ts noth'n else big 'nough ta hits."

Once Taylor was rodent-free, Zeus thumped the leechrat on his ankle.

Taylor picked up the towel and grinned, "My turn." He snapped at the leechrat on the orphan's shoulder.

Dr. Bentley hated rodents, especially ugly, pucker-lipped leechrats. She had picked her feet up off the ground the moment the first ones appeared. She cowered in the lawn chair. "Get those things away from me." She pointed to two fat rats smelling the grass, their thick tails twisting in the lawn.

Zeus pulled out his knife and threw it at the animal closest to Dr. Bentley. She screamed as the knife hit the target. The orphan grabbed the injured rodent and cracked its neck. He repeated the procedure for the remaining leechrats in her view.

"Good job, Malone," Sgt. Leiman said.

Yoggi and Taylor were pleased to see the orphan hunter in action. Zeus killed the last remaining rodent and tossed it into the pile with the others.

"I think it's safe now, Doctor," Sgt. Leiman said.

Dr. Bentley was hesitant to leave her safe perch and motioned to the pile of dead animals. "I don't want to look at those."

"Yes, Ma'am." Zeus picked up a towel and covered the carcasses.

"Not with my good towel." Cmd. Yoggi protested.

"Yes, Ma'am." Zeus never understood women's reactions to things. He pulled the towel off in one clean jerk. He picked up two rats in each hand and headed for the open hole.

"Not in there; that's my water," Cmd. Yoggi said.

"Yes, Ma'am." Since the rodents obviously came from the sewer, what difference did it make. As usual, Zeus was confused by other's comments. In desperation, he removed his shirt. As he leaned over to cover the carcasses, the others got a clear view of a large chewed-out section of his shoulder.

Dr. Bentley instantly changed from helpless female to doctor. "Come over here and let me have a look at that."

"Huh?"

"Your shoulder," Bentley stated

Zeus glanced around to see a gnawed hole with blood dripping from it. "Guess one gots a last meal. I's fine." He shrugged.

"Malone," the women exclaimed in stereo.

Zeus sat beside the doctor and stated the canned, "Yes, Ma'am."

The doctor could not see in the moonlight. "Come over to the house and let me get a better look. You'll be next, Taylor."

"Yes, Ma'am."

Cmd. Yoggi followed them to the garage. "What did you find out?"

"Commander, I's needs ta asks some questions firsts."

"Go ahead."

Zeus stood under the light. "Any a yous ever get the runs?"

"Yes," Cmd. Yoggi answered confused.

"Turn around and sit down," Dr. Bentley ordered.

Zeus complied. "Ever be's checks for parasites?"

"I've checked her and dozens of others on base for parasites," Bentley interjected.

"All overs the base?"

"What do you mean all over? Lots of people have come to me." Dr. Bentley swabbed the wound.

"Do's they's lives in one area?"

"No, in fact, some of those complaining don't even live on base."

"Yous ever done a biopsy or sent samples ta Triker Labs?"

"Triker Labs?" Dr. Bentley questioned.

"Yeah, they's specialize in detect'n insidious organisms."

"I'm aware of what they do." Dr. Bentley adjusted the laser sealer.

Yoggi stepped in front of her cadet. "Wait a minute. Are you saying I may have parasites from my water?"

"Yes, Ma'am. How long yous had the runs?"

"It started before last term. A year, maybe a year and a half. It seems to come and go. I have problems, then it just clears up."

"Don't clears up. Yous goes inta the dormant cycle. Get'n more frequent?"

Yoggi blocked the light with her hand. "Yes. I think I'm getting the picture. There shouldn't be leechrats running through my clean water."

"No, Ma'am."

"Leechrats carry dozens of parasites," Dr. Bentley said.

"I thought all the water pipes were sealed so nothing could get in except through the sanitation plant."

"Should be's."

"So how are the rodents and eels getting in?"

"Cracks or breaks in pipes. If they's ain'ts fixed, then lots a animals goes ins."

"Good work, Cadet," Yoggi said. "Sgt. Leiman, delete his demerits from earlier."

"Thank yous, Ma'am." Zeus was bursting with pride. Demerits could only be removed by an officer and it rarely happened. Zeus had never had a strike against him deleted anywhere for anything. The people at OTS continued to baffle him.

Zeus had been given more than his share of demerits by numerous officers. Leiman gladly whipped out her InfoPad and deleted the demerits. "Good job, Malone."

"You learned we have animals in the pipes and they are giving us parasites. Did you find out anything else."

"Anybody complain'n of be'n lightheaded, trouble wak'n up, mood shifts?"

"Yes, my daughter, Sheila." Yoggi had a sinking feeling in the pit of her stomach.

Zeus looked at the intake hole and followed the grass to the house. "She's sleep some place over theres?" He pointed to the corner of the house above the outside pipes.

"Yes, how did you know that?"

"First floor?" Zeus asked.

"Yes."

"Yous ever take her ta Bentley?"

"Yes, a number of times." Yoggi towered over the seated cadet. "Malone, what's wrong with Sheila?"

"Gots a parasite, plus probably gots carbon monoxide or methane gas exposure." Zeus twitched as the doctor bandaged his shoulder. "Maybes all threes, Ma'am."

"What?" both Yoggi and Bentley yelled.

"I's use ta it. Took me's awhile ta note the rush."

"Is that why my head feels weird?" Taylor asked. "I thought I was getting a headache from smelling that crap down there."

"Why would Sheila be exposed to carbon monoxide or methane?" Dr. Bentley turned Zeus so his arm was facing the light.

"Chemicals used ta purify the water and keeps the sewers clean ain't right. Byproducts can be carbon monoxide. Methane's produced by decay'n organic matter."

"I've checked her blood; there was no evidence of either."

"Oxygen content ons this planets is high, plus CO and CH four dissipates fast when exposed ta oxygen."

"That's true," Dr. Bentley stated.

"If it's coming from the sewer, why wouldn't it be worse after she has been in the bathroom or after taking a shower?" Cmd. Yoggi inquired.

"Basic physics, Ma'am. Each physical space can only holds so

234

much; don't matters if it's liquid, solid or gas. At night, when yous pipes is empty of water, they's fill with gas. Yous wake up, turns on the water, and CO or CH four is replaced by H two 0. Plus, more stationary the water, faster gases builds up."

Bentley suctioned the animal saliva out of the orphan's arm. "So because she's over the main pipe, Sheila is being more affected than the others in the house?"

"Right, Doc." Zeus answered.

"I'll check Sheila after I'm through with these two."

"Waters been run'n all night, and now the mains off."

"Oh, that's right. I'll have a monitor hooked up tomorrow," Dr. Bentley said to Cmd. Yoggi.

"She's had terrible diarrhea. Why haven't you detected the parasites?"

"It's because, like Malone said, Triker labs is one of the few places that can detect parasites within the cells. We're usually looking for extracellular organisms. A few insidious ones deprive their hosts from inside the cells. Some actually mimic cell walls. Only the most advanced and sophisticated equipment can detect these things."

"I want Sheila admitted tonight."

"I'll take her over to the infirmary as soon as I'm done." Dr. Bentley finished Zeus's left arm and moved to his right.

"Same water supply," Zeus snarled, frustrated they did not understand the severity of the problem.

"Oh, I guess it would be," Yoggi said. "Have her admitted to Lathen Medical Center off base."

"Sames budgin water supply," Zeus yelled in frustration.

Leiman's temples bulged. "Drop it, Malone." No cadet of hers was going to cuss at the commander of the base or in that tone.

Zeus immediately complied. Sgt. Leiman got down in the grass and yelled at her pupil about respecting senior officers.

Dr. Bentley tossed her medical scanner into the box. "Great, so much for the laser seal on his arms."

Sgt. Leiman stood. "Malone, you just keep counting."

"Yes, Ma'am. Thirty-three, thirty-four. . ."

"Long night?" Yoggi patted Leiman's shoulder.

"Yes, Ma'am."

Dr. Bentley pointed to Zeus. "You know, he's also been affected by the gas. It gives people headaches and distorts their judgment."

"I don't care how he feels, Doctor. No cadet of mine speaks to a superior officer that way, especially the commander of the base."

Dr. Bentley rolled her eyes.

"Doctor, I want Sheila off this planet and admitted somewhere tonight."

"I'll take care of her, Commander." The doctor cleaned Taylor's bloody arm. "She'll be fine now that we know what to look for."

Zeus began to slow down. Leiman let him struggle for another ten, hoping he would not appear to be seething with anger when he was done. "Get up, Malone."

Zeus stood and hung his head. "I's sorry, Commander."

"It amazes me how much you sergeants indoctrinate these kids." Bentley waved the laser sealer over Taylor's arm.

"The good ones do." Yoggi smiled at Leiman.

"Thank you, Commander."

"Malone?" Cmd. Yoggi crossed her arms. "How do you know it's the same water supply at Lathen Med?"

"Most planets got purify'n plants ons each continent. Ain'ts no reasons for the Corps ta haves a separate supply."

"You mean everyone on the continent would be affected?"

"Ain'ts positive. Gots ta checks the blueprints and trace the source."

"What do you think would cause such widespread problems?" Yoggi asked.

Zeus pondered how to explain the situations without using any forbidden words in front of the commander. After a long pause, he responded. "Ain'ts no way the sewers gots this bad unless some bastards ain't do'n theys jobs. All them leechrats down there's was alive. Means somebody ain't flood'n the system with pesticides. They's suppose ta clean out the dead crap, too. Choppers and sieves probably gots overloaded and brokes. That's why's the methane gas is build'n ups, cause all the decay'n crap is stay'n in the sewers. Someone's skim'n the supplies and sell'n thems for profit."

Yoggi scratched her head. "So why hasn't the water department been able to figure this out?"

"Cause they's the ones skim'n, Ma'am."

"This makes sense so far. Now that you've identified the problem, how do we fix it before anyone else gets sick?"

"Ain'ts that simple, Ma'am."

"I don't care. I want this fixed immediately."

"Ma'am, yous gots a big problem here."

"We have a big problem. Remember, you live here, too."

"Commander, I's use ta be'n bud. . ." Zeus saw Leiman's eyes flash and stopped abruptly.

"How do we fix it?" Yoggi snapped.

"First gots ta gets a copy of the sewage system for the whole region."

Yoggi nodded. "Do I get that from the water department?"

"They's ain't likely ta gives it ta yous, since one or more of thems is the skimmer."

"Good point. They haven't exactly been helpful in the past." Yoggi stared at a drop of Zeus's blood in the grass. "Well, where does that leave us?"

Zeus hated to offer his services. He thought of Emily and mumbled, "Hack'n."

She lifted her head. "Can you get in?"

"Probably." Zeus sighed. He might as well be signing his own discharge.

"What do you need?"

"Computer and time."

"Get on it, Malone."

"Yes, Ma'am."

"Do you want Capt. O'Donnell's help?"

"No offense, Ma'am. Capt. O'Donnell's a brilliant computer scientist, but she's ain't no hacker."

Yoggi smirked. "An oversight, I'm sure. You're dismissed. Hit the showers, then go to the computer lab. Report to me the minute you've got something."

"Yes, Commander." Zeus saluted.

CHAPTER 18

AFTER HIS SHOWER, Zeus raced to the computer lab. He was thrilled to be testing his renaissance theory uninterrupted. He was mesmerized as he quickly and easily accessed the sanitation department's protected files. He could hardly sit still it was so invigorating to combine Capt. O'Donnell's rebounding-waves work, his own knowledge and the power of the mega mainframe. What used to take him months or years to access appeared on his screen in a matter of hours, and this was his first complete attempt. Once he perfected the system, the time needed to access protected information would be negligible.

Zeus sifted through the information, located the skimmers and called his sergeant.

"Leiman," she answered, groggy.

"Malone, Ma'am. I's found them skimmers. Ain'ts certain if I's should wakes Cmd. Yoggi or wait 'til morn'n."

"What time is it?"

"Oh four, twenty."

"None of us have had much shut-eye. Do you have any idea who we go to get this mess fixed?"

"They's a group of thems in it tagether. They's all high up, and I's think those below 'em ain't gots the authority ta approve a cleanup."

"Great. That's not what Yoggi wants to hear. See if you can figure out how we can get things fixed. Who do we need to go to? What do we need to do? Remember, if you can, it's always wise to report good news to your company commander."

"Yes, Ma'am."

"I'll check on you before our morning drill at oh five- thirty. Leiman out."

Zeus chewed his fingernails while he considered how to locate the information he needed. His renaissance theory allowed him to access and read anything he could locate, but he still had to locate the renaissance waves he wanted. He programmed the computer to follow up on all transmissions and files associated with the five skimmers. He set the parameters for the files he wanted flagged and waited for the computer to sift through the information.

While he waited, his thoughts wandered to the sewers. He had enjoyed working with Sgt. Taylor, but the memories of Emily and the sewers on Velcron plagued his mind. Tonight the sulfuric smells made him cringe. The stench had never bothered him before. Now they smelled like fear and death, Emily's fear and death. The leechrats had never bothered him, either. He had always viewed them as a blessing. Frequently, leechrats were the only meals he could count on. Bentley's paranoid response reminded him of Emily and how she panicked when rats or insects touched her. On Velcron, Zeus had viewed the darkness as a friend who hid him from his enemies. Tonight the darkness felt like a wet blanket smothering him with painful memories.

He was relieved when the computer stated it had found numerous files within the stated parameters. He checked the facts and was disheartened by the information.

Zeus checked the time; Sgt. Leiman would be arriving soon. He would have to decide quickly where his loyalties were and what to do. On the one hand, he had the knowledge and experience to fix the water problem. However, he could not fix the sewers without using a number of his Kalopso skills. He was already concerned his hacking abilities would be interpreted as an admission of previous guilt. The Corps was looking for reasons to discharge him; flaunting well-known network techniques did not seem prudent. On the other hand, he did not want to disappoint his superiors. They were counting on his expertise to help an entire continent of people sick from drinking polluted water. He thought of the thousands of helpless women and children being affected. As always, he was trapped by circumstances beyond his control. To not help would go against his conscience and everything Emily had taught him. To help would probably give OTS the reasons they needed to discharge him. He bit hard on his thumbnail and spit it out. Cmd. Yoggi opened the door. Zeus stood and saluted his superior.

"At ease. Leiman left me a message; you were going to report to her at oh five-thirty. I wanted to hear your report first hand. What did you find out?"

"Thems skimmers is the top five at the sanitation plant. Director a sanitation and his four department heads."

"So because all the departments are involved, no one's ever going to look into our complaints?"

"Yes, Ma'am."

"What needs to be done to clean up our water?"

Leiman and Taylor entered and saluted.

"Ma'am," Taylor waited for her nod to continue, "if you'd prefer me to leave."

"No, I'm glad you're here. You seem to understand Malone better than anyone."

"Yes, Ma'am."

"Malone was just starting to tell me what we needed to do to clean up our water. Go ahead."

"Yes, Ma'am. Gots ta first flood the system withs a high concentration of chemicals and pesticides. Gots ta shuts off all the continent's water ta do thats cause at the levels we's talk'n, it's poisonous."

Yoggi listened as she stared at the computer code jumble on one of the screens. She wanted some insight into both Malone and the sewers. With any luck, she would have received enough information to solve both problems. "Where can we get the chemicals and pesticides?"

"They's controlled substances. Gots ta have legislative approval or gets 'em ons the black market."

"Is there currently enough of those available at the sanitation plant?"

"Won't be 'nough chemicals after taday. They's gots a deals go'n down tomorrow."

"How soon before they or we could get another shipment?"

"Ain'ts certain, Ma'am."

"Give me a range. One week? Two? What are we talking about?"

"Ain'ts certain. If I's guess, few months. Gots ta gets approval, then gets the chemicals made, then they's gots ta be delivered, and thens flood the system."

"You're right, that doesn't sound like it would take a few days."

Yoggi paced momentarily thinking. She would have to rely on her subordinates for a solution. It was one of her greatest strengths as a leader. She did not allow her ego to stop her from taking advice. She had learned, those who perform the jobs are often more qualified to give workable solutions than those who order the tasks to be done. "I'm in an area where I have no expertise. I am open to suggestions."

Zeus chewed his fingers to the bone. He felt obligated to help the innocent victims who might be ill or die from parasites or toxic gases before the bureaucracy got around to solving the problem. He racked his brain for a way to clean up the continent's water without incriminating himself further.

"Can we 'borrow' the chemicals we need before they're sold on the black market?" Sgt. Taylor suggested. "It wouldn't really be stealing, since we want to use them for the purpose they were originally bought."

"Won't do's no goods without be'n able ta shut downs the system ta do's the flood'n. Then yous still gots ta get all the crap cleaned outs and repair the broken choppers and sieves. Whole systems gonna needs work. Gonna take time and money."

"Who can shut down the system?" Yoggi asked.

"I's check. Here's only the director of sanitation."

"And since he's profiting from not doing it, he's not likely to approve it."

"Yes, Ma'am."

"My guess is if we confront him, he'll skip town long before our problem is fixed, and he probably wouldn't do the first flooding, either."

"Yes, Ma'am."

"How much would it cost for the Corps to fix this ourselves?"

"Ain'ts certain, Ma'am."

"Hundreds? Thousands? Millions? Guess."

Zeus did a few calculations in his mind. "Whole continent's affected. Millions, Ma'am."

"I certainly don't have that in the budget."

Zeus lowered his head. He had probably said too much already.

Sgt. Leiman watched as her cadet fidgeted. That was not like him. "Malone, do you know how to get around the system and start the repairs?"

Zeus paused. He wished she had not asked.

"Malone, out with it."

"Yes, Ma'am." Zeus swallowed hard and thought of Emily. In the long run, it would not matter. They intended to kick him out anyway. "Ain'ts exactly Corps methods."

Yoggi crossed her arms. "I'm willing to be flexible."

"Redirects the funds them skimmers been steal'n for the last couple a years before they's leaves. Use thems funds ta pay for the repairs. And likes Taylor says, we's use the chemicals ins a warehouse. Gots ta gets them before thems bastards sells tamorrow."

"That seems fair to me," Cmd. Yoggi stated. "What about shutting down the system and all that other stuff?"

"Gets director of sanitation ta approve them things befores he leaves and gives authority ta some that ain'ts skim'n."

Leiman eyebrows met. "Can you do those things?"

"Yes, Ma'am. Thinks I's can."

Yoggi clapped her hands behind her and paced for a moment. "How long would it take you to find and redirect the embezzled funds?"

"I's already finds 'em and gots 'em tagged, Ma'am. Only gots ta sets up an account and makes the transfer."

A smile spread across Yoggi's face. "Really?" She was impressed and concerned. Considering how quickly he had accessed the funds, it was unrealistic that the orphan had never done it before.

"How much have you found?" Leiman asked.

"Theys a bunch of accounts total'n 'bout two point three million drayka."

Yoggi put her hand on her head. "Did you say two point three million?"

"Yes, Ma'am."

"Wow!" Taylor exclaimed.

"That would certainly help pay for the mess they've created. It is going to take a great deal of money to supply water to an entire continent while this is corrected. Plus all the other things you stated. What do you propose we do to convince the director to cooperate?"

"Ain't likes no negotiation Maj. Patterson teaches."

Taylor instantly understood. "Is this the kind of negotiation you and the Little Lady do together?"

"Yeah," Zeus nodded to his friend.

Taylor grinned. "Commander, request permission to assist Malone in the negotiations."

"After listening to you two last night, I'm certain I'm going to regret this, but permission granted. Get a working plan on my desk in an hour. We will want to strike today, before our chemicals are sold."

*   *   *

Cmd. Yoggi and Sgt. Leiman were parked in a flyer outside the sanitation director's office. The commander was uncomfortable allowing Malone off base with permission to negotiate as he saw fit. Zeus had assured her his methods were extremely effective. She had ordered him not to hurt anyone.

Yoggi checked her watch for the umpteenth time. "What could be taking so long? I hate the idea of giving Malone free rein."

"Taylor will keep him in line," Leiman said, trying to convince herself.

"After hearing them last night, that's not very comforting."

"Yes, Ma'am. I see your point."

Zeus and Taylor jumped into the flyer. "Gets us outs a here," Zeus yelled. Leiman swiveled her seat and jerked the flyer into motion. The men stumbled before taking their seats.

"How did it go?" Yoggi asked.

"Malone got everything we wanted," Taylor proclaimed. "He has very effective negotiation skills. He and the Little Lady."

Yoggi observed her cadet from head to toe. She was relieved he appeared uninjured. She did not want to have to explain that to her superiors. She frowned at Zeus's trousers. "How did your pants get wet?"

"Idiot tooks a leak on me's."

"You let him take off his pants?"

"I's cuts 'em off."

"I'm afraid to ask, but start at the beginning."

"Malone was amazing!" Taylor unhooked his pack and slipped it off. "I asked the guy nicely for permission to use the clean-up supplies. He said he would look into things, and the sanitation department would fix any problems they found. That's when Malone yanks him out of his chair, picks him up and throws him against the wall. Malone lifts the director up by his neck and cuts his belt, pants and skivvies until they drop to the floor. Then he gives the guy an intimate introduction to the Little Lady."

"And that's when he took a leak?"

"No, Ma'am. He took a leak when Malone demonstrated how easy it was to castrate someone. When the guy saw himself bleeding. . ."

Yoggi whipped her head toward Zeus. "Malone, you didn't?!"

243

"I's barely nicks him, just scare'n hims." Zeus removed his back-pack. "I's make sure I's hit a vein, so he sees lots of blood."

Taylor squeezed his legs together. "I'm a little nervous that a friend of mine has performed such delicate surgery."

"Ain'ts never done it, only sees it, and it ain'ts delicate."

Leiman swiveled her chair to see her cadet. "So, did it work?"

"Yes, Ma'am," Zeus bragged.

"Once the guy's bladder was empty, he was extremely coopera-tive," Taylor stated. "The guy babbled like a baby. He couldn't ap-prove the supplies fast enough."

"I can see why you didn't think I should be present." Yoggi cov-ered her mouth and controlled her laughter. "OK, so where are we at?"

"I's had the director order toxic levels of chemicals flushed through the system and our man assigned complete authority. Now yous got ta do yous part."

"Good." Yoggi pulled out her ComLine and began coordinating the rest of the plan. She finished giving her initial orders as they flew onto base. She tucked her ComLine into her belt and updated her people. "Three of the skimmers have already been apprehended. The other two will be soon. The Corps is setting up temporary water sources, and the cleanup will be started as soon as those are in place."

"Ma'am?" Leiman asked.

"Go ahead."

"Do you want me to take you to HQ?"

"No, drop Malone at the computer lab." Yoggi turned to Zeus. "Make certain those funds are in the account we setup."

"Yes, Ma'am."

Yoggi pointed to Zeus and Taylor. "You two did a good job. I think I'll leave it to the public's imagination as to how you convinced the sanitation director to cooperate. And we need to consider that infor-mation classified. Understood?"

"Yes, Ma'am," they answered.

The flyer jerked to a halt in front of the lab. Cmd. Yoggi opened the flyer door. "Malone, dismissed." Zeus saluted her and got out. She shut the door and waited a moment. "Taylor, what do you think of Malone?"

"I like him. He's a good guy." Taylor scratched his neck. "But his methods and techniques have network written all over them."

"You think he's a member of the Kalopso?"

"It's possible." Taylor slid in his seat as the flyer lurched forward. "I can't see how he learned both the hacking and the fighting without their help."

"Could he be affiliated without being a member?"

"I don't know. From what I learned in jail, members are supposed to be ruthless. Malone doesn't fight like that. He doesn't seem to enjoy inflicting pain. Even so, I'm surprised he helped us with this. No matter how you look at it, it seems to incriminate him."

"I'm a little perplexed about that myself." Yoggi drummed her fingers on the arm of the chair. "We can only speculate. I wonder if he's in over his head and wants to get out. He could see us as his only chance."

"That makes sense, except he's not asking for help."

"Not yet. Keep talking to him like you did last night. See if you can get any more information out of him. Allude to the fact that we'd be willing to assist him, if he wants out."

"I'll do my best."

"You're doing a fine job. Keep it up."

"Yes, Ma'am. Thank you, Ma'am."

*　　*　　*

"Emily." Galahad burst through the door. "I's gets ta proves my's self while yous at yous contest!"

"Why can't you come with me?" Emily begged. She pulled her hair and twisted it nervously.

"Ain'ts got no ID. Boss says I's get taken away if I's leave. I's leave I's not see yous again."

"I don't want to go with the director. She's mean to me." Emily ran over, buried her head in his chest and cried.

Kindness had not produced the desired results from the old director, so the new director used fear and intimidation. She had made it clear, Galahad would pay for Emily's failure with a level-four fate worse than death, and Emily would be forced to watch. The thought of watching someone else she loved being tortured reminded her of the terrifying memories of her family's deaths. "But what if I lose? They'll hurt you, too."

"Yous not lose. Yous gots best idea."

"I'm scared," she muffled into his torn shirt. "What if I forget my presentation?"

"Looks at yous notes." He patted her reassuringly. "Ain'ts judge'n yous speech. They's want yous ideas."

"What if the model breaks or doesn't work? You won't be there to fix it."

"Director helps yous."

"She doesn't like me." Emily clutched her stomach and ran to the sink.

"Ain'ts got ta like yous. Boss make her pays if yous loose. She's gots ta help yous win." Galahad cupped his hands around her long soft hair and pulled it out of the basin. He loosely knotted the silky strands and held them in place.

"I'm afraid of her." Emily choked on the burning acid in her throat.

"I's asks the boss ta tell her yous not do's good when she's yells." He stroked her hair as she vomited. Galahad whiffed the putrid smell. He could not wait for this contest to be over. Emily was beside herself. She could no longer sleep at night or keep her food down during the day. The director was giving her intravenous supplements daily and sleeping aids at night.

"I don't want you to get hurt," she sobbed into the sink.

"I's not gets hurt. Boss takes cares of us. Protects us so I's don't gets taken away. Director, she wants ta take me's cause she don't care if I's taken aways. Boss good ta me's. Says I's special. Don't wants ta lose me's. I's try'n ta tell yous, I's finally be's K when yous come backs."

"What do you mean?" She lifted her head, and he released her hair. "Water on." She placed her hands under the faucet, then wiped her mouth and cheeks. She filled a glass with water, took a gulp and swished it around in her mouth.

"I's gets ta prove my's self while yous gones. Man's a police and try'n ta gets K people. Once I's kill him, I's a member. Then I's can takes better care a yous."

Emily spit the water into the sink. "You're. . .you're supposed to. . .to kill somebody?"

"Yeah!" He stood proudly. He had worked long and hard to receive this honor. "Gets ta proves I's loyal."

She pivoted and met his eyes. "Murder is wrong. It's one of the Ten Commandments."

Galahad turned away. "Thems ain'ts K rules."

"God is our creator. His rules are the most important."

"God makes yous so yous gots ta follows His rules. Me's, I's belong ta K, so I's got ta follows thems rules."

"No, Galahad, please don't do this."

"I's waits long time ta be's a member." He turned and held her shoulders. "I's works hard for us."

She dropped her head. "It's wrong."

He grounded his jagged teeth. "Ain'ts wrongs ta be's strongs and loyal ta Kalopso. K wants him dead. I's kill him."

"You're not mean and cruel like they are. You can't even be mean to your girls."

"I's kill him fast, so he's don't suffer none."

"What about his family?"

"Huh?"

"They'll be left behind like I was."

"NO'S." He stomped his foot. He refused to think about who else was affected. "I's be's member. I's take care of yous."

"Don't do this for me," she begged him. "I don't care what they do to me. I'm already crazy. Don't make other kids come here because of me."

He had waited so long to be able to protect Emily properly. To stop her pain. Galahad pounded his fists on the counter. "I's be's K," he screamed.

Emily shrunk away in fear. He never yelled at her.

He softened his voice. "I's sorry." He opened his arms.

She ambled cautiously over to him. "Please don't," she cried into his shirt.

He was stopping this ridiculous conversation. What did she think he had been working so hard for? "Yous needs ta sleep." He picked her up and carried her over to the bed.

"They don't care about you. They only want to use you."

Galahad got her sleeping medication out of the cabinet. "Boss says I's special. He takes care a me's."

"He doesn't care about you. He doesn't help or comfort you when you're hurt."

He placed the injector on her scrawny arm. "Don'ts want me's weak."

"He makes you do things you hate. He won't help your girls.

247

He's. . ." she trailed off as the sleeping potion took effect.

Galahad was thankful for the silence. He took off his shoes, pulled down the covers, tucked Emily in, then slipped in beside her. He held her as she mumbled restlessly in her sleep. He tried hopelessly to push Emily's comments out of his brain. He would not let her stupid, imaginary God person prevent him from achieving his goal; to give Emily safety and happiness. Her useless God had never done anything for either of them.

He stared for hours at the ceiling. The vision of Emily stepping away from him in fear haunted him. What if Emily viewed him as a murderer similar to the members who killed her parents? Would she trust him after that?

CHAPTER 19

CMD. YOGGI MARCHED IN and stood at the head of the conference table. The Malone puzzle continued to frustrate her. Nothing about the orphan made sense. She was late because three of her superiors needed extra time to reprimand her for failing to remove Zeus from OTS. Yet if she had done so earlier, their water problems would still be undetected. However, he had used network methods to solve the problem, and she could see why they wanted him discharged. However, he had volunteered at every step in the processes. Why had he helped them knowing they intended to discharge him? What was in it for Malone?

Yoggi glanced around the table and realized everyone was waiting for her to speak. "I'm sorry I kept you all waiting. I have reviewed Malone's final test scores. He can pass today and would obviously improve as the year progressed. The only possibility is flying."

"It's too bad we don't have minimum flight requirements until November," Lt. Cmd. Zeigler grumbled.

"I don't want to have to deal with him for that long." Yoggi sat rigidly in her chair remembering her superior's orders. "Sato, tell me you got something useful out of him."

"I'm sorry, Commander, I have nothing additional to report. My conversations with Malone are futile. He's angry, uncooperative, and reminds me, under ethical standards and OTS rules, I can't force him to answer."

"Why not?"

"Unfortunately, my role is supposed to be the cadet's advocate. I am not allowed to rate, score or officially comment. That way they feel safe talking to me. We use a separate person to do the stability testing before graduation. I'm certain he'll pass that. He understands the system too well to flunk. I do have some personal theories and opinions."

"All right, we'll get to that in a minute." Yoggi frowned. Sato was new to OTS. She was not impressed. "Dr. Jones, did you get anything out of Malone?"

"Not much you haven't heard before." She shrugged. "He enjoys reading technical journals and reports. Loves computers and is thrilled to be on an advanced computer system like ours. He came to OTS as a last resort. Said he was anti-military before he came and is now a strong believer in the system."

"I'd like to add to that," Sgt. Leiman stated.

"Go ahead."

"From what I can tell, Malone was shocked he was allowed to take the entrance tests and dumbfounded we admitted him. Malone's as surprised as we are that he's still here. He never assumed we'd give him a chance or treat him fairly. That's one of the big things that impresses him about the Corps. The fact that even if he's not wanted here, he's treated fairly and given the same opportunities as the other cadets."

Zeigler pounded the table. "So he expects to graduate?"

"No, Sir. He's not naïve. He knows his odds are slim to none."

"Then why keep trying?" Yoggi asked. "What's in it for him?"

"Our food, clothing and medical care are more than he's ever had," Dr. Bentley interjected.

"I don't think that's why he stays." Sgt. Leiman shook her head. "He enjoys the computers, flying and classes. But I think a lot of it is intangible. We treat him with basic respect. We give him feedback, compliments and positive reinforcement. I don't think he got any of that in the past."

"For example?" Yoggi asked.

"I told him how impressed I was after seeing the disk of him in Zeigler's class. Malone said he was amazed he was allowed to go up to the board. My impression was, in the past, he was allowed to sit in class but not respond, ask questions or interact with the students or teachers. I asked him very specifically about having a mentor, father figure, guide or leader, anybody like that. I've asked numerous times and ways." She pointed to the other sergeants. "He says Baker, Taylor and I are the closest thing to that he's ever had."

Zeigler fiddled with his laser quill. "What else have you talked to him about?"

"I talked to him about getting along with his roommate better."
She shook her head. "He and Christiani have discussed it, and he's
trying. He helps Christiani study the sciences, and Christiani helps him
in speech class and with social stuff."

"What does Christiani say about getting along with him?" Sato
asked.

"I asked Christiani this morning. He feels things are going better.
Malone has never talked much to others. They actually count the words
Malone uses to answer. According to Christiani, they respect each other,
it's no longer awkward, and he enjoys Malone's unique approach to
life."

"Anything else?" Cmd. Yoggi sighed.

"Nothing you haven't heard before."

"Thank you, you did pretty well." Yoggi turned to Baker and Taylor. "Do you two have anything to add?"

"No, Ma'am," they both answered.

"I'm opening up the floor. Anyone who wants to speak, can." Yoggi
sipped her water, wondering if she would be discharged before Malone.

"How are we going to get rid of him?" Chung asked. "I need to
start dealing with the rest of my students. I don't have time to keep
playing 'kick the orphan out.' "

Yoggi put down her cup. "As far as that goes, from here on out,
regardless of what we do about Malone, start concentrating on the rest
of this class. Treat Malone like everyone else. We need to remember
there's over a thousand other cadets in this class. I'm especially concerned about the flying practicals. These men and women have to be
up to speed on their flight duties. Someday their lives may depend on
what we've taught them. You flight people need to give him the same
amount of time you would any other cadet in his position. No more,
no less. If he's to improve on his flying, he'll have to count on his unit
mates to help him, same as anybody else would. No special treatment,
good or bad. Got it?"

The officers nodded. "Yes, Ma'am."

Dr. Jones tossed her laser quill on the table. "Well, it's about time.
Why shouldn't Zeus be treated like everyone else?"

"Because he's an orphan, Doctor," Haden stated sarcastically.

"OTS and the Corps have both instituted non-prejudiced doctrines,"
she reminded him.

"That's the official doctrine. The reality is, what we do and say for the press is a little different from what happens in here." Haden tapped the table with his finger. "You're naïve."

"Is that so?" she leaned toward him. "I faced his knife, and even in his hungry, delusional state, when he thought I was going torture him, he didn't hurt me. I've had no cause to be frightened when he comes into my office. I've listened to everything being said today and in the past weeks, added that with my own experience, and I don't think this is a bad person."

Dr. Jones had a chance to speak freely, and she was not giving up the floor until she had said her piece. "The first day, when he was groggy from anesthesia, he immediately said it would take him months to pay for his dental work. He couldn't have thought that through while sedated. You see people as they are in that state. Those aren't the comments of a liar, a cheater or a thief. That's an honest man."

"Thank you, Doctor." Zeigler ground his teeth and hissed through them. "I think we've heard enough."

"No." Yoggi waved to Zeigler. "Dr. Jones, you seem to be his one advocate. If nothing else, you give me a whole new perspective. I want to hear everything you have to say."

"Thank you." Jones glared at Zeigler. "I've heard of a number of fights where Zeus could easily have hurt his opponents. Some of those people have been cruel to him and deserve to be put in their place, yet Zeus never hurts them."

"Sgt. Taylor, have you seen or heard of any fights where Malone was vindictive?"

"No, Commander, and he's had plenty of chances."

"He's hard-working." Jones waved to Leiman and Baker. "You sergeants were mad when Dr. Bentley said he could take it easy and disappointed when he didn't. Capt. O'Donnell says he's asking for additional, more challenging work. You flight people say he's practicing at all hours of the night. What a horrible person to be dedicated to something he wants to succeed at. If it were any other cadet, you'd all be thrilled with his persistence and commitment.

"He wants his sergeant to be happy with her boyfriend. He wants his unit mates to be successful and is willing to stay up at night helping them. Why does everyone keep thinking he is so terrible?

"I know he's gruff. His language and culture are different than ours.

But I say his actions speak louder than his words. Why are you so afraid of him?" She eyed Haden and Zeigler. "We don't need to get Zeus out of here. If he can do the work, why shouldn't he stay?"

"You've made some good observations," Cmd. Yoggi hated to admit. She wished the pressure to discharge Malone were not so great. "Unfortunately, there are a lot of people affected by an orphan graduating from OTS. We have highly sophisticated equipment, codes and ideas to protect. Every person in this room has taken a oath to protect our worlds and, as OTS personnel, to produce the best, most honorable officers in the universe. I have to speak to the family members of people he may lead into battle and be able to say, 'Your loved ones are in good hands, and I'd be willing to put my daughter in those hands.' I am duty bound to make decisions based on more than what's right for one person."

"Here's a thought for you, Dr. Jones." Zeigler waved his quill in her face. "If Malone is so honorable and innocent of all crimes, then why won't he answer our questions?"

"He has answered. He just hasn't answered the way you wanted him to. Maybe he never had anyone else's help, and he isn't hiding anything."

Sato smacked the table. "That, I don't agree with. I'm positive he's hiding something. I monitor his emotional responses while we're talking. When I ask about secrets or hidden information, the monitor goes off the scale. He's hiding something. That's a fact. I've asked him who taught him to read. He won't answer, but the recorder goes crazy. I'm certain he did not teach himself."

Well it's about time Sato offered something helpful, Yoggi thought. "Sato, when else does the recorder go nuts? What other types of questions cause strong emotional responses?"

"Women, as everyone has said. He has strange responses to and about women's issues. Probably the most intense responses I've ever seen are when I've asked him about rape."

"You think he's raped someone?" Yoggi twisted her wedding ring.

"Well, that's what I think," Sato stroked his graying beard. "Unfortunately, that's not the only possible explanation. In theory, he could have participated in raping someone, been raped, seen a rape, had a person close to him raped; anything like that could account for the intensity of his emotions." Sato noted Yoggi nervously fiddling with her ring. He hated Malone and would exploit the Commander's fear to rid the Corps of this orphan scum.

"In my professional opinion, I think he's a vicious animal. Certain psychopathic profiles fit him exactly. Serial rapists and killers are often brilliant. They thrive on being able to trick experts. Ninety-nine percent of the time, they're loners. They often view themselves as being rejected by society and victims." Sato stared at Jones. "Does any of this sound familiar, Dr. Jones?"

His gaze pierced her confidence. Jones bit her lip. "Yes. But being brilliant and a loner hardly makes him a psychopath."

Yoggi noted Jones's reaction. Now they were making progress. "What other characteristics do these people have?"

"In most profiles, these men, because they usually are men, had a painful childhood, with little or no positive role models, especially male role models. They hurt people to feel powerful. They are sick, twisted and feel no remorse. The more the victim suffers, the more the tormentor enjoys it and feels powerful."

Yoggi drummed her fingers. She paused and processed the information. "Why so protective of women?"

"There are a couple of explanations. One, he's trying to hide his propensity to dominate and hurt women. Two, and this is what I think is most likely, he's setting up future victims. The more his victims trust him and willingly fall into his trap, the more powerful he feels. These psychopathic types like to get into people's heads. It bad enough for a woman to be raped, but it's worse when it's by someone she trusts, for example, in the case of incest. If it's an adult, the victim may never learn to trust again. She believes she's incapable of good judgment."

Dr. Jones felt chills run down her spine. "Zeus may fit the description, but I still keep thinking about that first day. Why didn't he choose to hurt me then?"

"Because that's not his M.O. You didn't trust him. He hadn't gotten into your head yet," Sato offered.

"Think about what Malone did to get the director of sanitation to cooperate," Zeigler said. "His methods were definitely Kalopso. Where would he have learned that? Only the network trains its people to be unfeeling, fighting machines."

Yoggi turned to her corporal. "Simb, what did our experts say about his hacking abilities?"

"No one has been able to get funds out of the institutions Malone hacked into. They say they could probably do it if they had enough time. Everyone said he couldn't have gotten in so fast without previous experience."

Bentley was more curious than ever. Malone was a mystery she wanted to solve. "If he's so smart, why was he starving?"

"These people are crazy," Sato responded. "Who knows? It may have been to prove he could control even his own body's need for food. It's obvious with his fighting and hacking abilities, if he had wanted to, he could have eaten more. For some strange reason, Malone chose not to. That, in and of itself, is a sign of instability."

"Well, at least your explanations make sense," Cmd. Yoggi commented. "Is there anything else you can tell us?"

"My guess is, he was down in the sewers, on his computer, finding victims. These weirdos spend hours meticulously finding the right victim. It's never by chance. She may have to have a certain hair color or eye color, go to a certain place, say a specific word; it could be anything. The only common denominator is the choices are never random."

"Unfortunately, we have no proof."

"What about hacking into restricted bank files?"

"We would be implicated, too. I authorized the acceptance of those funds. Plus, it's not against the law to seize stolen funds and return them. We have no proof Malone stole anything."

"I don't like the idea of having him anywhere near my people." Zeigler rocked his chair on its two rear legs. "I don't want to be responsible for one of our people getting hurt because we didn't get rid of him before he snapped. He can't keep this up forever."

"I agree. Malone will snap." Sato snapped his fingers at Jones. "Even if he currently has a clear sense of right and wrong, and I don't think he does, there are mountains of evidence that when orphans are under extreme stress, they become violent and dangerous. Years from now, if we send him into battle, hundreds will pay. If you'd like, Commander, I'll go though the experts' reports on orphans and highlight the pertinent sections."

"Yes, do that. Get it to my office immediately."

"Yes, Ma'am."

"We're starting the bulk of our training in the next few weeks. All the cadets have been assigned as pilots or NGs. In the next week or so, we'll assign flight teams." Zeigler huffed. "I don't care what it takes, he's got to go before we start teaching confidential information."

"Why?" Dr. Jones questioned. "Because you're prejudiced?"

Zeigler nostrils flared. "You're a good dentist and you obviously believe what you're saying, but you have no experience with the stresses of combat. Have you ever been in battle or had to defend yourself?"

"No, it doesn't come up much in dental school, but basic judgment does."

"I know you have good judgment," Zeigler stated diplomatically. "You proved that the first day you met Malone, but it's not the same. I've been in battle, and sometimes it's not the training that matters. It's experience and trusting your gut. My gut tells me this kid is bad news. If he graduates, we're going to regret it. I don't mean just OTS. I mean the whole Corps. Somewhere, somehow, Malone's going to double-cross us, and it won't be on something little. He's too smart for that. He's going to cost lives, lots of lives. I'm not going to sit around and let that happen."

"I agree." Yoggi respected her second in command's opinion. She, too, constantly had a bad feeling about Malone. Something just was not right about him. Nothing ever made sense. It had to be because he was hiding pertinent facts. She was always uncomfortable around him, and after hearing Sato talk, she was convinced he and Zeigler were right.

"Before I make a decision, Dr. Jones, where are you with getting his teeth fixed?"

"I'm done. I only saw him this week because you asked me to."

"Good. And you've documented the before, during and after?"

"Yes, Commander."

"About how much did his mouth cost the Corps?"

"I haven't done the exact figures, but I'd estimate somewhere between a hundred and ten and a hundred and twenty thousand drayka. That includes my time."

"Good, good. Patterson, take notes."

"Yes, Ma'am. I understand what you want." He smiled. The press would be given the total amount of money and time invested in Malone to show how hard OTS had tried to help and keep him.

"Dr. Jones, I want you to get exact figures to Patterson in the next forty-eight hours."

"Commander?" Patterson waited for her approval to continue. "I could also use the total number of hours she worked on him, the experts she consulted, and, of course, the pictures."

"And you want the same things from me?" Dr. Bentley interjected.

"Right. Get on it immediately."

"Yes, Ma'am."

"Now, what to do." Yoggi drummed her fingers. She considered what Sato said and decided her first duty was to protect the Corps' secrets and its personnel. Although she was uncomfortable forcing the issue, she could not avoid it any longer. No matter what, that kid has to go. I cannot live with myself if he attacks one of the woman here or costs dozens their lives.

Yoggi stood and clasped her hands behind her. "All right, everybody, it's time to close the orphan chapter and get on with the rest of this class. He will either answer my questions directly, or we'll push him into a discharge."

Zeigler suppressed his smirk. He had finally gotten what he needed. "How?"

"We drive him until he drops, quits or starts talking," she snarled. "We know he's not going to march into my office and start talking. Leiman, what's the daily maximum number of hours we can push a cadet?"

"Twenty." She gulped.

"What's the minimum food requirements?"

"For Malone," Dr. Bentley said loudly, "it's three high-fat meals a day." She softened her voice. "Besides, it won't make any difference. He's used to eating nothing. Whether he's fed one meal a day or five, it won't change what you're trying to accomplish. I think it will look worse if his fatty curve is down when he leaves."

"You're probably right," Cmd. Yoggi conceded. "But I want him broken, and I want him broken now." She slapped the table. "Hitler, get on it. I want him going twenty hours a day, around the clock. Give him four one-hour sleeping periods; that will give him less quality sleep."

"Commander," Leiman reluctantly interjected.

"Yes."

"They have to be consecutive hours of rest."

Cmd. Yoggi nodded at Leiman. "I know you wouldn't be mistaken about something like that. You heard her, four consecutive hours of sleep a day until he breaks. I want him pushed to the limit. Every muscle in his body better hurt. He should be falling asleep in class and half dead when he flies. I want him driven at least sixteen of those twenty hours. Rearrange all the classes so the Alphas never have more than one day until Malone is gone. Also, no more than an hour in the simulators. Give him three fifteen-minute eating times, some breaks for the can, and other than that, he moves around the clock.

"Leiman, go find Malone and bring him to my office, now! Tell him he's got one last chance to answer honestly, or we start pushing."

"Yes, Ma'am." Leiman jumped up, saluted and trotted off.

"Hitler," Cmd. Yoggi ordered, "the minute he leaves my office, you're on. You use whoever and whatever you need. The rest of you, if you see him falling asleep in class or during drills, you're to be merciless. Bentley, check him once a day, then give him back to Haden. You're dismissed."

*   *   *

Sgt. Leiman poked her head in Zeus's room. He was tutoring Victor. Both men rose and saluted.

"Petroff, I'm afraid you'll have to study alone." She could not make eye contact with Zeus. "Malone, you need to come with me."

"Yes, Ma'am," Zeus replied. "Requests permission ta speak."

"Yes?"

"Can I's give him a few equations ta works on?"

"Quickly."

"Yes, Ma'am." Zeus explained a space anomaly, marked some problems, gave Victor some instructions and fell in abreast beside Sgt. Leiman.

They walked briskly down the hall. Leiman struggled with what to say. "Petroff's going to miss your tutoring."

Zeus instantly understood. "They's kick'n me's out?"

"Basically." They rounded the corner to the stairs. "Yoggi's waiting for you in her office. She giving you one last chance to tell her the details of your past. If you don't answer her satisfactorily. . ." Leiman stopped on the first step. Her heart ached. She mumbled, "She's turning you over to Little Hitler. Hitler's ordered to drive you 'til you drop, talk, discharge or lose it. Twenty hours a day."

258

Zeus stormed down the stairs three steps at a time. "What the budge she wants ta know?"

Leiman scurried behind her cadet. "How a starving orphan is so well educated."

"I's studies a lot."

"That isn't going to cut it. Who helped you? What were you doing in the sewers? Why the strange, protective reactions to women?"

Zeus stopped abruptly at the bottom of the stairs. "Huh?"

"Malone, listen to me." Leiman paused on the last step and stood so she was eye level with the orphan. "If something happened before, and there were extenuating circumstances, tell me about it now. Let me at least try to help you."

"Don'ts matter what I's say." Zeus dropped his head. "They's already decides, I's gone."

"Yes, that's probably true. I don't think it will matter. But I want to know for myself what you're hiding. What's so terrible that you can't even talk to me about it?"

Zeus raised his head and fixed his jaw. "Ain'ts done noth'n wrong."

"Please, talk to me now. I can't control Hitler, and I'll have to follow orders when he tells me to push you."

Zeus pushed his face to hers. "Budgin yous. Ain'ts done noth'n wrong."

"Malone, how did you get here? They've checked it out. Few people on Orphan's Row can read. How is it you're doing advanced physics?"

"I's study lots."

"Who taught you to read?"

"Ain'ts been tolds it's against a law ta reads, Sergeant." He whipped around and marched to the door.

"It's not the reading part that concerns them." She raced after and grabbed his arm. "It's your connection to whoever taught you and what you owe them."

He jerked away. "Don't owes nobody, noth'n."

"You answer Yoggi like that, and she'll throw you right into Hitler's eager hands. He can't wait to tear you apart."

"Ain'ts none of yous gonna believe a thing I's gots ta say."

"Try me. You might be surprised."

Zeus said nothing.

259

In frustration, Leiman yelled, "Don't you trust me at all?"

Zeus faced her. "Yous ever think a me's as a potential officer?"

"I wish I could say yes." She hung her head. "But I'm sorry, I won't insult you by lying. The answer is no. "

"Then what budgin difference does anything I's say makes?"

"The reasons matter to me. I know and respect you. You're a decent guy. I'm trying to make sense out of all of this."

"Calls prejudice, Sergeant."

"I'm not prejudiced," she insisted.

"Budgin yous."

Leiman put her hands on her hips. "I've treated you fairly since the day you arrived."

"Ain'ts just 'bout treat'n me's fairly. Yous prejudice in the way yous think. Yous can't imagine me's as an officer. Why not? I's can do everything. It's cause I's ain't gots no parents. Ain't gots a home. That's why I's not goods 'nough."

Leiman stared at the floor like an ashamed child. "I don't know what to say."

"Ain'ts noth'n ta say." Zeus pushed the door open and marched toward Cmd. Yoggi's office.

"Malone." She raced after him

"Yoggi and Hitler is wait'n."

CHAPTER 20

ZEUS DRAGGED HIMSELF to his room after two days of Hitler's torture. He glanced at Apollo's alarm clock. It was after three in the morning. His muscles ached so much they twitched. He slowly removed his shirt and pants, then flopped down on his cot.

Apollo rubbed his eyes and sat up. "How are you?"

"Fines."

"Your appearance is terrible." Apollo stumbled out of bed, went to the closet and found his muscle-relaxing gel. Apollo reminded himself not to speak intellectually. "Allow me to rub some of this on you." He showed Zeus the tube. "The advertisement says, 'It will make your muscles melt.' "

"Leave me's the budge alone."

Apollo ignored his roommate's attitude and calmly answered, "For an intelligent man, you can be amazingly foolish. A rubdown with this relaxant and some sleep, and you would be far better off. If you would cease your stubborn and untrusting attitude, you would not suffer as much. Now roll over before you twitch yourself to death." Apollo sat beside Zeus on his cot.

Even that small movement caused Zeus to groan in pain. "Budgin yous." He smacked the tube. "Touch me's and I's kill yous."

"And give Hitler the perfect reason to discharge you. That is not a possibility. You do not frighten me. Now roll over, before I roll you over!" Apollo grabbed Zeus's shoulder. Zeus ground his teeth. Apollo twisted the orphan's body slightly and held firmly. Zeus grudgingly cooperated. He did not have the time or energy to resist.

Apollo squeezed the bluish gel onto his hand and worked it into Zeus's aching shoulders and back. Zeus had never used a muscle relaxant before. He felt the deep, penetrating warmth. It did seem like his muscles melted. The aching and twitching subsided.

"For a rich bastard, yous ain't so bad," Zeus mumbled into his pillow.

Apollo chuckled at the orphan's attempt at a compliment "Thank you. I have been amazed how impressed I am with you as well."

"Huh?"

Apollo kneaded the gel into Zeus's lower torso and legs. "I never anticipated you being intelligent or an excellent tutor, or that I would care if they forced you to discharge. For what it is worth, I do not agree with the commander's actions. What they are engaging in is immoral. I only wish I could assist you."

"Thanks."

"I am aware you do not believe in God; however, I wanted to inform you, a group of us are praying for you. That you be shown compassion and treated justly. That Yoggi would somehow become convinced you deserve to remain. You may perceive praying as foolish and a waste of time; however, I do not. I have personally witnessed the power of prayer dozens of times."

Zeus could not figure out what to say. He appreciated them praying for him, whether he believed in God or not. As was his habit, when he did not know what to say, he said nothing.

"Roll over."

Zeus strained to comply. His body felt glued to the mattress.

"Here." Apollo tossed the tube to Zeus. "I will allow you to apply it on your stomach and thighs. Just be cautious; you would regret getting this stuff around any sensitive spots."

"Yous ain't kid'n. This craps burns."

Apollo laughed heartily. "I recall once in high school, one guy put this gel in another friend's cup." Apollo crossed his legs. "It hurts me to contemplate it; however, it was humorous. My friend starts running around screaming, jumps in the shower. . ."

Zeus listened while he finished rubbing in the relaxant. He was amazed Apollo could babble so freely about any subject. Zeus flipped the top closed and tossed the tube to Apollo. "Thanks a lot." The orphan held up one finger then another.

"That is actually three words." Apollo smirked as he slipped into his bed.

* * *

Apollo checked the clock. He waited until the last possible second to wake his roommate. He was careful not to touch the orphan. Zeus was jumpy about surprise physical contact. Apollo had learned that the hard way. "Zeus, it is time to arise."

"Yeah, OK." Zeus's legs felt like lead as he forced them to the floor. "What we's do'n now?"

Apollo reminded himself to speak informally as he yanked on his boot. "The good news is, you will not be suffering alone. The bad news is, we are going on a 10K, full-pack hike."

"Budgin." Zeus rubbed his bloodshot eyes. "I's appreciate all yous do'n for me's, the rub-down, even the prayers thing. "

"I would assist you on the hike if I were allowed; however, I apologize in advance. Just so you are aware, Hitler has ordered us not to intervene. No one is allowed to step in for you or take your pack."

Zeus slowly dragged himself out of bed. He was too tired and depressed to remember to make conversation with Apollo. The orphan struggled to put on his boots and strained to lift his pack.

Apollo helped ease the pack on Zeus's aching shoulders. "You cannot continue at this pace indefinitely. Your treatment is unfair; however, the abuse will not cease until you are gone or speak to Yoggi."

"They's ain't gonna believe noth'n I's say. Don't understand why Yoggi's even ask'n." Zeus clipped his pack around his waist. He had forgotten to make his bed. He hung his head as he leaned over the cot.

"I will take care of the bed." Apollo stepped in front of him. "Yoggi's questioning I can explain. She is not being given many options herself." Apollo straightened the sheets. "People are fearful of the unknown. Since Yoggi cannot answer any pertinent questions pertaining to you and she has no proof you are not a Kalopso member, she has to assume you are. Without proof, she must err on the side of caution. In her mind, and more importantly, in the minds of the top brass, they must protect the rest of the Corps. Even if Yoggi wanted you here, and I am not privy to that information, she has no choice." Apollo tucked in the last corner and faced Zeus. "I do know Cmd. Yoggi is an honest, moral person."

"How yous know?"

"My family has a few connections." Apollo led Zeus out the door. "As I understand it, Yoggi insisted all written Corps policies be strictly adhered to. It is amazing she's done things by the book this long. As far as you are concerned, it does not matter who is doing the ordering.

However, I thought you may want to be informed it was not Yoggi's choice to force your discharge. She is taking enormous amounts of criticisms for your success here."

Zeus took the first step and groaned. He leaned on the banister for support. His legs felt like weights and his thighs burned with each step down. "What yous mean?"

"If you stay, there are people who will destroy her career because she failed to get you discharged. If you leave now, with no blatantly obvious reason, like grades, there are people who will blackball her for that. Plus, her husband has moved into an apartment off base. Now she only sees her daughter every other day."

"Cause a me's?"

"I am uncertain if they previously had marriage problems; however, this term has certainly made it impossible for her to focus on her family. It is not much of a consolation to you. However, her career is on the line. Now, no matter what the outcome, she is probably out a job." Apollo took his place in formation.

Zeus slumped beside him. Yoggi's situation was not any consolation. Until recently, Yoggi had forced her staff to treat him fairly. It did not seem right that to help himself and other orphans, Zeus was destroying an honest woman's career and marriage. Why were things always so complicated? He could not figure out what to do. The one thing he was committed to was never telling the truth. It was too dangerous. He would go to his grave with that information. Zeus had learned his lesson; he would never cross the Kalopso again.

The Alphas marched single file up a rocky cliff. Apollo stumbled numerous times, then fell over his feet and landed flat on the path.

"Apollo, yous OK?" Zeus knelt beside the crumpled body. No answer. Zeus turned his friend over. "Apollo." Zeus shook him.

Sgt. Baker squatted by the body and placed two fingers on Apollo's throat. "His pulse is good. He must have hit his head." Baker unclipped his ComLine and called for a medevac.

* * *

Galahad paced frantically. They had one chance to escape, and Emily had not returned. He had to get them out of the K-Club building before daybreak. The next day the boss would be sober, and it would be too late. Most of the girls were with customers celebrating the million-drayka prize. The boss had been generous and drugs were available for everyone. Even the guards were high. That night was their only chance. Why had Emily not returned? The director was supposed to be here for the party. The party had been going strong for hours, and still no director and no Emily. Finally, they arrived with only three hours of darkness left.

Emily rushed into the room and threw her arms around him. "We did it. I won."

"Yous did great." Galahad returned the hug. He did not have time for niceties. "Boss's wait'n for yous at the party," he lied to the director. He hoped the boss was too drugged to realized he had not said it. "Emily and me's, we's ta stay heres."

"Where's he at?" the director demanded.

"Last I's sees, he's in the dancehall," he lied again. The longer it took her to find the boss, the better their chances of escape.

"Make sure she gets some rest," the director ordered. "She has a big press conference in the morning."

Galahad nodded as the director walked to the door. "Boss gives us extra food ta celebrate," he said for the director to overhear. As soon as the door was shut, he pushed Emily out of his arms. "We's gots ta goes. Ain'ts gots much time."

"Go where? I just returned."

"I's fails. Don't kills my's guy."

"You told me. I'm so proud of you. We both did good this week."

"We's both dead if we's don't leaves." He packed the things on the counter.

"You told me the boss said it was OK that you failed. That you were special, and he'd give you something else to do."

"Boss lies so yous not worries 'bout me's and wins. Whippy overhears the boss talk'n. They's wait'n 'til after yous done talk'n ta the press and make'n speeches. When it's clear, and theys gots the money, we's gets killed. Yous firsts, I's watch, thens me's."

Emily trembled as her words cracked. "Why? I. . .I didn't fail."

"Yous know too much 'bout here." Galahad yanked the sheet off the bed and laid it on the ground. "Yous ever talks, they's get caught. They always planned ta kill yous once the contest was done." He grabbed all the medical supplies out of the cabinet and threw them on the sheet. "Yous supposed ta go work for the company that's build'n yous model. K can't control yous there. Too risky from thems. Yous

265

was right. Boss not cares. Uses us. Now we's gots ta gets out."

"How?" She opened the cabinet over the sink. "What else do you want packed?"

"Take everyth'n that ain'ts breakable. Ain'ts had time ta plans. We's gets in the sewers and then make plans on the computer. Whippy helps us. Says customer takes her downstairs ta the bathhouse. They's repair'n in there. Gots a hole in the wall. I's check, we's can gets out and in ta the main sewers."

"I thought they closed up the entrance."

"They's did. They's work'n on it." Galahad tossed a towel on the sheet. "When I's ins the vents, they's all interconnects. I's went froms the sewer pipes ta the air vents. K uses the sewer system ta flush the boorix gases outs of the mines. Remember yous had me's mark the way ta yous. I's been in 'em. They's goes a long ways from here."

"Where will we go?"

"Computer says main sewer pipes goes offs K property and inta the ghetto."

"My portable computer is still in the director's flyer. They'll never let us out there."

"I's stole boss's and already tooks it ta the vents. Tooks all the power packs and flashlights I's could find."

"How are we going to get out without anyone noticing?"

"Guards is fly'n fire. Boss gives everybody extra drugs ta celebrate. Whippy, she helps us. When we's gone, she tells boss she sees us sneaks inta the back of a flyer befores it leaves. Puts this ons." He threw her one of the dancer costumes.

Emily held up the flimsy, black teddy. "Why this?"

"Yous got ta fit in when we's go through the club."

"What if it doesn't work?" She unzipped her powder-blue dress and slipped it over her head.

"We's gots ta try. We's dead if we's stay." Galahad tied the sheet in a knot and threw it over his shoulder. "Come ons." He grabbed her arm. "Gots ta goes tanights while they's all too tripped ta stop us. Can'ts cross ta the sewers ins a light." He opened the door.

Emily peered down the hall. "Galahad, I'm scared," she whispered.

"Call me's Red Top 'til we's out a here." He pulled her out the door.

The entire club was a sea of drunken, drugged people partying.

They meandered through the halls down to the bathhouse. The escapees were stopped only once.

"I's take her ta a customer in the baths," Galahad lied to the challenger. "Boss says get her there nows."

The challenger waved them on as he took another drink from his bottle. Within half an hour, the pair was retreating in the sewers.

*　*　*

It was after midnight when Sgt. Baker ordered Zeus to take his rest period. Zeus hauled himself up the steps. He entered his room quietly, assuming Apollo would be asleep. Apollo was not there. Zeus checked Apollo's locker; his pack was not where it belonged. Apollo must have stayed in the infirmary for the night.

Zeus went to the bathroom to brush and floss his teeth. No matter how poor he was, he would never let his teeth deteriorate again. He meticulously brushed and flossed two or three times a day. Zeus popped his fatty booster pill and went to find Victor.

Victor was asleep in his quarters. Zeus lightly shook him with his aching arms. "Gets up. It's early, why yous not study'n."

"Zeus, go to sleep. You only have a couple of hours."

"Gets a budge up." Zeus jerked the covers off him. "Yous retake is tamorrow and yous study'n tonight."

"Zeus, you need to sleep." Victor pulled his covers over himself. "I decided to get a good night's sleep. I'll just have to do the best I can tomorrow."

Zeus yanked the covers off the bed. "Yous budgin gonna study."

"Guys," Victor's roommate snarled. "I'm trying to sleep. Go fight someplace else?"

"Sorry." Victor dangled his bare feet off his cot. "This will only take minute. Zeus, I appreciate your help. I just don't feel right keeping you up when you're pushed all day and you haven't slept."

"I's sleep plenty when I's gone. Now get yous budgin butts outs a bed." Zeus popped open the Little Lady and waved the switchblade in Victor's face.

Victor ignored it. "What difference does it make to you if I pass?"

"What difference does it makes ta yous if I's tired?"

"I'm serious, why do you care if I stay or go?"

"Yous gonna makes a good officer. Now get yous butt outs a bed." Zeus pressed the blunt edge of the knife in Victor's throat.

267

"Thanks." Victor batted the blade away. No one was saying he would make a good officer. "What makes you think so?"

"Yous honest and fair." Zeus swiped the blade against his pants until it snapped shut. His thigh cringed from the pressure. "I's don't want bastards like Richard run'n the Corps."

Victor was elated. He leaped up, grabbed his shirt and pants and followed Zeus across the hall. "Do you think you will be around to care which officers are in the Corps?" Victor sat at Apollo's desk.

"Nope." Zeus scooted his chair in beside Victor. "What problems yous work on?"

Victor accessed the problems he had completed. "I think you deserve to graduate, too."

Zeus spoke while he reviewed the work. "Don't matters what I's deserve."

"I know, that's why I'm surprised you care."

Zeus ignored the comment. He was too annoyed at Victor's homework. "What the crap yous do'n here?" Zeus thumped the screen.

"I gotta little lost."

"This ain'ts a little lost." He was tired and had hoped they could move on to a new subject. Instead he re-explained how to calculate the answers. After assigning Victor some new equations, Zeus went over to his own desk and terminal.

He needed to be aware of the staff's plans for him, especially if any of those plans could be fatal. He hacked into the communication system and programmed the computer to search for transmissions referring to "Malone." A transmission was in progress. He put the headphones on and listened. Leiman and Taylor were discussing the last few days.

"Brian, I think you're being too hard on yourself," Leiman said.

"Sues, you didn't see the look Malone gave me when he realized I'd betrayed him."

"You did NOT betray him."

"Yes, I did. If I were Malone, I'd be ticked off, too. I didn't handle things the way you did. I wish I had. I always implied I thought he'd be around for the All-Militaries, when I knew he wouldn't. I wanted him to teach me how to fight, and I lied to get it. Plus, he knew everything you heard was going straight to Yoggi. That's not what he thought when I talked to him. I asked him everything Yoggi told me to, and he knows it."

"I just think you're exaggerating your intent. You never meant to take advantage of Malone. We can't help it that Yoggi ordered us to get him out."

"I could have been honest with him. That's why I'm so mad at myself. If I'd told him the truth, he still would've sparred with me."

"I wish I was there to give you a hug."

"Yeah, me too."

"I understand why you're upset," she said, "but I don't get the part about withdrawing from the All-Militaries. If you don't tell Malone, what does that accomplish? He'll never know how sorry you are."

"Sues, this has to do with me. I need to remember. I've told you before, I used to be like that. In the past, I wouldn't have cared that I used Malone, not as long as I'd gotten what I wanted. I don't want to be that way again. I didn't think of Malone as another cadet. He was a friend, only I didn't treat him like a friend. I can't win the All-Militaries knowing I got there by cheating a buddy."

"Then why not tell him?" she insisted. "Let him know how much you care and how sorry you are."

"No, you just don't get it. If I were Malone and some guy spent weeks lying to me and milking me for information, then told me he was sorry, I'd be more insulted and mad. It's not the way guys do things."

There was a long pause.

"Brian, I'm not certain I can do this anymore."

"What do you mean?"

"I may not re-enlist." She sighed heavily.

"What?" Taylor exclaimed. "When are you up?"

"A little more than a year from now."

"Oh, what about us?"

"Don't give me that pathetic look. It wouldn't change anything between us."

"How do you figure?"

"I was going to ask you, when exactly are you up?"

"I just re-upped for another three. It would be two and a half years for me. Sues, what are you thinking? The Corps has always been your life."

"I know, but I've always been proud of what I do, at least until this week. I'm not saying I'll do it, and I certainly wouldn't leave without working things out with you. I'm just thinking about it."

"I still can't believe you'd leave the Corps. Have you ever thought about this before?"

"No, not really. But then again, I've never been ashamed to admit what I'm doing. I wouldn't do anything immediately. After Malone leaves, I figure I've got until graduation to decide."

"Why graduation?"

"I'd want to tell Yoggi before she started planning for next term; that is, if she's still here. It's not only what they're doing to Malone that bothers me. No matter what happens now, Yoggi's career is in the crapper."

"Why?"

"She's in charge. She'll be the one to take the blame. The way things are going, I wouldn't be surprised if the upper brass forced her to resign. Yoggi's one of the best commanders I've ever had. To destroy her career because Malone's not the idiot we expected him to be seems so unfair. I think Yoggi's handled this whole orphan thing pretty well."

"Do you really think her career is ruined?"

"Somebody has to be the scapegoat, and as far as I can tell, Yoggi is the only choice."

"Yeah, I guess you're right. The military definitely likes to blame someone for its mistakes. There's no such thing as it being nobody's fault."

"Between that and the fact that all the rhetoric about giving everyone a fair chance being BS, I'm not certain I want to be a part of this anymore."

"You know what's sad?"

"What?"

"Remember how you teased me about the way I talk about fighting?"

"Yes."

"That's how Malone was when he talked about studying and computers and all that other intellectual stuff. He was loving it. It was the most excited I'd ever seen him."

"That's what Christiani said about him and computers."

"He deserves to be here. He's as smart or smarter than most of the others. It's kind of funny, thinking about all the times we sparred.

Malone was constantly lecturing me on being a smarter fighter. He was always telling me he didn't win because he was faster or stronger, just smarter."

"You never told me, did you end up fighting with him this morning?"

"Yeah, we sparred."

"So what did Dr. Bentley treat you for today?"

"Amazingly, nothing."

"You must be getting better!"

"No, I wish that were it." Taylor's voice dropped to a whisper. "Malone didn't take one extra hit. If I dropped my guard, he tapped my ribs or face, same as he always does. Not one malicious hit. If you eliminate the kidding around we used to do, everything else was the same."

"You're going to miss him, aren't you?"

"Yeah, a lot. Not that he'd speak to me now, anyway."

"I wish I could give you a hug."

"I could sure use you in my arms right about now."

"I should get a little shut-eye before I have to get Malone going again."

"Look on the bright side, Sues, he's still speaking to you," Taylor teased.

"I guess. Amour."

"Amour, Sweetheart."

* * *

"Ten hut," Victor said when Sgt. Leiman entered the room.

Zeus stumbled out of bed and saluted.

"Come on. Straighten your bed and let's get going."

"Yes, Ma'am." Zeus fixed his bed. "Ma'am?"

"Yes."

"What shoes yous want me's ta wear?"

"Track shoes. You're going jogging."

"Yes, Ma'am." Zeus's knees creaked like an old man's as he sat on his cot. His stiff fingers slowly laced his tennis shoes. He stood with the aid of the metal bed frame.

"Good luck," Victor said.

"Yeah, yous, too."

"I think you need it more than I do. Thanks again for all your help," Victor said.

Zeus walked silently through the hall wondering if Victor could pass Capt. Ritz's test.

"There's a lot of people who care about you here," Leiman said. "Petroff is one of them. Christiani, too. I know what he did was pretty stupid, but his heart was in the right place."

She was about to add that Taylor's was, too, when Zeus interrupted. "Huh? What stupid thing?"

"Nobody told you? Christiani is in the infirmary?"

"Knows he trips on the hike. What's that gots ta do with me's?"

"He didn't trip." Leiman scurried in front of her cadet and faced him. "I thought you knew. He was fasting for you."

"Huh?"

"Some prayer thing. He doesn't eat as a, I don't know. Somehow it's supposed to help you with God."

"How's Apollo not eat'n help me's?"

"How should I know? I don't understand it. All I know is Christiani said he did it for you. Why don't you ask him yourself?"

Zeus resumed walking. "Yeah. Next time I's gots some free time, I's ask him."

"If you want, I'll arrange for you to eat breakfast with him."

"Thank yous, Ma'am."

*   *   *

Galahad's and Emily's life in the ghetto settled into a predictable routine. After months of searching, Galahad had found a safe place for them to live. Since they had moved into the condemned building, Emily was doing better. She was no longer attempting suicide. They spent their days hunting and foraging for food. Once food had been obtained, they studied and worked on the computer. When money was needed, Galahad tried to find day-labor jobs. Otherwise, the junkyard was their shopping center. They kept to themselves and were careful not to run into the gangs on the streets, especially the Kalopso's gang. As they became comfortable with their surroundings, they ventured farther away from their building.

"Looks, Emily." Galahad ran over and climbed up the small crab apple tree. "Just like I's tell'n yous. An apple tree. We's collect apples at night and carry 'em back. Eats for week!" He chucked a piece of fruit down at her and she caught it.

She took a bite of the little green apple. "Where are we?"

"Park I's tell'n yous 'bouts. Place I's get foods out of the trash. Gots ta look hard, but it's here."

Emily twisted and turned, looking at the dilapidated park. "Is it safe?"

Galahad swung down out of the tree with an apple in his mouth and two in his pocket. "Only had a few fights. Ain'ts too bad."

"Look Galahad." She waved to an old playground in disrepair.

He saw nothing of use in that direction. "Huh?"

"It's a swing." She leaped and pirouetted over to the playground. "I used to have one in my backyard. I'd swing for hours."

Galahad followed, perplexed. "Huh, swing."

"I'll show you." She hopped on the uneven equipment. She pumped and kicked for some time. "I feel so free," she squealed as the wind rushed through her hair. Exhilarated, she jumped off. "You try it."

Galahad sat and kicked his legs out. It did not go.

"I'll push you." Emily gave him a shove. "Now move your legs out when you go forward and bend them when you go back."

Once he mastered the technique, Galahad lost interest. To him it was a useless activity. "Yous do's it. I's gets the apples."

For days, the teenagers returned to the swing at night. Emily would swing for hours as Galahad collected crab apples and killed squirrels. He had never seen her this happy. Galahad could hardly contain her until dusk, when she could return to the swing. The swing had become her greatest joy.

Unfortunately, it was also the instrument that severed their friendship. The park had a sensor across from the swing. Emily's retina scan had been detected by the Kalopso. Galahad had never been scanned and could not detected. The K wisely assumed they were together and sent their gang to capture the escapees. The Kalopso intended to exact its revenge.

CHAPTER 21

GALAHAD WAS UP in the tree collecting apples in an old brown purse when he heard Emily scream. He dropped the purse, and green apples fell to the ground like hail. In the moonlight, Galahad saw two teenagers grab Emily.

The taller one cupped his hand over her mouth and held a pocket-knife at her throat. "K's gonna give yous a level four fates worse than deaths for leave'n thems."

Emily squirmed as her tears fell on the filthy hand of her attacker.

The smaller one grinned a toothless grin. "Yeah, but we's gets ta rocks her first." He squeezed her breast and forced a wet kiss on her lips.

Galahad stuffed his hand in his pocket, spilled the apples out, re-trieved his knife and popped open the blade. He leaped out of the tree and charged the man holding Emily. The toothless one blocked Galahad. Galahad round-kicked him squarely, and he fell into the taller man and Emily. Galahad prepared to thrust his knife, but was cracked across the back with a broken pipe.

Emily's cry pierced through the darkness as he fell to the ground. Galahad glanced around. There were three other gang members hold-ing weapons. He quickly surmised he was outnumbered and could not win. His only goal was to save Emily. Like an enraged, rabid animal, he charged the man holding her, yelling, "Emily, runs."

The tall one removed the pocketknife from Emily's throat and jammed it into Galahad's gut. With one clean jerk, he yanked the knife upward and pulled it out with his blood-soaked hand. The life-giving fluid exploded forward as Galahad dropped to the ground clutching his belly. He laid in a swelling sea of oozing red. Emily sobbed as her brother's hot blood splattered her face and dripped from her hair.

One of the gang kicked him. The soundless, still body sent chills through Emily's spine. She could not take her eyes off the motionless blob.

"Deads." The gang member wiped his bloody boot on Galahad's shirt.

A beat-up flyer pulled up and stopped. "Gets in," the driver called.

The tall one dragged Emily over and forced her into the souped-up flyer. The other members jumped in behind them.

"Good-bye, fair knight!" Emily cried as they sped away.

*　　*　　*

Zeus regretted saying he wanted to eat with Apollo. What was he supposed to say to someone who fasted? It was the stupidest thing he had ever heard of. Zeus carried two trays of food into the infirmary. He stopped when he saw Apollo on his knees praying.

Apollo motioned him in, stood and brushed off his pants. "Please enter. God is always available. I understand, your time is limited."

"Yeah." Whenever Apollo spoke about religious things, Zeus felt uneasy. At times Apollo reminded him of Emily speaking the same way. The trays clanked when Zeus set them on the table.

"Room service." Apollo grabbed a chair. "Is that your final fate; they demoted you to waiter?"

"Yous a budgin idiot." Zeus sat opposite Apollo. "Why yous not tell me's yous think'n of do'n something that dumb?"

"Praying and fasting are supposed to be private. That is assuming one does not faint in front of forty other people. However, in theory, it is between oneself and God."

"How long yous go without eat'n?"

Apollo sat up straight, proud of himself. "I abstained from everything except clear fruit juice all day yesterday."

Zeus smiled for the first time in days. "Really yous idiot, hows long yous goes?"

"I'm not joking, about thirty hours."

Zeus studied Apollo's face. He did not appear to be joking. "Yous pass out after only thirty hours and yous had fruit juice?"

"Yes," Apollo defended. He consciously spoke using simple words. "How long have you gone without eating?"

"Least a week, maybe ten days." Zeus popped a muffin in his mouth.

"We were expending a great deal of energy yesterday."

"Crap, Apollo. I's use ta jog 'bout seven kilometers to and from works. Then I's works in hard manual labor. Ain'ts no different than what we's do here."

Apollo cut his ham and laid his knife neatly across the plate. "How frequently did you eat when you were that physically active?"

"Every other day, if I's lucky. Once every four or five, if I's ain't. And I's don't haves no fruit juice. I's count that as a meal."

Apollo melted into his chair. "I apologize. I have no inkling what it is like to be truly hungry. How could you possibly endure that on a regular basis?"

"Yous body gets use ta it." Zeus chugged his milk, scrunched the empty carton and tossed it onto the table.

"It is no wonder you have been at this relentless pushing for what, five days now, and you are showing no signs of discharging. This resembles normal for you."

" 'Cept I's ain't hungry."

Apollo swallowed. "How long could you sustain your present rate?"

"Crap, forever, if I's sleep the four hours and don't tutor." Zeus lifted the tray to his lips and scooped his runny applesauce into his mouth.

"Yoggi will not be pleased to hear that." Apollo ate a piece of ham. At least he thought it was ham. The Corps food was often difficult to identify.

"I's just told Haden they's ain't bother'n me's. He's mads." Zeus grinned from ear to ear.

Apollo laughed. "I am not surprised. What was his reply?"

"Says he's be glad just ta kick my's butt outa heres."

Apollo wiped his mouth with the napkin. "Where will you go?"

"Back ta noth'n." Zeus jabbed his ham with his fork and stuffed the entire contents into his mouth. He loved the Corps food. He was eating more and of a greater variety than he could ever have imagined.

"No, seriously, where will you go, and what will you do?"

"I's serious," Zeus mumbled with the food in his mouth. "Ain't gots no place ta goes or noth'n ta do's."

Apollo meticulously trimmed the fat off his so called meat. "Do you have any friends you could stay with for a while?"

Zeus glared at Apollo in frustration. Apollo simply did not understand, and Zeus had no desire to explain it to him. In another few days,

Zeus would be gone. What difference would talking to Apollo make now? "Nope," he bluntly answered.

Apollo finished chewing his ham and placed his fork diagonally across his tray. "Do you have any job opportunities?"

Zeus wished they would talk about something else. He did not want to think about how empty his life would be after he left. He answered curtly to discourage the conversation. "Nope."

Apollo picked up on Zeus's frustration and ignored it. "I can assist you with employment. There are numerous family businesses that would benefit from your expertise in computers, especially with a physics compliment. Forward me a copy of your resume, and I will arrange something for you."

Zeus wanted to accept the offer. It was exactly why he had originally taken the OTS exam, to get someone to notice him and give him a chance. Unfortunately, after hearing the comments about Yoggi and some of the Kalopso's transmissions he had intercepted, Zeus was convinced anyone who helped him would be threatened by the network. He would not be responsible for anyone else receiving a fate worse than death.

In the last few days, Zeus had accepted that he faced the remainder of his life alone and trapped. He could not even return to the ghettos. The Kalopso intended to hunt him down and make an example of him. Anyone who assisted him would also become a victim. Zeus stared at the floor. "Yous can't help me's."

"Yes, I believe I can. I personally have controlling interest in two companies. If I instruct my people to hire you, they will."

"Nope." Zeus banged the table.

Apollo casually wiped his spilled milk with his napkin. "It would not be an act of charity; you are exceptionally proficient in computers. You would be an asset to any company. I have seen you work and, quite honestly, it's difficult to hire qualified technical people. I would be doing myself a favor and assisting you simultaneously."

"Look, I's know yous can. I's ain't interested." Zeus licked the last bits of food off his tray, then tossed it on the table. He was going to miss the meals here, too. He would soon be returning to garbage and game as his only means of sustenance.

Apollo rose, opened the nightstand drawer and took out some paper and a pen. "I will give you my personal numbers, in case you change your mind. I am also writing down Tom Green's. He is my personal secretary. If you cannot reach me, contact Tom, and he will take care of you." Apollo handed Zeus the paper.

Zeus pushed the paper away.

"Please take the numbers. It will not harm you to carry our numbers around." Apollo again held the paper out, and Zeus shook his head. "Why must you always fight assistance?"

"I's gots a conscience, too." Zeus was furious Apollo forced him to say things he did not want to say. "Ain'ts let'n innocent people gets hurt cause of me's."

"Estimate how many other orphans you will assist by succeeding?" Apollo shot back.

"Why yous always so budgin nice? What's wrong with yous?"

"That is amusing. Victor is wondering the same question about you. Why lose sleep over whether he is discharged or not?"

The orphan burped loudly. "That's different."

"No, it is not. Please keep the numbers." Apollo forced the paper into Zeus's hand.

"Thanks." Zeus stuffed the paper into his pocket. He would not let the K find Apollo's private numbers in his possession. He would throw the paper away as soon as he left.

Apollo cut his muffin in small pieces and ate a chunk. "At least contact me and inform me how you are faring."

"Huh?" Zeus checked the time. He was only supposed to have fifteen minutes for breakfast. Twenty-five minutes had gone by. Where was Baker? Exercise would be welcome, compared to this conversation.

"I would like to correspond with you and remain friends. We can send messages and visit one another now and then." Apollo finished the Corps poor-excuse for a muffin.

"Yous don't get this." Zeus rose abruptly, toppling the chair behind him. "Yous can't have contact with the likes of me's!"

Apollo calmly scooped up some runny applesauce with his spoon. "I can associate with whom ever I choose to."

"Nope, yous can't, anymore than I's can!" Zeus picked up the chair and forced it under the little table. The table rocked as the trays slid on top.

Apollo patted his lips with his napkin. "Why not?" He had consumed all the Corps food he could handle for one meal.

Zeus looked up at the clock. What was keeping Sgt. Baker?

Apollo noticed. "God will arrange your time here until everything which needs to be communicated is done so."

"Oh, yeah." Zeus rolled his eyes.

"I am serious. How frequently in the previous five days have they allowed you to accidentally relax for an extended period?"

"None, so whats? Coincidence."

"You believe what you want to. I will believe what I want to." Apollo hopped up on the bed.

Zeus shrugged. "Why we's discuss'n this? Don't makes no difference."

"Very well." Apollo opened his arms. "You may pick the topic."

"OK, I's will." Zeus definitely did not want Apollo choosing a topic. The room became silent. Apollo smiled, raising his eyebrow. "I's think'n," Zeus defended. He did want to ask Apollo something, but how? Apollo relaxed on the bed and clasped his hands behind his head.

"Yous remember what yous was say'n 'bout Yoggi?"

"Are you referring to Yoggi taking responsibility for your continued presence?"

"Yeah." Zeus took a deep breath. He hated revealing anything about himself. Unfortunately, he had no other alternatives. "What if, when I's leave, I's don't talk ta the press?"

"That would be disastrous. You must give a statement, or everyone — the other orphans you are paving the way for, OTS, Yoggi, even you — will be cast in a negative light. It will appear you were either paid off or threatened. Saying nothing implies some type of wrongdoing and leaves room for speculation. Everyone involved will become the target of negative speculation."

Apollo observed Zeus's reaction. The orphan was obviously distressed. Apollo said a quick prayer for guidance. "Do you want my advice on how to deal with the press?"

Zeus turned away. He was hopelessly confused. "Yeah, I's guess."

"First, what do you hope to accomplish? Your objectives will determine your response."

"I's don't wants ta hurt Yoggi or OTS, but I's want others like me's ta have a chance."

"Those are noble goals. I am certain Yoggi would appreciate your desire not to tarnish her or OTS."

Zeus whipped around. "Yous gonna tells Yoggi?"

"I have no personal agenda. None of this conversation has to leave this room."

"Keeps it's here. Crap, I's don't even wants it here."

"I appreciate your trust in me." Apollo sat up and dangled his feet off the bed. "I realize this is difficult for you, and I give you my word, I will not break your trust."

"Thanks." Zeus pulled the chair out and sat down.

"Let us discuss your goals. You cannot realistically accomplish them all. If you want, I will discuss your various options. Then you may make an informed decision."

"OK." Zeus tilted his chair on its rear legs.

"One, we have already discussed, leave and say nothing. That is potentially destructive for everyone. Two, leave, articulating the whole truth, without deleting anything. That is beneficial for you and other orphans. It is proof an orphan can succeed. That you were physically able, intelligent and capable. It has positive and negative repercussions for Yoggi. It is good she attempted to treat you without bias, bad she eventually would succumb to political pressure. Some will praise her for your forced discharge; others will condemn her. You could lie, saying you were incapable of handling the pressure."

Zeus crossed his arms and frowned.

"I agree. I do not think it is believable. Too many cadets and OTS personnel will question the validity of such a statement. They have all been sending communications home and talking to friends and family. That explanation will probably be refuted and, therefore, it does not help anybody. Once the truth surfaces, everyone will speculate about why you were dishonest. It is also potentially the worst option for other orphans. Many people will use you as an example of the fact that orphans cannot be trusted. They will say things such as 'Even when he was capable and intelligent enough to succeed, he still lied. Orphans are incapable of telling the truth.' "

Zeus dropped his chair back onto all four legs. "I's ain't do'n that one. Exactly what the K wants."

"You could leave saying you realized you did not belong, or that you discharged for personal reasons. There are positives and negatives to that option. Yoggi may not take the blame; however, the press will attempt to determine why you could not integrate. Then we return to other cadets and staff members giving their personal, often biased, opinions. It can also be construed as orphans and non-orphans having nothing in common and therefore can never intermingle."

Zeus stuffed his hands in his pocket and fiddled with the Little Lady. He could always count on her cool, comforting embrace.

Apollo stared out the window as he considered other possible options. "You could fake a medical reason or set yourself up on an Honor Violation. A medical problem could work; however, it has the potential to harm Dr. Bentley. There will be inquiries about your medical condition; when and how it arose; if it was pre-existing; why it was not diagnosed earlier; and the press will want proof the problem existed. Obviously, if you do an Honor Violation, it is disastrous for other orphans." Apollo rubbed his jaw up to his cheek. "I cannot think of any other options at the moment."

"They's alls stinks." Zeus kicked the leg of the table. "Those ain'ts choices."

"The fact remains, they are forcing you to discharge. No matter what happens now, the universe will realize that. Yoggi and OTS are going to have to take responsibility for their actions, and in my opinion, they should be held accountable. I will not bend the truth to accommodate immoral actions. I have been sending communications home about my impressions of you since the beginning. Most of the other Alphas have as well. As the saying goes, 'You can't hide the truth.' "

Zeus dropped his chin to his chest. He was profoundly distressed. Why was he always trapped by lousy options. "Crap, what I's suppose ta do?"

"May I ask you something?"

Zeus nodded while staring at his uniform shirt. Soon, he would not be wearing it anymore or the matching shoes.

"Why are you refusing to speak with Yoggi?"

"Ain'ts gonna believe noth'n I's gots ta say."

"You may be correct. Obviously, whatever happened occurred under extenuating circumstances. If you confide in me, perhaps I can assist you with her. If you are displeased with my suggestions or I cannot help, then I give you my word, I will not discuss anything we spoke about."

Zeus put his head in his hands. His head ached worse than his body. He was not used to working with people or the press. This situation was not just about Zeus Malone, so many others involved. If it were only him, he would take his lumps like he always had. Finally, Zeus raised his head. "What if it's 'bout something like an Honor Code violation."

"Did it happen before OTS?"

"Yeah." "

"And I assume there is a good explanation for your actions?"

"I's thinks so."

Apollo rubbed his cheek some more. "Were innocent people harmed?" Apollo would not go against his moral beliefs to protect Zeus.

"Nope, don't thinks so."

"Then I do not foresee my having to recount your secrets. For what it is worth, I am an excellent judge of character. You are a decent man. I am actually considering discharging myself."

"What?" Zeus leaped up.

"I am uncertain if I wish to associate with a hypocritical system that victimizes individuals like you."

"Budgin stupid idiot. This is a only system I's ever seen that in theory was supposed ta be's objective, not subjective. Ain'ts nobody like me's ever gonna gets no chance in a subjective system. If all yous honest guys quit, the Corps won't never be's like it's supposed ta, cause all the bastards like Richard and Hitler will be's run'n it."

"I never considered that perspective. Your view makes sense, and that, of course, answers the perplexing question of why you are fighting to remain. It also answers one of my prayers. I have been praying for guidance on whether to stay or discharge. My honest desire is to assist you and others like you."

"Then goes for the ring, yous idiot."

Apollo put his right hand out in front of him. "I do have the perfect size hand for one."

"Perfect." Zeus twisted the chair around, sat and dangled his arms over the seatback.

"We should proceed with the problem at hand. Perhaps your secret could aid you with the press. It depends on what you refuse to disclose."

Zeus rested his chin on the top of the chair. He cared what Apollo thought about him, and he needed the advice. He took a deep breath. "I's brokes inta the library ta study."

"It is a public facility. What would possess you to break in?"

"I's ain't part a the public."

"What? Are you implying they refused you access to the library?"

"Ain'ts imply'n. It's true."

"On what grounds?"

"I's orphan."

"That is outrageous." Apollo flopped back on the bed and stared at the ceiling. "The entire universe is indignant because orphans are supposedly uneducated and unmotivated. When in reality, the system refuses you access to anything that would promote your becoming productive. That is ridiculous." Apollo sat up. "The good news is, Yoggi would be crucified if she tried to discharge you on that revelation."

"Why?"

"Imagine the news." He framed an imaginary headline. " 'OTS Kicks Out Orphan for Using Library.' Not favorable to the OTS image. I assume you never stole anything?"

"Nope, don't matters. I's still guilty of break'n and enter'n."

"Technically, yes; however, it would be political suicide for Yoggi to discharge you on those grounds."

"She ain'ts got ta. Corps gets the library ta press charges, and I's go ta prison. But let me's guess, it's the only way Yoggi and OTS comes out look'n good?"

"To a degree. You were still treated improperly and against official policy. That disclosure can only undermine other orphans looking for opportunities. I promise, I will never repeat this conversation. You must feel as if you have no reasonable alternatives."

"Ain'ts no different than every other place I's live. What I's supposed ta do's 'bouts the press?"

"In my opinion, your best option is honesty. It demonstrates Yoggi and OTS tried to be impartial. They can state truthfully their concerns about your personal affiliations. You come across in a strong, positive light, and that bolsters orphan causes. No one will get caught making false accusations since numerous others around here will substantiate your story. In my opinion, it is the best option for achieving the bunk of your objectives."

"I's guess. Thanks."

The door opened and Sgt. Baker walked in. Both men stood and saluted. "Sorry about the mix-up. The schedules got crossed. I thought you were with Leiman, and she thought you were with me. We didn't figure it out until we ran into each other. Come on. I'm kind of glad you got a good break."

"Yeo, Sir." Zeuo walked out the door.

"Please contact me so we can communicate with one another," Apollo called after him.

*   *   *

Zeus attempted to determine what actions to take while he jogged around the track. His head throbbed. No matter what he did, people were going to get hurt. The longer he stayed, the more people he negatively affected.

The Kalopso intended to hunt him down and give him a level-four fate worse than death. Any place with sensors was dangerous. The only choices were sewers or uninhabited planets, assuming he could get to either. Neither prospect was appealing.

Since Emily had been killed, Zeus had convinced himself he hated people and was a loner by choice. OTS had forced him to face the truth; he was lonely. He was returning to nothing with nobody. He was through with people. . .forever. The emotional costs were too high.

Zeus stared at the moon. He finally accepted that he must leave soon. He would not be seeing Leiman or Taylor or Apollo or the obstacle course or the Alpha barracks or any of the other people and places of OTS again. His heart ached more than his muscles. He trotted over to Sgt. Leiman on the bench.

"Requests permission ta jogs around the base, Ma'am."

"Sure." She rose. Leiman sensed his attitude had changed. "You lead. I'll follow."

Zeus trotted slowly around the base, memorizing everything about the only decent place he had ever lived. He passed the flag pole. In his head, he could hear the trumpet blasts and the drum beats of the Corps anthem. He could almost smell the sweat as they rounded the corner of the gym. He led them down Yoggi's street. Cmd. Yoggi pulled into her driveway. Zeus abruptly stopped on the front sidewalk. His heavy heart anchored him firmly in place.

Leiman stopped, too.

Cmd. Yoggi parked and walked over as her two subordinates saluted. "At ease."

"Ma'am?" Leiman waited for her to nod. "Malone hasn't hydrated in a while. Do you mind if he uses the spigot on the side of your house?"

Yoggi caught her drift. "Malone, the spigot is on the left. Be sure you drink enough."

"Yes, Ma'am." Zeus wandered to the house.

Yoggi waited until he was out of hearing range. "Are we getting close?"

"I have a gut feeling, Commander. I think he maybe ready. We were at the track, then about thirty or forty minutes ago, Malone asked if he could jog around the base instead. It's almost like he's taking one last look around."

"Then he hasn't said anything about talking to me?"

"No, Ma'am."

"You have good instincts, you always have." Yoggi checked her watch. It read 23:06. She was in for another long night. "Let's not blow this chance. Do you think I should I play it hard or soft?"

"Soft, definitely soft. He's tired and depressed. Besides, every time Malone comes up against anger and aggression, he becomes defensive. I was hoping we could quietly lead him into talking. He knows what he needs to say."

"Sort of a covert intelligence operation." Yoggi nodded. "Let's give it a try. Nothing else is working."

"Do you have some furniture you need moved or some other excuse to get Malone in the house?"

"Why, yes, of course." Yoggi winked at her. "I'd almost forgotten. There's a broken credenza in the study that needs to be moved out."

"Yes, Ma'am." Leiman followed Yoggi over to Zeus. "How convenient we happened to be here when you remembered."

Zeus stood as he heard the footsteps behind him.

"Malone, I have a few things I need moved," Yoggi said. "As long as you're up, you might as well be useful."

"Yes, Ma'am." He fell in step behind the women.

Yoggi led them into her study. "I need to get rid of this." She motioned to an antique hand-carved white credenza. "Two of the drawers have been broken for years, and now it's wobbly. I keep thinking it's going to break. Help me get this stuff off the top."

They moved the items off the piece and onto the desk. Each time an item was removed, the top shifted and the items bobbled. "Let's just take the drawers out. I'll go through those things later."

Sgt. Leiman tried to take the top drawer out, but it stuck. "Here, let me do it," Yoggi stated. "You kind of have to jimmy it." Yoggi bumped it with her hip and yanked it out.

After everything was removed, Yoggi ordered, "Let's get it out of here."

Sgt. Leiman and Zeus each took a side and picked the credenza up by the top. They heard a snap, and the top jerked into their hands while the base of the piece remained on the floor.

"I knew it was going to break someday."

"Ma'am, requests permission ta asks a question."

"Go ahead."

"Yous want me's ta screw it tagether before we's move it?"

"Yes, I think it will be easier to move that way." She wanted to buy a little time. "I've always liked that piece. That's why I kept it so long. If it looks like it can be fixed, I'll probably pay someone to do that."

Zeus moved the base of the credenza away from the wall and picked up three screws. He took the knife out of his pocket and twisted the screws he had found back in place. Sgt. Leiman picked up another screw and handed it to her cadet. Yoggi got the power screwdriver and gave it to Zeus.

"Ma'am?" Zeus paused for her to nod. "Yous got any extra screws?"

"Let me see what I can locate." Cmd. Yoggi returned a few minutes later with a handful of miscellaneous screws.

Zeus quickly matched the screws and continued repairing the credenza. When he went inside the drawer area to finish securing the top, he found three other screws on the inside ledge of the drawer base. He attempted to use one on the top. It was too small. After completing the top's repairs, he realized the smaller screws were from the drawer tracks. Two were from the side tracks, and he replaced those. The third fit on the slider piece at the bottom of the drawer. When he was done, Zeus put the drawer in to see if it worked. The drawer glided in and out smoothly.

"That's amazing," Cmd. Yoggi exclaimed. "Can you fix the other one?"

"Yes, Ma'am." Zeus finished the last drawer and straightened up. "I's fixes it, Ma'am."

Cmd. Yoggi checked each drawer. They opened perfectly, and the top did not wobble. "I can't believe it. How did you fix the wobble?"

"Yous gots a screw caughts between the base and the top. I's gets that screws outs and puts thems all taghter."

"That's great." Cmd. Yoggi picked up a pile of computer discs and put them on the credenza. "Now you don't need to move it. I can't believe I've put up with broken drawers for years, when all it needed was a few screws. Thank you, Malone; I appreciate your help."

"Yes, Ma'am."

"Doesn't that drive you crazy?" Leiman said, trying to set up a chatty atmosphere. "Taylor did that to me a few months ago. The interior lights on my flyer haven't worked for at least a year. Whenever I needed to see something, I used a flashlight. Taylor used it once and returned it fixed. All it needed was some cheap little circuit that took him about thirty seconds to replace."

"I know what you mean," Yoggi followed suit. "I can't believe what we tolerate to avoid determining the problem."

Zeus added nothing as he followed them into the kitchen.

"Have a seat." Yoggi motioned to the table. "Let's celebrate my favorite credenza's repair." She took out a bottle of Haley's Brandy. It was expensive, but she hoped a little alcohol would loosen up Malone. She would have given him something more manly, but brandy was all she had in the house. She poured three small glasses and passed them out.

Zeus had no idea that little glasses were for brandy. He was thirsty and gulped his in one swallow. He coughed. He had not been prepared for the burning in his gut. "Crap," he gasped. "Tastes likes alcohol."

Both women laughed. Zeus appeared confused through his watering eyes.

"It is alcohol," Yoggi said. "I thought you knew."

"No, Ma'am." Zeus sniffed as he regained his composure. He was embarrassed he had handled his drink like a wimp.

"Don't you drink?" she asked.

"No, Ma'am."

"Never?" Leiman asked surprised.

"Never hads a money. Couple a times."

"Would you like a little more, now that you're prepared?" Yoggi held up the bottle. "And sip it this time."

Zeus did not want to appear weak. "Yes, Ma'am."

"Malone, when is the last time you ate?" Yoggi asked. She wanted an excuse to offer him something. She hoped he would appreciate the gesture. Anything she could do to make him feel comfortable and get this whole ugly business over with was worth a try.

"Dinner, seventeen hundred, Ma'am."

"Did you take your booster pills or whatever it is Dr. Bentley has you on?"

"Yes, Ma'am, before I's went run'n with Sgt. Leiman."

"Good, you better eat something. Dr. Bentley is already pestering me about your fatty curve. I want to tell her I fed you while you were here." She opened the cabinet and pulled some bread out. "How about a sandwich? I've got ham and Tageen."

"Ain'ts picky, Ma'am."

"Oh, yes, so I've heard. Anything but liver. You'll be relieved to know, I don't have any liver in the house."

"Yes, Ma'am," Zeus felt a little light-headed. He figured he was tired and took another sip of brandy.

"I appreciate your fixing my credenza." Yoggi slowly made the sandwich. She wanted to give him some time before she started asking her questions. By then the alcohol would have taken effect, and Malone would be as relaxed as he was going to get.

CHAPTER 22

CMD. YOGGI AND SGT. LEIMAN CHATTED around the kitchen table while Zeus silently ate his sandwich. He was feeling lightheaded and dizzy. The women's voices seemed distant and echoed slightly in his ear. His vision blurred, unless he concentrated on focusing.

Yoggi noticed his face was flush. She nodded to Leiman.

Leiman took her cue. "Malone here was able to tutor Cadet Petroff so he can stay in the program. He obviously knows how important a good tutor is."

"Well done," Cmd. Yoggi exclaimed. "I guess you didn't have any trouble going from student to teacher."

"No, Ma'am."

"Who was your favorite teacher over the years? The one who taught you the most?"

Zeus heard his own voice saying, "Emily."

Both women remembered he had mumbled that name while stunned.

"Oh," Leiman said, "what did Emily teach you?"

"How ta read, physics, chemistry, computers, alls the important crap." Startled, Zeus shook his head to clear it. He must be dreaming. He never answered questions like that.

"How long did she tutor you?"

"Six years, four months and twelve days."

"Was she your girlfriend?"

"Budgin bastards, NO!" He banged his glass on the table.

Yoggi waited until he relaxed, then cautiously asked, "What's Emily's last name?"

To his surprise, Zeus answered without hesitation, "Malone, Emily Malone." Zeus pounded the heel of his hand on his temple as he reminded himself not to answer questions like that.

Yoggi was surprised. "You have family?"

"Ins a orphanage, we's adopt each other as brother and sister. I's took her last name."

"What was your last name before?" Leiman asked.

"Ain't gots one. Didn't have no name before Emily. She calls me's Galahad, so I's use it as my middle name." Zeus rested his chin on the table. He struggled to focus on the glass. "After she gone, I's spend years hack'n until I's can gives myself an ID. Had ta make sure I's couldn't be track by thems budgin bastards."

Yoggi drummed her fingers. "Emily Malone. That name sounds familiar."

"Maybe yous read 'bout her in InterPress."

"I guess. I can't remember the article," Cmd. Yoggi replied.

"I don't recall ever hearing the name." Leiman shook her head. "Do you have any of the stories written about her, Malone? I'd love to know about the woman who kept you in line for six years."

"In InterPress network."

"Could you show me some?" Leiman hoped she was not pushing too much. She was surprised he was answering so freely.

"Huh, computer yous want me's ta use?"

"There's one right over here," Yoggi offered, hopeful.

Zeus stumbled over and sat at the built-in computer center in the kitchen. He turned it on and squinted to focus on the screen. "Yous got periodical reference?"

"No," she answered, disappointed.

Zeus slowly pulled the knife out of his pocket. He dropped to the floor, laid under the desk and adjusted something under the computer.

"I think he's rigging it so he can hack," Leiman whispered.

"Let's not interrupt him," Yoggi insisted.

Zeus fiddled with the system for about fifteen minutes, going from the controls underneath to the keyboard on the desk. When the screen read "InterPress Periodical Reference Systems," he sat at the desk. The women stood behind him. Zeus went to the "find" screen and typed in "Emily Malone." Numerous references appeared from years before.

Cmd. Yoggi thought she saw a familiar headline, tapped it on the screen and ordered, "Pull that one up first." The minute she saw the picture on the screen, Yoggi turned pale, gasped in horror and stumbled backwards. Leiman held her arm and steadied her.

Zeus was oblivious to them. He was in his own world, mumbling, "Emily, Emily." He gently touched the little girl on the screen. Emily was in front of a crowd explaining an underground aquifer system.

Sgt. Leiman was uncertain who to deal with first. Both were profoundly upset by the teenage girl in the blue dress. She tried to guide Yoggi over to a chair.

The commander jerked her arm away. "I'm fine. I want to read this."

Leiman squatted beside Zeus. "Are you OK?"

He turned to her. His head wandered, and his eyes followed slowly. "I's dizzy."

"Commander, look at his eyes."

Yoggi bent over. Zeus's pupils were severely dilated, his face flush and his head bobbed as he stared at her. "Malone, are you all right?"

"Dizzy," he strained to say. His head fell back onto his shoulder blades; unable to lift his head, he twisted it around and let it drop. "Dizzy."

"Come on." Cmd. Yoggi took one of his arms. "Let's get him to the couch and call Bentley."

*　　*　　*

Yoggi opened the front door. Dr. Bentley entered. She was wearing pink sweats and an almond T-shirt. Dr. Bentley took the med kit from around her neck and knelt beside Zeus on the couch. She examined Zeus as Yoggi and Leiman returned to the kitchen.

"Perhaps the doctor should check you when she's done," Leiman said.

"That won't be necessary. I was just shocked to see the image of Emily."

"Do you know her?"

"Not exactly. I've seen her before." Yoggi slid into a chair at the table. "I know Malone is telling the truth about Emily teaching him how to read. She was a child prodigy who lived in the orphanage on Velcron. I once heard her refer to a Galahad."

"Where and when did you see her?"

Yoggi closed her eyes. She shuddered as the memories flooded her thoughts. "I've never told anyone about this before. I've never talked about it, written it down, or dictated it, so there is no way Malone hacked his way into this information. I was too ashamed I never did anything to help her."

291

"What happened?" Curious, Leiman sat across the table.

"Years ago, I was at a large convention center. I got a terrible pain in my side and went to the bathroom. I thought I was constipated or something. I was sitting in one of the stalls, raising my legs up and down because it helped the pain. It turned out my appendix had ruptured. Later I was taken to the hospital.

"Emily must have checked under the stalls while I was raising my feet, because she thought she was alone. When I noticed her through the crack in the door, she was taking something out of her pocket and rubbing it on her wrists. The odd thing is, she was smiling. It didn't occur to me she was hurting herself, until I saw the blood on the floor."

"She was slitting her wrists?" Leiman questioned in disbelief.

"Yes. I started to get up, when someone burst through the door. She yelled, 'Emily.' I was relieved someone who knew her came to help her. Except the woman grabbed her by the hair and slapped her across the face."

"Why?"

"She wanted Emily to win an Agricultural Contest worth a million drayka."

"Who was the woman?"

"The director of the orphanage. She said someone named Galahad would get a fate worse than death if Emily didn't win. Emily promised to win. She was put in a clean, powder-blue dress, the one you saw in InterPress. I'll never forget what it looked like. It had long sleeves to cover her freshly sealed wrists. Once she was cleaned up, she was forced to compete in that contest. I went and watched her dissertation. I'm not certain Ritz or Kong would understand everything she explained. I read a few days later, she had won by unanimous decision. I looked up her accomplishments. She was touted as one of the most brilliant children in history. Soon after I saw her, she disappeared. I read she'd run away and was never seen again. I'll bet it was at the same time Malone disappeared into the sewers."

"Malone was in the sewers from about twenty-two fourteen through twenty-two sixteen, give or take," Leiman stated from memory. She had read his file dozens of times.

"Let's check InterPress to see when Emily disappeared. That sounds about right." Yoggi went to the terminal. She accessed the last available article. As they suspected, Emily had disappeared at the same time Zeus started living in the sewers.

"Emily easily could have taught Malone everything he knows. And that explains why the person teaching him wasn't feeding him, because she was a child trapped in the system as well. They wouldn't be on the network's side."

Leiman read the screen from behind Yoggi. "How do you know that?"

"Well, I guess I can't be certain, but I'd be very surprised. It's probably in InterPress, too. Emily's parents were killed by the Kalopso. Her father prosecuted one of the network leaders and supposedly was going after others. They brutally mutilated and killed her parents. As far as I can remember, they heard the network coming up the stairs and everybody hid. Emily was hidden in a kitchen cabinet, one that didn't close correctly, so there was a small crack she could see out of. She witnessed the murders."

"Eww, how horrible."

"Then this poor little girl was trapped in the cabinet, looking at and smelling those dead bodies for days. It was childproofed or latched, so it couldn't be opened from the inside. She was an emotional mess after that. She had to be kept in a special environment, because whenever she heard or saw insects, she'd kick and scream uncontrollably. Bugs reminded her of the ones that feasted on the dead bodies of her family."

Leiman grimaced and chills ran down her spine.

Dr. Bentley entered the kitchen holding her scanner. "How much brandy did you say you gave Malone?"

"Two small glasses," Yoggi answered. "Why?"

Bentley frowned at her recorder perplexed. "There is almost no alcohol registering in Malone's system."

"What?"

"How long ago did you give it to him?"

"Not that long ago. About an hour or so, wouldn't you say, Sergeant?"

"Yes, that sounds right. We both saw him drink it."

"There are only small traces in his system now." Dr. Bentley pushed some buttons and read the scanner. "What I think happened is the alcohol combined with the fatty boosters and somehow turned into Quakalin."

Yoggi's eyes grew wide. "The truth drug?"

"Yes, actually something chemically similar."

Leiman scratched her chin. "I thought it was odd Malone was answering us so freely."

"Is he in any danger?" Yoggi asked.

Bentley flipped through a number of screens on her scanner. "I'm not certain. I don't think so, but I need to run a few tests at the lab."

"Will it hurt him to answer a few more questions?"

"I'd rather wait on that," Dr. Bentley said.

"I didn't ask you if you'd rather wait. I asked if it was a health risk," Cmd. Yoggi snapped.

"Commander, I just. . ."

Yoggi spoke over her. "Listen to me. If I'm going to kick this man out, I need concrete reasons. I no longer think he's a network plant, but I don't know what else, if anything, he's done. All Malone wants is to stay in this program. I might be able to let him. If he were coherent, he'd want that chance."

Dr. Bentley sighed. "How much time do you need?"

"I'd say five, maybe ten minutes."

"Do it now. I'd rather be here to monitor him. Please keep it at five minutes."

"I'll try."

"Let's bring him into the kitchen. I want him to get some more food in his system. Sugary items will be best. Sodas, candy, cookies, juice, table sugar, honey, anything that metabolizes quickly. Leiman, help me bring him in."

Zeus stumbled in leaning on the doctor and Leiman. Cmd. Yoggi set out all the sugary items she could find. Zeus sat at the table. His head wobbled as he strained to focus through dilated eyes.

Dr. Bentley poured a soda, added some sugar and handed it to Zeus. "Here, drink this."

"Yes, Ma'am."

"Make it fast, Commander," Dr. Bentley begged.

"Malone, have you ever raped anyone?"

"NOPE!"

"Why so protective of women?"

Zeus pushed the chair out from behind him, jumped up and leaned forward. His hot breath pulsated in her face as he yelled, "I's swore after them budgin bastards said theys gonna rock Emily, I's never watch another man hurt a girl. An I's ain't never gonna." He pounded his fists on the table. "I's wish I's killed thems budgin bastards." He slapped the glass of soda across the floor.

Dr. Bentley leaned over and whispered to the commander. "This is what I was afraid of. Quakalin and similar drugs force the patient to experience the same intensity of emotions as the original experience. In some cases, the emotions are more intense. Hurry up and finish your questions."

"Ever killed anyone?" Yoggi asked.

"Nope."

"Have you ever broken the law?"

"Yeah."

"What did you do?"

"Budgin bastards ats the library wouldn't let me's in, so I's breaks in at night ta study."

"Did you ever steal anything?"

"Nope." He kicked the leg of the table. "All I's want is ta study like everybody else."

Cmd. Yoggi threw her hands up. "I can't kick you out for trying to use a library."

"That's what Apollo says."

"Then why not tell me the truth?"

"Cause it don'ts matter. Lt. Cmd. Zeigler gets the library ta press charges for break'n and enter'n, and I's go ta jail for that."

"What does Zeigler have to do with this?" Yoggi demanded.

"He's a K contact here."

All three women's jaws dropped. "What?" Yoggi exclaimed. "You can't possibly expect me to believe my second in command, a person I confide in and trust, is a member of the crime network?"

Zeus shook his fist at her. "I's can prove it."

"If you wanted to stay here, then why not prove it to me before?"

"Too dangerous. I's ain't let'n nobody else get hurt cause a me's. Budgin K finds out yous know, they's kill yous or worse."

"The reason you wouldn't talk was to protect us?" Leiman waved her hand at the other women.

"Yeah. Hurts too much ta watch."

Yoggi crossed her arms. "You said you could prove Zeigler's a member of the network. How?"

"Gots copies of the budgin bastard's B-file, and him talk'n 'bout me's."

Bentley scrunched her face. "What's a B-file?"

"K keeps copies a all the illegal crap members do. Then they's can be blackmailed inta cooperat'n, if theys ever want ta get out."

"I want to see that file," Yoggi ordered.

"Yes, Ma'am." Zeus turned around, tripped and fell into the counter.

Leiman put her arm around his waist and steadied him. "Where is it, Malone?"

"Computer." He staggered to the terminal.

While Zeus hacked, Bentley whispered to Yoggi, "I know I can't stop this. I need to go run those tests."

"Yes, go ahead. Return here as soon as you're done."

"I'll hurry." Bentley slipped the med kit over her shoulder and scurried out the door.

In minutes, they were listening to Lt. Cmd. Zeigler speaking about Malone and how he would convince Yoggi to force him out. Everything they discussed, Yoggi realized, in one way or another, Zeigler had said to her. She listened, stunned, as the extent of his betrayal became more personal.

"Where is her weak link?" the unidentified network man asked.

"Sheila. Definitely her daughter, Sheila," Zeigler answered.

"You think she'd roll for her?"

"Without a doubt." Zeigler snapped his finger.

"Can you get access to Sheila?"

"I've already arranged it," Zeigler bragged. "I spoke to Yoggi. I told her if there was ever a reason to be concerned for her daughter, I'd watch out for her. That we could easily hide Sheila at a fishing cabin I have on New Atlas. Yoggi was very appreciative of my concern." He laughed mischievously.

Cmd. Yoggi could contain her anger no longer. She picked up the plate of cookies and smashed it onto the floor. The crash startled Zeus, who turned to identify the noise. Both he and Leiman stared at her.

"I'm sorry." Yoggi shrugged. "It's kind of a family tradition. My family owns Yoggiware, a china and stoneware manufacturer. If a batch is flawed, it has to be destroyed. It's a long story, but the gist of it is, we always had these factory reject plates at home. When we got upset, or had a bad day, my parents let us smash a plate or two in a box. It helps release the anger. You'd be amazed at how well it works." Yoggi went to the cabinet and pulled out some mismatched plates. She picked up the top one and smashed it to the floor. "That bastard Zeigler is definitely a two platter."

In his drugged state, Zeus found the plate explanation completely reasonable. Leiman, on the other hand, thought it was bizarre.

The computer continued to run Zeigler's communication. The three turned and listened again. Nothing new was being said.

"I've had enough of this," Yoggi declared. "Let me see this B-file you were talking about."

"Yes, Ma'am," Zeus slurred. In moments, the screen listed Jeffrey Zeigler's B-file categories. The first files showed Zeigler had cheated on his taxes and embezzled money from two military accounts. Yoggi had suspected money was missing from one account. Unfortunately, she had assigned Zeigler to check into any possibility of foul play.

Zeigler had also framed an innocent orphan of murder.

"I remember that case," Yoggi commented. "Zeigler had to take off to testify. Why would he do it? What does Zeigler get out of framing an innocent man on another planet? He didn't even know the victim."

"Standard K practice. They's constantly frame innocent orphans ta keep the public paranoid. The more honest a orphan, the more K targets thems for a frame-up. That way society believes we's can't never knows right from wrong. And even if we's do now, theys keep prove'n we's can't be trusted. They's always make'n studies ta prove we's psychologically impaired for life."

Leiman scratched her head. "Why?"

"They's get more drayka that way. First government appropriates more ta ORA ta contain orphans. K pockets that, then forces us ta work for noth'n and takes thems profits, too."

Yoggi pulled a chair over and sat beside Zeus. "Talk about working both ends."

"We's ain't gots a chance."

"What's a K-Club?" Yoggi pointed to a file on the screen.

"That's where members goes ta rocks orphans and gamble." Zeus accessed the first K-Club folder.

Dr. Bentley returned. She stood behind Zeus and beside Leiman.

The women were horrified as they witnessed Zeigler sodomizing a young girl. Zeus randomly flipped through the folder to other dates, other girls, and more illicit acts.

Tears streaked Dr. Bentley's face.

Yoggi wrapped her arms around herself and tried to hold in the whirlwind of emotions erupting inside her. "It's no wonder he's adamant about getting Malone out."

Sgt. Leiman closed her eyes and shut out the images.

Dr. Bentley put her arm around her. "Are you all right?"

Leiman pulled away and asked Yoggi, "Can I have one of those plates?"

"Sure." Yoggi motioned to the stack on the table. "Smash as many as you'd like."

Leiman picked one up and threw it to the floor with a crash.

Bentley jumped back. Yoggi explained the odd family tradition again. Bentley decided she, too, would try this new stress reduction therapy. Crash went another plate.

"It does make me feel a little better," she proclaimed.

Zeus's dilated eyes stared at them. Yoggi offered him a plate. He took it and threw it Frisbee-style into the wall. The plate shattered and fragments flew in every direction.

Yoggi motioned the doctor over to the living room door. "I never asked. Is it safe for Malone to continue?"

"Yes. There is nothing I can do to minimize the effects of Quakalin or make it dissipate faster. His mind will force him to keep remembering things, if we don't keep him busy. We can't sedate him; that could be fatal. Quakalin has a stimulating effect, so he can't sleep until his blood levels drop substantially."

"Why can't you filter it out of his blood?" Yoggi asked.

"Unfortunately, it isn't pre-programmed into blood filters, and I don't have the exact chemical formula to program it in. Plus, it isn't exactly Quakalin. The original drug caused intense emotions; often unpredictable, violent responses, and some patients couldn't be controlled. The drug has been banned. It's odd that the combination of fatty boosters and brandy would produce it. I'm sure that's never been documented. Let's face it; it's rare for a patient to need fatty boosters these days."

"If we hit upon a bad topic, we'll change the subject." Yoggi walked over to the terminal. "Malone, go to another file."

"Yes, Ma'am." Zeus rubbed his eyes to clear his vision. He randomly accessed another K-Club entry. The little girl was about twelve years old. She had blue eyes and shoulder-length auburn hair, just like Emily had at that age. Through his blurred vision, Zeus thought it was Emily. As soon as Zeigler began molesting her, Zeus grabbed the terminal and screamed, "Don't yous touch her, yous filthy bastard." He shook the terminal, then smashed it onto the desk.

The women stepped back. "Any suggestions?" Yoggi asked the doctor.

"Stay out of his way."

The image remained on the screen. Zeus punched and yelled furiously at the computer until it was a lifeless pile of broken metal and glass. As the cork containing his emotions popped, he banged and kicked at the desk long after the computer fell silent. He swung around and faced the women. His nostrils flared and eyes burned red with rage.

Yoggi grabbed the five remaining plates off the table. "Here, you want to break another plate?"

Zeus snatched the plates and one by one threw them against the wall. Then he stomped on the larger pieces until they shattered into tiny fragments.

"Let me try to calm him," Leiman offered. "He's most likely to listen to my voice. He trusts me more than you two."

Yoggi rolled her shoulders. "Go ahead."

"Malone, could you come over here and help me?"

"Yes, Sergeant." He swayed as he walked to her.

"For once I'm thankful for boot camp brainwashing," Bentley said.

Leiman was not prepared for him to respond so quickly. She had to think of something for Malone to help her with. "Who. . .who can I get. . .to tutor Petroff? He'll never make it through without help."

"Ronner."

"You think so?" Leiman led Zeus to a chair and sat him at the table. She took the chair beside him and continued to discuss various other Alpha cadets.

Yoggi squatted by Zeus. "Malone, are Baker and Taylor connected to the Kalopso?"

"No, Ma'am."

"Then you trust them?"

"Don't trusts nobody."

"They have no network affiliations?"

"K ain'ts interest in enlisted. Don't makes 'nough money."

Yoggi rose and pulled the doctor aside. "Call Baker and Taylor. Tell them to come over and stay out of sight. I don't want to provoke Malone, but I want them here in case we need them."

Bentley nodded. "I'll let them in the front door." Dr. Bentley walked into the living room.

Yoggi pulled up a chair on the other side of the table. "Malone, I still don't understand why you wouldn't tell me all this. Obviously, I wouldn't have been so hard on you. I would never have told Zeigler anything you told me. Why not come to me?"

"Cause Zeigler bugs yous office. And cause if yous wasn't confide'n in him, he's suspect yous on ta him, then he's. . ."

"Wait. Back up. Zeigler bugged my office?"

"Yes, Ma'am."

She turned and scanned the room. "What about here?"

"Yous study in the house, computer terminals and yous ComLine."

"Leiman, go see if the study door is open or shut. Leave it the way it was and tell me if you can hear us."

Sgt. Leiman returned a few minutes later with Dr. Bentley. "The study door was shut and I couldn't hear anything you said."

Yoggi leaned across the table. "What types of bugs did Zeigler use?"

"Standard issue C32's in yous office and study."

"Audio and visual?" Yoggi drummed her fingers.

"Yes, Ma'am."

"What about the computers and ComLine? Are they hooked to work only when in use?"

"Yeah."

Panic swept over Yoggi's face. "Then he'll know all the things you showed us tonight?"

"I's bypass the links on this end and they's can't trace where I's gots my's information from."

Leiman returned to the seat beside Zeus. "Why not?"

"I's don't goes inta any files. I's recapture renaissance waves and reads thems."

"I don't understand." Yoggi wanted to be certain they were safe.

"All computer information transfers in the form of energy. Energy has waves that ebbs and flows likes water, 'cept we's don't sees it. Don'ts matter where the energy originates, all artificial energy waves is retrievable, least in theory."

"Keep him talking," Bentley mouthed, circling her hand.

"Start at the beginning and explain it to me in detail," Yoggi said.

"Emily and me's, we's figured out how ta trace specific waves, retrieve 'em and reads 'em. We's could only do it if we's close ta the source and knows exactly what we's look'n for. I's ain't been too successful with it 'til Capt. O'Donnell shows me's how ta harness the power grid from the mega main on Tallien. I's take her ideas and use Tallien's frequency and power ta trace and retrieve any files I's want. Since I's ain't retrieve'n from either a source or a destination, ain'ts no ways ta even know I's gots in or ta track me's."

"That's fascinating," Leiman said. "If it's so simple, why can't you teach the other Alphas to do it?"

"Gots ta be able ta read ins computer language. Wave energies ain't in software formats. In energy formats or sort of like computer language. . ."

Yoggi leaned over to Bentley and whispered, "Do you understand what he's talking about?"

"Me? How would I know? I'm so lost I wouldn't have known he was talking about computers."

"Well, now we know why his roommate says this stuff is boring."

Cmd. Yoggi waited until Zeus quit talking. She still was not certain if they were safe. "Then Zeigler won't know anyone saw his B-files?"

"No, Ma'am." Zeus laid his head down.

"And he doesn't have to know you were here?"

"Gonna knows," Zeus mumbled into the table. "I's in yous study ta fix the desk thing."

"Can you disconnect the sensors?"

"Ain'ts gonna."

She slapped the table. "Why not?"

Zeus gradually lifted his head. His reactions were in slow motion or none existent. "If they's ain't transmitt'n, Zeigler will know yous on ta him. I's ain't gonna be responsible for what the K does ta yous or yous family."

"Why would you protect me, when I've treated you so badly?"

"I's ain't like yous or thems. I's don't budge people ta gets what I's want. None of yous want me's here. Crap, even yous, Leiman. If yous can't see me's as an officer, ain'ts nobody never gonna. I's was budged before I's gots here."

"Then why fight to stay?" Leiman questioned.

Zeus rested his chin on his arm. "I's leave here, K gots a level-four fate worse than death wait'n for me's."

"What's a level four?"

He stared off into space. "Worse, most painful, budgin long drawn-out torture they's can come up with."

"What makes you think you're safe here?" Leiman asked.

"K wants OTS ta have clean reputation. Corps can'ts afford the negative press. I's gots ta take the bad press."

"Why?" Yoggi asked.

"They's take part of the funds from OTS and Corps. But K's gets big drayka from what them bastards takes from ORA. I's look bad, more drayka appropriated ta keep orphans contained."

"Oh."

Yoggi shook the table. "Sneak out while you can?"

"Ain't gots no place ta go. K can have me's. And I's wanna help the other kids they's budgin over. Woman at school told me's, longer I's stay, and the less valid a reason I's kicked out for, the better it is for other orphans look'n ta gets out. Apollo says the same thing. Only I's wanna way out that don't budge all yous careers. I's try'n ta get crap set, ain'ts had time."

"What do you mean that won't hurt our careers?"

"Apollo and Leiman's think'n of quit'n. And if Apollo don't keeps his budgin mouth shut, they's gonna kill him. Taylor thinks he's withdrew from the All-Militaries. And yous," he shook his finger at Yoggi, "is taken the fall for my's still be'n here."

The Commander dropped her head in shame. Despite trying to act fairly, she had been blinded by her bias against orphans. She had never given Malone a fair chance. Dr. Jones had been right. He was an honest, decent man. She raised her head. "You let me worry about my career."

"Yous daughter?"

"I see your point." Yoggi drummed her fingers. "How do I ensure she doesn't get dragged into this?"

"Yous do what Zeigler tells yous."

"He wants me to sell you out."

"Yes, Ma'am." He nodded. "Yous do it."

"You don't seem too concerned."

"I's already dead. Ain't noth'n yous can do ta helps me's. Ain't no reason ta let thems hurt yous, too."

"And my integrity?" Yoggi raised her eyebrows.

"Budge it. Ain't worth yous daughter's life."

"You're protecting us?" She waved her hands at Leiman and Bentley. "Including me, my family and my career?"

"Yes, Ma'am."

"What am I supposed to do to help you?"

Zeus slapped the table. "Do what Zeigler tells yous."

"And if I don't?"

Zeus shook his fist in her face. "They's budge yous daughter 'til yous wish yous is dead."

"Thanks for caring what happens to Sheila." Yoggi rubbed her temples. "I can't bear the thought of Sheila being hurt, but I have a duty to you and the Corps. Maybe it wouldn't be that bad."

"Disloyalty and rat'n on the K is always a level four. I's know."

"How do you know?"

"They's do it ta Emily, and I's wish I's dead." Zeus laid his head down and covered his tear-streaked face. "I's. . .I's supposed ta kill a guy as my's initiation inta K. Emily, she believes in Jesus likes Apollo. Always talk'n like him. She teaches me's it wrong and bads ta murder for the K. I's goes and can't kill my's guy. They's mads I's failed after invest'n two years of train'n me's ta be K."

"What do you mean training you?"

"Teach'n me's ta fight, ta use knives, ta survive attacks, ta sleep with my's eyes opens, crap like that."

"Were you a member of the network?"

"Nope. Budgin selfish, lying bastards, all of thems. I's tell them after I's fail I's don't want ta join K. I's goes back ta work'n in the mines. K boss lies and says I's ain't gots ta kill nobody. Only I's find out boss has ordered me's a fate worse than death for fail'n. Wait'n ta give it 'til I's done help'n Emily wins her contest. I's pay. Cause if K wants yous ta suffer, ain't no way ta escape. We's sneak out before my's fate. I's still wish I's dies." He wiped his running nose with his sleeve. "Why Emily? She don't hurts nobody. It's my's fault. I's fail, and Emily pays."

"What happened?"

"Whippy, she helps us escape inta sewers. Emily can't handle small dark places, reminds her of the cabinet at home. Emily screams at bugs and leechrats when theys touch her. Ain't no ways ta avoid thems in the sewers. I's carry her when we's in the water and let her sleep on top of me's, so they's ain't so many touch'n her at night. Don't help much. Emily, she's wants ta die. Tries ta kills herself. After we's out of the sewers, K finds us through Emily's retina scan and the sensors they's access in the ghettoes. They's want us ta suffer. They's think they's kill me's, and I's ain't in the universal ID system then." His voice dropped to a hush. The women leaned in to hear him. "They's give Emily a fate worse than death. Level four."

Leiman put her hand on Zeus's shoulder. "If she believed like Christiani, she's at peace in heaven now."

Zeus pushed her hand away. "It's all my's fault." He banged his head on the table. "They's made her suffer and suffer and suffer all cause a me's." Zeus picked up his chair and hurled it at the door.

"I's weak. I's couldn't let her die with me's. I's fail, and she pays with a level four. I's budgin weak. WEAK. WEAK. WEAK!" He beat the table with each word.

Sgt. Leiman put her hand on Zeus shoulder. "It wasn't your fault."

Zeus swung around. He stopped and the room continued to spin. Through his tears, he jabbed at one of the three Sgt. Leimans he saw. His fist passed centimeters from her face as he stumbled into the wall. Bentley pulled Leiman away while Zeus round-kicked a hole in the wall.

"But he could hurt himself," Leiman objected to Cmd. Yoggi.

"He's there now," Bentley said. "In this state, Malone could easily mistake any of us for a Kalopso member. If we try to interfere, he may hurt himself more or hit someone next time. As long as he's attacking inanimate objects, I think it's best to leave him alone. He'll sustain minor injuries, and none of us will get hurt."

"I agree," Yoggi stated. "Let's try to redirect his thoughts."

"Be careful." Bentley looked at Leiman. "From the brief overview I read, you need to redirect within his memory. Forcing him to stop reliving a traumatic memory could cause him to be stuck in that place for weeks. That could potentially be more devastating to his mind than allowing him to continue. I'd like to check his blood levels. I wish I could continually monitor, but I have to filter each sample manually."

"How long do you think this will go on?" Yoggi asked.

"I haven't taken enough samples to determine how quickly the Quakalin is dissipating." She winced as Zeus flung himself into the computer desk.

He kicked and punched at the remainder of the desk until he fell down in exhaustion. Zeus hugged his knees to his chest and sat motionless amid the rubble.

CHAPTER 23

"MALONE. MALONE." Dr. Bentley knelt beside him. Zeus's eyes were open, but whatever he was seeing was far, far away. "I'm going to take a quick blood sample." Zeus did not move or respond. She cautiously swabbed his forearm and extracted a small sample. She left him still frozen like a statue and went to her bag to run the test.

"Malone?" Leiman squatted in front of him.

"I's weak. It's all my's fault."

"It's not your fault. You're not weak." Leiman tried to reassure him. "It takes great strength to do what's right in the face of adversity."

"Yous don't watch Emily's suffer'n. Yous don't have ta see her in pain and hear her screams in her sleep. I's should a let her dies."

"He's in the present for now," Bentley whispered to Yoggi. "I wish I knew if that was good or bad."

Leiman sat on the floor. "Doing what's right isn't always easy or painless, but it's still right."

"Ain'ts right ta makes Emily suffer." He picked up crumpled disc of broken metal and flung it across the room. "I's a one who should a suffered."

"Malone, you did, and you're suffering now."

Cmd. Yoggi looked at her watch. "How much longer before this stuff wears off?" she asked the doctor.

"I don't know. I've checked his blood twice since I returned. It's dissipating at different rates. I think it depends on his emotional intensity. It dissipates slower when he's talking about computers and faster when he smashing them."

"It's after four now. Do you think he'll be done in the next couple of hours?"

"If I were to guess, yes. Am I positive? No. Why?"

"I want this kid protecting the truth before Zeigler shows up in the morning."

"Why would Zeigler come here?"

"He often runs in the morning and then stops here for coffee. He's usually early." Yoggi rubbed her forehead. "Never later than oh seven hundred. The past few days, he's been checking with me every morning about Malone. I thought it was considerate that during his busiest time, while the cadets are pairing off into their flight teams, he took the time to check in on me. The past few years, I haven't seen Zeigler during partnering time. Now I know he was checking on me for the network." She clenched her fist. "I want to kill that bastard."

"But you can't." Bentley held her by her upper arms. Their gazes locked. "Everything Malone says makes sense. If you in any way imply you don't trust him, he's on to you."

"I know, I know." Yoggi bobbed her head up and down. "I need to be completely composed before I see him."

"You go upstairs and rest. We can handle things down here." Bentley released her grip.

Yoggi stepped away. "I'm not leaving until Malone's head is clear."

"I'm not certain he'll be himself before six or seven. I suggest we ask him general stuff about Emily. Nothing too traumatic. My guess, and I'm afraid it is a guess, is that the Quakalin will dissipate faster than it is now, but slower than when he's smashing things. Let's get him eating more sugary items. That helps a little. Not much."

"OK." Cmd. Yoggi walked to the cabinet to get another glass and plate. "Malone, how about another bite to eat?"

"Yes, Ma'am."

Sgt. Leiman rose and offered Zeus her arm. He tried to stand alone, faltered and fell into her. Leiman steadied him and led him to the wobbly table. Dr. Bentley picked up one of the chairs and guided it in behind Zeus.

Yoggi poured another soda. "Malone, tell me how you met Emily."

"I's chase'n a leechrat and gots lost in a sewers. I's ends up at Emily's."

"Here." Yoggi handed him a cookie and the soda.

"Yes, Ma'am." Zeus lifted the glass. He misjudged the distance to his mouth and dribbled the clear liquid down his chin.

"Did you stay with Emily after you met her?" Yoggi questioned.

"First year, I's sneaks in ta the lab at night ta learn. Then I's gots caught. K boss likes me's. Says he's train me's if I's helps Emily with her aquifer and keeps her happy."

"Why don't you start at the beginning and tell me all the wonderful things you remember about her."

Zeus told them how he would sneak into Emily's lab through the sewage and ventilation systems after he finished working in the mines. He and Emily played and she would tutor him. They still had struggles. She hated being forced to compete in contests. He was always hungry. Each time Zeus recalled a painful memory, Cmd. Yoggi let him break another dish. She no longer cared that he was breaking her good dishes. The doctor's theory was working. The Quakalin was dissipating quickly enough without agitating Malone too much.

One by one, Zeus broke every plate, bowl, glass and dish in the house. It was after five, Yoggi had nothing breakable left in the cabinets to offer the orphan. Zeus's eyes appeared less dilated. Yoggi was hopeful he would be Quakalin-free by six.

"What do you remember most?" Leiman asked.

"Them budgin bastards take'n her." Zeus abruptly lunged across the table, toppling the chair behind him. "They's took her say'n they's gonna rock her, then K gonna gives her a level four." Zeus grabbed the chair and pounded it against the wall until it splintered into pieces. "I's promise Emily I's never let them hurts her again." He seized another chair and threw it at the women. "None of yous tries ta helps her." He nabbed another chair and charged them. The women raced to the door and retreated to the living room. Leiman yanked the door shut as a chair splintered on the wall near the door.

"Do you want us to go in, Ma'am?" Sgt. Taylor asked.

Dr. Bentley raised her arm in front of Taylor. "I think we ought to leave him alone for a few minutes. If you go in there now, someone is bound to get hurt. Let him unwind. Then we'll decide what to do."

They heard a loud shattering of glass. "There goes the cooking surface," Yoggi guessed aloud.

Bentley sank into the recliner. "So, now that the demolition is done, when does the remodeling start?"

They laughed nervously as they listened to the pounding, kicking and breaking noises echoing from the kitchen. They could hear Zeus calling, "Emily. . .Huh is yous? Emily. . . Emily. . ." Over and over he called for her.

The group remained silent until another extremely loud crash sounded. "When does this drug wear off?" Taylor asked.

"The last time I checked, it appeared we were getting close. Plus considering the intensity of his current emotions, he should be almost done."

Ten minutes later, the noise became less frequent. Leiman finally stopped pacing. "Let me go in by myself. He responds best to me. We don't want to upset him anymore."

Cmd. Yoggi glanced at her watch. She guessed Zeigler would arrive in about an hour. "All right, but no unnecessary risks."

"Yes, Commander."

Leiman waited for a lull in the sound and pushed the kitchen door open cautiously. The door opened halfway, then got caught on a broken chair leg. "Malone, are you all right?" she asked softly.

"All my's fault." He stumbled into the wall.

"No it's not." She moved closer to him

"Yous don't understand." Zeus banged his head against the wall.

"I know you loved Emily very much."

"Yeah. For thats she gets raped and a fate worse than death."

"Your caring for Emily is not what hurt her. The sick and twisted people in the network did that."

"She begs me's ta let her dies." He slid down the wall and crouched on the floor. "I's couldn't let her goes. I's afraid ta be's without Emily, and the budgin books and computer." Tears rolled down his freckled cheeks. "She's begs me's, over and over, ta lets her die. I's too budgin selfish and afraid. I's don't wants ta be's alone and without no study'n." Zeus pulled his knees up to his chest. "Emily and read'n was all I's had ta keep me's go'n."

Sgt. Leiman knelt beside him. "You were probably all Emily had, too. You can't blame yourself."

"I's couldn't lets her die. I's stop her whenever she tries."

"Don't blame yourself," she whispered in a soothing voice. She put her arms out and motioned him in.

He looked at her through his bloodshot eyes. "I's couldn't let her go."

Leiman cautiously put her arms around him. He resisted slightly, but she held him firmly. He was too ashamed and tired to fight her.

"I's too budgin afraid."

"It's OK now." Leiman pressed his head to her shoulder and held him like a child. Zeus tried to pull away, but she held him tightly, quietly encouraging him. "The tears are good for you. Let it out. You've kept this in too long."

"I's didn't wanna lose her teach'n as much as Emily," he whimpered.

"Let it out. Tell your sergeant all about it."

Zeus took a large deep breath in an effort to gain control. Just when he thought he had succeeded, he exhaled, and the floodgates opened. He sobbed uncontrollably.

His sobs shook them both as she held him and patted his back. "Let it out. Sgt. Leiman's here."

"I's. . .I's. . .I's couldn't. . .I's. . .couldn't. . ."

"It's OK. Tell Sgt. Leiman all about it."

She continued to comfort him as her shirt grew wet with his tears. Zeus finally settled into an erratic post-crying breathing pattern.

"Doctor," Leiman called.

Bentley entered the kitchen, cleared a spot on the floor and knelt beside her patient. Zeus had a glass cut underneath the left eye. The drips from the cut made it appear he was crying blood onto Leiman's shoulder. Bentley raised the laserseal to repair his face.

Zeus's mind flashed to an earlier time. He grabbed the sealer and slung it across the room. "Yous ain't touch'n her, yous budgin bastard." Bentley realized too late she was in danger. Zeus struck her with a left cross and screamed, "I's kill yous for what yous done."

Sgt. Leiman used all her strength to restrain Zeus long enough for Dr. Bentley to retreat into the living room.

"Is yous OK, Emily?" Zeus asked Sgt. Leiman.

"Yes, I'm. . .I'm fine," Leiman pretended to be Emily.

"I's won't let them hurt yous. I's kill'em first, thems budgin bastards. Yous know yous safe withs me's. Ain't gonna lets nobody hurt yous. They's come, I's kill'em. Here," he removed his tear-soaked shirt. "Yous wear it. Yous gets cold out here. Yous won't be's cold with me's. And I's ain't gonna let yous touch the grounds even once tanight."

Leiman covered her mouth, trembling. She could no longer contain her emotions. The roles reversed. Zeus held her while she wept.

310

"I's wish I's could stop 'em," he whispered. "Gangs is strong here. I's sorry I's can't keep 'em away." He put the shirt over her head.

"That's all right." Leiman pulled the shirt off. "I don't need your shirt."

Zeus forced it over her head. "I's not gets cold like yous. Can't starts a fire, they's finds us again. Yous needs ta keep warm." He guided her right hand through the sleeve.

Leiman put her left hand through the hole. "Thank you," she choked out, feeling strangely better with his shirt on.

"Come on, I's help yous sleep." Zeus put his arms out. Leiman assumed he would hold her as she had held him. Instead, in one fluid motion, he laid on his back and pulled her on top of him with her head on his shoulder and her legs between his. Zeus held her tight and swayed from left to right.

Leiman felt like a sick child in her father's protective embrace. She also felt awkward lying on top of one of her cadets. She tried to position herself to lie beside him. Zeus would not allow it. He held her firmly, swayed faster and pleaded, "Don't hurt youself, Emily. I's take care of yous, just don't hurt yous. . ." Zeus's breathing grew even and quiet.

Leiman waited until he was asleep and then slipped onto the floor. Even in his sleep, when she tried to move off, Zeus stopped her, swayed and said, "Don't hurt youself, Emily."

Cmd. Yoggi peered cautiously into the kitchen and returned to the living room. "He appears to be quieting down. I think we'll give Leiman a little more time before we go in."

Dr. Bentley had a large bruise under her cheekbone. She looked at Taylor and rubbed her sore cheek. "Tell me again why you enjoy fighting so much."

"Well, Doc, the goal is to hit the other guy and NOT get hit yourself."

"Yes, I can understand why."

"Commander," Sgt. Baker asked, "what are we going to do about Malone tomorrow, I mean later today?"

Taylor leaped out of his seat. "You wouldn't kick him out now, would you?"

"Not if I don't have to." Yoggi again peered at her watch. "Baker brings up a good point. What are we going to do? We have to justify him staying without Zeigler becoming suspicious."

"Can't we just tell the truth about Emily?" Dr. Bentley offered. "Say Malone showed you the InterPress information on her, and she taught him to read."

"Yes, that works for the mentor questions. InterPress will verify they were in the same orphanage, at the same time, and disappeared at the same time. Unfortunately, that doesn't take care of the crime network and Zeigler, or the bugs in my office and study, or how my kitchen got completely destroyed. Besides, who's to say, even with the InterPress articles about Emily, that Malone hasn't broken the law or isn't the psychopathic rapist Sato says he is. Plus, I'll have to give some form of a statement to the press."

"That's a lot of things to work out." Baker cracked his knuckles.

Taylor flopped in the recliner and rested his chin in his hand for some time. "Doctor," he raised his head, "did you take readings and samples of Malone's blood?"

"Yes, of course."

"And you still have those?"

"Yes." She shrugged.

"Then there is proof that there was a truth drug in Malone's blood?"

"Yes."

Yoggi crossed her arms and frowned. "What are you getting at, Taylor?"

"The way I see it, Commander, we should tell Zeigler, the press and everyone else the truth about tonight, minus the details about Zeigler and the Kalopso stuff."

"I see your point. Malone won't be held accountable for what he did in his drugged state, especially since Quakalin is known to make people erratic. That way, we have definitive proof Malone is not a network member and has never broken the law." Cmd. Yoggi paused. "We'll also have to omit the part about him sneaking into the library. No one would question his motives or why I allowed him to stay."

"What about the fact that you gave him the brandy?" Sgt. Baker questioned the commander.

"She couldn't possibly have known it would combine with the booster treatments to make Quakalin. That phenomenon has never been documented," Dr. Bentley stated.

"I don't mind if people know I gave him the brandy. If anything, it would be viewed as a minor lapse in judgment. It's not like I made him chug it or forced him to drink it. I gave him two small glasses and called the doctor as soon as I suspected there was a problem."

Baker played the devil's advocate. "Why didn't you take him to the hospital, Doctor?"

"He was too agitated. Once I knew there was nothing I could do to treat him and he insisted he wanted to say here, I was afraid he'd accidentally hurt himself or," she brushed to her bruised cheek, "someone else."

Yoggi drummed her fingers on the cushion of the couch. "Doctor, go in and carefully recheck Malone's blood. See if there are any traces of the drug left in his system."

"Yes, Commander."

Yoggi checked her watch for the umpteeth time.

Bentley returned, ran her sample and read the scanner aloud. "The Quakalin level has dropped to a negligible amount; however, he's still being affected to some degree."

"Explain that," Yoggi asked.

"He still thinks Leiman is Emily and won't let her go. Apparently to prevent her from attempting suicide."

"What do you mean, won't let her go?" Taylor walked to the kitchen and entered through the damaged door.

Yoggi followed him in. "Is he asleep?"

The doctor filed into the kitchen behind the others. "Yes, out cold."

Zeus was still on his back with Leiman on top of him. Anytime she spoke or attempted to move, he held her tighter and mumbled about Emily not hurting herself.

"Brian, it's not sexual," Leiman explained.

Zeus resumed swaying.

Leiman felt her face turn as red as Zeus's hair. "It's sort of paternal."

"Have you tried to get off?" Taylor asked.

"Yes, he won't let me go. Emily must have tried suicide a number of times."

Taylor kicked some debris with his boot. "Why can't you just lay beside him?"

"He won't let me. It really kind of sweet," she explained. "He wouldn't let her lie on the cold ground. She got cold and was afraid of the bugs. It probably felt safer this way."

"All right," Taylor crossed his arms. "I know Malone thinks you're

Emily, but I still don't have to like it."

"Why won't he stop swaying or whatever it is he's doing?" Baker asked.

"It must have comforted her. He does it whenever I talk or move," Leiman answered.

"Then I guess you'd like to remain silent?" Cmd. Yoggi picked up her grandmother's broken holo-picture and sighed.

"Yes, Ma'am."

Cmd. Yoggi conveyed their plan for keeping Malone in the Corps. Leiman was pleased; however, she felt ridiculous with everyone standing around staring at her. "Doctor, how long before he stops this?"

"I don't know. Quakalin was never widely used. As far as I can tell, he should be in the present right now. It may be that he fell asleep this way and is now in a dream-type state."

"Can we wake him?" Yoggi questioned.

"In theory, yes, but I wouldn't exactly call Malone predictable, in this state or his regular state. I heard he pulled a knife on Christiani when he tried to wake Malone. Plus, we didn't actually give him Quakalin. Who knows if there are differences, because of the way the drug formed in his system."

Yoggi checked her watch again. "Best guess, Doctor?"

"I'd say it's worth a try. I'd let Leiman do it herself."

Taylor motioned to Zeus. "I'm not leaving her alone with him."

"Bulldog, I'm fine," she replied as Zeus swayed her again.

"The rest of us will step away and remain quiet." Yoggi and the others moved to the farthest wall. "Leiman, go ahead when you're ready."

"Yes, Ma'am." She took a deep breath. "Malone, wake up," she said into his ear. Zeus returned to the swaying behavior. "Malone," she said louder, trying to shake him as he rocked her.

After a number of tries, slowly Zeus's eyes opened. As soon as he was coherent and realized he was holding Sgt. Leiman, he jumped up, throwing her to the floor. "Yous budgin bastards. I's hope yous gots everything yous want," he screamed and bolted out the rear door.

Sgt. Leiman instinctively ran after him. "Malone," she called. "Malone, stop." She easily caught up to the groggy orphan and ran in front of him. "Halt. That's an order."

"I's ain't gots ta listen ta yous crap no more. Yous gots me's out, now leave me's the budge alone." He shoved her aside, teetering from the motion.

"Malone, you weren't kicked out last night, and you're not going to be."

"What?" He whirled around and stumbled; his body stopped and his mind continued spinning.

She steadied him with her arm. "Come in and let me explain."

"What yous give me's last night?" He rubbed his pounding head.

"It's kind of complicated." She led him inside and steadied him near the wall.

Dr. Bentley explained the chemical reaction.

Zeus shook his fists. "Budgin bastards, all a yous. . ."

"Shut up, Malone," Yoggi ordered. "I haven't got time for this. Zeigler's been stopping by my house early every morning."

"What yous knows 'bout Zeigler?" He leaned against the wall.

"Everything, I think. You showed us Zeigler's B-file."

Zeus's knees buckled and he slid down the wall. "They's gonna kills us all."

"Not if we don't tell them," Yoggi insisted. "And I sure don't plan to!"

"I'm certainly not going to," Baker echoed.

"None of us are." Leiman squatted beside her cadet.

"How yous gonna explain me's stay'n?"

"Why, we're going to tell everyone the truth, minus a few pertinent details. I, of course, will confide completely in my second in command or at least he'll think that. The only things we can't talk about, to anyone, is that you broke into the library, and that Zeigler is a spy. Everything else is relatively provable, and five reliable witnesses heard you state you'd never broken the law, raped, killed or hurt anybody. Getting drugged may be the best thing that ever happened to you."

"Doubts it." Zeus chucked a mangled pot at the door. It skidded and slid a broken plate against the door frame. "K don't likes people go'n against them. They's ain't gonna let me's stay."

"If OTS is to look good and not get tarnished, then they can't kick you out. I will start preparing a carefully worded press statement, and we'll face the rest as it comes alone."

"Ain'ts gonna works."

"Listen, Malone." Yoggi knelt in front of him. "I know you are more familiar with the network's ways than I am; however, at this juncture we don't have any other choices. Unless you have a suggestion, we'll have to deal with each problem as it arises."

"How yous gonna know 'bout any problems?"

She waved her open hand toward him. "Because you're going to tell me."

"How?"

"That's a good point." Yoggi stood up and glanced around at the others. "We'll have to think of a system, since we can't meet in my office or study. You're certain they aren't monitoring any other conversations?"

"Ain'ts so far. Don't mean they's won't start. They's get suspicious if yous talk ta me's."

"Yes, that's a good point, too. I could talk to you once or twice, but that would be it. Does anyone have any suggestions?"

"Malone can send messages through all of us," Taylor offered. "He reports or talks to us constantly. I see him privately at least every other day, Baker and Leiman see him daily, and the doctor sees him, what, once a week?"

"It depends on how many fights you children get into, but usually once or twice a week."

"Well, for now that's our only choice," Yoggi stated. "Malone, make sure you check regularly on exactly what they're monitoring and anything else they are suspicious of."

"Yes, Ma'am." Zeus squeezed his temples. He was not comfortable sharing his secrets with others.

Yoggi saw Lt. Cmd. Zeigler jogging up. "All right, folks, the rest of this will have to wait. It's show time. Doctor, examine your patient."

Bentley knelt and began another examination. Zeigler knocked on the door. When he looked through the window, he was surprised to see the others in her kitchen. Yoggi opened the door until it stuck on the plate fragment, and Zeigler squeezed in.

Zeigler stared at the demolished kitchen. "What happened here?"

"Malone happened." Yoggi waved her hand in his direction.

"Gees, I thought he'd go peacefully." Zeigler kicked at the trash.

"Malone is not leaving," Yoggi stated.

Zeigler's head snapped up. "What?"

"This is kind of my fault." Yoggi gestured around the kitchen. "I accidentally gave Malone the truth drug Quakalin."

"Accidentally?" Zeigler raised his eyebrows.

"I gave him a little brandy. The brandy combined with the booster treatments Bentley's giving him, and together they make something similar to Quakalin."

"You're kidding."

"No, let me explain."

"Commander," Dr. Bentley interrupted, "I'd like to finally get him over to the infirmary and check him over completely."

Yoggi towered over her cadet. "Malone, are you ready to cooperate with the doctor?"

"Yes, Ma'am." Zeus sighed. His head was pounding. He could not think of another solution in this state. He would have to clear his mind and then devise a better, safer plan.

"He's still disoriented." Bentley stood and turned enough to be certain Zeigler got a clear view of her bruised cheek. "But I think the drug has dissipated enough for us to get him safely to the infirmary."

"Go ahead, Doctor."

Bentley tucked the scanner into her med kit. "Baker, Taylor, help him up?"

"Yes, Ma'am." They each took a side and steadied Zeus. Zeus leaned heavily on the men.

Yoggi kicked a blue cup fragment out of the way and opened the door. "Be careful, and steer clear if he flashes back. Doctor, I want a full report as soon as you're done."

CHAPTER 24

YOGGI ARRANGED a staff meeting for 13:00 and decided to take a quick nap. She had tried to clean the kitchen while she spoke to Zeigler. He was too agitated. Four times, he verified Malone was answering under a truth drug. He asked over and over if there was any other way to get Malone discharged. He was frightened, almost terrified, as she informed him Malone was staying. From observing his reaction, she realized how much danger she and the others were in. His reactions made the bare-bones truth a walking, breathing dragon that burned a hole in their friendship. She could never look at him the same again.

She needed to rest, but her mind was reeling. Yoggi decided to take a hot bath. She poured some sweet-smelling oils into the tub, put one foot in and waited for it to adjust to the temperature before standing with both feet in the tub. She slowly moved more and more of her body in until she was relaxing comfortably on a gel pillow. She took long, deep breaths, slowly breathing in the sweet aroma of a spring-time garden. She felt the soothing effects of the warm water and let her mind wander. She was drifting to sleep when a problem popped into her head. She jumped out of the tub, pulled on her robe and called Sgt. Leiman to come over.

Yoggi opened the front door. "I'm sorry to call you out." She stepped aside.

Leiman entered. "I couldn't sleep anyway, Ma'am."

"I couldn't, either. Let's go upstairs." She pointed to the study. "Thanks to Malone, my lower back is killing me. Bentley said I should lie flat as much as possible."

"Do you want me to bring the Alphas over and clean up your kitchen?" Leiman followed her upstairs.

"Yes, but not today. It seems the insurance people are having difficulty believing one man could be as destructive as I described. They want to do a visual before it's cleaned up." Yoggi led them into the bedroom. "They promised someone would be out tomorrow."

"If they still don't believe it, have them watch Malone fight the infamous Eric Ryan and Taylor. . .together," Leiman joked.

"That's not a bad idea. I may have to. That assumes, of course, they decide accidentally drugged orphans are covered under my policy."

"I never thought about that. What exactly would this come under?"

"Homeowner's stupidity comes to mind." Yoggi motioned Leiman to sit in the rocking chair.

Cmd. Yoggi sat on the bench at the end of the bed. "I had this terrible thought as I was soaking in the tub."

Leiman sniffed the air. "I wondered what smelled so good."

"Springtime Enchantment. My daughter gave it to me for my birthday."

"She has good taste." Leiman fidgeted, feeling a little strange sitting in the commander's bedroom discussing bath oil.

"Yes, I think so, too. I'm concerned that Christiani could be in danger."

Leiman rocked in her chair. "Why?"

"Call it a hunch," Cmd. Yoggi explained. "You didn't see Zeigler's reaction when he realized Malone was staying. He was scared. He went right home, I assume, to discuss it with his Kalopso boss."

"Remember what Malone said the minute he heard we knew about Zeigler? He said they'd kill us."

"After hearing and seeing the things the Kalopso do and seeing Zeigler's reaction, I don't think Malone was exaggerating." Yoggi twisted the belt on her robe. "What if they decide, with Christiani fasting and the other stuff, that Malone has confided in him? They'd eliminate anyone Malone might have talked to."

"This is getting complicated." Leiman stopped rocking. "I wonder if Malone purposely tries to be disagreeable, so no one will get close to him."

"I wouldn't put it past him. Not after hearing how much he was willing to suffer to protect us, and we weren't even being nice to him."

Leiman stared at the floral carpet. "What about his flight partner?" She raised her head. "If Christiani is at risk because OTS roommates have a reputation for getting close, there is no way they'd ignore Malone's flight partner."

"I hadn't thought of that." Yoggi dropped her head and sighed. "Hours and hours together, one on one, completely uninterrupted and presumably unmonitored. Starting with a twenty-hour get-to-know-your flight partner drill. They'd be fools to assume that risk. I wouldn't, if I were in their position."

"Me either." Leiman stared at the blue floral carpet until her eyes went blurry. "What are we going to do?"

"I don't know. I keep thinking about the other children, like Malone and Emily, who are counting on him to succeed. Malone's probably their only hope in the near future."

"I hadn't considered that." Leiman rubbed her eyes to clear her vision. "I've been so preoccupied with my own little world, I forgot about everybody else's."

"It's easy to do, but we must remember the whole universe is watching what's going on here. And there are going to be long-term effects, no matter what happens. One thing I am committed to is giving Malone a chance. He deserves it, and so do those other kids." Yoggi paused. She could not look Leiman in the eye. "I blew it with Emily. I called the orphanage and reported what I saw. They didn't even take my name. They had no intention of looking into my allegations. I rationalized I'd tried to do what was right. If other people didn't do their jobs, it wasn't my problem. That decision has haunted me as the most shameful thing I've ever done. I won't do that again."

"I agree. I haven't been too comfortable taking the low road this last week."

"I'm sorry about that."

Leiman shrugged. "I understand. I know Malone and Sato practically had me convinced he was a psychopathic rapist."

Yoggi nodded. They sat silently thinking of some practical solutions. Ones that did not endanger others. Yoggi drummed her fingers while Leiman rocked.

After a long silence, Leiman said, "I hate suggesting this, and I know it's against policy, but Christiani should probably be Malone's flight partner. He's already at risk, so what difference does it make?"

"That's a good suggestion. I'll arrange it. If there are fatal repercussions, at least that will contain the damage."

Leiman rested her chin in the palm of her hand. "Christiani's one of the best cadets I've had in years. Baker agrees."

"Does he have the potential to get bumped up to second lieutenant?"

"Yes, Ma'am, but you know how unpredictable that can be."

"I'd hate to take that possibility away from him." Yoggi leaned back and propped herself on her elbows. "Malone's not that great an NG. Zeigler says he's a good navigator, but his shooting is below average, and he can't pick up any of the flying slack. No matter how good his leadership scores are, Christiani won't have a chance if he's teamed up with Malone. Flying counts for too many points."

"Commander, it's not just his leadership or flying or grades that makes Christiani a good prospect. It's his integrity. My guess is he's going to view the moral and ethical sides to this as much as the prestige of getting a ring. I'd be happy to talk to him."

"No, thank you. I appreciate you're offering. If I'm going to ask someone to chuck his chance at a higher ranking commission, I need to do that myself." Yoggi touched her chest.

"Yes, Ma'am."

"Sgt. Leiman. . .Susan, I'm glad you're one of the people I'm in this with. I can trust your judgment, Baker's, too. I want you to know I feel confident having you as my frontline person."

"Thank you, Commander." She was flattered by both the compliment and being called by her first name. Officers did not routinely call enlisted by their first names. When it did happen, it was because the relationship had developed beyond the professional level.

"I'll inform Zeigler I'm concerned about the press and Malone's social development so I want you to continue to report weekly. That way they can receive the edited version of what's going on. We need to come up with a code, when you need to add something unofficially."

"It should be something simple, that appears natural." As the chair rocked forward, Leiman flexed her feet and rocked again. "What if I cross my arms sometime during our conversation and sometime before I leave, you can cross yours, as a way of acknowledging the signal?"

"Agreed." Yoggi crossed her arms with an exaggerated motion. "If you cross your arms, I'll bump into you outside the office by the end of the day. How will you let me know if there's an emergency?"

"I don't know." Leiman stopped rocking. "That's going to be a lot tougher."

"Malone also needs to be able to contact me in an emergency. He's the one hacking into their communications, probably late at night."

"He should be able to contact all five of us. Any one of us could be at risk, some of us, or all of us."

"You're right. But how?"

"Let's ask Malone. He's the computer expert."

"Good point. Try to get him working on it ASAP. I want us to be able to contact each other without alerting anyone else. That needs to be Malone's top priority. He's the only one who could rig something. I want to know if and when Zeigler, or the network, intend to deal with Malone. . .or us."

"Yes, Ma'am."

"I hate to wake him up, but we need to be informed about what Zeigler is doing." Yoggi rose and tightened the belt on her robe. "See if Malone can work off the computer in your office. I don't want him to be seen. Let everybody think he's still asleep and you're in your office working up a report from last night."

"Understood. How will I contact you?"

Yoggi plopped on the bench in frustration. "Right where we started."

"We've bumped into each other at the commissary before," Leiman offered.

"Let's both have an uncontrollable urge for a candy bar in, let's say," Yoggi looked at her watch, "in about an hour an a half. I'll meet you at the commissary at eleven-thirty. If something is urgent, call Bentley. Tell her Malone is concerned that other things he eats or drinks might turn into a truth drug. She can call me laughing about how funny it is Malone asked. Bentley calls, I'll bump into you at the commissary ASAP. I want it to be public, in case we're being watched. Nothing should appear sneaky or hidden. None of us should meet secretly; it could alert them. Once we meet, we can talk generally about last night until we're outside and clear."

"What if they decide to start using audio scanners? Then they could monitor anything we say, anywhere. We could use blockers, but they'd know we were suspicious."

Cmd. Yoggi massaged her tension-filled neck. "Good point, Susan. See if Malone can figure anything out with that, too. For today, let's hope they don't pull it together before eleven-thirty. Better get Malone started; he's going to need all the time he can get."

*   *   *

322

At 11:30 the two women purchased candy bars and walked out of the commissary. As soon as they were out of everyone's hearing range, Leiman reported. "First of all, at least for now, they're not using audio scanners. Malone's certain of that. Secondly, no one's certain what to do. They're waiting until after your press conference before deciding. Lastly, everything we discussed can be accomplished. Malone needs a computer and time. He can make it possible for us to leave untraceable messages. He can do it from any computer, anywhere."

"How much time does he need?" Yoggi opened the wrapper on her candy bar.

"Lots. Baker suggested we send him on his twenty-hour flight. The problem is he hasn't been assigned his flight partner yet. Once he's assigned, just like everybody else, the team gets thrown up there for twenty-plus hours." Leiman tugged on both sides of her candy wrapper until it opened. "The best excuse we could come up with for assigning Malone now was you wanting Malone off-base and inaccessible to the press. In theory, it would give you time to prepare his press statement and Malone time to practice it."

"It's a good plan. We need communications immediately, and no one will suspect he's up in space clearing communications for us. It also stops Zeigler from checking on him." Yoggi nibbled on her chocolate.

"There are a few glitches. When Malone overheard we planned to assign Christiani as his flight partner, he shot through the roof. He said we were practically giving Christiani a death sentence, and he wasn't going to be a party to that."

"Did you explain his limited options and the fact that Christiani's already at risk?"

"Yes." Leiman rolled her eyes. "Malone agrees that unless he flies with someone he doesn't get along with which, of course, would be suspicious because we never assign people like that together, anyone he flies with is at risk."

"So, he's not happy, but he agrees."

"Malone didn't say that." Leiman took a bite out of her candy bar.

"Did he have a better suggestion?"

"No, Ma'am."

"Then we need to get Christiani to make up his mind ASAP. I'd like to get them up and flying before our meeting. That will give Malone a few hours head start. Have Christiani report to me now. If I have to, I'll postpone the staff meeting."

"Commander, I'm concerned about Malone. He has a nervous habit of biting his nails. Now he's practically chewing his fingers to the bone. He's always been strung tight, but I've been around him and he's on the edge. Except for Emily, he's never trusted or confided in anyone else."

"You have good instincts, Susan." Yoggi touched her arm. "I trust your judgment. If you don't think he can handle what we're giving him."

"No, I'm sure he can accomplish what we've discussed. If anything, I'd say Malone's not going to rest until he feels we're protected. I'm just not sure how long he can keep this all bottled up. I suggested he see Sato. It seems the Kalopso used a therapist to manipulate Emily. Malone would rather die than talk to Sato. He needs to talk to someone, someone just to bounce ideas off. Someone who knows what's going on, and he has time to talk to. Not only today, but for however long this goes on."

"The way I see it, there's only one possibility."

Leiman nodded.

"I guess I'll need a little more time with Christiani than I thought."

"Yes, Ma'am." Leiman twisted the top of her candy wrapper and stuffed it into her pocket. "I'll find Christiani and have him report to you."

"I want you both to report. He'll be more comfortable with someone he trusts present."

"Christiani is closer to Baker."

"All three of you, then. Zeigler will be there, too. I'd never assign a flight team without consulting him. I'll see you in my office in fifteen minutes."

"Yes, Ma'am."

*　　*　　*

Leiman saluted as she entered the commander's office. "Baker and Christiani are on their way. They will be a few minutes late. I forgot Baker was wetting down the course today. Christiani was covered with mud, and Baker wasn't much better. I told them to clean up and then report."

"Thank you." Yoggi dropped her laser quill on her desk. "I don't need another room trashed right now."

Leiman looked over at Lt. Cmd. Zeigler. He made her extremely nervous. She hoped he did not notice. "Would you prefer I wait outside until they come?"

"No." Yoggi motioned to an empty chair. "Have a seat, Susan. We're reading over the press release."

"Susan?" Zeigler questioned.

"Yes," Yoggi snapped, then softened her tone. She had to remind herself to act as if she still trusted him. "We've been through quite a bit together lately."

"I just wondered." Zeigler shrugged.

"Susan, you were there last night. How much information should we give the press about Emily? Do we tell them everything, or let them look through InterPress and come to their own conclusions?"

"I have no idea, Commander. I've never had to deal with the press. And to be quite honest, I can't say I'm sorry."

"I don't blame you." Yoggi picked up her dictation wand and spoke into it. "Simb, make a note. All staff having regular contact with Malone need to be briefed on press procedures. Have Patterson prepare anyone the press might want statements from. Yoggi end transmission." She smiled at Leiman. "I wouldn't want you or Baker to miss out on any of the fun."

"Gee, thanks."

Baker and Apollo entered, stood in unison and saluted.

"At ease, Gentlemen, have a seat." Yoggi looked Apollo over. He was big, hairy and dark. The Black Bear nickname was an accurate description.

Baker took the seat furthest away. He was only there for moral support.

Apollo was left the seat closest to the commander. He surmised he was either in trouble for fasting and praying, or the meeting was related to Zeus. Either way, he was nervous. Cadets did not usually speak to the commander, plus both his drill sergeants and the second in command were involved. Apollo was certain the meeting was serious. He took a deep breath and sat stiffly in the chair.

"I've heard many good things about you," Yoggi said to Apollo. "Your sergeants, Lt. Cmd. Zeigler and a number of other officers have mentioned you're an outstanding cadet."

325

"Thank you, Ma'am." He waited to hear her say, "But you need to keep your religion private."

Yoggi checked her watch. She wished they had more time to get acquainted. "I understand you're an excellent pilot and have outstanding leadership skills. The rumor is you have a good chance at one of the two second lieutenant commissions."

Apollo eyed each person and tried to read their expressions. He knew he was in trouble. No one was relaxed.

"I assume that's a topic you're interested in?"

"Yes, Ma'am." Apollo smiled nervously.

Yoggi could not find the words, so she bought herself some time. "Have you run into your roommate since this morning?"

"Yes, Commander."

"Then you know he's staying?"

"Yes, Ma'am." Apollo exhaled, relieved they weren't discussing his faith.

"How do you feel about that?"

Apollo was uncertain what she wanted. As a natural-born diplomat, he did not like to answer directly until he knew the other person's expectations. "Ma'am, are you inquiring if I am pleased Zeus is staying?"

"Yes. That and how do you feel about continuing to room with Malone?"

"I am pleased Zeus has not discharged. I do not mind rooming with Zeus. Adjusting took awhile; however, it is no longer an issue." Apollo added what he believed Yoggi wanted to hear. "If you are concerned that Zeus will be detrimental to my scores, I can assure you, the opposite is true. Zeus tutors me in a few of my weaker subjects, like navigation." He cleared his throat and turned to Zeigler.

"I'm glad to hear you two are getting along. Baker and Leiman were confident you could handle it. Just as we're confident you can handle what I'm about to propose." She leaned toward him. "However, that is not the issue. You need to consider what I'm about to suggest carefully. No matter what you decide, it will not go against your ratings. I want to be certain you're clear on that."

"Yes, Ma'am, I understand," Apollo answered.

"I'm sure you're aware that Malone has not had an easy life."

"Yes, Ma'am, I have gathered that from some of his reactions."

"Did Malone tell you anything we discussed last night?"

"No, Ma'am. I had to pry out of him the fact that he is staying."

"What I'm about to tell you is going to become public knowledge; however, until it does, I'd like you to keep it to yourself. Understand?"

"Yes, Commander."

Yoggi quickly summarized last night. She concluded with, "Malone is concerned that anyone he befriends could become a target of the Kalopso." She paused to let him absorb what she had said.

"Then you perceive I am at risk as his roommate?"

"Possibly. I honestly don't know. Lt. Cmd. Zeigler," she waved to the traitor, "is personally trying to find out and assess the risks to us all. Even if it's a small risk, it should not be taken lightly. These people play hardball and for keeps."

"I do not need to change rooms." Apollo glanced around at everyone's reactions. He was confused no one was relieved he had offered to stay with Zeus. What did they want?

"Don't be too hasty," Zeigler stated. "You should take some time to consider this."

Apollo turned and faced Zeigler. "With all due respect, Sir, I want to assist Zeus, and I am in the most advantageous position to do so."

"I'm not finished," Yoggi said. "If the network decides to take action against individuals they perceive Malone might have confided in, whether he did or not, then both his roommate and his flight partner are at risk."

Apollo nodded. Now he understood why Zeigler was there. He was responsible for approving all flight teams. Apollo was finally certain what they wanted to hear. "Lt. Cmd. Zeigler, I would like to request Cadet Malone as my flight partner."

"Christiani," Zeigler huffed as he crossed his arms, "you need to take a little time and think about this. Malone is not at your level. Not only are you in danger, but without a top-notch partner, you can kiss that ring good-bye."

"Sir." Apollo stood and faced him. "I do not need to ponder this. There are more important issues involved than rank-jumping. I would gladly forego the higher rank to assist Zeus and others who are less fortunate."

"I appreciate your volunteering so quickly." Yoggi opened her hand at the empty chair and Apollo sat. "I want you to understand the type of risks you're taking, before your final decision. Let me tell you a few of the things we heard last night. First, it's common for the Kalopso to blackmail people by threatening their families. They infect people with incurable diseases, violently rape women, cause people to be paralyzed in accidents. The Kalopso uses fates worse than death to persuade people. And from what I saw last night, most people would rather die than suffer as much as they did at the network's bidding."

Apollo slumped in his chair. The room was tense as everyone stared nervously at the cadet. He put his head in his hands and prayed desperately for courage. He raised his head high and in a strong voice said, "Lt. Cmd. Zeigler, I would like to request Cadet Malone as my flight partner." Apollo was as shocked as everyone else at the strength and conviction in his voice.

Zeigler stood, went to Apollo and rested his hand on Apollo shoulder. "Son, you need to consider this carefully." He squeezed Apollo's shoulder. "I don't believe you understand what you're saying."

"No, Sir, you do not understand." Apollo rose abruptly, knocking Zeigler's hand off. "I am aware my faith makes you all uncomfortable." Apollo made eye contact with each one. "However, I have been praying for guidance on how to assist Zeus. I have my answer. I do not need to deliberate anymore. My desire is to bolster Zeus's position and ensure his graduation. His achievements will set an example that reinforces other orphan causes."

Zeigler locked his gaze on the young cadet. "Aren't you afraid?"

"Yes, Sir. I am terrified. How do I articulate my faith? I am required to do God's will, even when I would prefer not to. Besides, I surmise you have discussed this and there cannot too many other possibilities. Meetings of this type are rare in OTS. I can sense the seriousness of this request."

"That's because we're concerned for your safety." Zeigler patted Apollo's shoulder paternally.

"Sir, I am honored by your confidence in me. However, I am forced to assume, given the public scrutiny on this issue and the pressure you all are under, you would not have made such a unique request unless you wanted, or more accurately, needed me to accept." Apollo stepped away from Zeigler. "Now, since Cmd. Yoggi has looked at her watch numerous times, I must postulate that our time is limited. I suggest we conclude this discussion and move forward."

Cmd. Yoggi raised her eyebrows. "Well, I guess that's what you all meant when you said he had natural leadership ability. Cadet Christiani just started running our meeting."

Apollo cleared his throat and sat down. "I apologize, Commander."

"No, no need," she corrected him. "You're right on all counts. There aren't any other choices and, of course, we wanted you to accept. I want to verify we're clear on a few points, and then we'll move on."

Apollo nodded.

"You understand you are probably throwing away a chance at a higher commission?"

"Yes, Ma'am. Except for the honor, a commission will not change my future opportunities. Between the businesses I own and my family's businesses, my future is secure. All I am sacrificing is something to boast about."

"You realize both you and your family could be in danger? If you wish, you can call your family and discuss this with them."

Chills ran down Apollo's spine. The threat must be real. He had never heard of an officer allowing a cadet to contact his or her family. Apollo took a deep breath. "This decision does not necessitate me contacting my parents. We have been communicating. My mother's last words of advice were to listen and trust God. I believe that is worth heeding."

"You realize Malone will not be happy about this. He does not want you in danger. In fact, the biggest reason Malone refused to speak with me earlier was to protect us." She waved her hand around the room. "He will not want to open up to you, not because he doesn't trust you, because I know for a fact he does, but because he's concerned for your well-being. Even without the potential danger, Malone will not make this easy. He's going to fight you, kicking and screaming the whole way."

"I suppose it is a good thing I am charming." Apollo grinned.

"Yes, you're going to need all the charm you can muster to subdue Malone." Yoggi returned his smile. She was pleased this had gone so well. She flipped open her outer office ComLine and said, "Simb?"

"Yes, Commander."

"Page Cadet Malone and have him report to me immediately. He's probably in the Alpha barracks."

"Yes, Ma'am, right away."

She flipped the switch off and returned her attention to Apollo.

"Now, as the chairman of the board has stated, we need to move on."

Apollo laughed, shaking his head.

"Zeigler, assign them as flight partners and get everything arranged for their twenty-hour flight. I'll have them report over there as soon as we're through here. Leiman, Baker, go straight to the conference room. Tell them I'm running late. Start at the beginning and explain what happened last night. I'll join you as soon as possible. I'm going to make certain Malone understands what Christiani is going to do and that our orphan friend cooperates. You three are dismissed."

"Yes, Ma'am." They stood, saluted and left.

Yoggi titled in her chair. "I can see why they've been so impressed with you."

"Thank you, Ma'am."

"Do you have any questions you want to ask before Malone arrives?"

"Exactly what are your expectation of me? What do you want me to accomplish with Zeus?"

"He's not had much experience trusting and confiding in people. I want you to become his friend and confidant. Obviously, we're here to help you. If you need something, you can come to any one of us. That includes me. You're not doing the same things the other cadets are. I will not be upset if you wish to speak to me personally. It's a big responsibility. I'm certain I'll want to chat with you to see how things are going."

"Yes, Ma'am."

Yoggi grabbed the InfoPad off her desk. "For today, he may have to make a statement to the press. That's one of the reasons I want you two up and flying, ASAP. Then the press can't get at him right away. Once we get things worked out here, if he needs to speak to the press, and that is definitely a last resort, I'll contact you with what he's to prepare for. Then you can run some drills with him."

The door opened before Apollo could answer. Zeus entered, saluted and remained at attention.

"At ease, Malone. Take a seat."

Zeus hung his head. "Yes, Ma'am."

"Gee, I'm glad to see you, too."

Zeus answered by glaring at her.

330

"Malone, meet your new flight partner."

Zeus answered by glaring at Apollo.

"I want you to listen to me carefully," Yoggi said. "I've thought a great deal about this. One of your problems is you don't trust people or confide in anyone. So I'm ordering you to tell Christiani everything you told us last night."

Zeus jerked his head up. "What?"

"You heard me. You are going to open up to somebody, starting today. I'm going to give Christiani a list of general topics. If you don't speak openly and honestly, I'll give him the bottle, and we'll do it the hard way." She shook her finger at him. "You will learn basic trust. It is essential to the Corps and you personally."

"Yous crazy." Zeus had a splitting headache and squeezed his temples.

Yoggi turned to Apollo. "Topics for discussion: How did Emily get to the orphanage? What happened to her family?"

Zeus jumped up. "I's told yous that last night?" He had not realized how effective the Quakalin had been.

"Yes. Now sit down. I'm not through." Zeus complied. He squirmed in his chair each time she added to the list. "How did Malone meet her? What did they do together? What work did he do?"

"Did I's not shuts up?"

"As a matter of fact, you were very cooperative." Yoggi turned to Apollo. "Why did they go into the sewers? What were they doing there? How did they survive? What. . ."

"Crap, did I's ever budgin shuts up?"

Cmd. Yoggi ignored him and continued her list. "What was Malone doing in the orphanage? What was his life like? Why is he so protective of women? How he felt when they took Emily away to be raped and . . ."

"Shuts up." Zeus lunged at her.

Apollo leaped up, grabbed Zeus at the shoulders and pushed him away.

"Don't yous budgin say noth'n else."

Apollo forced Zeus into his seat. He kept his muscular arms securely on Zeus.

Yoggi closed her eyes and held in her tears. "I think you get the gist of it," she whispered.

"Yes, Ma'am," Apollo answered quietly. "Are you all right?" He squeezed Zeus's shoulders.

Zeus's body relaxed a little. "Yeah." He dropped his head.

"Are you certain?" Apollo loosened his grip.

Zeus tried to control his feelings. Apollo hovered around him for a few minutes. When he was convinced Zeus had calmed down, he returned to his seat.

Yoggi waited until the tension eased a little and then said to Apollo, "You'll need to take it slow. Let him rest today. He definitely has a great deal of unresolved anger, although I'm hoping that my kitchen's sacrifice has helped a little."

"Kitchen sacrifice?" Apollo questioned. Zeus also appeared bewildered.

"Malone, don't you remember anything about last night?"

Zeus rubbed his throbbing temples. "Little withs Leiman this morn'n."

"You don't recall trashing my kitchen?"

Zeus shook his head. He was too upset to remember to answer verbally.

"Come on, let's go for a walk." Yoggi rose and lead them through the door. She had been waiting for an excuse to get them out of her office and speak freely with the cadets. Zeus and Apollo followed her outside. As soon as she was away from the building, she turned and asked, "Malone, are they using audio scanners?"

"No, Ma'am, not yet."

"Good, be sure and tell Christiani about Zeigler — today!"

Zeus's nostrils flared. He yelled in her face, "Yous budgin crazy. Yous gets him killed."

"It's too late for that. I originally agreed, but now he should know. He basically implied to Zeigler that you do confide in him. At least enough that they won't take a chance."

"Why don't yous shoot him yourself?" Zeus grabbed her shirt and yanked up. "What the budge gives yous the right ta decide my's life?"

Apollo pushed Zeus away.

Yoggi had had enough. She regretted being lenient with him. She thought of how Leiman controlled Malone with the power of her voice. "Stand down, Malone," Cmd. Yoggi bellowed in her most authoritative voice. She pushed her face up into his. "You see this?" She tugged at the commander's insignia on her collar. "This gives me the right. I've put up with your insubordinate crap because I know you're tired and half-drugged, but it stops here and now. I'm in charge, not you. When you enrolled, your butt became mine, and don't you forget it. I decide what my people need to know, not you. Got it?"

To her surprise, he immediately gave a compliant, "Yes, Ma'am."

"Christiani," she barked, "we sunk you in way over your head. The reason Zeigler was discouraging you is because he is the Kalopso plant here on base. My office, communicators and study are bugged. Malone is going to brief you on everything during your twenty-hour flight. Don't start him talking until he's finished the jobs we've assigned him. I need clear communications."

"Request permission ta speaks," Zeus demanded through clenched teeth.

"Granted, but watch it."

"They's ain't gonna let this goes on. Yous all in danger."

"So are you." Yoggi resumed walking to her house and the men followed. "We're in this together, whether we like it or not."

"They's always gonna kill me's. Don't makes no difference why. I's don't wants ta be responsible for anyone else get'n budged over."

She rounded the corner to her house. "I understand and I honestly appreciate what you were willing to sacrifice to protect us. But it's too late for that. If you quit now, it will look worse, and everyone will suffer. I have to react as if I didn't know about Zeigler. My job is to make you the best officer I can, for as long as you're here. Even if they do terminate you, if everyone here says you would have made a good officer, that will help other orphans. We have to look beyond ourselves at the big picture. There are a lot of other kids like you and Emily out there. I intend to do everything I can to make their lives better."

Cmd. Yoggi opened the kitchen door, turned sideways and entered. The men squeezed in. Apollo's jaw dropped as he surveyed the destruction. Zeus was as shocked as his friend. Broken plates and shattered glass were everywhere. The kitchen table was lopsided and two of the chairs had been splintered into pieces. The computer and its internal components were strewn throughout the room. The stovetop was destroyed and the front panel gone.

Apollo finally sputtered, "You demolished all this?"

"I. . .I's guess."

Yoggi picked up a broken platter and displayed it to Zeus. "You don't remember trashing my kitchen?"

"No, Ma'am."

"None of it?"

"Nope."

Apollo scanned the room, shaking his head. "I will state this for you, Zeus, you never do an inferior job of anything, mass destruction and all."

Zeus kicked a table leg at his roommate. "Shuts up, Apollo."

Apollo ignored the comment. "Cmd. Yoggi, if you do not mind my asking, what exactly were the rest of you doing while Zeus was demolishing the place?"

"Taking cover." She placed the broken platter on the chipped countertop. "I've got to get to that meeting. Malone, get those communication lines open. If possible, I want to be able to listen in on Zeigler and the Kalopso."

"Ain'ts possible, Ma'am. Gots ta secure a line every time, and yous can't read computer language."

"All right, work out the rest." She led them out of the house. "Take care of yourselves, Gentlemen."

CHAPTER 25

APOLLO MANEUVERED the ship out of the dock and into space.

Zeus clutched his gut, grabbed for a barf bag and threw up. Watery brown fluid sprayed the outside of the bag, the control panel, his seat and pants. Zeus opened the bag and held it over his nose and mouth as his stomach continued to expel its contents.

Apollo tried to fly smoothly. "Is there anything I can do to assist you?"

Zeus shook his head between his legs.

Apollo headed slowly out into open space.

Zeus dry heaved. He lifted his head and wiped his mouth on his sleeve. "Launch us out'a here."

Apollo spoke softly, "If you are nauseated now, hitting the interspace shift will make you violently ill."

"They's monitoring us. We's don't goes ta warp, they's be suspicious." Zeus opened a clean barf bag.

"Affirmative." Apollo pushed the turbo button on his joystick.

Zeus fell forward between his legs. Apollo set his course to open space and engaged the autopilot. Apollo pulled the monitor and saline kit out that Dr. Bentley had given them. "I am going to strap this monitor on you and administer some fluids."

Zeus dangled his right arm out beside Apollo. Apollo rolled up his partner's sleeve, attached the saline and strapped the monitor on. Ten minutes later, Zeus lifted his head and leaned it against the cockpit window.

"How are you feeling?" Apollo asked.

"Likes crap." Zeus wiped the sweat from his face.

"We have twenty hours. May I suggest you recline your seat and rest for a few minutes. You will be unable to accomplish anything in your present state."

"Yeah." Zeus tilted his seat. His eye lids felt like weights. In moments, the exhaustion overpowered his instinct for preservation, and he fell asleep.

Apollo hated the silence. Normally he would have turned on some music, but he was afraid even the slightest noise might disturb his friend. For more than an hour, Apollo's mind wander to the unknown fears and challenges ahead. Then a terrible thought crossed his mind. "Zeus."

"Huh?"

"I apologize for waking you. When was Cmd. Yoggi going to conduct the press conference?"

"How I's know?" Zeus snapped, annoyed at the intrusion for such a stupid question.

"It is of vital importance. Did she mention any time frame?"

"Nope," Zeus snarled. "What yous talk'n about?"

"Contemplate what will happen if Yoggi makes a public statement describing the conditions the orphans were, and presumably are currently, subjected to on Velcron? Even without a public statement, the Kalopso have been monitoring our conversations. They realize people in authority know the truth."

"Oh, crap." Zeus raised his seat to an upright position.

"That is what I am concerned about. We must prevent Yoggi from conducting a press conference until after those children are rescued."

"How we's gonna do's that?" Zeus demanded, upset more innocent bystanders would be hurt because of him.

Apollo explained his idea for helping the children. Zeus was enraged at the stupidity of the plan, until Apollo asked for a better suggestion. The two of them discussed the best approach, given the limited options, and devised a strategy for saving as many of the kids as they could. It was foolish to assume none of them would be sacrificed.

"You are committed to your top priority being others' protection?" Apollo was uncomfortable with a plan that left Zeus as an easy target.

"Yeah! They's gonna kill me's, anyway. Plus I's tooks an oath and I's keep'n it!"

Apollo nodded, unhappy with their limited options. "We need to contact Yoggi immediately."

"I's hate this," Zeus grumbled as he rigged the ComLine to bypass Yoggi's voicemail and ring on her portable unit.

"I concur."

336

"Yous gonna do the talk'n?"

"If that's what you desire."

"Remember yous can be heard by Zeigler."

"Remember." Apollo winked and clicked his tongue. "I am counting on it."

"Yous hack everybody." Zeus popped two of Bentley's pills in his mouth and chewed them.

The men heard Cmd. Yoggi's confused voice. "Yoggi, here."

"I apologize for disturbing you, Commander. This is Cadet Christiani, and it's imperative I speak with you."

"Go ahead." She was puzzled by the request coming through on her bugged line.

"Are you still conducting the staff meeting?"

"Yes."

Apollo piloted the ship away from the gravitational pull of a nearby star. He did not want any turbulence to upset Zeus's queasy stomach. "Have you contacted the press yet?"

"No, why?"

"Because children's lives are in jeopardy."

"What? Get to it."

"Yes, Ma'am. If you make a public statement about what transpired last night, including the conditions of the Velcron orphanage, people will demand an investigation."

"Oh, my."

"Yes, Ma'am. You understand."

"Is Malone there with you?"

"Yes, Commander, who do you assume patched me straight through to you?"

"Of course. Malone, can you hear me?"

"Yes, Ma'am." Zeus leaned against the window. He concentrated on making his voice sound strong. "I's hear yous."

"Have you come up with anything we can do, or should we talk about it later?" Yoggi asked to verify if they could speak freely.

"We's gots a plans."

"Go ahead."

"Yes, Ma'am." Apollo looked to Zeus who nodded. "With your approval, I could speak to the entire group in attendance. It is more time-efficient than your repeating our conversation."

Now Cmd. Yoggi understood. They wanted Zeigler to hear the plan. "I've switched you to speaker; everyone can hear you now."

"Thank you, Ma'am. I assume you have briefed the others about what transpired last night?"

"Yes, they know."

"I have not been privy to the complete details; however, I surmise, if you make a public statement, hordes of reporters and curious people will want to investigate. Sooner or later they will stumble upon the truth. That orphaned children are being forced into prostitution and slave labor."

"That's ridiculous. Malone, you must be delusional from the Quakalin last night," Zeigler snarled.

"Ain'ts noth'n wrong with me's. I's lived there. I's know." Zeus's stomach tightened. He had to concentrate on relaxing or he would be vomiting again.

"Malone, where are they hiding these slave laborers?" Zeigler asked.

Zeus ground his teeth. "Ins the mine and K-Club."

"We're supposed to believe there is an entire mine and building on Velcron that has never been detected?"

"Yes, Sir." Apollo caught Zeus's eye and tapped his own chest.

Zeus gladly nodded and allowed Apollo to speak on his behalf.

"I also inquired about that. Orphanages are surrounded by force-field bubbles. The Velcron orphanage has a large amount of land. Scanners will ignore the bubble, because it is an authorized field."

"People go in and out of orphanages all the time. I myself volunteered at one. People would notice the things you're talking about," Zeigler said.

"At Velcron, three force fields are activated. Two smaller bubbles within the larger bubble. Scanners only detect the larger bubble, and since the size has remained unchanged, no one has any reason to investigate. The children in the real orphanage have no knowledge of their abused counterparts. They stay within their force-field limits. The mine workers and girls are equally unaware of the front orphanage, because they, too, must stay within their bubble."

"How can we be certain Malone hasn't imagined all this?" Zeigler asked.

"Because he talked about it last night under the influence of the

Quakalin," Dr. Bentley answered.

"Why not let the press investigate?" Zeigler questioned.

"Because the individuals who run the illegal operations will not want witnesses to testify against them." Apollo maneuvered the flyer.

"Are you saying I shouldn't make a public statement?" Yoggi asked.

"No, Ma'am, the situation is significantly more complicated. You should not make any immediate public statements. Zeus believes the Kalopso are monitoring him. If or how, he has not determined. If the Kalopso are aware of what transpired last night, or will be soon, they will presume the Corps will investigate."

"What do you two suggest?" Yoggi asked.

"We must rescue the children immediately, before the guilty parties have a chance to react. The Kalopso will assume the Corps will follow the usual slow bureaucratic process, and they have time to control the collateral damage."

"You two cadets should be commended for your concern for those innocent children." Zeigler had to get control of the situations. "I realize you are trying to help; however, you're not qualified to understand how these things work."

"I think we understand it, Sir," Apollo answered diplomatically.

"Son, I know you believe what you're saying, but you need to leave these things up to us. I give you my word, we will deal with this. You don't have experience with any of this," Zeigler spoke in a paternal tone. "Your concerns are real, but you don't understand what's involved. You two are both twenty-one or two. Neither of you has ever worked in a leadership capacity. You can't understand the problems associated with what you're proposing."

"That is incorrect. I have worked in leadership," Apollo answered calmly.

"Christiani, we're not talking about college clubs and things like that. This type of decision requires allocating money, resources and personnel. We don't do that overnight, especially when people's lives are stake. This type of decision requires being responsible for the well-being of others."

"Excuse me, Sir. I have been responsible for decisions involving money, resources and employees. My family owns and operates numerous companies. I personally have conducted my own meetings, approved and allocated funds, run press conferences and decided on employee contracts and demands. I have been required to fire employees who pleaded for their jobs because they had families to support. I know what it is like to make decisions that cause others to suffer. Everything I am stating can be substantiated in any financial journal. Feel free to verify my credentials. I have not succeeded by spending weeks making important, time-dependent decisions. Some decisions have to be made immediately, and this situation is an example. As you yourself have instructed us in class, sometimes you have to go with your gut instincts and react, or you will lose your only opportunity."

Sgt. Leiman and Taylor smiled at each other.

"What's so funny?" Zeigler demanded. He did not like being humiliated by cadets or snickered at by sergeants.

"I'm sorry, Sir," Leiman spoke in a remorseful tone. "I just can't figure out what I'm supposed to teach Christiani about leadership."

"Now you know how I feel about teaching Malone self-defense," Taylor quipped.

"Actually, Sgt. Leiman," Apollo replied, "I have gleaned a great deal from your example about leadership, like treating people equitably, regardless of background."

"Thank you."

"Taylor, I's ain't learn noth'n from yous," Zeus proclaimed.

The group laughed.

"Let's get back to business, people," Yoggi ordered. "Christiani, you make some good points. I'm open to your ideas. Exactly how do you two think this can be accomplished?"

"From what Zeus states, most orphans are armed, well. . .the way Zeus is, with knives and other Stone Age weapons. The children are controlled by denying them food and water, not powerful weapons. Securing the area would not require a great deal of resources or personnel."

"How are we supposed to get from the front building into the restricted areas?" Col. Peaks asked.

"That is where Zeus can assist us. He can lead a unit from the slums, through the sewage system and into the restricted area. That allows us the benefit of a surprise attack."

"We don't allow cadets off the base for any reason," Zeigler snarled.

"I am confident that breaking regulations to save hundreds of innocent children from malnutrition and abuse is acceptable both to the up-

340

per brass and the public at large. However, many will question decisions that bring further harm to children while OTS sat around and discussed options. This situation provides perfect PR for OTS and its sometimes self-centered image. Imagine on all the news broadcasts, OTS and Corps personnel carrying out weak, malnourished children into the arms of our own medical people. And do not forget the touching interviews the little darlings will give afterwards. You cannot purchase positive image building of this magnitude, and if it is done correctly, it can be perpetuated for years. Envision headlines like, 'Where are They Now, Ten Years After Their Daring Rescue from the Velcron Orphanage?' "

"You, Sergeant," Maj. Patterson exclaimed. "What am I supposed to teach him about PR?"

"Then you agree with Christiani's overall plan and its effect on our image?" Yoggi asked.

"I'm not certain if the military plan can be successful, but Christiani's right; you can't buy PR like that. It's one of the few ways to get enduring good press. Even if the casualties are high, the means will justify the hurried attempt, and some of the kids are bound to survive."

"I wonder about that," Zeigler stated.

"What do you mean?" Yoggi asked.

"If the Kalopso are monitoring Malone, or there is a spy in our midst, they could be hearing this transmission. In which case, if I were them, I'd blow the place up tonight."

"I do not concur, Sir," Apollo replied. "Should they have that much access, and we hope they do not, they will not expose their inside contact on a lost cause. The exploitation on Velcron is already ruined. It is strategically foolish. They will minimize their losses. They will attempt to dispose of children who can identify key members of the network without substantially reducing the number of orphans. If the network kills dozens of kids prior to the rescue, the survivors will state numerous individuals are missing. That directs our thoughts to only one possible conclusion; an inside contact. I was informed you personally, Lt. Cmd. Zeigler, verified the conference room was free of listening devices. Zeus secured this line, and I am positive of his abilities. His survival has continually depended on it. Process of elimination leaves only a spy. And we both know Cmd. Yoggi would not rest until that person was apprehended. No, Sir, if they are monitoring us, and they are smart, they will minimize their losses. They will each protect their own interests and not worrying about anybody else's."

"What do you think will happen to these kids, once they're rescued?" Zeigler asked.

"A few will be adopted; most will be divided among the other, non-corrupt orphanages around the universe. I am confident Maj. Patterson would agree, every public representative will be clamoring to sponsor legislation to appropriate additional funds to the Orphan Relief Agency."

"That's true," Patterson confirmed. "We're in an election year. Whether you're pro-orphan or not, this one's a winner. With such graphic pictures and stories, and with the victims being children, billions and billions will quickly be put into the system to take care of those kids and to ensure that this type of thing never happens again. No one's going to come out publicly against a program like that; it would be political suicide, especially when the visual images are still fresh in the voter's minds."

"You cadets seem to have thought of everything," Zeigler huffed. "However, I still think it's a poor idea. The casualties will be high, and it won't be us that gets hurt, it will be the kids in the crossfire."

"Sir," Apollo corrected, "there is no reason to kill anybody. We have rapid fire PSG's, even if we are forced to stun every child, it is better than their alternative."

"And what about the Corps casualties?" Zeigler continued.

"I am willing to risk my life to save innocent children, and unless I am mistaken, we all took an oath to that effect," Apollo shot back.

Zeigler glanced over at Yoggi. She had already made up her mind. The best thing he could do now was gain control of the operation. "Commander, I believe I'm the best person to lead this mission, and I'd like to volunteer for the job."

Cmd. Yoggi was trying to think of a reason why Zeigler could not lead the group when she heard Zeus's voice, "When do we's leave, Sir?" She understood Malone was approving Zeigler as mission leader.

"Thank you for volunteering. It's nice to know my best will be out there running things. Christiani, Malone, turn around and return here."

"We are approximately thirty minutes from the landing bay, Ma'am," Apollo stated.

"You two are making quite a team. Report to the conference room as soon as you land."

342

"Yes, Ma'am."

"The rest of you, it's going to be a long day. Everyone return here in half an hour. Simb, I'll need you to contact the upper brass. We'll need reinforcements. Zeigler, take anyone you want to help you plan this."

"I want to lay things out in my own mind first; then I can decide what and who I need. I'll be in my office, if you want me. Malone, are you still there?"

"Yes, Sir."

"Report to my office as soon as you land. I want a layout of everything you can remember. I expect a working sketch by the time I see you. Zeigler out. "

*   *   *

Zeus quickly hacked into Zeigler's ComLine. The two cadets listened to Zeigler explain what had happened in the meeting, emphasizing how he had tried to discredit the cadets and their plan.

"This better be a big success with lots of tenderhearted stories and sentimental crap," the network boss said. "I expect billions to be appropriated to the ORA, OTS and the Corps. The Corps better look good before the budget vote next month. Make sure you do a visual of the entire daring rescue and have lots of press people there when those kids come out. Plan it for the daytime, so the pictures are better. I'll make certain the kids aren't fed between now and then, just to make it a little more graphic. I'll also be certain no one of importance is in the club when you're there. You got that?"

"Yes, Sir," Zeigler snapped back. "Do you have a particular unit of the Corps you want me to use?"

"Use people from every branch. That's gets us the most funds."

"It's supposed to be a small sneak attack. How am I supposed to use three branches?"

"Make it work. If you had done what you were supposed to, then we wouldn't be forced to close down one of our most lucrative mines. Bring lots of shrinks and other medical people. Use a different unit for the club, and a couple to search the mines."

"I'll make it work, Sir," Zeigler assured him.

"You better. And make certain Malone encounters an unfortunate cave-in while he's in the mines," the K boss stated.

"I. . .I understand," Zeigler swallowed hard.

"You better not fail this time, or you'll pay the price. We've toler-

343

ated your failures, but you won't get another chance. I hope I make myself clear."

"Yes, very clear."

"I'll be watching you," the voice said before terminating the ComLine.

Apollo stared at Zeus. He was beginning to realize his friend had not exaggerated the potential risks.

Zeus, on the other hand, was not surprised by the ruthless comments. He was more accustomed to people like the boss than honest, caring people like Apollo.

Apollo did not know what to say; he could not forget Zeus was going to die. The orphan had told him, but he had not believed it.

Zeus gave Apollo a thumbs-up. "Yous the best budgin word hacker ins the universe. I's can't believe yous convinced thems of everything we's wants."

"Hum, Zeus, are you forgetting they intend to kill you?"

"Nope."

"You do not appear too distressed by the news."

"I's been tell'n yous, K always plans ta."

"Now that it is eminent, aren't you frightened?"

"Nope. What I's gots ta live for? Ain't gots noth'n or nobody."

"What about our friendship?"

Zeus took a swig of water, swished it around in his mouth and spit it into the trash receptacle. "Can'ts never be. Me's budgin the K over and shut'n down the Velcron operation is worth die'n for. Ain'ts die'n for noth'n likes before."

"Is that why you appear happy?"

"Ain'ts gonna die a meaningless death, and lots of people will know I's lives." Zeus sipped the water cautiously. "Yous think the Corps will give me's a burial and a marker?"

"I believe it is mandatory unless your will or family made a different request. If you die on a mission, you should be given full honors."

"And a marker?"

"Yes, probably on Tallien in Hero's Hollow, the Corps cemetery."

"Really? Hero's Hollow?"

"What is this obsession with your death?" Apollo adjusted the rear engine output. "I suggest you expend more energy contemplating staying alive?"

"Yous don't gets what it's like ta live and die with nobody know'n or care'n or ever being able ta tell yous existed. If I's got a marker, there's be a record I's existed. Ain'ts too many orphan able ta say that."

Apollo scrunched his face. "What is the cultural burial practice when an orphan dies?"

"Another piece of trash ta be's tossed."

Apollo was appalled by the blatant disregard for human life that Zeus and other orphans were subjected to. "On my oath, you will have a huge, impressive marker. One visible to everyone."

"Thanks." Zeus's face looked translucent in the dim cockpit lights. "I's don't care what. I's just wants proof I's here."

"I insist on the best for my friends."

"Yous assume'n yous gonna be alive ta insists on the best."

"I will leave instructions with my secretary, Tom. He will complete the task whether I am dead or alive." Apollo's mouth felt dry. "Do you think they will kill me, too?"

"Don't know. If I's guess'n, they's want yous alive. Yous got too much potential ta gets them money. Drayka has a tendency ta make bastards take risks. Yous rich, and they's always want more money. I's ain't heard nobody order yous dead."

"Thank you; however, I'm still concerned about you."

"I's told yous before, I's always gonna die. Lots worse things." Zeus flipped on the computer screen in front of him. "I's talk, now yous gots ta let me's do this sketch for Zeigler."

*   *   *

Zeus opened Cmd. Yoggi's bedroom door. He had to wake her without alerting Zeigler, who was outside her window watching her house. Zeus had checked, and Zeigler could see shadows moving in her room. Zeus would have to make certain neither of their heads lifted above the window. The only way he could be confident Cmd. Yoggi would not sit up or scream was to hold her down and cover her mouth.

The second Zeus covered her mouth, Yoggi's eyes snapped open. As soon as Zeus was convinced she was coherent, he whispered, "It's Malone. Zeigler's outside watch'n yous. Don't lift yous head up and don't make no noise. Gots it?"

Yoggi nodded, and he released her. "What are you doing?" she hissed.

"Gots ta talk ta yous. Ain't gots no other way. Rolls over ta this side and off the bed. Keep yous head below the window."

She complied, ending up on the floor beside him. "I take it this is important or you wouldn't have scared the crap out of me?" She started crawling. "Follow me into the closet." Zeus obeyed, and the two crawled into the closet. Yoggi shut the door, stood and flipped on the light.

"OK, you got my attention. What's this all about?" she demanded in a normal tone.

"Shh." Zeus stood.

"This room is practically soundproof. Don't ask me why, it just is. I come here to get away from Sheila's loud music." She grabbed her robe off the door hook and slipped it on. She was more comfortable talking to him with a robe on than wearing only a nightgown.

"Yous certain?"

"Yes, I'd stake my life on it, and if I'm not mistaken, I am. They're not using audios, are they?"

"No, Ma'am. Since yous ordered Col. Peaks ta sweep and monitor the base, they don't wants ta be's detected."

"Good. What do you have to report?"

"Yous gots ta let me's go with Zeigler and lead thems."

"No, I don't." Yoggi crossed her arms. "I'm in charge here. It's consistent with policy not to let cadets off base. I won't be responsible for sending you into a trap."

"Yous ain'ts gots no choice."

"Are you saying I have to choose between you or me? Is Zeigler planning to kill me and take over? Is that their plan?"

"Theys always plans ta kill me's."

"I took an oath to serve and protect, and I intend to keep that oath. I won't hand you over, even if they do plan to kill you. It won't be because I let them."

Zeus stomped. "Crap, that's what Zeigler says yous say. Theys already suspicious yous know too much. Ta keep yous in line, they's gonna infect Sheila with Intracellar Disintegrating Disease. Yous ever see anyone die of IDD? I's has. It's slow, painful and ugly."

"I've never seen it." Yoggi hugged her robe around her. "I've only read it's horrible."

"Send'n me's ain't gonna prolong my's life or saves it. I's want ta die on Velcron. Least I's die'n for someth'n, not starve'n for noth'n."

"Is that how you see it? That it's noble to die for a cause?"

"Ain'ts sure it's noble, but it's better than die'n for noth'n or nobody."

Yoggi sat on the blue carpet and leaned against the closet wall. "I need to think about this."

"Noth'n ta thinks 'bout." He sat across from her. "Yous saw how I's was last night and what keep'n Emily alive did ta me's. I's know what it's like ta watch someone suffer cause I's couldn't let her die. Ain't gots nobody or noth'n ta lose. Yous do. And they's gots ta kill me's. I's knows too much, and they's lose credibility if I's live. Look like they's lose'n control. I's ain't even gots a place ta goes. Last night I's plan'n ta make it ta the sewers here. And for what? Life of live'n in crap, never see'n nobody. After live'n here, ain't easy ta think 'bout go'n back. Yous tell me's, Commander, where I's go that be's safe?"

"Do they monitor everything?"

"Ain'ts a sensor in the universe theys can't plugs inta."

"I know you're right." Yoggi stared at a piece of lint on the carpet. "I still feel terrible that I'm going to be responsible for your death."

"Ain't yous fault. I's knew the K would contract me's as soon as I's applies ta OTS, and theys did. I's dead before yous run out of excuses not ta enroll me's."

She lifted her eyes to meet his gaze. "Have you known that long?"

"Yeah. I's only surprised I's ain't dead already. Theys mad yous let it goes this far. Yous could of assigned me's ta prejudice bastards, but yous don't. Yous believes in the system, even if yous don't like orphans."

"I'm sorry about the last few weeks. I've changed a lot since then."

"No, yous ain'ts." Zeus looked her in the eyes. "Yous decent and fair then and now. Ain't changed."

"Thank you." She grimaced. "How about you? Did we have any effects on you?" She wished they had more time to get to know each other.

"Two months ago, I's never believe I's die with a full belly, close'n the mine on Velcron, save'n them kids, know'n a few people care, and maybe have'n a marker after I's die. Ain't never talks ta anybody 'cept Emily 'til here. Bests place and people I's ever know. No matter how theys kill me's, I's got no regrets."

"I'm glad you've had a few happy days here, and I can promise you'll have a marker in Hero's Hollow. You won't be forgotten, Malone. I'm certain of that. All those kids will have you to thank for their freedom."

"Thanks, Ma'am."

"Do they plan to kill some of the kids, too?"

"Nope, want ta." Zeus moved his leg so he could rest his arm on his knee. "Theys can't figure out which girls can identify important K leaders. They's don't keep track a which girls the budgin bastards rocks."

"I guess that's a hidden blessing. But there are bound to be some who will remember visitors from the past."

"Theys plan ta adopt 'em, so theys can still control 'em. They's gonna try ta gets control of the adoptions."

"What?" Yoggi's body went stiff as a board. "Are we just taking them from one miserable life to another?"

"Ain'ts like that. Most members is men. Theys don't tell thems wives or kids or families. Theys gonna be adopted by the members, but I's hope'n them wives is gonna raise 'em. Plus, still be lots better than what theys used ta. Ain't no poor K. Them kids won't never be hungry. They's go ta school. K is order'n members that is adopt'n ta treat the kids good, ta make sure kids trust 'em. Then if theys ever want ta identify someone or crap like that, them families will discourage 'em."

Yoggi put her hand over her eyes and shook her head. "It's the perfect plan. All these bastards look like public heroes for stepping forward and offering to adopt an abused orphan, while secretly their only motivation is to keep control over the children. Zeigler hasn't thrown that one at me yet."

"Ma'am." He waited until she looked at him. "Yous gots ta let him do whatever he wants."

"Malone, I'm responsible for everything that happens."

"I's the only one theys plan ta gets rid a right now. They's gonna have expendable members in the club, and they's ain't gonna be no one armed, 'cept a few of the usual guards. Ain't nobody but me's supposed ta get hurt. Yous interfere, more get hurts and dies."

"You can't honestly expect me to give Zeigler a free rein."

"Yes, Ma'am, I's can. Two days ago, yous don't question Zeigler. Yous trust him before, and yous gots ta now."

Yoggi drummed her fingers. "Do you know he's talking about taking Christiani, too?"

"Yeah, theys figure with Apollo's big mouth, and the way he's so convince'n, he's convince the voters ta approve more funds ta orphan causes. They's try'n ta make up for the drayka they's gonna lose at Velcron."

She clasped her hands. "Then they don't plan to harm him?"

"Not now, but even if theys decide ta, noth'n yous do is gonna stop 'em."

"How are they going to kill you without endangering anyone else?"

"Zeigler's supposed ta arrange a cave-in. I's whats gonna be under the debris."

"They're going to bury you alive?"

"Basically." He shrugged.

"You must have nerves of steel. You don't seem afraid."

"Ain'ts afraid of die'n. Can't be's worse than live'n. I's suffocate in 'bout seven minutes. Easy way ta go. Lots less suffer'n than theys planned for me's before. Seven minutes of suffer'n ain't even a level two. Makes them mad, theys gots ta let me's die easy. Theys want me's ta be a martyr, so theys can get more money appropriated."

"It always seems to come back to the money."

"Money and power."

"I knew Zeigler was hung up on money, I just never knew how badly." Cmd. Yoggi sat quietly for a few minutes. She was struggling with what else to say before his suicide mission. After careful consideration, she decided Malone would not want anything sentimental. "I guess you should get some shut-eye." She rose.

"Yes, Ma'am." He stood and moved toward the door.

Suddenly, a deep belly laugh shook her torso.

Zeus frowned. "Huh?"

"The role reversal over the last few days. I haven't even been vaguely in charge. You've been running the whole show and taking responsibility for everything, and you're still answering me 'Yes, Ma'am,' and 'Thank you, Ma'am.' Dr. Bentley has joked about how well OTS indoctrinates people. I believe she calls it brainwashing. And I have to admit, Leiman and Baker have done a fine job with you. You are an excellent officer. I'm proud to have served with you."

"Thank yous." He beamed with pride.

"Just this once." She stood tall and saluted him. "Thank you, Sir," she stated proudly, then quickly turned out the lights before he could see the tears rolling down her cheeks.

CHAPTER 26

APOLLO WANDERED slowly around the base. He eyed a unit marching in formation. He stopped at the mess hall and leaned against the wall. He panned the area. Desperate, he bowed his head and prayed. He felt he should call out to Zeus. He looked around. There was no place for Zeus to hide. He must have gotten the signals crossed. Communication in prayer was such an inexact method. He decided to check around the supply warehouse.

Apollo walked a few paces, then stopped abruptly. He felt an uncontrollable urge to yell for Zeus. He was embarrassed to be calling out to nothing. "Zeus, where are you?" he yelled half-heartedly.

Zeus jumped off the roof. "What yous do'n here?"

Apollo jerked back. "Do not startle me in that manner." He exhaled loudly.

"How yous find me's?"

Apollo smiled as he looked piously up to the sky.

"Yous spooky."

"Zeigler sent me to locate you. I am joining you on the mission to Velcron."

"What? That bastard Zeigler can't order yous ta goes."

"He did not order me, I volunteered."

Zeus shoved his friend. "Yous budgin idiot. What yous think'n?"

"Me think?" Apollo shrugged. "Never. I can assure you, this is one time I wish I were not a Christian. I am a little apprehensive."

"Then don'ts go."

"You are better aquainted with me than that."

"Yous a pain in the butt. What yous gonna do ta helps on Velcron?"

"Zeigler assigned me to keep you emotionally stable. He said you were having outbursts in the meeting, to calm you down, and return with you. You appear stable enough to me."

350

"Budgin Zeigler." Zeus shoved his hand in his pocket and stroked the calming steel of the Little Lady. "He wants me's ta look crazy."

Apollo scratched behind his ear. "Why?"

"So he's can explain why I's caused the cave-in."

"Oh, I understand. You supposedly have some delusional fit, and indirectly cause your own tragic death." Apollo rolled his eyes and said sarcastically, " That is consistent with your personality."

Zeus growled and flashed his knife in Apollo's face.

Apollo chuckled at his frustrated friend. "Can you not overpower Zeigler when the situation is at hand?"

"Ain't gonna be's likes that."

"Would you expand on that."

"Apollo, yous ever seen a cave-in?"

"No, it is not exactly a daily occurrence."

"Not in yous life. Budgin common for me's. He ain't gots ta get near me's. Only gots ta shoot the rocks over my's heads."

Apollo made circles in the dirt with his boot. The reality of the life Zeus and the others endured caused a lump in his throat. Apollo fought to control his emotions.

Zeus could smell Apollo's fear. "Yous can't handle see'n them kids in the mines and K-Club."

"I will manage," Apollo's voice squeaked. He cleared his throat. "God will provide the grace I need, when the time comes." Apollo spoke without his usual conviction. "Do not concern yourself with me. You keep your eyes on Zeigler."

"Yous gonna see a lot worse if yous goes ta Velcron."

"I realize that." Apollo took a deep breath. "I am not thrilled about this. I have to trust God, even when I do not want to."

"Ain'ts never gonna change yous mind. Yous stubborn."

"That is a trait we have in common. Now, let us proceed to the meeting." Apollo turned toward headquarters. "They cannot continue without you."

"Yous go ahead. I's follow ins a minute."

Apollo almost protested, then wisely held his tongue. "I will see you in there." He walked away alone.

Zeus waited until Apollo had rounded the corner, then jogged over to the track. He had been waiting for Taylor. He wanted to die with their friendship intact. Taylor had loosened up and was running slowly. Zeus loitered behind the bleachers until Taylor passed him.

Zeus came up behind the sergeant, grabbed him and flipped him to the ground. Zeus triumphantly put his knife to the sergeant's throat. "Too budgin easy ta beat yous, ain'ts no fun."

"You stick." Taylor wiggled loose and knocked the knife out of the orphan's hand. The two men sparred until they heard a loud whistle.

"That's Sues." Taylor released his buddy. "I'd know that whistle anywhere."

"Crap." Zeus stood and prepared to salute.

Leiman jogged up. "Quit messing around. We've got to return to the meeting." Zeus obeyed and walked off the track. Taylor hesitated. She turned to Taylor. "What are you waiting for? I assume everything is OK and you want in."

Taylor smiled, nodded and fell in behind the others. He enjoyed watching her walk briskly ahead of him. He was too busy watching to notice Zeus stop. Taylor bumped into the orphan. "What are you stopping for?"

"Forgot my's knife."

"I kicked it over by the bleachers. We'll catch up," he said to Leiman, running over to find the knife.

"I's ought ta beat the crap out of yous for kick'n the Little Lady."

"Why do you call it that?" Taylor meandered over to a reflection in the grass and picked up the knife. He retracted the blade and tossed it to Zeus.

Zeus caught the knife and put it in his pocket. "Anything I's got ta have in my's pants all days, gots ta be a lady."

*   *   *

Zeigler flipped on his pen-sized pointer. "For the two of you that just joined us, let me quickly go over what was discussed earlier. Up on the screen, you'll see a rough sketch of the sewage system. That's how we intend to enter. The pink building," he shined the light on it, "is where the club is. The gray areas," he moved the pointer, "are the mines. Malone says there are no accurate maps of the mine shafts. The kids know how to get in and out of their territory, and things change frequently. We'll have to get the miners' help, once we're in."

"How can we be certain they'll help us?" Maj. Sato questioned.

"Yous offer food and water, they's help yous," Zeus responded. "Plus, ain't loyalty keep them down the shafts."

"What can we expect when we encounter them? For that matter, what's the approximate age range we're dealing with?" a captain from another base asked.

"Age ain't relevant in the mines. Done by brands." Zeus unbottoned his shirt to show his brands. "Bigger yous is, more work yous do, and the more brands yous got. One circle is a runner. Two, bag stuffers. Three, light loaders and haulers. Four, light diggers. Five, heavy loaders. And sixes do the major dig'n. One square is a small group taskmasters. Two squares, unit taskmasters."

"So it has to do with size, strength and ability?"

"Yes, Sir." Zeus buttoned his shirt.

Dr. Bentley was taking meticulous notes. The medical portion of the operation would be far more extensive than the military portion. "How small are the littlest ones?"

"Yous sees Capt. Weiss' kid? 'Bouts that size."

"Matthew is three." She dropped her laser quill. "What possible use could a three-year-old be?"

"Plenty, when they's hungry."

"What age group is the oldest?" Apollo asked calmly.

"Anybody ain'ts dead yet."

"At what age do you get released into society?"

"Nobody leaves."

"You got out."

"I's sneaks out through the sewer system. Ain't never mets nobody else from the Velcron mines."

Baker cracked his knuckles. "Who's on Orphan's Row on Velcron?"

"Low-life scum. Orphans froms a front orphanage. Druggies, trick turners, poor trash."

"So as far as you know, no one else has ever gotten out alive?"

"Yeah."

"Where are all these children living and sleeping?" Dr. Bentley asked without looking up from her notes.

"Shaft they's assign ta. Mosts only leave the shafts ta hunt food. Force field keeps us close ta the entrance. Ain'ts no other reason ta leaves."

"You kids weren't given breaks to go out and play?"

"Doc, yous ain't get'n this. Ain'ts no play'n." Zeus slapped the table. "We's work ins a mines."

"How many kids were in each group?"

"Depends on the size of the shaft yous in. Average, one master, couple runners, 'bout the same number of sixes, fours and two circles, 'cause they's work together. Usually 'bouts six of each and 'bout half as many threes and fives. 'Bouts twenty-five ta thirty a unit."

Bentley wrote down each category as he spoke. "How many two-square taskmasters do you think there are?"

"When I's there, I's know of three or four others."

"So about thirty per one-square taskmaster. About one hundred and eighty for a two-square taskmaster and four two squares. That's seven hundred and twenty!" Yoggi exclaimed. "They can't be hiding that many."

"Ain'ts done. Bunch of ones and twos sort the ore. Two squares gots surveyor who finds the next dig'n sites. And a fews at the body pool."

Dr. Bentley glanced up from her notes. "How often was the water changed?"

Zeus curled his face in confusion. "Huh?"

"Don't tell me, they never changed the water?"

"Ain'ts no water! Budgin body pool." Zeus breathed heavily. He panned the confused faces and stopped at Apollo. Apollo shrugged his shoulders and shook his head. "What's wrong with yous?" Zeus banged his fist on the table.

"We are trying," Apollo said calmly. "Describe what is there."

"Dead bodies."

Dr. Bentley covered her mouth and closed her eyes for a minute. "I'm sorry." Bentley dropped her head. "How many bodies?"

"Total? Don't knows. 'Bout one every other day. Sometimes there's a bunch, if we's gets a epidemic."

"Do any." Bentley took a deep breath and composed herself. "Do any." Her voice squeaked and she cleared her throat. "Do other kids ever go near the body pool?"

"Yeah." Zeus clenched his fists and ground his teeth. "Budgin goods place ta hunt. We's all go there if we's gets a chance." Zeus ripped a huge chunk of nail off his pinkie, tearing the flesh and wiped the blood on his pants.

"Commander, do you mind if we take a short recess?" Apollo requested.

"No, I think it's a good idea. Take all the time you need."

"Come on, Zeus." Apollo stood and pointed toward the window. "Let us get some fresh air."

Zeus slammed the chair into the table, saluted and marched out of the room. Apollo followed and waited to speak until they were outside. "I realize this operation is dredging up painful memories; however, we honestly do not understand what you are referring to."

"Yous all too naïve ta do's this."

"No, we are not. It will take longer for us to comprehend the situation since we have not encountered anything similar. That is as ridiculous a statement as saying you cannot adjust to OTS. It has taken you longer; however, you have proved to be more than capable. The same will be true on Velcron. Those of us who are determined to interact effectively may learn slowly; however, we will adjust, just as you have."

"Maybe."

"The children will need sensitive, compassionate people once they are freed. I am not arrogant enough to think I am going to be particularly useful during the military portion of this mission; however, I can be of great assistance once the children are freed. If your information is accurate, it will not be difficult to gain control of the area. Once controlled, we will need to interact with the children in ways they will respond positively to. Follow me." Apollo walked over to the bleachers. "Let us sit down. Walk me through this entire mission. Describe what we will see, what are appropriate interactions, and most importantly, what is inappropriate. I do not want to engage with the orphans in ways that will frighten or upset them. For example, waking you by shaking produced a knife to my throat. I should be knowledgeable enough to avoid those altercations or be prepared to de-escalate them when they arise."

The two men talked while the others waited. After half an hour, the cadets returned. Apollo asked permission to speak on Zeus's behalf.

"Go ahead," Cmd. Yoggi answered, hopeful things would progress more smoothly with Christiani leading.

"We are all confused by some of Zeus's terms. I have obtained the basics from him. I will attempt to explain things so you can understand; however, it is going to be imperative we know the orphans' slang. If someone informs us the rocking area is up a particular shaft, and we are unfamiliar with that term, then we will be endangering ourselves and the others in our unit."

Apollo checked his handwritten notes. "First, seven-hundred and twenty is not an accurate number for the mines. The numbers were never constant in either the mines or the club. To be conservative, we should count on between a thousand and twelve hundred."

"What?" Dr. Bentley threw down her laser pen.

"That is why I mentioned the count first. It will not require many units to take control of the area. Most of our resources should go to medical supplies, personnel, transports and trained therapists."

"Malone, why didn't you tell us that before?" Zeigler demanded.

Zeus leaned over the table at Zeigler. "I's tell'n yous. . ."

Apollo yanked his friend into his seat and spoke loudly. "Zeus is not accustomed to thinking in terms of ordering or allocating supplies. We should be mindful, he has not slept, he has been drugged, he is dealing with violent and abusive memories, and he is the sole individual who can make this mission successful."

"I have a couple of questions," the visiting captain said. "What are we going to do with these kids once we've captured the bad guys? Where are we going to put them? How are we going to keep track of all these children?"

"Don't they carry their ID chips with them?" Dr. Bentley asked.

"Doc." Zeus banged his fists on the table. "Yous ain't get'n this. Ain'ts none of them gots ID chips."

"So I need to keep their medical files by name only?"

Zeus smacked his forehead with the palm of his hand. "No names."

"What do you mean no names? What do you call each other? How do your taskmasters keep track?"

"We's keep track by's our work units." Zeus unbuttoned his shirt and showed them his shoulder. "I's a arrow."

"If your master wanted to talk to you, how did he identify you from the other four or five circles or whatever?"

"My's unit called me's Red Top." Zeus rubbed his orange-red hair. "Names gots ta do with something they's done or how they's look, like One Eye or Diggy. It can change, and they's a bunch of One Eyes or Nine Fingers."

"Malone, how do I keep track of which medical record goes with which child?"

"Don't knows. They's ain't gonna remember."

"I realize that. So how do we keep track?"

Zeus rebuttoned his shirt. "All I's knows is the brands."

"Can we tag them? Like a med bracelet or something?" Sgt. Leiman asked.

"Yeah," Zeus answered.

"We'll have to identify them somehow," Dr. Bentley stated. "Do we have enough med bracelets in supply?"

"Simb," Cmd. Yoggi ordered, "be certain there is at least fifteen hundred in the supplies."

"Yes, Ma'am."

"Once they're rescued," the captain asked, "will these kids line up and attempt to cooperate with us?"

"Noth'n likes this never happened. I's guess most won't resist. They's won't want ta get the new owners mad. Some be too drugged ta cooperate. Line'n up? Theys ain't gonna know what it means."

"We will have to count on there being a great deal of confusion," Apollo stated. "The children will be bewildered at best. They will be frightened and uncertain who we are or what our motives are. Zeus thinks we ought to assemble the children in their basic work units. The children in the mines have brands similar to Zeus's. Whatever brand is on their right shoulder identifies their unit. The ones from the club will be more complicated. They have floors and group rooms; however, they are moved around a great deal. We have discussed color coding, like different colored shirts. The problem is they may not comprehend our requests, or they will simply forget. We should each be assigned a small number of children to be accountable for; however, I would not plan on them remaining in an outlined area or sitting in an orderly fashion for meals. We should pitch camp near the entrance to the mines. It is completely surrounded by force fields and, therefore, provides a controlled perimeter. We will not lose any of the children; however, we maybe unable to keep track of them."

Bentley tossed her pen on the table. "How will I know when I've examined them all?"

"Either do not put on the bracelets until they are examined, or you will need to mark the bracelets once you have completed your exams," Apollo suggested.

"Will they resist having the bracelets put on?" she asked.

"I's would," Zeus answered.

"My staff will already be overtaxed. I'd like those put on before we see them. We'll mark them in red as we finish their initial screening."

Apollo looked at his list. "According to Zeus's speculations, a consistent location until placement will be best. The more location changes, the more disorientated the orphans will be. When their environment is unpredictable, they are. That could prove detrimental to our goals and possibly dangerous. We should keep them on orphanage property until they are permanently placed."

"Twelve hundred kids. ORA can't place twelve hundred kids that quickly, and they can't live on the grounds for months," Zeigler exclaimed.

"Sir, I am confident it can be accomplished," Apollo answered. "It has not been discussed; however, I assume once the area is secure, we will allow a limited number of the press corps in to report. I am certain, throughout the galaxy, there are more than twelve hundred loving families who would gladly take home a needy child, no questions asked. We use the press to publicize the children are available for immediate adoption."

"Son," Zeigler stated condescendingly, "I realize you're young, but you can't be that naïve. Adoptive parents have to go through numerous home visits and background checks. The process takes months and sometimes years."

"Yes, Sir, I am aware of that. However, statistics show the system cannot accurately predict how healthy and stable a family is. In fact, there was a scandal in the last year because children were placed in an inordinately high number of alcoholic and abusive families. Historically, government agencies are unable to determine whether people will make good parents or not."

"That assumes we get the right press people in there. What if someone who is anti-military or anti-orphan is assigned to report on Velcron?" Maj. Patterson asked.

Apollo cocked his head. "We ensure that reporters whose goals are contrary to our own are not permitted to report from inside the orphanage. We hand-pick the reporters allowed in."

"Christiani, that's not how the press works."

"Major, yes, it can."

Patterson rolled his eyes. "You cannot call up and request specific reporters."

"Yes, Sir, I can. Commander," he turned to her. "May I make an outside call?"

"Yes, I'd like to see this myself." Yoggi slid the audio/visual ComLine to him.

"Sally Russell is pro-orphan and pro-military. Does she meet with your approval?"

"Yes, she does," Yoggi answered.

Apollo punched in some numbers. A bleary-eyed man grumbled, "Hello."

"Tom. Apollo. I apologize for waking you. I need you to contact Sally Russell. Inform her she has five minutes to contact me or lose the story of her life."

"It will take me a minute to get her number from my files." He moved away from the screen.

"I will remain on this line. Connect her to me as soon as you reach her. I may have a couple other things I need assistance with, so would you mind staying awake?"

"Sure, I'm already up. Sally's number shouldn't take long."

Apollo's screen flashed, "Holding."

Cmd. Yoggi asked, "Who was that?"

"Tom Green, my personal assistant. We have been friends for years. He realizes I would not awaken him unless it was imperative."

"Oh."

They waited only a few minutes before the ComLine beeped and Apollo flipped it on.

"Sally Russell."

"Apollo Christiani, Ms. Russell. Thank you for responding immediately."

"Yes, I'd recognize you. What's the story of my life?"

"I cannot give you specific details at this time; however, as I am certain you are aware, my credibility with the press is extremely high. I have never contacted the press to make insignificant announcements. You will have to trust my reputation."

"I do. Any call from a Christiani is always taken seriously. Can you give me a topic?"

"Would you wait a moment, please?" Apollo turned the ComLine to hold. "May I inform her the topic is orphans?"

Cmd. Yoggi nodded. She was too amazed at what was transpiring to answer verbally.

Apollo reactivated the ComLine. "The topic is orphans, Ma'am."

"Since we don't know each other, I was a little surprised you called me. Now that I hear the topic, I understand. Count me in," Sally replied. "Tell me where and when you want me. I'll be there."

"Would you hold again, please?" Apollo pressed the hold button and turned to Yoggi.

Yoggi's eye were wide. "Wow! I'm impressed. I hadn't really gotten that far. Tell her we'll call her shortly."

"Yes, Ma'am." Apollo flipped back to the first screen. "Tom?"

"Yes, I'm still here."

"Where is Russell located?"

"On Igna."

"Thank you, I will return to you momentarily. Commander, she ought to begin assembling her supplies and preparing for transportation or she will never arrive on Velcron in time."

"Good point. Go ahead and take care of it."

"Yes, Ma'am." He returned to that screen. "Ms. Russell, I apologize for keeping you holding. You will need to leave by the end of today. Assemble your team and equipment, and I will contact you with specific coordinates as soon as possible. You will need to bring a full camera crew, satellite-feed people, interview capabilities, everything. Power-source plug-in may not be possible, so please provide your own generators and your own satellite links. The conditions will be crude, so be prepared."

"I can leave within the hour, but you realize I'm about seventeen hours from you."

"Yes, Ma'am. That is why you were given only five minutes to contact me."

"Thanks for the tip. I owe you one."

"I look forward to meeting you." Apollo smiled as the screen went blank. "Commander, what other reporters do you approve of?"

"Wesley Circuit and Don Little are always pro-military and they didn't oppose Malone's acceptance, but I don't know their overall views on orphans," she answered.

"I can obtain that information." Apollo pressed the ComLine button. "Tom, are you awake yet?"

"Yes, I made myself some coffee while I was waiting."

"Excellent, you will need it. Will you please cross-check all the top reporters. I need people who are both pro-orphan and pro-military. Compile the list and contact me as quickly as possible. The more popular, the better."

"How pro do you want them?"

"Rate them in both areas."

"I'll be in touch."

"Thank you, Tom." Apollo turned off the screen.

Cmd. Yoggi shook her head in awe. "I don't suppose you could teach our people to do that?"

"No, Ma'am." Apollo dropped his eyes, a little embarrassed. "I have not entirely earned my reputation. It is my family's name people respond to."

"Yes, and quickly at that." Yoggi drummed her fingers. "While we're waiting, let's go back to what we're going to do with these children. We can't announce open adoptions without the ORA's approval, and they have a reputation for responding slowly. Besides, no one could take a child without an ID card."

"Yes, Ma'am. My family also has a few contacts in the government. Would you like me to work on that?"

"Do you think you can work them like you did Russell?"

"Yes, Ma'am. I should be able to."

Yoggi leaned back in her chair, crossed her hands in her lap and smirked. It was enjoyable to have someone on her side who could work the system. She intended to utilize every angle she could. "Go ahead."

Apollo typed in another code. A sleepy voice said, "Hello," on a blank screen.

"Charles, it is Apollo. Please, activate your screen."

"Apollo?" the voice answered as an unshaven face appeared. "Nice hair cut."

"You are always amusing. I apologize for waking you."

"That's all right, the alarm was going off in a few minutes anyway."

"Are you alone?"

"No, just a second."

Apollo took a few drinks of his water and relaxed in his chair. He felt like a caged bird who had been freed to fly. This was what he was born to do.

"OK, I'm alone. What's up?"

"Does the job you have been appointed to involve issuing ID cards?"

"Yes, we verify births and give out cards."

"What if someone does not have a card?"

"We check them out. If it's lost, we replace it. Some people try to hide from their past. We usually catch them."

"What if an individual never had a card?"

"Apollo, what's up?"

"There are some children being exploited by the network. They have never been issued cards. Which is why nobody is checking up on them; nobody realizes they exist. We are preparing a rescue. I thought I might give my old friend an opportunity to be involved. I can arrange the situation, so you personally are there to ID these defenseless children."

"Is the press going to be there?"

"All top-notch people. I am hand-picking them myself."

"How many little darlings are we talking about?"

"Twelve hundred."

"What?" Charles twisted his finger in his ear. "I thought you said twelve hundred."

"You heard correctly. It will be one of the biggest stories of the decade. I surmised you would be interested in some free 'I care about the poor' PR to assist you with your campaign. As I understand it, you are struggling with capturing the middle and lower class votes."

"I'm going to owe you big."

"Yes, you are."

"Twelve hundred cards. Wow! The ID checks will take awhile."

Apollo shook his head. "I thought you wanted a reputation as a public servant who acts quickly."

"Yes, but I have to do background checks."

"When the universe sees the visuals of these children, where they have been and hears their stories, I am confident no one will question you IDing them and doing thorough checks at a later date. Besides, you are going to figure out there is nothing to check. They have all been locked away since birth. You will have to trust me. I would never mislead you. I personally guarantee you are not being misled."

"Your judgment on political things I trust implicitly. I can always track them down at the orphanage."

"That is not our intention. We are hoping to get them adopted, immediately."

"How?"

"That leads me to my next inquiry. Who are you acquainted with in ORA?"

"I know the director, but I don't think she'll speak to me."

Apollo chuckled and rolled his eyes. "You enrage another woman?"

"Mary Ann Fritsimmons. And she definitely has a temper."

"Does she have political aspirations?"

"Oh, yes! And the money to support it."

"Is she running a campaign this year," Apollo asked hopefully.

"Yup."

"Forward her code to me. I am certain she will be reasonable. She must be, she discarded you." Apollo pointed his thumb behind his shoulder.

"I dumped her. And I wouldn't tell her I gave you her code. It won't help."

"Your name as an introduction with women never helps."

"Hold on, let me look up her codes. I'll send her office and home numbers to your ComLine."

"Thank you."

"Where am I going for this PR gig?"

"Obtain everything you need. I will contact you with the coordinates later. Do not dress for success. The conditions will be rustic. You will receive more details later."

"Am I going to see you there?"

"Probably. One more thing, this is classified information. You cannot speak to anyone else."

"Classified? How'd you get involved?"

"I will explain the situation to you later. I must terminate this conversation." Apollo turned off the screen.

"I'm impressed again," Cmd. Yoggi commented. "I could have spent months cutting through the bureau's red tape. Christiani, you move on to ORA. The rest of you, take a break."

Sgt. Leiman strolled out of the room. "Wow! Have you ever seen anything like that?"

"Never," Taylor replied.

"What are we supposed to be teaching him?" Baker asked.

"We did teach him how to salute," Leiman stated.

"And march," Baker added.

Taylor jabbed his girlfriend. "All things I'm sure Christiani needs to get ahead."

CHAPTER 27

APOLLO'S STOMACH CHURNED like a washing machine. He felt
the contents spin and twist as he crawled through the sulfur-smelling,
sewage-filled sewer. His headlight shined on Sgt. Baker's boots in front
of him. He tried to keep his mind off the leechrat that had locked its
jaw on his calf and rode piggyback. He also tried to ignore the dead
animals, feces and huge water bugs slipping in between his fingers
and beneath his skin-tight gloves. How Zeus and Emily had lived down
here was beyond him. A half-eaten dog's head with one eye bulging
floated between Sgt. Baker's boots. Apollo jerked back. The brew in
his stomach jumped into his throat. He forced himself to choke it down
into the churning machine and crawled forward.

The train of human crawlers reached the abandoned sewers. These
pipes were drier and better smelling, but corrugated. Apollo's knees
ached. He had difficulty focusing as his mind wandered to the terrifying unknown ahead.

They reached a fork in the pipes. A captain gave them orders.
Apollo heard Sgt. Baker's voice over his helmet communicator.

"Christiani, follow me. We're heading up to the mine. PSGs on
stun. Remember, we may have to stun the children. They will be unpredictable. Do your best, but don't hesitate because they're children.
The unit ahead of us is in. No resistance yet. There's a shaft to the left.
We're to take that shaft and help gain control of one small cave. You
and I will stay together."

"Yes, Sir."

Apollo waited his turn, then followed Sgt. Baker into a small cave.
There was a hunched-over man with one arm sitting by a hole.

The man ignored the rifles leveled at him. "She's ain'ts founds
noth'n." He bent his scarred face at the hole.

"Christiani, check it."

365

"Yes, Sir." Apollo peered down the hole. It was a very narrow, deep pit. He adjusted his headlamp to a tight beam. A pair of eyes squinted at the bright light. "There is somebody down there!"

"It's Shuts-up. She don'ts says noth'n," the one-armed man explained.

"How do we get her out?" Baker asked.

"Can'ts." The man scratched the open sore on his thigh. "Two Square says Shuts-up gots ta stays 'til she's finds water."

Baker shoved his PSG in the man's face. "I say differently."

"I's ain'ts get'n beats for yous."

"Sir, may I?" Apollo asked.

Baker stepped aside. "Go ahead."

Apollo swung his rifle over his shoulder and pulled some food packets out of his pocket. He reminded himself to use simple words. "I will give you two packets of food to show me how to get her out." Apollo opened the dry rations and waved the brown bar in front of the man.

"Threes." The man grabbed at the packet and shoved the bar in his mouth.

"I agree, three." Apollo handed the him another packet. "What is your name?"

The man shook his stump. "One Arm."

"One Arm, how do we get her out?"

He stuffed the second bar in his mouth and muffled. "Threes is deal."

"Two now. The last one when she is out."

One Arm leaned to the side and revealed the rope he was sitting on. "Pulls herselfs outs."

Apollo raised his eyebrows at Baker, took the rope and tossed one end down the pit. "Please grab hold of the rope." Apollo held his end of the rope.

The rope went taut and the men heard scrapping for several minutes. The rope relaxed, and a whimper sounded from the hole.

"Too weaks," One Arm said.

"I am confident I can pull her out," Apollo said to Baker.

One Arm burped. "Cuts hers up goods. Two mores foods. No cuts."

Baker laughed at Apollo. "He works people as much as you do."

Apollo tossed two more ration bars at his fellow negotiator. One

Arm opened and forced both bars in his mouth. When he was done chewing, he got up and pulled the rope out of the pit. There was a ledge jutting out above the hole. One Arm tossed the rope over the ledge, made a slip knot in the rope and threw it down the pit. "Tugs yous ready." The rope wiggled and moved, then One Arm felt a strong tug on his end. He twisted his one hand around the rope and walked slowly away from the pit.

A tangled mop of hair appeared, followed by a filthy body. Apollo wrapped his arms around the child and pulled her away from the hole. Apollo set her on her feet and she collapsed.

"Can'ts stands yet."

"Why not?" Baker asked.

One Arm held out his hand.

Apollo gave him another ration bar.

"Beens down too longs. Takes awhile."

"How old is she?"

"She's a one circle."

"She looks about five or six to me," Sgt. Baker said.

Apollo knelt beside the tiny girl and lifted the rope over her head. Between the darkness in the cave and the layers of dirt, he had not realized the girl was naked. "Uh, excuse me." Apollo turned his face away. Apollo yanked another bar out of his pocket. "Where are her clothes?"

One Arm grabbed the bar. "She gots ta waits 'til body pool squares gives her somes." He shoved the ration down his pants to save it for later.

Apollo fought the tears welling in eyes. He removed his jacket, unbuttoned his shirt and offered the shirt to Shuts-up.

The child stared at him with blank eyes.

"Shuts. . .I cannot address someone like that. My mother would not even allow me to say it." Apollo sat across from the crumpled girl. "I will call you Angela, because you are a little angel to me."

The girl smiled meekly at him.

"Angela, I am going to slip this shirt on you." Apollo held it out in front of her. "You can wear it until we find you something else."

Angela was confused. She looked at One Arm. He was equally perplexed.

Apollo thought perhaps he was still speaking too aristocratically.

He would be careful with his vocabulary for the rest of the mission. "I am going to assist, help, you put this on." Apollo carefully guided Angela's hands through one sleeve and then the other. The girl remained passive as he buttoned her new "dress" and rolled up the sleeves. Apollo took a ration bar out of his pocket, opened and held it out to Angela.

She trembled and tears made clean little lines on her dirty face.

Apollo scooped her into his lap and hugged her warmly. She sobbed into his shirtless chest. "Shh. You are safe now." Apollo stroked her hair. "What was she doing down that pit?"

One Arm waved his palm in front of Apollo's face. Baker chucked a bar at the orphan man, and he stuffed it in his pants. "Ain'ts keep'n ups withs her works. Sents down cause Red Top's magic well dries up. We's look'n fors magic wat'r."

"We are with Red Top." Apollo released his canteen strap, popped open the top and poured some water on the ground.

One Arm leaped down and tried to catch some of the precious fluid in his mouth. Angela tentatively reached her scrawny hand out, but jerked it away when Apollo stopped pouring.

Apollo lifted the child's chin to look her in the eyes. "You can have as much as you desire, want," Apollo corrected himself. He held the canteen to Angel's lips, lifted it and let her drink.

"I's trades." One Arm offered Apollo a ration bar.

"I will make a deal with you. I have got lots of magic, food and water. You be my one square and tell me everything I need to know, and I will give you all the food and water you want."

One Arm's eye grew wide. "I's tell yous alls a secrets. I's be's yous two square."

"Deal." Apollo turned to Sgt. Baker. "Sir."

Baker removed his canteen and tossed it to One Arm. One Arm pulled the top off with his teeth and chugged the water, careful not to spill any.

Baker covered his ear. "They're calling for us to proceed to the entrance of the mine."

"One Arm, lead us out of here." Apollo handed Angela the open ration bar, picked her up and followed One Arm.

Baker patted Apollo on the shoulder. "Malone's right. You can hack anybody."

"I used to be considered charming and tactful."

"He had to put your skills in terms he understood. Besides, I kind of agree with him. You push each person's buttons perfectly. Where did you learn all this?"

"I majored in diplomacy, Sir."

"They teach this sort of orphan stuff at Hadley?" Baker sounded surprised.

"What I learned was always speak and negotiate within the native culture."

"Well, you can't get any more native than this."

*   *   *

Apollo stepped out of the mines. He squinted at the bright light. Angela closed her eyes and buried her head in his shoulder. Apollo panned the flat, dusty terrain. He walked beside One Arm. "Explain, I mean, tell me everything I see and all the secrets."

"Can'ts goes pasts a markers, gets zaps froms K magic." He waved his arm at the circle of stones outlining the perimeter. "Can'ts gets ta the good hunt'n."

"The force field," Baker stated.

One Arm pointed to a windowless building. "K-Club. Where's members goes ta rocks. Girls thats lucky an goods look'n can works there ifs theys gets picked."

"Who picks them and why do they have to be lucky?" Apollo asked.

"Mosts picks by two squares, somes by bosses. Alls girls wants ta be's picked. Works less, gets mores foods ins a club."

"Anything else go on in there?"

"Fights."

"Goods fighters gets ta works ins a ring an be's two square. Members bets on fights. Boss gives two squares foods froms that's door." He motioned to the only visible entrance to the club.

Apollo eyes stopped on six huge mounds of stones. "What are those?"

"Olds body pools." One Arm faced a large shallow hole. "News body pool."

Apollo caught sight of a lifeless leg under some discarded ore. Chills ran down his spine as he stared at the bottomless pits of inhumanity.

Lt. Cmd. Zeigler approached and Sgt. Baker saluted. Angela was in Apollo's right arm, and he attempted a salute while shrugging.

369

"Never mind. We'll need to be flexible while we're here."

"Yes, Sir. Thank you, Sir."

"The doctors are having trouble with the bracelet system. They can't keep track of the kids. Many of them have the same name, the descriptions don't fit into the computer field, and the kids aren't staying put. They want them named and IDed immediately." Zeigler handed Apollo his ComLine. "Your friend Charles wants to wait until the press arrive to start IDing."

"I will handle it, Sir." Apollo fumbled to use the ComLine with his left hand.

"Hello?"

"Charles, Apollo. Please bring your equipment and proceed with identifying the children. You will receive ample positive press. Trust me."

"It's taking longer than I expected to get things set."

"If it requires more than five minutes, I will announce to the public you were more concerned with PR than assisting the children."

"OK, OK. I'll be right there."

Apollo handed the ComLine to Zeigler.

"Well done. Let's set Charles and his ID team up at the north corner of the building. We'll put the bracelet people next to them. Now, how to identify each child?"

"We give them names; for example, I called her Angela." He winked at her. "We enter each name in the computer as we use it to avoid duplicates. We can label their bracelets."

"That won't work," Dr. Bentley interrupted from behind him. "They're taking off the bracelets."

Sgt. Leiman came up with a lift full of T-shirts. "Sir, here are the colored shirts."

"Start handing them out," Zeigler ordered.

"Yes, Sir. Sir?" Leiman waited for his nodded. "I think were going to need a lot more. The mine kids aren't staying with their units or responding as expected."

"Great."

Angela fiddled with Apollo's shiny name plate while they talked. "Sir, Angela has given me an idea."

"Go ahead."

"We obtain shirts and mark each child's new name on it. If we all address the children by their names, then they will know if we page them. The children are not accustomed to being addressed by a name; however, they will learn quickly. Right, Angela?" The little girl lifted her head. "See, she already knows when I say Angela I am speaking to her. It will not take a great deal of time or effort."

"How are we going to get them to keep their shirts on?" Bentley asked.

Apollo picked up a few shirts and stepped in front of the three girls walking by. "Hi." He squatted down while repositioning Angela in his arms. "Would you like to put these pretty new shirts on for me?"

"Why's should I's?" the tough blonde asked.

"That is a good question. You must be very intell, I mean smart." Apollo smiled, projecting all the charm he could muster. "Because if you are wearing a shirt, we know you are supposed to be with us and no longer belong to your old bosses. The ones who do not feed you like we do."

The girls grabbed the shirts from Apollo and yanked them over their heads.

"In a little bit, we are going to give you each a name and write it on your shirt. That way no one can take it from you and pretend it is theirs." Apollo moved Angela into his left arm. "Would you like that?"

"Yeah!" they exclaimed.

"You will remember your name, because it will be only yours and nobody else's. And you know only really, really important people get names, so I would hate for you to forget yours and not get another one."

"I's remembers," the thin one answered.

"Great. I know I can count on you." Apollo stood and turned to the doctor. "It is all in how you present it, Doctor."

"Wonderful. Convince them clean is good. They won't let us help clean them and I can't examine them under all this filth."

Apollo gave a mischievous grin. "I have an idea."

"Is that an I'm-thinking-like-a-native-look, again?" Baker said.

"Yes, Sir."

"Native?" Bentley asked.

"He hacks 'em," Baker said.

Zeigler's face scrunched up.

"Malone says Christiani re-programs people to think the way he wants," Baker explained.

"You are gifted." Leiman nudged her cadet.

"Proceed," Zeigler ordered.

"One Arm?" Apollo turned to the man who had waited patiently behind his new boss.

"Yeah."

"Go round up all the one and two squares you can find and bring them here to me."

"I's gets 'em." One Arm trotted off.

Apollo faced his superiors. "Did you all ever play in the sprinklers when you were a kid?"

"I don't have time for games," Zeigler snapped.

"With all due respect, Sir. Children enjoy games. One has to think like the locals." Apollo tilted Angela toward him. "And most of the locals are children."

"I'm listening."

"We brought our water tanks. We can set up huge showers behind large partitions. One side for boys; one side for girls. Then let them play in the water. These people have been experiencing a drought. They will be begging to cooperate if we lavishly shower them with unlimited water."

Dr. Bentley crossed her arms. "It would be clever, except they need to use soap."

Apollo turned way from her. "Would you mind retrieving the soap foam out of my pack."

Bentley unlatched the center pocket.

"It's always packed on the right," Baker stated. Doctors were a breed of their own.

She closed the center flap and stepped to her right. She removed a small canister and handed it to Apollo.

Apollo showed Angela a dirty spot on the palm of his left hand. He squirted a small amount of foam on the spot, rubbed and blew the foam away. "All clean."

Angel's eyes widened.

Apollo sprayed a mound of tiny white bubbles in his hand. "Touch it. It is soft and slippery." He pinched a little between his finger and thumb and rolled it around.

The child slowly moved her fingers to touch the strange substance.

She worked a bit between her fingers and watched in awe as the dirt fell away.

"It is magic and it is fun." Apollo wiped the rest of the foam onto his nose.

Angela's face lit up.

Apollo held the canister over his open hand. "You push the button." Angela squirted until Apollo's hand disappeared under the soapy cloud. Apollo grasped one of her tiny hands in his empty one and clapped his hands. The foam splattered and flew in every direction.

Angela giggled.

Zeigler frowned as he wiped some soap off his cheek. "Very amusing."

Bentley brushed some foam off her sleeve. "I think it will work."

"Fine. Make it work."

"Yes, Sir."

"They have to keep their bracelets on. I could overdose a child or worse, if I don't know if he or she has been treated."

All of them turned and faced the cadet. Apollo shifted nervously for a moment, thinking, then spoke directly to Zeigler. "We stop providing food or water to anyone not wearing a bracelet. No one will starve in the time it takes us to get them IDed and with bracelets on. Anyone who is sickly, we will move to the front of the line."

"Well done," Zeigler exclaimed, impressed. "I'll instruct our people not to give out food or water unless the orphans have bracelets." Zeigler noticed a press wagon arriving over in the distance. "You all take care of this. I need to deal with the press." He marched off.

"Yes, Sir," the group answered.

"Well, Mr. Native, what next?" Leiman asked.

"We must wait for One Arm." Apollo shrugged. "In the meantime, Doctor, would you please examine Angela?"

"Sure, what's the matter?"

"She cannot speak. Angela," he said to her, "do you ever talk?"

Angela shook her head.

"Sit down." Bentley unclipped her scanner and knelt.

Apollo sat on the ground and placed Angela in his lap. "I promise she will not hurt you."

Dr. Bentley ran the scanner over her throat. "Can you open your mouth for me?"

Frightened, Angela leaned into Apollo's chest. "It is all right." Apollo spoke in a soft, soothing voice. "Let me show you what to do. You open your mouth like this," he demonstrated. "Stick your tongue out real far, make an ugly face and then," he whispered in her ear, "blow some stinky breath in her face."

Angela giggled and followed his instructions.

"Good girl," Apollo said.

Bentley read her scanner. "As far as I can tell, her silence is trauma induced."

"There is no damage to her vocal cords?" Apollo asked.

"No, nor any deformities in her tongue."

"You are saying it is psychosomatic?"

"Basically."

"Angela, did you used to be able to talk?"

His only response was an uncertain look.

"Talks when she's little," the girl next to them offered.

"Thank you." He looked to the doctor. "How do we assist Angela?"

"It will take a safe environment and long-term therapy." The last word trailed off. One Arm and his group of men surrounded her. She could see why these were the taskmaster. They were a strong, fierce-looking bunch. Dr. Bentley stepped between the two sergeants.

"Good job." Apollo exclaimed to One Arm. He remembered how important feed-back and praise was to Zeus. "I belong to The United Corps. TUC has taken over this operation."

A large black man spit at Apollo's feet.

"We have more power and magic than you have ever seen."

"Don'ts see noth'n," the skeptic stated.

"What is your name?" Apollo asked.

"Hulk." He stared Apollo down. "I's a head two square."

"Good to meet you, Hulk." Apollo offered a handshake and Hulk batted his hand away. So much for being charming. They want proof, Apollo thought, I'll give them proof. "Get your knife out."

Hulk waved a bowie knife in Apollo's face.

Angela clung tightly to Apollo. Apollo maneuvered his tiny charge to his right side. He pulled his left jacket sleeve up to his elbow and shoved his bare forearm at Hulk. "Cut it."

Hulk raised his blade and sliced a six centimeter gap into Apollo's forearm.

Apollo focused on not wincing or showing pain. He gave a condescending glance at the red river. "Taste it."

Hulk pressed his finger into the gash and licked his finger. "Bloods."

Apollo raised his arm and slowly moved around the group. Once they had all seen his wound, he said, "Doctor, show them your magic."

Dr. Bentley cleaned the gash.

"A little abracadabra would help," Apollo whispered.

"I don't do abracadabra." Dr. Bentley laser sealed the cut and wiped away the excess blood.

Hulk stared at sealed skin. "Yous do's have magic."

Apollo pointed to a man with a large, red boil, oozing puss on his cheek. "Doctor, fix it."

The fascinated men pressed in around her from all sides. Dr. Bentley tried to ignore their hot, rancid breaths. She gently drained the infection, treated it and sealed the skin. The healed man's hand quivered as he brushed the smooth skin. "Yous a witch."

"A very powerful one." Apollo walked among the taskmasters. He stopped at a man who had two sticks tied to his wrist. "Broken?"

"Yeah."

"Doctor." Apollo stepped aside.

Dr. Bentley untied the sticks, surrounded his wrist in a caladrom wrap, read the scanner and made the necessary adjustments.

"It takes a few minutes," Apollo said, then let the seconds tick by in silence.

The group held its breath as Bentley removed the caladrom wrap. The man twisted and flexed his cured arm. "Fixes! Don'ts hurts none."

"Yous a big witch," Hulk gasped.

"I'm a doctor," she snarled. Years of medical school and training, and all they saw was a witch.

"We are planning on fixing you and your people. But doctors, they do not like dirt. It is bad luck." Apollo tugged at Bentley's jacket. "That is why they wear white; so they can see the dirt."

Dr. Bentley frowned at him.

"These are the new rules. You are going to get your people in their work units. One Arm will assign you each a spot for your unit to meet. You and your units will wear the shirts and bracelets the Corps people give you if you want food or water. We have magic that tells us if you are not wearing the right ones. Once your whole unit is assembled, we are going to start you with a soap-and-water party to celebrate the Corps taking over."

"Huh, I's goes ta party?" Hulk challenged.

"Sgt. Baker, would mind giving these gentlemen a six-caliber demonstration."

Baker adjusted his rifle and shot at the ground. Dirt and gravel flew ten meters in the air. When the dust settled, there was a crater big enough to bury a man in. The taskmasters moved away from Sgt. Baker. Angela wrapped her arms around Apollo's neck and clung to him.

"Why?" Apollo tapped Hulk's chest. "Because I like parties."

Hulk nodded obediently.

Apollo loosened Angela's grip. "You made us scare Angela." Apollo slowly annunciated each word. "Do not ever let it happen again or you will be sorry. Understand?"

Hulk gulped. "I's understand. I's make sure alls a workers do's what yous says."

"One Arm, start assigning units their meeting places. Hulk, go find the rest of your one and two squares. Have them report to One Arm for their meeting areas. Now move it, all of you."

The group scurried away, eager to impress the Corps.

"Did you see how puffed-up One Arm was when you put him in charge," Leiman said.

Baker cracked his neck. "That poor old guy's probably been taking crap from those taskmasters for years."

"I'm not questioning you, not after seeing what you can accomplish, but why pick One Arm as your assistant?" Leiman asked. "Why not Hulk?"

"It is my experience that with age comes wisdom. Plus, while Hulk and those other meatheads were impressing the Kalopso and fighting for power, old One Arm's been sitting around observing. He has been here for forty or fifty years. His knowledge of this environment and the taskmasters' quirks will prove useful. Don't you agree, doctor witch?"

"I am not a witch," she huffed.

"No, you are a big witch," Apollo corrected.

Bentley smacked his free arm and marched off.

CHAPTER 28

APOLLO SPENT THE NEXT DAY and a half organizing and implementing his plans, plus coordinating and obtaining supplies. He sat on the ground and Angela plopped in his lap. Apollo squeezed his stiff neck. Angela panicked any time he attempted to leave her. She refused to sleep except with her head on his shoulder and only while he was standing. Apollo prayed she would finally let him sleep. Angela was slowly falling asleep when Apollo's ComLine beeped. Angela's head popped up.

"Christiani," he snarled with a hoarse voice.

"Did I wake you?" Taylor asked.

"Not me, Angela."

"Worse."

"Yes, Sir. May I assist you, Sir?"

"Where are you?"

"Approximately six meters east of First Aid Six."

"I'll be right there." Minutes later, Taylor marched up fuming. "Zeigler is finally saying Malone is missing. We're not starting an all-out search. Instead, he's sending in limited teams. He's also posting pictures of Malone, and we're to ask our kids if anyone's seen him."

"What is that supposed to accomplish?"

"Absolutely nothing while publicly looking good. The mine is a maze of hundreds of tunnels and dead ends. Even the kids who live here get lost. The terrain changes constantly. He could be in any one of a thousand places. To make matters worse, just walking around, I don't think you could tell where a recent cave-in has been. That's why Zeigler waited. To make certain the debris and dust settled. One of the kids showed me a recent cave-in spot. I scanned it carefully from every possible angle. It looks and reads like the rest of the mines, because most of the work was done by manual labor. There is no chemical residue or machine tracks for the scanners to lock onto."

Apollo rubbed Angela's bony back. "In Zeus's case, there would be residue for the scanners to identify."

"But it's still a thousand to one. The kids led us out by the most direct route to the surface. It took over an hour. The unit's combined mapping data was given to the computer. Even the computer can't accurately map it. I lost contact with Malone early on, before I got to the group I rescued. Malone has to be more than an hour down, and Zeigler's not sending any groups that deep."

"Why not comb the entire area?"

Taylor rolled his eyes. "Safety reasons. Plus, the boorix is interrupting the scanners. Only very short-range scanning is accurate."

Apollo stared at the ground. "We will never even recover the body."

"Doubtful."

"Zeus informed me they planned that. Then there can be speculation he is still alive and money appropriated to find him. Plus, they want to create the possibility he is missing voluntarily. The Corps is cast in a positive light, and the network can still claim Zeus's deliberate disappearance as proof orphans cannot be integrated into society. Therefore, more money is appropriated to study why and how to improve the situation."

Taylor noticed Apollo's heavy stubble and the deep circles around his eyes. "You look terrible. When's the last time you slept?"

"Is that where I close my eyes and snore?"

"Have you rested since we left the base?"

"No, Sir. I have attempted to." Apollo glanced down at Angela.

"Let me take her." Taylor touched the child. Angela wrapped her arms around Apollo's neck and squeezed.

Apollo coughed. "Not so tight, Sweetie."

"I won't hurt you," Taylor said quietly.

She squeezed tighter.

"Angela, I am not leaving you," Apollo reassured her while trying to loosen her grip. "She is clinging for dear life," he said to the sergeant. "I think we will stay together."

Taylor nodded. "Get some shut-eye. Turn your ComLine to messages only. The supplies will have to wait. Leave a message that if they need things immediately to contact me."

"Yes, Sir."

"Dismissed, and turn that ComLine off."

Apollo pulled his ComLine out, dictated his message and turned the unit off. He laid down on his side and wrapped his arms around Angela. She watched him intently. "Shh. Close your eyes."

Angela sat up.

"Please lie down and rest."

She shook her head.

"You were tired just a minute ago. Why not try to sleep?"

A tiny tear was his only answer.

Apollo knelt and held her. What was upsetting her? Why would she not sleep unless he was standing and busy? He stroked her hair, thinking. Thinking what he would want, if he were a frightened little girl. Reassurance and security.

Apollo winked at his charge. "I have an idea." He slipped off his jacket and put it around her. He took his ComLine off his belt. "I will not leave you. I promise. You have got my jacket and I am going to give you this." He handed her his ComLine. "You know I cannot work without that. You keep it safe until we both wake up. OK?"

Angela hugged him and cried.

"Does this mean we can both go to sleep?"

She nodded into his hairy chest.

Finally, Apollo laid on his side, cradled her in his arms, and they fell asleep together.

*   *   *

Apollo awakened the following morning, reminiscing about Zeus. He stroked Angela's precious face and prayed for his dead friend. Apollo closed his eyes and took some deep breaths. Then his eyes snapped open. He felt around his jacket on Angela's limp body until he found his ComLine.

"Taylor."

"Zeus is alive!" Apollo stated.

"What? Where are you?" Taylor asked, excited.

"Still by First Aid Six."

"I'm on my way. Taylor out."

Taylor leaped over sleeping bodies, his heart pounding with hope. "How did Malone contact you?" he yelled to Apollo as he hurdled the last body.

"He did not contact me. I have not spoken to him."

Taylor breathed heavily. He stopped abruptly in front of Apollo. "Then how do you know?"

"I was praying. I am positive he is alive." He smiled at Angela rubbing her eyes and stretching.

Taylor wiped the perspiration from his brow. "Christiani, I know you were friends, but you have to accept the facts, same as the rest of us."

"Sir, Zeus is alive!" Apollo stood and towered over Taylor. "Do not discount the information because of the source."

"Where do you think he is?"

"In the mines. We need to find Sgt. Baker and Sgt. Leiman and rescue him."

Taylor gave him a paternal clap on the shoulder. "There's a lot of kids here who need us. He's at least an hour down in the shafts. We can't go on a three- or four-hour goose chase."

"Ponder the possibility that he is buried alive, awaiting our assistance. Even if I am mistaken, if you do not attempt to locate Zeus, it will haunt you the rest of your life. In fact, you are already feeling guilty you have not searched the mines."

Taylor's eyes flashed at him. Christiani certainly knew the right button to push for him.

"You are defensive because I am correct."

"I'll get my gear."

*   *   *

Apollo and Angela were sitting eating breakfast when Leiman and Baker arrived.

"What's up?" Baker asked.

"Zeus is alive," he said to his sergeants.

"Where is he?"

"Down in the mines, trapped in one of the shafts."

"How do you know?"

Apollo glanced at Baker for support. "God revealed it to me through prayer."

"What?" Leiman put her hands on her hips.

"Give it up." Taylor came up behind her and slipped his arms around her waist. "Even if Christiani is wrong, I want to personally search those mines."

380

"I know you do, Bulldog." Leiman wrapped her arms around his. "Malone didn't want anyone else to get hurt. I can't lose you, too. It's easy to get lost down there, even with the computer's help."

"We will not lose our way," Apollo insisted. He peeled a banana and offered half to Angela.

Baker cracked his knuckles. "What if Zeigler notices we're missing?"

"He will not." Apollo took a bite of the banana.

"How do you know?"

"I trust my Creator."

"Well, I don't believe in your creator." Leiman stepped away from Taylor.

Apollo rose and faced her. "With all due respect, Ma'am, in the last few days, I have delivered on every promise I have made. Trust me. I can locate Zeus."

"That was politics," she stated.

"Sues." Taylor held her hand. "I'm going. I've got to at least say I tried. I want you there with me."

"All right." She squeezed his hand.

They turned at Baker.

"I'm in." He shrugged.

They gathered their equipment and met at the mine entrance. "Haven't you forgotten something?" Baker pointed to Angela.

"No, Sir. Angela will be joining us."

"This is not safe for a child," Leiman insisted.

"We will need her assistance," Apollo answered.

"For what?" Taylor clipped his pack around his midriff.

"She has lived in these mines."

Leiman fastened her headlamp. "Christiani?"

"We shouldn't drag the kid into this," Taylor stated.

"Ma'am, Sirs, please trust me. This is difficult for me as well; however, it is a leap of faith."

"She's too small to help us," Leiman said.

"Let us make an agreement. You give me two hours of blind faith, and if we have not located Zeus, I will cooperate with your directives."

"I'm following Christiani," Sgt. Baker stated.

"Baker," Leiman protested.

"I've been watching Christiani for weeks. He has something I don't.

In two hours, I'll be able to find out if there really is a God. If it's as impossible as you say it is, only God, if there is a God, can lead us to Malone. I want to know. Not just about Malone, but if God exists."

"Baker, you're losing it," she said. "Taylor, what about you?"

"I'd like to know about the God thing, too."

"Brian." She smacked him.

"Aren't you a little curious?"

She ignored the question and pointed to Angela. "What about the girl?"

"There's no one armed but our own people. She's not going to get hurt," Baker said.

"I'm going to regret this, but let's go."

The three sergeants followed Apollo into the dark mines. Everyone but Angela wore a headlamp. The shafts to the digging sites were narrow. Angela rode piggyback as Apollo tried to keep her legs from bumping into the jagged edges. The digging sites resembled caves with piles of rocks stacked to make mini-mountains of scaffolding. Rusty shovels, broken picks and shattered axes were abandoned throughout the mines. Occasionally, one could see an unidentified bone. The mine was cool and dry. The adults' lights darted and danced on the rocky path. The group followed the map deep into the mine. Every few minutes, Leiman checked the scanner for life signs.

They entered another digging chamber. Apollo switched Angela and held her awhile. "I am thankful you forced me to practice walking with a pack for weeks," he joked to the sergeants.

"See how important seemingly senseless training is?" Baker watched the path as he followed the eerie yellow glow of his headlamp.

"Yes, Sir. I am beginning to understand."

"Wait, stop," Leiman exclaimed. "I've got a life sign!"

"Where?"

"This way. Follow me." She bolted to the front. The group followed as she read the scanner. Fifteen minutes later, she stopped. "The life-sign is behind this wall." She angled the scanner to a barrier of solid rock. "The signs are weak, but only about thirty meters away."

"Malone," Baker yelled. "Malone, can you hear me?"

No response. Taylor and Leiman each took a turn calling out. No answer.

"Maybe the life-sign isn't Malone," Baker offered.

"It is Zeus." Apollo switched Angela to his other arm.

"Can anyone hear me?" Leiman called out. No answer.

"Either way, we've got to get whoever it is out of there." Taylor unclipped his pack.

Leiman read the scanner. "This wall is solid rock and a meter thick."

"It would take us weeks to dig through it manually, and we can't blow it up without risking whoever is on the other side."

They all turned and looked at Apollo. "I am working on a solution." Apollo sat, positioned Angela in his lap and prayed.

"I've scanned this whole area," Leiman said. "Whoever is in there is in a very small area. This is the thinnest wall. There's one other side that is a possibility. I don't see an easy way to get in. That wall is about four meters thick, but not solid. My guess is that's where Zeigler shot the ceiling.

The sergeants discussed their options, while Apollo pleaded with God for guidance. Nothing. No inspiration. After numerous desperate pleas, he leaned on the rocky wall behind him and looked upward. His eyes focused on a small opening, meters from the ceiling.

Apollo rose. "It is Angela's turn."

"Angela?" Leiman questioned.

"See that hole up there?" Apollo directed them to a small opening near the rocky roof.

"We can't dig from that height."

"Angela, if we help you, can you go look through that hole up there?" Apollo shone his light on the opening.

Angela nodded.

"Come on, let's form a pyramid so she can get up there," Baker said.

"Where do you want me, Sir."

"You're at the bottom with Taylor. Leiman, you get up on their shoulders. Here's my hat with the light." Baker secured his large hat to Angela's little head. "Now let me help you up."

Baker lifted her up to Leiman's waist. Angela grabbed her shoulders and Baker steadied her from behind. She stepped onto Leiman's shoulders and balanced on a horizontal rock jutting out from the side of the cave. Little foot and hand holes made it easy for her to scale the rest of the wall. She peered through the thick wall, then crawled inside until only her new shoes glimmered in the light. She shimmied out, grabbed her shirt and pointed furiously at the hole.

"There is a man dressed like us in the hole," Apollo interpreted.

She nodded.

"Angela," Baker ordered, "climb back in. Tell us if he moves when I call his name."

Angela complied.

"Malone, Malone can you hear me?" Baker called.

Angela reappeared out of the hole shaking her head.

"He's probably dehydrated or worse. She needs to climb in and give him a shot of saline and a stimulant," Taylor stated.

"Angela, climb down as far as you can," Apollo said.

She climbed down carefully as far as the footholds lasted. She was still meters above Apollo's outstretched arms. "Jump, I will catch you. I promise."

Angela looked fearfully at Apollo. "I will not let anything or anybody hurt you. Just close your eyes and jump."

Angela squeezed her eyelids tight and leaped.

Apollo easily caught her and held her close. "I am so proud of you. You are doing a wonderful job."

"Was the man sitting or lying down?" Taylor asked.

She laid down.

"Show me exactly how."

Angela turned on her stomach, tucked her head under her arm and the put her other arm out in front of her. She pulled her legs up, picked up a large rock and put it on her leg.

"He's trapped under some rocks?" Apollo interrupted.

She nodded.

"Can you climb down and touch the man?" Baker asked.

Angela shook her head.

Leiman checked her scanner. "The other side is sheer or concave under the opening."

"We'll have to use the harness and coil." Baker removed the items from his pack and held it up to the child.

Angela quivered, barely breathing.

"I will help you." Apollo patted her. "I promise it will not hurt."

Angela protested.

"Angela, please," Apollo begged. "Zeus will die if we do not help him."

The child nodded reluctantly.

Baker handed the harness to Apollo. He gently coaxed his little heroine into it and snapped the safety shut. When she heard the clicking noise, Angela leaped up around his neck and squeezed for dear life. "I do not think this is a good idea," Apollo gasped.

"Give her a minute," Baker suggested. "She'll be all right."

Apollo comforted her until she relaxed. "Angela, are you ready?" She nodded.

"Do you see this?" Taylor showed her the medical injector. "Put it on his arm and push here." He demonstrated. "You try it." He handed it to her. "Good job. Make sure you don't touch any other button, OK?"

Angela nodded.

"I'm putting this in your backpack, so you don't have to carry it." Taylor programmed the stimulant and saline into the injector and placed it in the pack. He picked up his PSG. "Don't play with this. Give it to Malone as soon as he wakes up."

Apollo smacked the weapon. "A six caliber PSG! Are you insane?"

"I put the safety on."

"Where's your faith, Cadet?" Baker questioned.

"He may need it, and we won't get a second chance to send things over. If we pull Angela back through, we'll rip her flesh off," Taylor explained.

Apollo grudgingly agreed. "Angela, please, please, do not touch this. Once Zeus wakes up, give him the bag. That way you never have to touch this."

Angela nodded.

The human pyramid reformed. Sgt. Baker gave the last-minute instructions. "I'm holding the coil. I'll hold it nice and tight, so you can feel me holding you. When you're ready to go down, slap your leg. If you want me to stop, slap it twice. Are you ready?"

She nodded.

"This will let us hear you and Malone." Baker clipped the communicator on the harness. "You'll be able to hear us, too. OK?"

She nodded. Angela easily made it over the wall. Baker carefully lowered her to the ground and gave her enough coil to walk to Zeus. She took out the injector and gave Zeus the saline and stimulant shot. He stirred slightly.

"Zeus, can you hear me?"

"Apollo? Huh, yous?" came the confused reply.

"Angela's holding a bag with a medical kit. Give yourself whatever you need."

"Huh?" Zeus rubbed his blurry eyes.

"What yous name?" the rescuers heard on the audio scanner. Zeus took another shot of saline.

"She cannot speak," Apollo said.

"Types a roommate I's like."

The sergeants chuckled.

"I can see being buried alive for a day has not improved your disposition," Apollo joked.

"And a day in here ain'ts shut yous up."

"Well, we're sure it's Malone," Taylor quipped.

"Taylor, that yous?"

"You bet. Crap, Malone, you're hard to get rid of."

"Ain'ts no competition with the likes a yous."

"I'm only rescuing you so I can win at the All-Militaries."

"All right, Gentlemen," Leiman bellowed. "Enough male bonding. Malone, can you climb out of there?"

"I's can't move. I's trapped under the crap Zeigler shoots on me's."

"You've worked these mines," Taylor said. "How do we get you out of there?"

"Yous gots a scanner?"

"Yes." Leiman flipped it on.

"Scans the wall in front of me's."

"What am I scanning for?" she asked.

"Composition, mass, density."

Leiman recalibrated and read the glowing green box. "Composition is mostly corundum, quartz and boorix. Mass eleven point two. Density seven point three."

"Yous all goes ta another shaft. I's shoots a hole in the wall."

Taylor punched Apollo's upper arm. "I told you he'd need the PSG."

"All right, Malone, we'll clear out," Baker stated.

"Baker?"

"Yes."

"Doc, yous there's?"

"Just the five of us. Can Angela get back through the hole?"

"Not withouts get'n scrapped ups."

"Angela, I'm going to remove the long rope attached to you." Baker released the coil and retracted it.

"Please take care of Angela for me," Apollo said.

"She's be fine. I's needs the hat." Angela laid on the ground and let Zeus remove the helmet. "Yous go far aways on the other sides and cover yous face." Zeus steadied the light to the safest spot.

The sergeants and Apollo wandered though the shafts until Leiman said, "Stop. Here's a good spot. It has the most solid rock overhead. "Malone, fire at will."

"Yes, Ma'am." Zeus aimed and shot continuously until the ground rumbled and the wall caved in. He blasted the loose rubble and cleared an opening. The fine dust rose in the air like fog on a cold morning. Zeus focused the light around the edges of the opening. "It's clear," he said to his rescuers. "Be careful. Lots of loose stuff."

Baker cleared his throat and entered the thick cloud of dust. He squinted as Zeus's light caught his eye.

"Angela, clap so I can find you." Apollo waved at the dust and followed the sounds to his reluctant helper. "You did a great job." He scooped her into his arms. "You helped save Zeus's life."

Her body went limp.

"Did the noise scare you?"

She nodded into his chest.

"You are safe now." He tugged at the harness. "Do you want me to take this off you?"

Her head bobbed.

Apollo stood her on her legs, unsnapped the harness and helped her out. He removed his pack and set it on the ground. "You sit there while I help with the rocks."

Angela curled up on the ground and rested her arms on the pack. In moments, she was fast asleep.

"Malone, I'm glad to see you're all right." Sgt. Leiman squatted beside him. "I've been worried about you."

"Took yous long 'nough."

"You can thank Christiani. He convinced us you were still alive and led us in." Baker grunted as he lifted a large rock off Zeus's legs.

"Huh? How yous knows?"

Apollo raised his arms and looked piously upward.

"Yous spooky," Zeus said, uncomfortable with Apollo's faith.

"You is spooky." Taylor scrunched his pushed-in face. He related the details of the rescue while they lifted debris off the orphan cadet.

"I don't know," Baker chimed in. "He has me convinced about God."

Zeus quickly changed the subject. "What yous gonna says ta Zeigler when I's show up?"

"What are we going to say to Zeigler?" Leiman tossed a shovel full of stones over her shoulder. The rocks fell like hail and echoed in the cavern.

"It was my job to get us here." Apollo lifted a large rock and threw it aside.

"Did you see Zeigler cause the cave in?" Taylor forced his boot down on the shovel.

"Yeah. Budgin bastard was laugh'n and taunt'n me's before he shoots the ceil'n."

Apollo put his hands prayerfully together. "Perfect."

"Huh? I's hates when yous do's this."

"God bless the press." Apollo winked.

CHAPTER 29

THE PRESS CORPS ASSEMBLED in front of the mine entrance for a live press conference. Maj. Patterson stepped to the makeshift podium. "Good afternoon. We are still searching this mine for Cadet Malone. Lt. Cmd. Jeffrey Zeigler is in charge of the rescue operations." Zeigler stepped to the podium. "He will be happy to answer any of your questions."

Apollo pressed the signal button on his ComLine and waited for Zeus to appear. Ten minutes ticked slowly by, and no Zeus. Apollo checked his watch. Zeus must be having trouble getting to the entrance. Apollo's heart pounded. Zeigler was wrapping things up.

A woman screamed, "Look over there."

The cameras focused in on a lone figure, face down, dragging himself out of the mine. Zeigler and Patterson knelt beside the unidentified man. Dr. Bentley raced to the entrance and carefully rolled the man over.

"Malone!" Zeigler gasped.

"Budgin bastard." Zeus spit at Zeigler. "Yous try ta kill me's, yous K bastard."

Zeigler moved away.

"What are you talking about?" Patterson demanded.

"Lt. Cmd. Zeigler's a K spy. Causes a cave-in ta kill me's, but I's don't die. I's come ta makes yous pay."

Zeigler turned to run. Two rifles were leveled at his head.

"Take him away," Patterson ordered. "Malone, are you all right?"

"No, he's not," Dr. Bentley answered. "Get me a stretcher."

         *   *   *

Apollo and Angela went into the K-Club building where the infirmary had been set up. The curtain rattled as Apollo slid it across the chrome pole. "How are you feeling, my friend?"

Zeus lay flat on a thin green air pillow. "Fines." He was sick of people asking him that.

"Are you all fixed up?"

"Nope. Budgin Zeigler crushed my's leg." He leaned up on his bandaged elbow. "I's needs micro-surgery."

"Please do not cuss in front of Angela." Apollo brushed her warm cheek as they exchanged smiles.

"She's heard its before and worse."

"That does not make it acceptable now. The children here deserve the same respect all people do. We must set an example."

Zeus hung his head. "Yous right. I's sorry, Angela."

A tear caught the light and sparkled in the corner of her eye. She scrabbled out of Apollo arms, climbed up on the cot and gave Zeus a big hug.

Zeus held her. "Yous ain't never gonna be hungry again. Me's and Apollo, we's promise." What he had not achieved for Emily, he had done for Angela and the others. Zeus stopped the watery leak by forcing his eyelids shut. Angela kissed his cheek.

Zeus could not shut his eyes tight enough to conceal his emotions. Angela caught one of his tears on her finger and licked it. He brushed her wet face, passed his tongue over his finger and savored the salty taste.

"Angela tasted my tears earlier. What is the significance of that gesture?"

"Special pact. Exchange'n tears is a promise ta be there for each other. Likes a blood oath on the streets."

"Oh, Sweetie." Apollo sniffed as he leaned over the cot and wrapped his arms around them both. "I never meant to hurt your feelings. Of course, I will be there for you. I am going to make certain you are always taken care of."

Apollo had a cloud full of tears to share. Angela cupped her hand and drank in the safety. Apollo returned the gesture of lifelong friendship. She pecked him on his unshaven stubble. Apollo lifted her into his arms.

"Thank you, Zeus, for Angela and all the others who cannot speak for themselves."

Zeus turned away.

"You cannot always hide behind your stoic exterior."

"What yous talk'n about?"

"You are a bigger softie than I am."

"Just don't tells nobody. I's look weak."

"Does the tear oath include a code of silence?"

"Does now," Zeus answered.

*　　*　　*

The next morning, Apollo entered Zeus's partition with Angela asleep on his shoulder. Zeus set down his InfoPad.

"Do you mind if I sit?" Apollo motioned to the end of the bed.

"Nope."

"Thank you." Apollo sat and placed Angela's limp body on his lap. "My arms are aching from carrying her for days."

"Yous hear about Zeigler?"

"Just a few moments ago. I do not understand it. Why did they have to murder him?"

"Can't fails the K. Yous do, yous dead."

"I thought they would reprimand him; however, I never expected poison?"

"Stakes is a lot higher where I's come from."

"That statement is obviously true. How are you feeling?"

Zeus poked his cast out from under the sheet. "I's gots ta use crutches for awhile."

Apollo tapped the cast. "Perhaps this will hinder you enough so I can beat your times on the course?"

Zeus kicked his roommate with his cast. "Yous can't beat me's, even on crutches."

"Oh, because you are so much tougher than I am?" Apollo baited him.

"Don'ts takes much."

"If you are so tough, prove it."

"What yous talk'n 'bout?"

"Something that takes real courage, facing the press."

Zeus crossed his arms. "Ain'ts do'n it. I's already told Patterson, I's ain't do'n no press conference and no interviews."

"I am relieved we did not plan either one of those." Apollo squeezed his aching neck. "We were thinking of a round table discussion."

"Huh?"

"The public is clamoring for information about you. We have assembled a panel of individuals from your life. Each one will speak about a different time in your life. You will be present; however, you will not be expected to say a great deal. We will arrange the time so you will not have to answer many questions."

"Who yous gets ta talk 'bout me's?"

"There is a gentleman who remembers you from the arrow work unit." Apollo raised his arms over his head and stretched his sore triceps. "He told some amusing Red Top stories. There are two women who recall you working in the club. They continually speak about how kind you were. They stated you always attempted to assist them and take care of them."

"Who's says they know me's."

"A guy named Half Ear. . ."

"Half Ear?" Zeus rose on his elbows. "Kinda gots yella skin?"

"Yes, we call him Ron. The women were Whippy and Nut Cracker."

"Don't remembers no Nut Cracker."

"She is a teenager, so she had to have been a child when you departed. Maybe she had a different name then. She is called Robin now. Whippy is Denise."

"Yous gonna has ta do's some great hack'n ta convince me's."

"Thankfully, I am up to the challenge." Apollo arched his back. "The sergeants, Bentley and I will speak about OTS and you will keep quiet as much as possible, as if that is difficult for you."

"Why I's got ta be there?"

"You are the hero of the decade. One reporter even gave you the century. You are the only person who has to be in attendance."

"I's thinks 'bout it."

"Patterson has it arranged for this afternoon."

"What?"

"I assured him I could convince you to participate."

Zeus shoved his roommate. "Yous bastard."

"For effect, we are setting the stage near the mine entrance, where you toiled tirelessly for years and dragged yourself out after being buried alive." Apollo laid the back of his hand above his brow.

Zeus rolled his eyes at Apollo's theatrics. "What yous do'n with the kids?"

"They are the audience."

392

"Huh?"

"The other orphans want to catch a glimpse of the man responsible for ending their misery. You should hear them speak about you. You were a legend before the rescue. You could decipher the magic letters. You dug a well. You were an awesome fighter. And now they know you are the only person to escape alive. These people need to see you. It gives them hope. You are the only role model they will have in the near future. It is imperative you encourage them."

"What I's got ta do?"

"When you are introduced, walk through the crowd to. . ."

He sideswiped Apollo with his cast. "Bentley's gots me's on crutches."

"I am well aware of your medical limitations." Apollo thumped the stiff restraint. "It adds to the drama."

"I's ain't walk'n out likes no cripple. I's look weak and an easy target for the K."

"Zeus, the entire universe has been informed your leg was crushed. Dr. Bentley has given two or three status reports on your recovery. It is no secret you are on crutches."

"Has I's gots a choice?"

"The Corps always give you a choice. There is 'Yes, Sir; however, I hate it,' and 'Yes, Sir, I would be happy to comply.' " Apollo flipped an irreverent salute. "Which response would you like me to tell Maj. Patterson?"

*   *   *

The press conference panel was seated on a platform. The dark, hollow mine entrance provided the backdrop. Maj. Patterson sat in the middle with Sgt. Baker, Sgt. Leiman, Sgt. Taylor and Dr. Bentley on his left. On his right was an empty chair for Zeus. Next, Apollo sat holding Angela. Beside them sat Zeus's three orphan friends. The press representatives were at podiums off to the left. The crowd of Corps personnel and rescued orphans stood in the courtyard below the platform.

The ragged group of rescued men, women and children stared at the platform. They listened intently so they would not be punished inadvertently. After the last few days, they definitely wanted to stay under the new management. The owners' leader, Zeus, Red Top, was one of them. He knew their plight and had brought the new leaders to give them a better life. The spectators anxiously waited to welcome Zeus.

Showing their gratitude was imperative to making a good impression. The air was alive with electricity.

Patterson spoke to the floating camera. "This has been a joint TUC rescue operation. Many individuals have made this mission a resounding success. I am proud to serve with these courageous men and women. I'd like to thank those who have donated food, clothing, medical supplies, toys, money and other necessary items.

"As you know, all these free, hopeful faces," the camera cut to the orphan crowd as previously arranged, "have been made possible by the suffering, fortitude and courage of one man. He himself toiled tirelessly in this harsh mine." The camera focused in on the mine entrance. "He was also branded like an animal." The audience saw a close-ups of work brands. "He knows of their starvation, lack of medical care, sadness, loneliness and hopelessness." The lens focused on an elderly orphan woman with one tear in the corner of her eye.

"He has fought against social barriers, language barriers and prejudice to lead this mission. He has survived an attempt on his life, just days ago in this very mine." The booth cut to some footage inside the mine. "His leg is still healing from being buried alive and then dragging himself up to the surface. He is a man who has never given up or forgotten where he came from. This man, who brings hope and freedom to all of you," Patterson opened his arms to the audience, "is Red Top, Cadet Zeus Galahad Malone."

The crowd and camera turned to face the nervous hero. The Corps people cheered, clapped, whistled and yelled. Zeus laid his crutches against the building and limped down the stairs into the corridor banked on both sides by a wall of people. Zeus flinched from the noise and well-meaning pats on the back. He hobbled forward as people filled in the space behind him.

When he was twenty meters in, a blueberry muffin bounced off his head. Zeus felt relieved when a banana fell at his feet. In seconds, a colorful array of food came flying from every direction, landing on and around him. Two teenage boys ran up and dumped a serving tray filled with rice on him. A tray of applesauce quickly followed. The sticky goop meandered down to his waist and plopped into little puddles on the ground. Amidst the slippery food, limping on his cast and laughing, Zeus fell on his bottom as the shower of perishables continued.

"What is going on?" Patterson demanded, as he watched his well orchestrated press conference being ruined.

"Foods mountain," Half Ear yelled over the noise and confusion.

Apollo leaned over. "What?"

Half Ear explained the orphan tradition.

Angela threw crackers in Zeus's direction.

Once Apollo understood, he yelled, "Can you hear me?" to the sound people. No response. Apollo stood and pretended to hold a microphone. "Please get my voice on a target microphone. . .Can you hear me?" A sound woman gave him a thumbs up. "This is called a food mountain." Apollo returned to his seat. "It is the greatest honor that can be bestowed on an orphan. It is equivalent to being permitted to roll in money. Since food was scarce, if an orphan accomplished something extraordinary, the others would throw him their food as a reward and a sign of respect." Apollo laughed hysterically as he watched Zeus thoroughly enjoying his hero's welcome.

Zeus sat in the pile of chow. Some green gelatin hit him between the eyes. He was giddy as the delectable rain continued. In the end, he sat victoriously buried to his chest with a mountain of food surrounding him. A thick, pasty, multi-colored goop dripped off his matted hair. Then the orphans walked before his throne to lay their handmade knives, spears and arrows in front of him.

Apollo questioned Half Ear and again explained to the listening audience. "They are presenting Zeus with the best and often only items they have to protect themselves. It is an honor for Zeus. A sign of extraordinary loyalty and respect. . .There is an incredible sense of love and jubilation in the air."

When the presentation of the gifts was over, Zeus attempted to stand amid the sloppy mess. Two orphan men helped him off his throne as a crown of beans slid off his head. He stood, but could not walk unaided in the slippery cast. Plus, the confusion had closed the corridor up to the platform.

Patterson turned to Sgt. Baker. "Go and get Malone cleaned up. Then bring him up here. . .without going through the crowd."

"Yes, Sir," Sgt. Baker smiled.

"Cadet Malone, return to the building and wait for Sgt. Baker," Patterson ordered.

Zeus flipped a salute. His royal helpers lifted him onto their shoulders. Members of the court followed behind, carrying the booty for the king's treasury.

*   *   *

Zeus stood in his clean uniform and balanced on his good leg.

"Get your crutches," Baker said.

"Sir, I's don't needs them."

"Bentley had a fit when you put them down. She said she ordered you to use them."

"No, Sir. She's order me's ta lets the universe sees them. And I's did."

Baker chuckled. "Now you're getting the hang of the Corps."

"I's look weak."

"It doesn't matter. You can stand tall and proud out there. You've done a fine job and I'm proud of you."

"Yes, Sir."

The two men made their way around the crowd to the platform and up the rear stairs.

"Nice of you to show up, Cadet," Patterson said.

"Yes, Sir." Zeus sat and placed the crutches beside him.

As soon as Zeus was seated, Half Ear threw his open knife to the orphan. Zeus easily caught the blade between two fingers, nodded his thanks and closed the knife. Nut Cracker flipped him her sharpened rock. He caught it, nodded to her and put it in his lap. Whippy tossed the butter knife she had stolen off the serving table. Zeus graciously accepted it.

Little Angela melted into the crevice between Apollo's arm and chest. She twisted nervously. Her heart pounded as she prepared to pay homage to her redeemer. She took a deep breath, climbed off Apollo's lap and onto Zeus's. Angela offered the only things she had. She kissed him on the cheek and gave him a hug. Zeus held her tight as he choked back the tears and thoughts of Emily.

"Best thing I's got," Zeus whispered to her.

"Huh, yous turn'n softs?" Half Ear frowned.

"Nope," Zeus defended. "Ain'ts soft ta protect little girls."

Half Ear crossed his arms and nodded.

"Adoption of these children is what we all want," Patterson said. "We need to act in the best interest of the children. . ."

As he was speaking, Dr. Bentley quietly walked over and exam-

396

ined Zeus's cast. She wiped a small stream of red flowing from inside the cast. "Wiggle your toes," she requested of Zeus.

"Budgin yous softs." He motioned to Dr. Bentley and what he perceived as a minor injury that did not require the witch's magic. "Ain'ts hardly no's blood. Yous ain'ts gots a rocks ta throws a knife, gives it back ta me's." Half Ear shoved his hand at Zeus.

"Ain'ts soft!" Zeus opened the knife and threw it. It landed with a loud thunk between Sgt. Taylor's legs, only centimeters from his crotch.

Taylor jumped. "Malone!"

"Taylor, yous twitched." Zeus laughed. "Gives it ta him." Zeus tipped his head to Half Ear.

"Ain'ts certain I's wants. Huh her's?" Half Ear waved a hand at Dr. Bentley scanning Zeus's leg.

"Ain'ts gots no's choice. Bentley orders me's ta cooperate. She's outranks me's."

"Huh?"

"Likes a two square."

Half Ear pounded on his head. "Budgin woman?"

Sgt. Leiman was not about to let Zeus lose face with an old friend. She jerked the knife from between Taylor's legs, marched over and pressed the blade to Half Ear's throat. "Yes, a woman. I outrank him, too." She pushed the knife under his jawbone, forcing Half Ear to lengthen his neck. "You got a problem with that?"

Half Ear swallowed hard. "Crap. Nope."

"Good. Now be quiet." Leiman tossed the knife to Zeus and returned to her seat.

"It's time for our questions," one of the press people reminded Patterson. "I'd like to ask a question of Zeus?"

"Yes, go ahead. We have a few minutes left."

"Zeus, how do you feel about The United Corps and OTS?"

"I's like 'em." Zeus grinned from ear to ear.

"What about the fact they were forced to accept you and are renowned for being prejudiced?"

"Corps ain't prejudiced, peoples is. TUC has the only system I's gets a chance in. Theys setup ta grades and judges objectively, not subjectively."

"I'm not trying to change your loyalties, but as I understand it, even when you were doing a fantastic job and could obviously succeed, OTS was pushing you twenty hours a day, to make you quit. Why applaud an unfair, abusive system?"

"Budgin press bastards, don't understands noth'n." Zeus scowled as he leaned forward in his chair. "TUC has a duty ta protect yous. If theys ain't sure I's not K, theys better not let me's stay. I's gots access ta weapons, flyers, computers and strategies that can benefit our enemies. Be'n ninety percent certain of loyalty ain'ts enough. Yous press," he shook his finger at them, "complain if I's stay, say'n I's risk yous security and complains if I's out, say'n Corps is prejudiced. Ain'ts no ways ta please yous."

"Hoo Ra!" Apollo punched the sky. Hundreds echoed the sentiment.

"Give it up." Dr. Bentley rolled her eyes. "Those two," she pointed to Leiman and Baker, "are two of the best drill sergeants in the Corps. After only a few days of their brainwashing, Malone was incapable of a non-regulation thought. He is been hopelessly indoctrinated."

* * *

Zeus watched the flimsy curtain part.

Apollo and Angela entered. "Hi, how are you feeling?" Apollo asked cheerfully.

"Fines." Zeus wished people would quit asking him that.

"You would not believe the atmosphere out there." Apollo motioned to the courtyard. "It is incredible. God has answered your prayers."

"God ain'ts answered noth'n for me's."

Apollo hopped onto the bed. Angela sat beside her protector and handed him one of her dolls. Apollo smiled at her. Every time they sat, while he talked, they played dolls. "What about your rescue?" Apollo asked in a high voice. He was embarrassed to be playing dolly in front of Zeus.

"Luck."

"OK," he squeaked, walking his doll. "You hoped the children would be placed in good, loving homes, and that is happening? I am positive most of the children are not going home with network people."

Zeus shook his head at his weird partner. "I's hear."

Angela offered Zeus her doll with the purple polka dot dress. "That is Angela's special dolly." Apollo focused a stern glare on Zeus. "She wants to share her best with you, to show her appreciation for all you have done."

"Thanks." Zeus managed a weak smile.

Angela's face was aglow.

Apollo winked at his charge. "I am proud of you." He handed her his doll. "You be the pink one. I will be the puppy doggy." Apollo rooted in his pocket and produced a small, fluffy, stuffed pup.

"What about your staying in the Corps?" Apollo panted at Angela and rubbed the dog on her leg.

"Luck," Zeus said, without moving his doll.

Angela frowned.

"If the commander of the Corps of Engineers can play, so can you."

"Yous spoke ta the head a the Corps of Engineers ins a dolly voice?"

"He was in a hurry and Angela was upset. Besides, I will probably never have contact with him in the future. I am always going to be in a relationship with Angela."

Zeus rolled his eyes.

Apollo nudged Angela. "We will have to teach Zeus how to play. He has never had a doll before."

Angela tottered the pink doll over to Zeus. She patted him for encouragement, then waited.

"Thanks." Zeus rustled the purple dress.

"You have to do the voice too; that is the most important part."

Zeus's eyebrows pinched together. He was not doing a high squeaky dolly voices. His gaze met Angela's innocent brown eyes waiting for him in anticipation. "Oh," Zeus finally squealed as quietly as he could.

Angela's doll hugged Zeus's.

Apollo's smile was as big as the sun. "Now back to the coincidences."

"How come yous ain't do'n the voice?"

Apollo held up his stuffed animal. "I am the dog now. All I have to do is bark. Ruff, ruff." Apollo's pup pounced on the sheet. Apollo pinched the sheet in the dog's mouth, shook it and growled.

Angela giggled with glee as her doll skipped over to pet the puppy.

Apollo played as he spoke. "You are proficient at math, figure the odds of this. You trust and deal better with women."

With Angela's back to him, Zeus pointed to Apollo, then choked himself.

Apollo proceeded uninterrupted. "Only seven women have ever commanded OTS. Therefore, the odds of you being in OTS with a female commander are low. Most lead sergeants are men, at least sixty percent. And Dr. Bentley is one of only a few female OTS head physicians. The Corps is over sixty-five percent men. What is the statistical probability that you would have a female commander, head physician and lead sergeant?"

"Crap, I's don't know."

Angela turned and waved her doll at Zeus.

"You forgot the voice," Apollo said in a singsong way.

"Don't knows," Zeus snarled in a high-pitched voice, bouncing his doll on the bed.

Angela nodded her approval.

"Ruff. Fairly low, would you not concur?" Apollo panted as his brown puppy leaped up and licked Angela on the cheek.

Under Angela's watchful eye, Zeus did not forget his dolly voice. "Yeah."

Apollo ComLine beeped. "It appears to me like a great deal of coincidences. Perhaps too many to be explained away." Apollo laid his dog sideways as if it were taking a nap and answered his ComLine. He spoke as Angela demonstrated to Zeus how to make his doll sit.

"Angela, we have to get going." Apollo clipped his ComLine on his belt.

Zeus gladly held his dolly out to Angela. He could not believe the stupid things Apollo made him do. Angela pushed the purple doll to Zeus and hugged the pink doll. Zeus understood all to well the sacrificial gift she was offering him. He took a deep breath and held his emotions in check.

"Would you like Angela to keep your doll safe for you. She is keeping mine for me," Apollo said. "I explained to her that OTS does not allow us to have toys."

"Yous takes care of it's for me's. Plays lots with her." Zeus gave the generous child the doll. "It's gots a name?"

Angela shook her head.

"Can I's names her?"

Angela beamed as she nodded.

"Calls her Emily."

Angela threw herself into Zeus's arms. He held her tight and said, "Thanks," in his best dolly voice.

*　　*　　*

"Zeus," Apollo jogged in front of him. "I apologize for earlier."

"Huh?" Zeus asked annoyed he still could not follow the conversations.

"Are we still friends?" Apollo offered his hand. "If I promise not to be preachy again?"

Zeus balanced on his crutches and squeezed Apollo's hand. "Yous not promise'n ta shut up?"

Angela giggled in Apollo's arms.

"Thank you both. You are stuck with me as a roommate," he said to Zeus. "As for you, missy," Apollo touched her nose, "here come your new parents. I will inform them you like it nice and quiet."

"They's all set?"

"I think so. Thank you for verifying their affiliations or lack thereof. I could not bear to place my little angel with a Kalopso member."

"They's good people. They's love her."

Apollo choked back his tears. "I am going to miss you so much." He hugged Angela tightly. "I will send you lots of messages and come visit after I have completed school."

"We'll take good care of her." Angela's new father touched her head.

The mother wrapped her arms around Apollo and Angela. "The minute I saw you at the press conference, I just knew you were the one for me," the mother gushed. "You're my precious gift from God."

"Now I's know they's right." Zeus adjusted his crutches under his armpits. "They's spooky, just like yous." He positioned his crutches and limped off. "We's ship'n out in ten minutes."

"I will meet you on the transport. Please save me a seat."

401

Chapter 30

ZEUS LAY ON HIS COT staring at the watermark above his bed. He could not imagine living in a better place. All the other cadets were ready to return to the outside world, to see their family and friends. Zeus's heart was heavy. He did not want to leave. OTS provided everything he had ever wanted in life. Yes, he was finally free to create a future for himself, but for once, backwards seemed better than forward. He clasped his hands behind his head and reminisced. He wondered if he would see the officers, his sergeants and the other Alphas again. The only departure he had ever had to deal with was Emily's, and hers was too painful to ponder.

Zeus was deep in thought when Apollo's dirty undershirt hit him in the face. Zeus leaped up, startled and defensive. Apollo grinned. He could always get his jumpy roommate.

Zeus laughed. "Budgin bastard." He balled up the shirt and tossed the smelly garment at Apollo.

"I am going to miss irritating you." Apollo flopped down on his cot.

"Yous find some else ta bugs."

"No one could be as unpredictable as you."

Zeus sat on his bed and sighed. "Don't seems like we's been here ten months. Gone too fasts."

"Speak for yourself. I am amply prepared to return to the outside world. We have had some great experiences; however, there are a many things I will not miss."

"Likes what?"

"Number one, the swill OTS pretends is food."

"Yous spoiled. Ain'ts noth'n wrong withs the chow here."

Apollo shook his head. He had never seen anyone enjoy the Corps food. Zeus was a hopeless cause. "You are jealous because you do not have a discriminating palate. If an item even vaguely resembled sustenance, you are elated."

"I's don't believes in discrimination," Zeus shot back. He had frequently pointed out Apollo's prejudiced attitudes over the past semester.

Apollo ignored the bait. "I will be extremely glad to be done with school for awhile."

"What's wrong with yous. How's could yous not likes learn'n."

"I can enjoy intellectual stimulation as much as the next guy; however, cramming years worth of knowledge into one term was grueling. I cannot wait to relax, where the most challenging problem I have to solve is should I snooze by the pool or lounge in the entertainment room."

"I's gonna miss it all. Crap, I's can't believe we's graduate'n tamorrow."

Apollo pulled on his pants with the gold braided side seams. "Watch your language tonight."

"Why we's gots ta do this?" Zeus unbuttoned his shirt and shuffled over to his locker.

"It is a dinner party in our honor. It is not intended to be a punishment." Apollo zipped his dress green trousers. "When you enlisted, did you ever envision your graduation?"

"Nope." Zeus buffed his shiny black shoes. His mind wandered to his first day and how jealous he was of Apollo's shiny shoes. "They's wants us ta feel honored, why'd they's invite the press?"

"We are heroes. The Corps needs the positive press and intends to capitalize on our marketability. Most individuals appreciate positive press. I cannot wait to attend. They are going to feed us gourmet food. It will not resemble anything OTS serves. Your taste buds will be in culinary heaven. Relax and enjoy the experience."

Zeus laid his dress uniform on the bed. "What's ta enjoy?" He fiddled with the medals on his uniform. "Everybody look'n at me's, judge'n me's. Everything I's do. Everything I's say."

Apollo laced his last shoe and buffed the toe. "Stick close, partner. I guarantee I will hack the press. No matter what mistakes you make, I will run damage control."

"Crap, I's gonna hate this."

Apollo checked himself in the mirror. He picked a piece of lint off his sleeve. "Come on. Hurry up. I have not seen my family in ten months. I would prefer to be in front of the barrack when they arrives."

"I's ain't go'n for that. Catch yous later at the Officer's Club."

"I want to introduce you to my family."

"I's meets 'em over there."

Apollo paused. "I suppose that might be a better system." It would be nice to have a few minutes alone with his family, without worrying about Zeus being uncomfortable. "I will see you later." Apollo checked himself in the mirror one last time. I look great. Mom will be pleased, he thought, marching out the door.

Zeus planned to arrive at the party at the last possible minute. If Yoggi had not ordered his attendance, he would not have gone. He finished getting dressed. He examined himself from head to toe in the mirror. He had received dozens of demerits during OTS for uniform violations. He hated having his appearance picked apart. When he was certain he was perfect, he stared at his refection. He did not look anything like how he had arrived. He felt proud as he stared at his reflection in his dress uniform with all his medals. Finally, he could not avoid it any longer, he had to leave. On his way to the Officer's Club, he ran into Sgt. Baker, and they walked together.

"You're looking sharp," Baker commented.

"Thank yous, Sir."

"After tomorrow, I'll be calling you that."

"Yous ain't gots ta call me's that."

"Yes I do." Baker stepped in front of his cadet and stopped. "Malone, you listen to me." Baker shoved his face into Zeus's. "I didn't bust my butt training you to be an officer so you could tell sergeants they don't need to show you respect. You stand tall and proud and demand respect at all times. You got that?"

"Yes, Sir." He grinned, feeling taller than usual.

"You've earned it, and you deserve it. Don't you ever forget that." Baker resumed his pace. "I'm looking forward to saluting you. It will be an honor."

"Thanks for all yous done. I's never makes it without yous and Leiman."

* * *

The cocktail hour and dinner trickled slowly by for the orphan. He was beginning to think he did not want to be an officer. The K's

404

torture and abuse were nothing compared to this. How was he ever going to fit in? Apollo had rescued him so many times, Zeus had lost count. He was relieved to get up and walk around. How could anyone possibly spend so much time eating one meal? At the rate they were going, he would never get out of here. His uniform was soaked with perspiration. He was sweating more than when he ran the course in full packs in the hot summer sun.

Cmd. Yoggi kept a watchful eye on the nervous cadet. She cringed as a well-wisher patted Zeus on the shoulder. True to form, Zeus swung around, bumping two drinks and spilling one on a civilian man's suit. Apollo smoothly pulled his handkerchief out and obviously eased the tension, since everyone was laughing. Everyone except Zeus. Yoggi wished she could hear what Christiani had said.

"Excuse me, Commander." A tall, dark man extended his hand. "I am Matthew Christiani. We were introduced earlier."

"Yes." She shook his hand. "It's a pleasure to see you and your wife, Victoria, again." She shook the dignified woman's hand.

Victoria wore a shimmering blue-gray gown with a scalloped neck. The dress flowed over her shoulders and opened in a graceful scallop at the center of her back. "May we detain you a moment?"

"I'd enjoy chatting with you. I just observed your son rescue Malone again. Over the last ten months, many times, I wanted to meet the people who raised such a fine young man."

"Thank you." Victoria adjusted the diamond comb in her blonde hair. "Apollo speaks highly of you as well."

"It has been my honor. How can I help you?"

Victoria clearly articulated each syllable of each word. "Is there a quiet location where we could converse?"

Yoggi was silently amused at Victoria's Exodonian accent. Victoria personified the prim and proper Exodus person. "We can talk in the small conference room down the hall." Yoggi led them. "Is everything all right?"

"It is not concerning Apollo. It is Zeus we wish to converse about."

"Malone? What's the problem now?"

"May we inquire where is he going after tomorrow?" Matthew asked.

"I've been working on that." Yoggi held the conference room door open for them.

When the door shut, Victoria sighed. "Are you aware Zeus intends to live in the woods after you close the barrack?"

"What!?"

"I did not assume so."

"Tomorrow he's going to be an officer, and he still thinks it's normal to camp out." Cmd. Yoggi rubbed her temples. It would be a relief to finish this term. "I'm working on it. I'll see he's assigned quarters until I get something else arranged. I appreciate your bringing this to my attention."

Victoria sat regally in the chair. "If it is not offensive to inquire, what matter of things are you attempting to arrange?"

"Someone to teach him basic social skills, manners, things like that."

Matthew tugged the pant leg of his tux and sat beside his wife. "Do you have someone to undertake that endeavor?"

"No, not yet. Any suggestion?" Yoggi asked, hopefully.

"If I may inquire, what hindrances present themselves?" Victoria crossed her feet at her ankles.

"In his case, there are lots of problems." Yoggi pulled a chair near them. "One is finding someone qualified who the Corps can afford. Charm school is not in our budget. Malone can't even image normal social situations, much less respond correctly. Earlier, a woman stopped and asked him where the powder room was. He couldn't tell her, because he didn't realize the powder room was the can. He actually thinks our military jargon is customary in society. His speech is atrocious. Worse of all, he jumps or pulls his knife anytime someone touches him."

"Does he have a counselor?"

"We've sent him with only negative success. Everything for Malone is black," Yoggi held out her right hand out, "or white." She held out her left hand. "Therapists are black." She waved her right hand. "Emily had a counselor hired by the network to keep her in line. To say Malone doesn't trust counselors is an understatement. The experts we've retained believe forcing him into therapy now could be detrimental. He's not ready yet."

"I surmise Zeus needs to observe ladies and gentlemen interacting normally like this evening. Personal comfort in social situations is not a lesson anyone can memorize. It has to be experienced. All individuals are apprehensive in new environments."

"I agree. The question is, how do I accomplish that? Even finishing school teachers aren't qualified to deal with his idiosyncrasies."

Matthew spoke up. "I believe we can assist you."

Victoria smiled affectionately at her husband.

"I figured this conversation wasn't just small talk," Cmd. Yoggi commented. She was hopeful that with the Christiani's connections, they could come up with something.

Victoria squeezed her husband's hand. "It is unrealistic to assume Zeus can develop social confidence without an abundance of exposure."

"I agree, but I don't know how to achieve that."

"One cannot compensate a mentor and achieve your purpose. A paid professional detrimentally changes the social dynamics. We have been praying about this matter. We were not confident until this evening; however, we believe we can assist Zeus."

"Great! How?"

"We wish to extend an invitation for Zeus to grace us with his presence during his three-month break." Victoria crossed her long, thin legs. Her knee poked out of the slit in her skirt. "I intend to work daily with him on manners and grammar. We would expose him to dozens of social situations and then discuss issues as they arise. The majority of these situations cannot be anticipated. We will deal with each encounter as it presents itself."

"Trust me, no one can anticipate Malone's reactions."

"In addition, it is imperative for Zeus to experience healthy family dynamics. Apollo has conveyed in his communications that Zeus has a fascination with the concept of mother. Except he is unable to comprehend the relationship. He perceives me as a lifelong drill sergeant to my offspring."

Yoggi smirked as she pictured a Exodonian drill sergeant. The statement alone was an oxymoron. "For Malone, that's a compliment. His drill sergeants are the first authority figures who didn't take advantage of him and who honestly cared about him."

"It was apparent the comment was a compliment. However, it is appalling that Zeus would journey through life with so skewed a conception. He cannot read about families and fathom the bonds between them. It has to be observed and hopefully experienced."

"Your offer is more than I could have hoped for. I've spent weeks attempting to place Malone. Thank you for your more-than-generous offer. It is a relief. I think what you're proposing has a much greater chance of success than anything I could arranged. I am curious. What happened tonight to convince you?"

"I was not confident I could assist him. This night, we were situated for dining. Zeus was not occupying his seat. I requested Apollo to escort him to the table. He stated Zeus was not accompanying us during the meal due to his poor table propriety. Apparently, Apollo had unsuccessfully attempted to convince Zeus to participate. I took it upon myself to locate him. He was on the outside steps studying 'et a que.' "

Yoggi scrunched her face. "Et a que?"

"Etiquette."

"Oh." Yoggi shook her head. "I keep telling that boy to turn on the audio."

"Why does he not use audio?" Matthew asked.

"He's used to noise giving away his location. I think he's gotten used to reading and now prefers it."

"Anyway," Victoria continued, "he was reading this disk. When I approached, he said, ' 'Tis lovely to see you again.' "

"Lovely?" Yoggi grimaced.

"Yes. When I seemed perplexed by his statement, he returned to his disk and consulted the text. He reread, then verified his statement to me. I confirmed his salutation. Then, since he had properly memorized the greeting, Zeus was annoyed I did not respond appropriately. He insisted on clarity. He wished an explanation of his or my error."

"So it was his tact that impressed you?"

"No, obviously not." Victoria laughed. "I was impressed with his studious endeavor and devotion. In addition, it grieved me that he did not recognize a distinctly feminine statement. The topic was bantered about. Zeus is of the impression everything in 'et a que' is less than masculine."

Yoggi pinched her fingers together. "He's a little on the Neanderthal side."

Matthew opened his arms wide. "Just a little."

"I requested he accompany me to recline at the table," Victoria continued. "Zeus insisted he was not attending. Since I could not force him, I simply lingered beside him. Subsequently, ten minutes passed and he relented. He accompanied me to the festivities. His solution was to recline at the table; however, he would not partake. Hence, no one would be offended by his atrocious table manners. I, too, decided not to partake."

Cmd. Yoggi could not stop smiling as she pictured this odd stand-off. "How did our self-proclaimed protector of women respond?"

"He conceded."

"And then proceeded to drink out of the finger bowl," Matthew added with a chuckle.

"Why did that change your mind?"

"I have educated my offspring that impeccable manners stem from one's desire to accommodate others so they experience a sense of comfort and serenity. There is no justification for social customs. As an example of such, I could not justify the acceptability of keeping one's hands in one's lap at meals. Zeus substantiated his hands above the table as a reassurance to others he was not concealing harmful weapons. In his opinion, it was extremely rude we were not as considerate."

Yoggi shrugged. "Seems logical to me."

"Logic cannot assist in grasping or defending social customs. It is an impossibility. No such explanations exist. Zeus desires his social training to be scientific and exact."

"That's his computer and physics mentality. Are you certain you want to do this?"

"Yes, now that I am convinced Zeus is committed to others feeling comfortable. That is the only justification I need possess."

"There are so many people you would be helping," Cmd. Yoggi stressed. "All those adopted children need a successful role model. Malone has to integrate and succeed so they believe they can, too. It's also proof to the skeptics it's possible. He is paving the way for thousands of others. Malone is aware of this, but it may be helpful to remind him now and then."

"Apollo has informed us how intense Zeus's concern is for other underprivileged children."

Yoggi checked her watch. The press would be wondering where she was. "One last thing. You are not committed to this. If things don't work out, call me. I'll arrange something else."

"Thank you. I do not anticipate circumstances demanding that alternative."

"Then I'd say it was time to break the news to your new pupil."

She called Zeus and Apollo on her ComLine and asked them to come to the conference room. Once they were on their way, she said, "Be prepared. Malone will probably not to be pleased with your invitation."

"We shall manage," Victoria said as Apollo walked in the door.

"Manage what?" Apollo asked.

"He doesn't know?" Yoggi questioned.

"No, Apollo has not been involved in this decision."

"Involved in what decision, Mother?"

"We shall inform you momentarily." She smiled at her son. He was so handsome in his uniform.

Zeus entered, stood at attention and saluted.

Cmd. Yoggi's gold dangle earrings jingled as she moved her head from side to side. "Malone, you don't salute at a party."

"What? Why not?" Zeus asked, still at attention.

"This is a social setting, not a military one," Victoria offered.

"She still my's commander."

"At ease, Malone," Cmd. Yoggi insisted.

Zeus spread his feet shoulder-width apart and placed his hands behind his torso.

"No, I mean relax."

"Huh?" He glanced at Apollo casually leaning against the conference table. "Oh." He did his best at an informal stance. Between Cmd. Yoggi and Victoria Christiani staring at him, how could he possibly relax? Mrs. Christiani, with her formal high speech and ways, made him more nervous than the press.

"He definitely requires a familial-type setting," Victoria stated. "Preferably a great distance from the military."

"What?" Zeus snapped.

"Malone, meet your new social tutor." Yoggi motioned to Victoria.

Victoria smiled. "Matthew and I would like you grace us with your presence while you are on leave."

Apollo hugged his parents. "Thank you, Mom and Dad."

"Apollo, yous bastard." He shoved Apollo into the table. "I's ain't go'n."

"I did not have anything to do with it," Apollo defended.

"The Christianis have offered to let you live with them so you can see how a healthy family interacts," Yoggi said.

"What good's that's do me's?"

410

"Malone, you have to learn some social graces, and a large part of that is how various individuals interact."

"Don't mean I's gots ta live with thems." Zeus stuffed his fist in his pocket and held hands with his trusty friend. "What's watch'n a family gots ta do with anything?"

"Victoria is going to tutor you in grammar, table manners and social customs while you're there."

"I's pay her for her time and lives somewhere else."

Victoria smooth a wrinkle on her dress. "I do not intend to be compensated. You would be an honored guest at our residence."

"What?" Zeus bit his nail.

"I volunteered because my desire is to assist you."

He spit the nail at her diamond-clasped shoes. "I's ain't no charity case."

Victoria crossed her legs away from the disgusting chewed nail. "I never implied you were. Many of my offspring's friends have resided at our home. We shall learn from one another."

"Ain'ts go'n," Zeus snarled at the commander.

"We've talked about this. You have to learn it," she said, perturbed at his rudeness.

"No. I's keep study'n."

"It's not something you can read about," Cmd. Yoggi stated.

"I's find another way."

"You're going," she insisted.

"Nope, I's ain't. Yous can't orders me's in my free time."

"Don't push me, Malone." She tried again, softly, "You don't have a choice. You need their help. The other orphans out there are counting on you."

"No!" Zeus marched to the door. "I's ain't discuss'n this no mores cause I's ain't go'n."

"Malone," Cmd. Yoggi bellowed, "you were not dismissed."

Zeus turned, glaring at her.

"Stand at attention," she demanded.

"Yes, Ma'am." He stood seething, with his eyes facing forward.

"Malone, you will go."

Zeus fixed his fiercest glare on her. "Requests permission ta speak."

"Go ahead, but watch it."

"Yous can't orders me's on my free time, Ma'am."

Cmd. Yoggi ignored him. "Matthew, Victoria, are you still certain you want him?"

"Yes, more determined than ever," Victoria responded as Matthew nodded.

"It's a mistake to push me," Yoggi snarled. "Malone, your next assignment will be on. . .what's your home planet?"

"Aqua," Victoria answered.

"Your next assignment is on Aqua. You will be stationed there until Victoria says you are ready for further duties. Do I make myself clear?"

"Yes, Ma'am," he grumbled.

"Think of Matthew and Victoria as admirals in rank," she snapped. "You report after graduation. Got it?"

"Yes, Ma'am."

"Ouch," Apollo joked, "she pulled rank on you."

"Apollo, do you not have something else to occupy your time?" Victoria asked politely.

"Yes, Ma'am." He grinned, kissed her on the cheek and went out the door.

"Do you mind if we converse alone?" Victoria asked her husband and Cmd. Yoggi.

"He's all yours," Yoggi gladly exited.

Matthew winked to his wife. "I will meet you inside."

Victoria observed her new pupil standing rigidly at attention. "Please relax."

Zeus dropped his head and stuffed his hands in his pockets. "Yes, Ma'am."

"It is not my intention to upset you. I greatly desire to assist you."

"Then tells Cmd. Yoggi yous changed yous mind." Zeus squeezed the Little Lady for strength.

"Surely in the ten months of dwelling with Apollo, he has mentioned my fortitude once I feel a conviction to proceed. I am not easily deterred."

"Why do's this?"

"Because it is God's desire."

Zeus rolled his eyes. He hated that argument. He never had a defense. "Then I's pay yous, Mrs. Christiani."

"No, I thank you for the gracious offer. And you may address me as Victoria."

"Can't calls yous that. Not if yous in charge."

"Would Lady Victoria be more to your liking?"

Zeus stared at the floor in defeat. "Yes, Ma'am."

"Then, shall we go and enjoy the rest of the festivities?" She rose gracefully, offering him her arm.

Zeus frowned at her arm raised as she had done outside. "Not thats again."

She smiled sweetly, saying nothing.

He sighed and took her arm. It was going to be a long break, and she was going to be impossible to deal with.

*   *   *

Zeus strolled to the East Gate in his dress green uniform. He had been assigned guard duty. There was a long line of fliers waiting for the gates to open. In keeping with OTS tradition, the gates remained locked until 07:00, when family and friends were allowed to enter and see cadets for the first time in ten months.

At precisely seven, Zeus opened the gate, stood at attention, saluted the driver and yelled, "Welcome ta Officers Training School. How may I's direct yous, Sir?"

"I'm here to see my daughter, Sally Brown."

"Sir, Cadet Brown's a member a Beta unit. She's at her's barrack. Follows this road straight. Beta Barrack is a second build'n on yous right, Sir." Zeus stood at attention and saluted the driver. A procedure he would be repeating over and over. He did not mind the repetition or the monotony. It was easier than the alternative — to watch the other cadets cheerfully embracing their family and friends, when he had no one to greet. Zeus anticipated an uneventful day of saluting, greeting and giving directions.

The sixth driver asked, "Where can we see the orphan?"

It had not occurred to Zeus that people would ask to see him. Fortunately, the manual had a section covering gate protocol and similar situations. "Sir, yous currently speak'n ta said individual. How may I's assist yous, Sir?"

"Oh, I should have recognized you." The man's face reddened as he flew quickly through the gate.

Zeus was confused. He had not sensed anything negative or antagonist in the man. Oh, well, there were plenty of stranger guard gate stories. He ignored what he assumed was an isolated incident. How-

413

ever, many people were looking for and at him. Visitors stared and pointed. Some of the young girls giggled at him. Zeus was perplexed by their gawking, but continued his duty in a professional manner.

One flyer stopped and the man asked, "Can I take a visual of you with my daughter?" A pre teen girl in the rear of the flyer waved at him.

Zeus paused, confused. There was no protocol for this. "Please waits here, Sir." Zeus did a half turn, marched into the gatehouse and called Sgt. Leiman.

"Well, Malone, the order of the day is to be friendly and helpful. Cmd. Yoggi wants everyone to have a positive orphan experience. . ." she trailed off, hesitated, then asked, "Does it bother you to do it?"

"Why she wants it?" he asked.

"Think of it as a compliment."

"Ma'am?"

"The girl wants her picture with you to prove she's met you. She can show it to all her friends and impress them with the picture. You should be flattered. Thousands of people wish they were famous enough to have people ask for their picture."

"Yes, Ma'am," came the unhappy, but compliant response. Cmd. Yoggi had given him a stern lecture about not speaking freely today. "What I's says ta her? Ain't noth'n in the handbook."

"How about, 'This cadet would be happy to comply with your request.' "

Zeus nodded.

"Don't forget to smile and show off those famous dimples all the women are talking about," she instructed him as he broke off the transmission.

Zeus exited the gatehouse and smiled for the visual. He hoped the experience would not be repeated. Unfortunately, when the next flyer saw he was granting pictures, those passengers requested a visual, too. After that, he was smiling for picture after picture. He could not wait for his two hours of guard duty to end.

Cmd. Yoggi wandered over to check on him. "How are things going?" she asked as he saluted her.

"Fines, Ma'am."

"You're doing a great deal of good here. This type of interaction is a big boost to your image as well as the Corps."

"Yes, Ma'am. How longs it take for everyone ta arrive?"

"Normally the gate would be slowing down by now. People are leaving and returning through your gate, just to get a picture with you."

Zeus eye widened. "What?"

"You're a celebrity." She grinned at his frustration. "What time are you supposed to be relieved?"

"Oh nine hundred."

"I may keep you here a little longer."

"Yes, Ma'am," he grumbled.

"Remember they helped pay for your education, and they'll be paying your salary."

"Yes, Ma'am."

She winked at him. "You better return to your adoring fans."

"Yes, Ma'am."

Cmd. Yoggi kept a watchful eye on her cadet as she meandered over to chat with the press. She was trying to decide how long Zeus could handle the situation.

Zeus snapped to attention for another flyer. "Welcome ta OTS," he said to a flyer of teenage boys. As they flew through the gate, Zeus felt SPLAT, SPLAT. His left cheek and chest stung as two balloons filled with yellow paint hit him.

"Go back where you belong," one boy yelled.

"Orphan trash," another called.

Zeus instinctively pulled his weapon and leveled it at the moving vehicle. Yellow paint dripped on his trigger finger. He saw the boys laughing, realized there was no real danger and lowered his gun.

Yoggi came running over. "Are you all right?"

"Yeah." Zeus tried to wiped the paint off his cheek. It smeared under his eyes.

"I'm proud of you. You handled it like an officer."

"Thank yous, Ma'am." His heart sank. His uniform, medals, commendations, all ruined.

"There will always be a few narrow-minded idiots."

"Yes, Ma'am." He wondered how many in the viewing audience were cheering his humiliation. He could not even stroke the Little Lady without defacing her as well.

"Come on, let's get you cleaned up."

"I's can't leave my's post without a replacement."

"Very good. Always keep thinking, even in a crisis." Yoggi pulled out her ComLine and punched in Leiman's code. "I guess it's Christiani's turn to smile for the cameras."

"Sgt. Leiman," she answered.

"It's Yoggi. . ."

"I saw it on the news," she interrupted. "I've sent Christiani to relieve Malone."

"Good job. Pick us up here in a truck. It smells like permanent paint. I'll get Supply to give him a new uniform and order security to track down those kids. They will not be on this base for long," she added to Zeus.

"I'm on my way. Leiman out."

Cmd. Yoggi checked her watch. "We've got an hour to get you cleaned up, in a uniform that fits and with your unit. I will not be the only commander in the history of OTS to start graduation late. The entire universe will notice if you're not where you belong. Thankfully, as the top unit, the Alphas are the last ones to march in."

"Yes, Ma'am." Zeus's cheek stung from the paint. Graduation or not, hero or not, he would never be anything but an orphan to some people.

Apollo marched over and saluted Cmd. Yoggi. "At ease. You two go wait behind the gatehouse," she ordered.

Zeus hung his head.

Apollo stared at the bright golden paint dripping on the gravel. "What happened?"

"Kids throw'n crap at me's." He shrugged, pretending it did not bother him. Zeus did not want to discuss his current humiliation. He quickly changed the subject. A trick Apollo had taught him. "Was yous with yous family?"

"Yes and Angela."

"How's she do'n?"

"Her appearance is wonderful." Apollo frowned. "She has gained a great deal of weight. Her parents state she is sleeping better."

"Yous don't seem happy."

"Angela still has not spoken. She cries and screams in her sleep; however, when she is awake, she does not speak. I thought, hoped she would be conversing by now."

"When she's ready. She. . ."

Yoggi motioned Zeus into the flyer.

"I's gots ta go."

"I'll see you at graduation."

*   *   *

Cmd. Yoggi started the graduation at precisely 10:00. Zeus's heart pounded as he heard the band play the first drumbeat of "We are Proud to Serve."

Zeus was charged with emotions as the cadets received their ensign bars and insignia. He forgot about the trashed uniform and painful prejudice. He savored each memory as it flashed like a fairytale before him.

"The last two cadets we'd like to honor have been quite a pair," Cmd. Yoggi announced. "The press is calling them The Gods." The large screen behind the podium displayed a series of pictures of Zeus and Apollo over the previous ten months.

"As a team, they have achieved more than any cadets in the history of OTS. As an individual, Cadet Malone has received more honors than many receive in a lifetime of service. I'd like to introduce you to The Gods, Zeus and Apollo."

They marched in unison onto the stage. The crowd rose to its feet. Yoggi proclaimed, "Ensign Apollo Christiani and Ensign Zeus Malone."

After the noise subsided, she said, "I'd also like to introduce the sergeants who managed to keep these two in line for the last ten months, Sgt. Susan Leiman and Sgt. Dennis Baker." The monitor pictured Leiman and Baker with their two famous cadets. "I can assure you, no one deserves more credit for Malone's success than these two. Malone was a challenging task at best."

The crowd chuckled as the screen filled all four quadrants with stills of Leiman and Baker yelling at and instructing Zeus.

"Let me start by saying each man has already received a number of commendations. If you watch the monitor, it will display each ribbon and medal. Malone placed first in our annual All-Military maxor competition." A yellow-and-blue-striped ribbon appeared on the screen.

"Both men and their sergeants received the Humanitarian Service Medal for Operation Rescue on Velcron." A round brass medal dangled from a kelly-green and white ribbon.

"Christiani received the Achievement Medal for his leadership before and during Operation Rescue." A silver cross on a solid teal ribbon was displayed.

"The Gold Fleur-de-lis hangs from a crimson and gold ribbon. Red always represents bloodshed or suffering for the Corps. Malone received the Missing-In-Action Medal and a Gold Fleur-de-lis with a Valor Star for being buried alive at Velcron. He has also been given the Bronze Service Medal for his unique participation in correcting our planet's tainted water supply."

"Lastly, Cadet, excuse me, Ensign Malone has received the Corps' highest tribute, the Silver Star or Medal of Honor." The screen showed a close-up of a three-tiered bow. At the center of the bow was a pyramid of small glistening stars. The bow clip held a large silver cross that sparkled with diamond dust. "For Malone, Operation Rescue was supposed to be a suicide mission. Prior to leaving for Velcron, Malone had obtained intelligence that the Kalopso intended to kill him. It takes a great deal of courage to die for a cause. Malone insisted he was not only willing to die to stop the horrors there, he demanded he be allowed to go and ensure its success. If there is one thing that has impressed me about both these men, it's their willingness to serve, regardless of the price."

"On to grades. Christiani." She shook her head at him. "You passed, and not with flying colors."

Apollo made an exaggerated swipe of his forehead. "Woo."

"Malone, somehow you managed to receive an Academic Excellence Commendation." The screen displayed the cream-and-purple ribbon. "Your scores were the second highest in your class. You would have been first, if you hadn't completely flunked press and PR. In fact, you're the only person ever to flunk press and PR. I saw your press conference; I can't imagine why you did so poorly."

The large screen displayed Zeus throwing the knife at Sgt. Taylor's crotch.

Zeus fidgeted at the visual behind him.

"It's tradition in TUC that commendations be given by family members or significant others. Due to the circumstances, we made other arrangements. Today's awards will be given by two children rescued from Velcron. Sergeants, if you would assist the children. Our final order of business is to promote our two outstanding ensigns to the rank of second lieutenant. This is a lifelong honor. This ring has been given to OTS's two outstanding cadets for the last one hundred and fifty-seven years."

The monitor displayed a heavy gold ring with a round center emerald. The Corps insignia was on one side of the jewel and the year 2222 on the other. The sides were outlined in rare ruby crystal paint. Inside the ring, the person's name was engraved.

"These men have proven themselves willing to do their duty with courage, dignity and honor. I am proud to present this ring and the rank of second lieutenant to Zeus Galahad Malone and Apollo Matthew Christiani."

A ten-year old boy stepped up and slid Zeus's ring on his right ring finger. With tears in his eyes, he said, "I won't never forget you. I gots a home and a family."

Zeus closed his eyes and wrapped his arms around the boy. He attempted to respond, but the lump in his throat refused to let him speak.

Angela skipped out in the pink embroidered dress Apollo had sent her. She handed Apollo his ring, and he slipped it on his finger.

Angela's heart pounded as she took a deep breath, kissed Apollo on the cheek, and clearly stated, "I love you."

"Angela!?" he scooped her into his arms. "You talked?"

"My present for you," she said slowly.

"Thank you!" Apollo proclaimed loudly, "She talked! She talked!"

"What?" Zeus turned to them.

"Say something for him."

Angela leaned into Zeus's arms, kissed his cheek and said, "I'm never hungry."

"She talks!" Zeus yelled.

Angela hugged him warmly. "Thank you."

ORDER FORM

Please send _____ copies of

"Duty Honor Deceit"
by
J. Lissner

Name _____

Address _____

City/State/Zip _____

Price . . . . $15.95 per book _____

Taxes, Shipping and Handling $4.00 per book   _____

Total $ _____

☐ Check   ☐ Visa   ☐ MasterCard

Card No. _____ Exp. Date _____

Signature _____

Use this form or photocopy and mail to:
Leathers Publishing
4500 College Blvd., Suite 180
Overland Park, KS 66211
or
you may contact J. Lissner at:
jlissner@eternal.net
Web Site: http://www.eternal.net/jlissner